INCARNER

Book 3 in the Oracle, Tailor, Curator trilogy

Halli Starling

Halli Starling Books

CONTENTS

Author's Note

THIS TRILOGY BEGAN AS a mishmash of ideas. New York, turn of the 20th century, the history of queer and gay culture, the history of the rare book trade, and the history of occult groups. Despite physical proof otherwise, *Coup de Coeur* was meant to be a standalone story, one that ended in a masked ball and a frightening gallop through Rosehill to evade agents of The Golden Order and their extraplanar assassins.

It would have been a fine book. But it wasn't the book I wound up writing. It also explains why each book gained more and more avenues for the horrifying and profound (for me, as a writer and someone who is both enamored with language and often horrified by its capacity for true awfulness). The romance between Calix, Ethaniel, and Aubrey only grew. The blossoming of other relationships came from out of nowhere.

I enjoyed every moment, and I hope you do, too.

I'm never writing a series again.

I don't say this in jest, at all. Tracking every little whim my brain wanted to add into the story was next to impossible, because by the time I've written in some detail, my brain has moved on to the next piece, eager for everything. I can claim this trilogy to be a truly eye-opening experience for how I (don't) plan what I write, outside broad brushstrokes, and even those are eroded by whatever thing has currently captured my imagination. I'm certain there are a few minor details that might not line up book to book, and I do apologize for that. It is my job to find those and I hope your enjoyment of the book wasn't ruined by my inability to shut my brain up for five seconds.

After all that said, I hope this book ends the series satisfyingly for you as a reader. And if it doesn't, and you want to know what happens next... there will be another book. There are already short stories written and more planned as of this writing (late 2025). I know what the fourth book will entail because those questions you have by the time you reach the end of this installment? I had the same ones, and then I wanted to provide the answers. So if you want to stop after this book, you get the always-promised happily ever after. If you want to continue on, there will still be a happily ever after, but not without more bumps and obstacles.

Finally, I wanted to say thank you. I've been honored by every reader who has ever given these books a chance, even if they weren't the right fit. If all media and art was meant for everyone, it wouldn't make a difference from this book to that song to this indie film. *Art* itself would have no value, because art is individual. The true beauty and loneliness, the desolation and the joy, of being human is experiencing the familiar, the urbane, the sacred, and the damned with our own minds and senses. We feel sounds and see stories and color the world in our particular views all for the sake of feeling *something*, and our best work is the expression of all of that and so much more through art. I think about this all the time, and what happens when we replace art and culture with soulless technology. A question many of us are grappling with currently, and a question that all humanity has grappled with for as long as we've been making art.

So thank you, kind reader. Thank you for giving this trilogy a chance and, if you're so inclined, continuing on this journey with me. I promise to do what I can to make it worth your time and energy.

—Halli Starling, August 20, 2025

List of short stories in the OTC universe as of now (links below, QR codes on next page):

- **"You Absolute Bastard": a snapshot of Calix and Lawton's relationship during their university years.**

  - ○ Read it HERE

- ○ **Toxic relationship, power dynamics, boundaries, sex**

- "A Place Like Home": takes place months after this book ends as **Calix, Aubrey, and Ethaniel prepare for a masquerade benefit on behalf of the Collectio**

  - ○ Read it HERE

  - ○ **Fluffy and smutty in equal amounts**

- "To Us and the Night": a closer look at Aubrey and Calix's end of the relationship, takes place in an amorphous time when Ethaniel is out of town

  - ○ Read it HERE

  - ○ **Fluffy and smutty in equal amounts**

"A Place Like Home"

"To Us and the Night"

"You Absolute Bastard"

Content Warnings

- Horror elements, including gore, blood, and vivid descriptions of brutal death

  - This includes mentions of spiders, tendrils, eyeballs, and black holes

- On-page animal death (birds falling out of the sky)

- Cosmic horror (multiple limbs, claws, ichor, etc.)

- Threats and evidence of self-harm (intentional and unintentional)

- Discussions of magic and the occult

- On-page sex

- Foul language

FOLIO ONE:

WHAT RARIFIED GLORY

"The boundaries which divide Life from Death are at best shadowy and vague. Who shall say where the one ends, and where the other begins?"
— **Edgar Allan Poe, "The Premature Burial"**

CHAPTER ONE

At the heart of magic as we know it is a black, unyielding nebula of questions swirling about like flies over a corpse. "Where did it come from?" we ask the air and stars, our gazes as expectant as our minds. "What little we know! What more we seek to understand! Won't you only tell us? Won't you let us know what secrets lie beyond your veil?"

And then we wait.

We have waited since the beginning of our time here, and yet what we know could dance upon the head of a pin. As we uncover our own world's secrets with microscopes and x-rays, we do not have the same level of scientific curiosity for the arcane. We have become most human in this way. We got a little of what we wanted and, satisfied, sat back like a lion, patted our engorged bellies, and said, "Well, how marvelous. I'm quite full, aren't you?", and then died snoozing in a patch of hot sun.

My god, what we could have discovered by now if we'd been willing to push. If we hadn't stayed seated after admiring the little baubles and trinkets, the enchanted embroidery and buttons that never fell off, and marked the occasional burst of magic as a sad accident, instead of looking at that person's work and vowing to fix where they went wrong.

Science has always been brave. Bold. Ceaseless in the desire to explore, to roam, to know. Why do we not feel the same about magic? And why haven't we organized any effort to know more about something as equally bold and brave and ceaselessly uncapitulating, a steady churn of discovery and innovation powering the wheel of actual, true improvement for society?

I aim to fix this. No, to repair it. After all, a fix is often merely a bandage, a patch for whatever below still burns and seeps. But to repair is often to replace, is it not? I will build the Order in my vision, and replace what is outdated. Replace those who sat by; greedy, slothful lions too slow to hunt again with those more nimble. More hungry. More driven. And I will read the tomes and texts, the dusty scrolls and forbidden manuscripts, and piece together the real story of how magic came to humanity, and how we can begin to know it more intimately.

—From the journal of Vincent de Laine, 1896

Pictured below the entry is a half-completed runic circle, the pencil lines faint but steady. Runes of unknown origin sit in each segment of the circle save for one empty spot. Runic circles must be complete and comprehensible to work.

CHAPTER TWO

ETHANIEL

Its smile was a thing made of nails. Like splinters dug in around the knobs of his spine, forever pricking and itching and dying to be cut out. Ethaniel wondered if this was what it might feel like to be flayed open, skin curling like ribbon away from muscle, from bone. And if he felt such a way, the expression on Vincent's face spoke of far bloodier tortures at the hands—*claws*—of Uzala.

Uzala loomed impossibly large before him, its shadow bitterly cold and all-encompassing.

No escape. No escape.

It echoed in Ethaniel's mind again and again.

No escape. No escape.

And then, just as suddenly, a new thought: *No escape now. Could be soon. Stay small and quiet.*

Said in the voice of an eight-year-old girl, who had disappeared when Ethaniel was sixteen.

Ethaniel flinched, but Maria's words stuck in his mind, pulling like taffy against the fear and disbelief. It cushioned him from the painful *lack* of Calix that came on like a wave, as if Ethaniel had felt the door they'd cut into the *demimonde* collapse in on itself. Forever closed. Forever gone.

"You may feel the pressure of this place on your mind, but give it time," Uzala whispered in a strange, almost musical tone. "Your family line is etched into its fabric, this place between realms."

The being stared at him, its lack of eyes not lessening the *sensation* of being looked at. Like a thousand pairs of eyes across a crowded room, and half of them looking at him. Ethaniel tried to speak, tried to *think*, but the essence of the *demimonde* dug fingers into his mind and blotted out all higher thought.

small and quiet

small and quiet

Maria's voice was a litany of those three words, and with her third repetition, Ethaniel felt the pressure of the *demimonde* go slack.

He could see her now, nearby but blending into the gray all around them; only her dark hair and dark eyes in shocking contrast. Not a thing had changed about her, after nearly twenty years. Was she a tiny immortal being now? Was she in this land of her own choice, or had she been lured here?

And worst of all: *Had he been the one to help put her here?*

Memories flashed before him, tattered bits giving him a second or two of remembrance, but those shards were enough to make that old wound reopen once more.

Dropping his books on the kitchen table to find his father frantically folding Maria's tiny dresses, his steady hands shaking, his face pale.

His questions going unanswered, his father's mouth a tight line all the way through the smoke-clogged train station, to a dock far too grimy to play host to such a shiny new ship.

Their tiny room on the ship, all his father could afford, and how Maria's voice filled it as she flitted between excitement and confusion. A new adventure in Father's homeland! But why must they leave Mother behind? Wasn't she ill? That's what you said, Da, that Mother was ill and...

Her hand tucked into his as they walked the ship's hallways, quiet as could be so they didn't get yelled at again by a porter.

Her joy at seeing the apple trees in their new backyard, and so many questions about the wildlife.

The nights when he found her window open, her tiny boot prints in the frosted grass the only indication of where she'd gone. Her joy at seeing him in the woods, and her insistence that he meet her new friend.

The way the mists clung to their shoes, their coats. How it seemed to almost toy with her braids, tightening its grip on her. How he swore, more than once, that there were actual handprints on Maria's shoulders, their impressions left in the fabric of her wool coat. But he'd blink, and they were gone.

And then that day she disappeared...

The memories surged through him, leaving behind a corona in his vision and the taste of ash on his tongue. Ethaniel choked, gagging against it. Vincent turned a wide-eyed stare toward him, and all Ethaniel could do was give a miniscule shake of his head.

small and quiet

He thought about those words, then balled up his intent and lobbed it at Vincent like one would a wadded-up newspaper. Not to harm, but to make it known. He only hoped Vincent was listening.

"Ah, I see what plagues you. Not me or your relation here," Uzala said, its presence no less intense now as it lowered itself a few feet and let Vincent drop to the ground. Vincent was a tall, strong man but now discarded, he was a slumping pile of limbs decorated by shallow cuts. "Not that I believed there was any love lost there between the beatings of such strong wills." It was suddenly above Ethaniel, its face so close to his, he feared it would breathe on him. But it loomed there, impassive, emotionless, and yet vibrating with such self-satisfaction. It sent a chill down Ethaniel's spine, to be seen in such a way.

A toy, a trifling pleasure which would pass the time but quickly grow mundane.

I cannot afford to be mundane here, in the face of such terror, such power. Ethaniel recognized that logic as not solely his own, but flavored with the quick wit and quicker mind of the first man he'd ever fallen for. That was *Aubrey* in his mind now; a gift, such thoughts, but oh, what a curse as well.

Ethaniel pulled on whatever source of courage he had left and met the thing's gaze, such as it was. "And what is it that plagues me?"

One clawed finger, jointed at least six or seven times, the nail more shard of glass than anything else, carefully traced Ethaniel's jaw. There was no helping the shudder that went through him. Revulsion, yes, but the touch itself was colder than any ice Mother Nature could conjure. "You're wondering... what could have been if you'd let those rune circles simply go to ash. If you'd activated the failsafe, as it were, and ruined your chance to go to the *demimonde*. If you'd never come here, you'd be together. Safe."

Uzala wanted something. Obedience? Acquiescence? Acceptance? It had mentioned a twin and revenge. It wanted them here for *something*. His mind whirred, spinning in five directions trying to figure out the puzzle before Uzala handed him the solution.

He couldn't afford to be mundane here.

Ethaniel cut his gaze to where Maria stood, seemingly obedient, wreathed in gray mist. And the moment he did, she smiled ever so slightly. And he made a choice.

Ethaniel drew a tight fist around his courage and said, "I hadn't thought about it that way yet, but you're right. I charged forward without a thought toward the simplest solution. Because... what I wanted was to give in. After so many years of fighting, I knew I couldn't toe that line anymore. Not when the ones I cared about were threatened."

He looked down at his hands, the way the mists twined around his fingers like thread. The call of this place wasn't some accident. Maybe he'd fallen victim to suggestion, or maybe he'd simply wanted to. "I wanted to take the leash off. The one that I put on so many years ago. The one I knew would put a chokehold on my magic. My blood."

Ethaniel kept his eyes on Uzala the entire time but the burn of Vincent's stare was a bodily thing, raw with disbelief and at its center, a well of hope. Examining what that look meant would take more focus and time than they had right now. "This place speaks to me," Ethaniel continued, his voice softer now. It wasn't a hardship to acknowledge this, after all; the moment he and Calix had stepped through the door, he'd felt *reborn*. The tingle of it — magic, its very essence — danced over his skin even now, distracted as he was.

And gods, Calix... I hope he made it back.

"Cast him from your mind," Uzala said with a wave of its hand. "He is out of your reach for now. I want to know more, little patterner."

Ethaniel froze in place as Uzala's face, that thing of hard, unyielding stone, featureless but emanating power and curiosity, came within inches of his own. "We have much we could do together and we shouldn't tarry here. We will travel back to my domain. Let your sister lead us."

Maria nodded and began to walk in... some direction. There was no North here, no horizon. No sky, no ground, though what he walked on was firm under his shoes. He felt the mist cling to his skin, saw the way Maria's braids swung as she walked, her hand wrapped around one of Uzala's fingers. He had no way of knowing where the door they'd opened had been, so he had no way of escape. He could follow and hope, or stay and doom them all. The implicit threat was *Uzala*; there was no need for magic or manacles to force him to trail after them like a lost dog.

And as Ethaniel shuffled forward, careful to stay out of reach of the creature's long arms but close enough to appear obedient, he also didn't miss the way Vincent looked back at him, the blood on his face doing nothing to hide the keen light in his eyes.

CHAPTER THREE

CALIX

Calix groped the gray air, desperate in his reach, his heart lodged firmly in his throat as he called out Ethaniel's name over and over again.

Nothing.

He was in the middle of a shifting wasteland. Ethaniel was gone. And that creature...

Calix shuddered and looked down to see his hands were covered in dust. A few bruised lavender petals clung to his fingertips.

It was a land of nothingness. An endless chasm filled by what it lacked. But he couldn't panic. Ethaniel had slipped a thin silver band onto his thumb right before they'd walked through, with hardly a whispered, "For luck." Calix ran his opposite forefinger over the band, feeling how the silver was pitted and dented with age. This was a beloved thing now in his care, and seeing how large it was on his own hand made Calix want to cling to it evermore.

Panic was threatening to settle in. He couldn't afford that. Instead, he held Convergence up and said, "Where are we?"

Immediately, Talbot was there, but gone were the claws and fangs. His eyes were still wild, unruly orbs, but now they fizzed and popped with power instead of their previously fathomless pools. He looked almost *human*. "In the *demimonde*," Talbot rasped. "Good. Very good. But you've lost your guide."

And of course, Talbot had done nothing but remind Calix he was still a cozener. Bastard. "I didn't *lose him*. He was... ripped from me. It's this place."

Talbot seemed to shrug. "Harkness blood runs in the veins of *this place*. They were the first, you know. The first ones to delve here."

The bottom dropped out of Calix's stomach. What had been a wild theory he'd kept to himself, barely even thinking on it lest he somehow manifest it into reality, now lingered on the edges of his mind. Eager. *Hungry.* "Spit it out," Calix snapped, trying to sound more like Aubrey. Talbot clearly respected him, or feared him; as he should. Aubrey was a force to be reckoned with.

Talbot leered at him, smugness radiating off his visage. "Harknesses were the reason John and I knew about the *demimonde*. They opened the first door, made deals, gained mighty powers. Then squandered it on petty schemes and rivalries, instead of making intelligent moves."

Calix had become so numb to shock over the last few days that it was anathema at this point, and yet here he was gaping toward Talbot's visage.

And yet it made all the sense in the world that a family with an ounce of power and a heaping of ambition could do such things like research ways into the *demimonde*. Ethaniel had said their influence dripped with darkness and malice, and that the Harkness power was not what he wanted to claim as his sovereign right.

And yet... Ethaniel had fought the call of his blood with honor, giving in only when they needed help the most. Calix had never asked for that and he knew Aubrey didn't want it, either. Was Ethaniel more helpless to it than he'd thought?

"That information doesn't assist me right now," he snapped.

Truth hovered ever closer. He needed to play on Talbot's ego, or at least his sense of self-importance. It wasn't all a bluff; Talbot needed to come here, and they needed to be rid of him one way or the other. *It's what Aubrey would do.* "And you know this because... ?" he asked while biting down on the urge to toss the book in any direction, find Ethaniel, and return home.

Instead of immediately answering, Talbot cocked his head, eyes narrowed in intense study for a moment far too long to be comfortable or proper. "When you first found me, I thought I was touching someone powerful. I could feel it, the beating of your wings against my prison. *Freedom.* But when you brought me to *him*, I thought it was a fevered dream thrust upon me by one of the soul-bits trapped in these pages with me." His tone turned cold, vicious. "It's all that was left of them once John fed them to Uriel."

Calix didn't have it in him to be shocked. He was standing in the *demimonde*, an actual place between realms. And realms were *real*, as much as magic was real. After everything that had happened — every mistake, every taste of terror, every bite of elation, and the sheer harrowing they'd all been through? *This* was too much.

"I can't bring myself to care much about people your old master offered up as sacrificial lambs to a literal otherworldly denizen." Calix was shouting by the end, his free hand shaking with anger and frustration and fear as he held the book up. "You made your choices, and you and Dee are dead. We were willing to trade for the return of my mother, but you've done so little to assist in our plight, one that was for *your* benefit, and now I've lost someone in this awful place. I need him *back* so we can go *home*."

He wanted to fling Convergence into the space, watch it disappear into the gray mists. He wanted to be free of it.

So why didn't here?

The conscience in the back of his mind, the one he'd let Lawton gag into silence many times, screeched to life. *But what could happen if you do that? Utter unknown. You stand in a place you do not understand and that should terrify you. It is no opportunity. You and all the others would be responsible for what happens after that, but they'd all know you were the one to make the decision for them. And they may resent you for it, even if resent was the bare minimum.*

Calix gripped the book until his hands ached with the effort. Could they really be free of Talbot and all the problems around him with a single toss? But as his thoughts rioted and his chest grew tight with the strain, Calix noticed Talbot wasn't answering his question. But he was providing information, even if it was the kind that made him seize up in dread. Anything with Dee was now tied to his mother, based on her obsessions with his writings and rituals, and by Talbot's own admission, it was all tied to Ethaniel's family as well. He had no good choice, only one he hoped was the wisest one in the moment. "Can you help me— " He bit down on his cheek with a grimace, shook his head. "Can you find Ethaniel? Can you sense him? I can't go back without him."

The buzzing of the door he'd come through, held open by sheer will, was a persistent fluttering against his own magic; butterfly wings against skin, but maddening. "We've little time and these mists are thick," Talbot said, his voice gone contemplative. "Try to call him to you. Or perhaps...ask your mother for help."

Ah, there it was. There was Talbot's real entreaty. *Ask your mother for help.*

Yes, he should ask his mother for help and hopefully draw her to the scene, and if he could do that, surely he could find Talbot's essence floating in this space? Talbot was, all at once, complimenting him and drawing him further into a web Calix only wished to be free of. What Calix wanted and needed was to get Ethaniel back. If that meant giving up on this wild plan to bring Talbot to the world of the living and possibly his mother along with the old necromancer, then so be it.

Ethaniel was worth ten of them, many times over. He loved his mother, yes, but how much had she taken from him in her self-satisfying, self-edifying need to "save" him from an older version of himself? How many times had she lied? Stolen things from him? And why should he have to suffer her jabs even now?

"I think perhaps speed is best here," Calix bit out before closing his fist tightly—tight enough that the silver band Ethaniel had gifted him cut into his flesh—and thought about Ethaniel. He thought about hazel eyes and a crooked nose and wide lips that smiled with everything they had. He thought about Ethaniel's kindness, his gentle touch, his hesitation and how it bumped up amicably against Aubrey's forthrightness. And Calix thought about all the ways Ethaniel had, in such a short amount of time, burrowed into his heart.

He thought about joy. And equal admiration, one that felt like the first burst of autumnal fire across trees as the seasons changed and the winds began to sing home their bones. It felt quite a bit like the beginning of love, of hearth and warmth, but also safety and surety.

Something in the mists answered his call.

"I said call the Harkness, not the beasts!" Talbot exclaimed as he reached toward Calix. "Strong emotions are like a beacon here and you've called them to you!"

Fear jumped in his veins. "I called what?" Calix asked as he looked around, as if he could see into the very mists. The moment Talbot had begun to shout, his magic had risen to the challenge, but something was *different* about it in this land. It wasn't lavender on the back of his tongue, coating his sinuses as if he'd buried his face in her dressing gown; once more a child sitting at her feet as she combed her hair.

No, this was *fire*. It licked a path along his skin like a lover's tongue, fierce and unyielding, sending shivers down his spine. Calix had to blink against the rush of tears as his sight blurred.

There in the mists, something was charging toward him.

Hulking bodies, stout but rippling with a frantic kind of energy.

"They hunger," Talbot said. Calix thought he heard fear in the specter's voice. "You are a beacon of power here. I suggest you *run*."

Calix didn't need to ask for a direction. He knew.

To the door. To the door. And back, back, back home again, but this time alone. Only a possessed book and a dented silver ring to keep him company.

"You must go!" Talbot screamed, his voice pitching higher as Calix dashed with mad intent toward the faint glowing outline of the door. He could feel its energy, too; another source of power not his own but still intrusive somehow. This entire place felt strange and unwieldy and with each breath, he felt the pull and tug of a thousand strings trying to tie him down, bind him here.

We should never have come here, he thought as he ran.

The door grew closer still but surely he should have reached it by now?

"The mists are fickle," Talbot said, eyes rolling in their sunken sockets. "Be clear in your intent, boy!"

And behind him, the growls grew louder. Calix didn't dare look back.

He focused what little energy he had, through the shock and despair and pain, on going *home*. Again and again, always returning to that place where his mother's footsteps echoed still and the malingering ghosts of their shattered bond creaked with every change in the wind. Was it their presence that rankled him so, or was the very house itself trying to tell him something? Was Rosehill the real beating, bleeding heart behind his losses and grief?

Or was it her?

Calix reached out and let his power push forward, as if to shove away the mists and forge a clear path. He was desperate now, the acrid taste of it foul.

"Aubrey!" Calix yelled, praying his other companion heard. "Please! The door!"

Through the mists came an echo, like a distant yell reverberated through glass. And behind him came a snarl, then hot breath on his neck. He ducked but was too late, and something swiped across his forehead with what felt like jagged glass.

"Through the door!" Talbot yelled, but it was lost in the cacophony of growling and teeth and Calix trying to cover his face from the assault. The very touch of these beasts *burned* and he could feel his flesh sizzle. But more than the pain was the anger. It rushed through him, unstoppable; another assault.

But this time, Calix gave in.

"Enough!" he screamed and threw his hands out.

The magic that poured from him was not a swell; gentle but constant. This was a tidal wave, and he was left helpless in its wake. Only able to watch and *feel* as it left his body in a torrent and crashed into the shadow creatures that had been trying to rend his skin from his bones. He felt the magic in his head, behind his eyes, reverberating through his teeth and rattling the cage of his ribs. It was sound in his body and the scent of colors and so much more.

Calix felt *alive*.

Time seemed unimportant. He was it, and it was he. The magic. The endless loop of it. He began to feel heavy and light-headed all at once, his vision drawing further and further away from his own body, but he couldn't break the chain between himself and the magic.

A funnel. A flood. Ceaseless. Colossal. Immortal.

And in that space where he saw nothing and everything, she found him.

"I knew you'd figure it out," Lily said.

Are you in my mind, Mother? Or is this merely another wisp of your soul meant to torment me?

" I am here," she replied. "But you have to take me with you. You must undo what I've done."

Why? What matter is it to me? Your mistakes are yours.

"And yet, even my best intentions left pain behind. I would fix that. Calix. Please."

That's your plea to me? To help you again? This coming from the woman who took so much from me. My mother. The one person I trusted more than anyone.

"Please, Calix."

Before him appeared her face, sad and pale. But the familiar ache echoing in his bones upon seeing her once more was muted. Aborted longing for something that had been a half-truth.

Calix frowned but didn't approach her image. "Tell me where Ethaniel is," he said, struggling to keep his voice even. "Find him and I'll take you back with me."

It was the slightest of tells, but her slow blink told Calix everything he needed to press his advantage. "I'll even go through this insane plan you have to be… what? Resurrected? In some vain hope you can help me control my powers? Powers which I inherited from *you*, Mother."

Her face bore an entreaty her tone did not match, but he felt that guilt anyways. It bore the weight of familial bonds but took on the form of a fire-haired woman who looked as timeless as he'd remembered her to be and had, once, been everything to which he'd aspired. They could have been inches from each other, on opposite ends of a mirror, and he would have felt the distance between them.

Calix bit back its sour taste as she said, "I know. And I made those mistakes but I did it for you. Please, Calix. I'll do anything."

He didn't bother to bite back a scoff at that. "I told you what I want. Find Ethaniel so I can take him back home."

"All right. I will."

The moment she blinked away, Calix was thrust back into his body. And he was alone in those gray mists but now it smelled of sulfur and burnt wood and tiny bits of black floated around him. Convergence was at his feet, its front cover now marred by a scorch mark that curled the fine velvet and had blackened the long edges of the pages.

Calix scooped up the book, examining it for more damage, when Talbot said, "What a pity John was right."

Part of him didn't want to engage in conversation right now. The other part of him was eager for an answer. The latter won out. "Care to explain?"

What sounded like a laugh dragged over rusty railroad spikes left Talbot. "My boy, he'd been right from the moment he'd started studying this place. Magic? It's not of our world. It's from here. There's no other explanation for what you just did."

Calix paused his inspection of the book to lift an eyebrow. "And what did I just do?" He gestured at the black specks floating like volcanic ash before him. All that was left of the creatures. "Other than apparently destroy three very frightening shadow beasts."

"Exactly!" Talbot cried. "You destroyed something from another realm. John had long posited that magic came from a source outside our world, that it was energy from somewhere else that blessed humans who were most pious. Superstitious nonsense, but the man took a Bible to bed every night, so I wasn't going to change his mind. But Uriel.... "

A sound like a thundercrack shook the ground, the sky, the air, and then his mother was before him once more. Her outline looked tattered, as if someone had taken a barber's razor to it, and in her wide eyes Calix saw panic. "We must go! He knows, he knows! Through the door, my son!"

A braying he now recognized sounded all around them; a certainty there were more shadow creatures. Dozens of them. "But Ethaniel!" he said as he started for the doorway.

Ethaniel's voice called out to him. Reached for him. He felt it was sure as a touch, a caress, and when he blinked once more, Calix was staring at the man himself. His mother had disappeared, even if her presence lingered, and Ethaniel stood before him, the panic on his face like a punch to his stomach.

Calix had never been so relieved. "Ethaniel?"

In the blur of confusion that followed, Calix could hardly track one moment from the next, the weight of the *demimonde* and its putrid mists pushing on him from every angle.

And in those same moments, he lost Ethaniel to this place between realms; to its mists and terrors and he was left, once again, with only the voice of his mother for company.

"The door is further off than it looks!" his mother said as she tore through the mists. "We need to go, now! Your patterner is with Uriel's twin, there's no saving him!" His mother ran ahead of him and Calix could only run and watch in horror as she started to flicker and fray more and more. And all around them came the sounds of braying.

Convergence grew hot in his hands. Talbot yelling. His mother yelling encouragements to *keep running, keep running, don't look back.*

Calix's gaze got stuck on the book, stuck on all the problems it had brought into his life. All the possibilities and wonderful things, too. But the door was just up ahead. Fifteen paces. Ten paces.

Five.

Four.

Three.

"Help him if you can, and we'll set you free," Calix said before he threw Convergence into the mists and dove through the door as it snapped shut.

CHAPTER FOUR

AUBREY

Calix collapsed in his arms and for a long moment, there was nothing but relief in his veins.

Reality was a long, slow blink of Aubrey's mind's eye, to catch up to what Calix had just said. When it settled through him, Aubrey began to shiver and through that uncontrollable movement, he held Calix tighter.

"...Aubrey?"

A firm, warm hand on his shoulder. Aubrey turned his head but it was as if his neck was made of molasses. "Aubrey? Did you hear me?"

Magnus, now kneeling beside them. Calix's arms a vise around his waist. Something wet against his shirt. Aubrey looked down and saw blood, saw Calix's tears. Time was sticky, clinging to them by both millimeters and miles.

Then his mind caught up with what was happening, and what had happened. What Calix was saying, what Magnus was saying. Aubrey could sense how close they were, how damaged and afraid. Bruised and broken.

But all he could focus on was how Calix had returned alone.

"I'm so sorry, it's my fault. Aubrey." Calix was staring up at him with the most pained expression, caught somewhere in a deep valley between grief and guilt. "He saved me. There was this thing, this monster, and it had that man we've seen before. Ethaniel's brother?" Calix sounded unsure and it made Aubrey's own memory give a watery ripple. Dark hair, like Ethaniel's, but a narrower face, more powerful build.

The feeling of Calix's fingers fluttering, barely touching his neck, finding purchase in the overgrown scruff of his hair, made everything snap back to *now*. Aubrey immediately felt sick, stomach upending, bile threatening to sear the inside of his throat. He pulled away to cough and retch as the truth of it all dangled above his head, its string waiting for the swing of the reaper's scythe.

Tears stung his eyes and his lungs felt as if a band had been wrapped around them. Every breath *burned*. Every thought was an unending echo: *Ethaniel, Ethaniel, Ethaniel.*

Through eyes that didn't feel like his, Aubrey watched as Magnus rushed from the room and as Calix, who had slumped to the floor in shock, now crawled to him. A trail of dust and blood and tears left in his wake.

You need to be there for him. For both of them. And you can't do that if you're incapable.

Fuck, he hated that word. *Incapable.* The only barb in his father's bandolier of insults that ever truly landed. A direct hit to the small, dark orb of insecurities he kept buried beneath viscera and caged in his ribs. The cage was always there to protect his heart, and there had never been any reason for it to not play jailer to that orb, too.

Aubrey curled his hands into fists, let the fine wood of Rosehill's floors imprint into his knuckles, then took Calix by the wrist and pulled him in. Gods, he was so thin. It was some instinct of his, some twisted part of himself, that made Aubrey want to keep Calix safe and warm and well-fed, but far, far out of reach of anyone who might hurt him. And that fierceness, that protectiveness, was what reached out to him now, through the gray mists of the *demimonde* and the quiet, choking sobs of the man in his arms.

"I'm so sorry," Aubrey managed to say, his throat already far too tight, his eyes on fire. "I'm so, so sorry, Calix. We'll get him back. I swear it."

"Please," was all Calix managed to say before sobbing, shaking with every breath. "I would have never let him go with me if I'd known... "

Aubrey looked to the ceiling and the movement unearthed old, long buried instincts. To pray to a God he no longer believed in. To ask the spirits for guidance.

He stamped it out, a well-heeled shoe on a fire-hot cherry, and tightened his grip on Calix. "You cannot blame yourself, Calix. Please don't. Ethaniel needs you. And I need you strong to bring him back."

Magnus found them like that some untold minutes later. The rain outside had slackened but the gray clouds rolled, tumbling over each other. Something about the sight made Aubrey's stomach drop. "Here," Magnus said as he handed Aubrey a tumbler half-full of golden liquid. "It's not going to do much more than calm either of you down."

Then Magnus paused. Thinking. The light in his eyes was dimmed and Aubrey couldn't help but focus on his mentor's face, the lines and planes of it. Magnus had always been an elegant man, but age had brought a sageness to his demeanor. He'd been the older confidant Aubrey had yearned for his entire life, and now he was seeing Magnus fully take up the mantle on his own terms. Defining their path forward with all the wisdom and cleverness he kept smothered between velvet lapels and tied up in ascots burning with autumn color.

What he saw now was Magnus of ten years ago, the steel in his spine now once again polished to an impossible shine.

Magnus pulled a thin cord out of his pocket, from which a speckled pendant swung. Aubrey couldn't see what color it was in the time it took Magnus to toss the thing into the air. The pendant glittered briefly, then a mass of sunset-hued magic spun and spun, in the very space in front of Magnus opening up like a cat's slow yawn.

A familiar face, both human and not, appeared, followed by a ruffle of down and the scent of cinnamon. "Magnus? What the devil—"

Magnus cut Agrippa off with a hand. "No time. I need you here now. Hence the emergency communication."

Aubrey realized he was still holding the cup and handed it to Calix, who downed half before returning it. Aubrey drank the rest, unable to tear his eyes away from the creature Magnus had apparently called *friend* for some time. "It's not safe here," he managed to say as warmth spread through him. The effect was immediate; he felt Calix's shivers slow, stutter, then stop, and his own head felt less heavy, his eyes no longer blurry with tears.

Agrippa stuck their head out of the portal a bit more, their nostrils flaring as they scented the air. "Bah. *Demimonde.* Like rust on the air. Nasty stuff." Their eyes, a swirling miasma of galaxies, blinked rapidly, and then Agrippa hissed, "Your patterner isn't here. He's trapped. Ah, wait… "

Calix shivered again and Aubrey clung to him, rubbing his palm up and down the slighter man's back. A mimicry of intimacy but not lacking in care. Aubrey needed the contact just as much, if not more, than Calix did. A reminder to stay safe, but also sane.

The next word that left Agrippa's pale lips was more snarl than anything. "*Uzala.*" Then they straightened, adjusted the fussy little bow that sat in place of a necktie, and said, "Well, that clears some things up. Come, come. It'll be less roomy than your current quarters but far safer."

Aubrey stared at them. "Where are we going?"

Magnus gave him a wan smile. "The Collectio isn't one building, Aubrey. It's several, broken up between our realm and little… bubble planes built very carefully to avoid interference from places like the *demimonde.* Agrippa lives in one of them, and has been the caretaker of many more."

He and Agrippa exchanged a look, and Aubrey saw something pass between them. He couldn't name it, not now or perhaps ever. But it was *something* that made him trust Agrippa a bit more.

"Many of the *unstable* artifacts the Collectio has picked up through the generations are housed in spaces like mine." Agrippa gave them all a nod, then pulled back into their side of the portal. "Well, come on!" they said, voice an echo from within.

Magnus got them to their feet and with Lawton following close behind, waved them forward into the portal. Aubrey didn't bother to look back at the place that had been the source of so much strife over the last few days. Rosehill wasn't his, and if he knew anything about Calix, the young earl wouldn't claim it as home anymore, either.

Too much ash on the walls and blood built into the roots of that place to be considered safe.

"I should stay here, with Richard," Calix said, sounding far more steady after Magnus's concoction. "Lawton and I should stay, I mean."

Aubrey turned to Lawton, who immediately said, "Calix, you have to go. Whatever ill will between us, whatever damage I've done, I'm not going to do anything other than mop the man's brow and make sure he's still breathing. If he wakes up, I'll ensure he eats. You should go, but you won't need me there. I'll stay." Lawton's face, already pale and wan, looked even more drawn out and despite his hesitance about Lawton's moral barometer, Aubrey believed him. Perhaps the veins as dark as ink under his skin helped him believe Lawton didn't have the energy to argue much. It was clear the path they were headed toward involved him, too.

But real sincerity was hard to forge in the midst of dire straits.

And his Ethaniel was trapped. *Ethaniel Ethaniel Ethaniel.* A heart ripped free of its earthly moorings and left to drip upon the floor. His name a metronome, so full of sound and life but so far away.

Agrippa seemed to do their own version of truth seeking while staring down Lawton like a vulture over a carcass, but they eventually nodded and said, "He'll be fine. He's not lying. He doesn't know who he is exactly, given the extra passenger bouncing about his body, but he won't do more harm than he already has."

Aubrey turned to Calix, whose gaze was darting between Lawton and Agrippa. "It's your call, Calix, but I think you'll be needed wherever we're going."

Calix swallowed hard. "I know. We should go."

Aubrey led him over to the portal, through which Agrippa had already disappeared, but Calix paused in front of Lawton to hand him a key from his pocket. "For the front and back doors, just in case," was all Calix said before following Magnus through the portal.

Aubrey turned his attention to Lawton. The other man was gripping the key in his fist, eyes fixed on it. A gift with teeth.

"No threat?" Lawton asked as Aubrey passed him.

Aubrey merely shrugged. For him, the urgent need was Ethaniel. Getting him back. Lawton was barely tertiary right now. "No need. I think you have much to reflect on, and the time we're gone may be the right nugget of peace for it."

But it didn't feel right to leave him like that. Trapped in a house of the flimsiest cards. "Magnus, hold it for me," Aubrey said before darting down the hall to Calix's private study. They'd locked the gun away in the safe the moment they'd arrived; all of them wary around the damn thing and for good reason. There was no better time in his eyes to let it see the light of day once more.

"In case the time we're gone isn't peaceful," Aubrey said before setting the gun on a side table and passing through the portal.

That was a petulant, dangerous thing to do, Aubrey thought as the world swirled around him, patterns of blue and purple and silver impossible as they filtered through his mind. He was moving, traveling, and then suddenly... not.

Come to a sudden, dizzying halt in a completely unfamiliar place, his own chastisement like a burned tongue. *You gave Lawton a weapon. An enchanted weapon.* There were only three no-miss bullets in the chamber, the others standard fare. And he had no idea if Lawton knew how to wield such a thing.

All thought of Lawton blinked out as Aubrey stared up at the shelves mere inches from his face. Boxes and bins, trays and jars, all neatly labeled in a language that made his third eye flick open. He slapped a hand over it, frowning as everything around him began to speak. Most of it he couldn't understand.

....over the river...

....sounds like morning raiders...

No, we can't. But yes, we should...

...the master seeks the student seeks the master seeks the student...

It was all too much. Aubrey winced and began to turn away, when something cold touched the back of his hand.

"This will keep them from chattering at you," Agrippa said. Aubrey realized the creature was a solid foot taller than him, but spindly as a willow tree, and the thing against his hand was actually pressed into his skin. And the moment it touched him, Aubrey's vision cleared completely and all he could see were endless rows of shelves packed to the brim with objects. Bizarre, mundane, disturbing, ethereal. But whatever it was marking his hand kept the roar of their magic at bay.

"The things Agrippa watches over have a very... eh, let's say *peculiar* sense of humor." Magnus was beside them now, with a red-eyed Calix in tow. "Keep that on until we leave." He held up his hand to display the greenish circle stamped into his skin. Runes flickered past Aubrey's third sight, but like so much in recent memory, he could only understand snippets before all meaning was yanked away. "It's harmless to us, but the artifacts aren't fond of it."

It was telling that neither he nor Calix asked exactly what it was. It didn't matter. They were too exhausted, too terrified, too consumed with the ashen taste of dread to care.

Ethaniel was gone.

"Not gone," Agrippa said as they shooed them all away from the shelves and toward a cheerily flickering fireplace and a circle of overstuffed chairs in mismatched patterns of the palest blues and yellows. The flames, reflected in their strange eyes, brightened and Aubrey could *taste* the magic command on the air. The same scent he'd been hit with upon Agrippa's appearance: down and cinnamon and the long dark kept back by a steel trap mind. Faintly, Aubrey wondered how Agrippa had heard his thoughts but realized it didn't matter. Another mystery on the pile.

"Come sit," Magnus said, his hand firm under Aubrey's elbow. "I'll explain what I can, but our priority is Ethaniel."

"And the book," Agrippa said. They moved closer to the fire as a gold tea cart slowly wheeled into the room. There was no one steering it, and Aubrey realized such a thing would have been a fascination for him, had his attention not been split in so many directions.

Ethaniel and Calix and the book and Vincent and whatever happened on that side of the unknown. They should have never tried it, never been so bold, so arrogant—

Aubrey found himself sitting, a delicate teacup carved out of what looked like jade gently placed in his palms. The cup's warmth was a kindness to his entire being at this point.

It hit him all at once and was confirmed by the way Calix was staring down at his untouched tea. Hands at his sides, clothing rumpled and stained but empty of any odd shapes.

The book.

Agrippa sat across from them, very human-shaped legs bending in very human ways as they crossed one over the other. Something about the way they sat made Aubrey feel as though their body were far larger, maybe even *too large*, for the chair, but that feeling defied what he saw.

"You're not wrong. A little nosy, but then again, so is Magnus. I'd expect you to be a bit like him." Agrippa wasn't smiling, their very human mouth downturned not in disappointment or anger, but in thought. The expression made their already sharp nose stand out more prominently. "And yes, here, I can pick up on your thoughts. Not in words, necessary, but feelings, flashes of images. The hard-beating heart of someone terrified. The blood vessels near to bursting of someone screaming at the top of their lungs in anger... " Agrippa shrugged and the heavy wool knit of their gray sweater shifted again, like someone wearing a size or two too small. "I've gotten rather good over the centuries at understanding nuance."

They paused, gaze roving. "What I don't understand is," Agrippa finally said, leaning forward, eyes narrowing in Calix's direction, "is why you had the book and not Ethaniel. He's the patterner in your trio. Oracles are powerful, yes, but Ethaniel has the direct connection to the *demimonde*, not you."

Scattered jigsaw puzzle pieces finally assembled into a whole picture. But the final image wasn't what he'd expected, nor did he expect Calix to say, "I left it there because if Talbot was going to help anyone, it was going to be Ethaniel." Calix turned to Aubrey, desperate, seeking... what? Absolution? Forgiveness? Empathy? If only their minds were connected still. Calix would see all of it there, out in the open and his for the taking. "It has caused all this grief and I couldn't... stand it any longer!"

Calix's last words were a mangled shout and in the shocked silence that rang out around them, as full as a void, all Aubrey could do was reach over to take his hand. Feel the fine bones of it, the soft skin, and hold on tight. Calix was practically vibrating with energy, but Aubrey could taste his magic, too; could sense it deep down, could feel his third eye flicker open briefly in response.

"Oracles aren't meant for places like the *demimonde*," Agrippa said not unkindly. "The book would have made you a target, Calix. And I'm guessing it did, if I'm assuming correctly in how you got those scratches on your arms and face. All manner of amorphous things live there, half-remembered dreams of ambitions and envies that led others to their doom. Leaving it in that place was the smartest thing you could have done."

Aubrey now understood. He had nothing but circumstance as evidence, but it made *sense*. "So Talbot didn't need Calix. He needed Ethaniel." He stared at Calix, who had gone even more pale, practically ghostly against the dark red leather of his chair. "You said something in your head took you right to safety after Lawton's little escapade with the thug he was selling books to. It was Talbot. He led you right to Ethaniel."

Calix nodded. He was gripping the arms of the chair so tightly, Aubrey feared he'd snap a finger, so he gently put his hand over one of Calix's. Lending warmth and strength where neither of them had enough on their own. "It...*Talbot*...took me directly there. Said there was safety."

Agrippa seemed encouraged by Calix's words. "I doubt anyone involved in that little equation truly understood what they were doing, Talbot was drawn to

Ethaniel the way the Harknesses are drawn to the *demimonde.* They're all of the same nature."

The clink of a teacup drew Aubrey's attention to Magnus, who was now sitting forward in his overstuffed chair, his right fist balled up under his chin in a pose Aubrey knew very well from their years working together. Magnus had a plan. Maybe not an entire one, not yet, but something was brewing in his mentor's mind.

"Calix, can you tell us everything that happened once you passed through the doorway? No detail is too small, and nothing is inconsequential." Magnus's gaze was bright as he honed in on Calix, who was far too still in his own chair. When Aubrey tried to reposition their hands, Calix only clung that much tighter to him.

"I'll try," Calix said softly. He looked to Aubrey with pain written in every line of his face and it made Aubrey's heart twist into knots all over again. "Could you… could you help me focus? I don't need to borrow any magic, I swear. I only want to be tethered."

Aubrey knew he had the fortitude for it and didn't hesitate. Anything. *Anything* to get Ethaniel back, to bring him home so they could be whole again. "Of course."

The moment Calix had finished his tale, he'd slumped forward and, alarmed, Aubrey dashed to his side. His head still rang with all the things Calix had told them, and his heart might as well have shriveled to a husk with Ethaniel trapped in the *demimonde,* but he wasn't going to give up. And he wasn't going to abandon Calix.

"He's exhausted," Magnus said as they watched Agrippa conjure walls and a floor and a nice, if not a bit small, bed into some semblance of a space where Calix could rest. At Magnus's insistence, Agrippa added a small fireplace, a lamp, and a table to the room before stepping out, claiming they needed to locate a few things to better help them work on a plan to get Ethaniel back.

Bundling Calix into the bed had been more of a fight than Aubrey had expected. Not concerning Calix, but himself. Because he was going to stay up and figure this out and bring Ethaniel home, and that was the end of it.

"You're no use to anyone, Ethaniel included, if you're drained," Magnus said gently while Aubrey watched Calix bury his face in a pillow and cry softly to himself, too exhausted to lift his head. "He needs you. You need him. Trust that Agrippa and I have some control here. And that I'll tell you more when you wake up."

"What about you?" Aubrey asked. He'd not missed the strain on his mentor's face.

"That's a secret for me to keep, I think," Magnus said, his tone lacking any joviality for once. "But I want to make one thing very clear, Aubrey. You are, without a doubt, one of the most skilled magic practitioners I've met. But you're human. You cannot push yourself past the point of breaking. I know you want Ethaniel back. We will ensure that happens." Magnus paused, put his hands on Aubrey's shoulders, and said, "I will ensure this happens. Do I have your trust in this?"

Aubrey frowned. "Of course you do. Always."

"Then do me a favor, and rest. And remember your promise to me when things start to become a little... strange."

Aubrey felt a tiny, hysterical laugh bubble up in his chest. This was all *so much*. And he didn't have a fucking clue what Magnus was hinting around at. But yes, he trusted Magnus more than anyone else. So he would rest. He would hold Calix close and stroke his hair and make sure that whatever fight was next, they were ready to face it.

"Good. I see the determination in your eyes and I admit, it's a relief. These last few days have been hell, and the next few won't be any easier. But we'll get through it." Magnus gestured toward the Calix-shaped lump under the covers and said,

"Go to him. And don't let him think any of this was his fault. You've all handled this with as much grace as could be afforded, given the circumstances."

Aubrey let him get a few paces away before saying, "You're planning on doing something truly stupid, aren't you?"

Magnus smiled at him. There was still no humor anywhere on his face. "I'm not about to throw myself on the pyre, if that's what you're worried about. I like living too much. But there are things… " He sighed; his expression drawn down into a mask of reticence. "I've worked for the Collectio since I was twenty-two. Fresh out of university, ready to dive into all the occult world had to offer. I met Agrippa quite early on in my work, and the things they've shown me rival the greatest fantasy stories. I always suspected the *demimonde* was both a funnel and a graveyard. A place full of monsters and bones. And the frailty of humans becomes food for their ugly maws." Magnus gestured to the strange space around them, and Aubrey watched the walls and floors ripple in response. "I think we can work the funnel part to our advantage. And luckily, Calix has given us a target to aim for."

"The book. Of course." Something like *hope* fluttered under his ribs, but all Aubrey could do was laugh when the realization hit him square in the chest. But the laugh burned like fire. "What a route we've taken to hell."

Magnus smiled grimly at that, but it only lasted a few seconds. "Hell and heaven and everything in between are just matters of perspective. But that's a conversation for another time. Rest, Aubrey." He stuffed his hands into his pockets and ambled back down the hall, leaving Aubrey to stare after him.

Aubrey carefully slipped his shoes and vest off, then slid into bed behind Calix. Immediately, the tight line of Calix's body relaxed against him, but Calix began to cry all over again. Wounded, aching, sad beyond measure and worried out of his mind, Aubrey wasn't going to be sleeping anytime soon, but he could keep Calix safe if they were this close.

"You don't give yourself enough credit," Calix finally whispered after what felt like eons in the dark together. "I can hear the gears turning, Aubrey. Powered by worry and guilt."

"I can't help it," he admitted, "but neither can you. You're so tense, you're practically vibrating. I fear if I let go of you, you'll shiver up to the sky and not come back down."

Calix nestled in closer, entwining their arms and legs in a mockery of the absence they felt so keenly. Aubrey was a man of extremely precise tastes, and he'd barely managed to wrap his mind around all that was Ethaniel before he'd found himself alone once more, victim to another kind of practicality, of his own making and one that didn't often make room for emotion. He was the very *opposite* of that, really, but from the outside, his veneer kept others from thinking him a living, breathing, *feeling* thing.

And the moment he'd shoved his pride into a hole and was a day away from apologizing again to Ethaniel (and this time on his knees, speaking aloud all the things he'd tried to write down and had failed at), he'd been drawn into the orbit of not one lover, but two. Because of a book.

Because of *magic*.

Because humans always wanted to know *more more more*, hungry for knowledge with open throats and hearts. If he truly wanted to lay blame at someone's feet, he'd tear it to shreds and toss it all before the withered bones of John Dee, to point accusingly while saying, "Look what your malice and greed did."

Look what it made me lose. Look what it brought me.

Aubrey pressed a kiss to the top of Calix's head. *Look what it brought me.*

Chapter Five

After the rush of activity, the sudden quiet at Rosehill left Lawton jumping at every shadow. He could still feel Lily but faintly now, though the black lines across his skin hadn't faded. Somewhere deep down, their twinned heartbeats were slowing. In fact, he looked even more sickly; eyes sunken, mouth a red, bitten slash, his nails practically gone with how he'd chewed them away.

And despite his appearance, Lawton's main concern wasn't his own health. Or the safety of Richard, who had seemingly disappeared; Lawton had conducted a search of the rooms and found no sign of the man aside from mussed bedsheets and a few bandages covered in dried blood and left to fester on a nightstand. No, he was concerned about Calix.

And now, a few hours later, Lawton sat in Calix's study, at the pristine desk dotted with all the trappings of a wealthy man, and marveled at how distant his friend felt. Calix had been a known quantity in Lawton's life for so long. Dependable, if not a little needy from time to time, and easily swayed into most things. Calix had been as lonely as he but together they were able to withstand the brute force that was life. Calix had the money while he provided the wit and charm, and the city (or town or university, wherever they were together) was their playground.

And now.... everything was upside down. Everything was wrong, but in the middle of all of it were his shortcomings. He'd never been the most introspective person, but Lawton knew this farce of the last few weeks had been a long time in the making.

He looked down at his arms resting on Calix's desk, amongst his friend's things, and saw ugliness. Not physically, though the black marks Lily's prolonged possession had left were no comfort. He was simply an ugly human being, barely scraping at being moral or upright. But if he was good at anything, it was getting out of a jam. Ugly or not, he still had some of those wits about him, and if there was nothing good for him at the end of this journey, then at least he wanted to do everything he could to set it right.

But that didn't mean he couldn't hold out hope that an opportunity to save his own neck would arise. He could be repentant and survive.

"Still clinging to my bones, Lily?" Lawton said to the still, empty air. He'd waited until the moments between their heartbeats, on the every third *thump* where his was a smidge faster, a bit louder, before speaking. Hoping that even in her weakened state, she might have answers.

Like about that coin he'd kept out of Calix's pocket, the one Lily had given him and the same one he harbored deep doubts about.

Lily trembled as she slid into existence; a shard of cold wedged somewhere between his lungs and just below his heart. *I am here.* A beat of hesitation, and then, *Lawton, what did you do?*

"Call me a suspicious bastard, but I couldn't help but feel as though that coin was for you, and not Calix," he said. He realized he looked like a fool, but since there was no one around to watch him, Lawton rose from the desk, Calix's fine fountain pen in emerald green and silver between his fingers, and paced the length of the room. Holding the pen was Lawton's way of tethering himself to Calix, even if the connection didn't feed back to him. He wanted something of Calix's close to him. A reminder of days long gone and not yet bitter with regret.

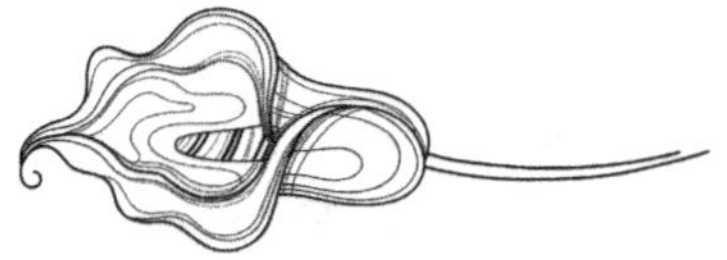

"It's a fine thing," Lawton said as he leaned closer to the box that was in Calix's hands. "You said your father sent it? Seems strange."

Lawton straightened, expecting to see his friend's face twisted with an avalanche of emotions, but there was only muted anger in Calix's brown eyes. Calix swiftly replaced the lid to the black velvet box, and tossed the thing onto his bed as if it were a ratty winter scarf.

"He only cares now that his last living heir died," Calix spat. "I want nothing to do with him."

Lawton couldn't stop himself. The idea was too ridiculous. "Calix... you're the only heir left. Your father has to leave it all to you. It's– "

"I don't want it!" Calix was practically snarling in Lawton's face now. "He never helped when Mother was ill, and he's never once set foot on this side of England to even dare to visit. Mother stopped making excuses for him ages ago. Why would I want the money of a man who held me in no esteem higher than that of a stable boy?"

The words were quicksilver on Lawton's already sharp tongue. Surely Calix wouldn't... "Are you disturbed?" Lawton said, nearly shouting himself. "Your father is wealthy beyond, even above most in line for the Crown! You'd have to be a fool to turn him down, Calix! Think of what you could do with the estate!"

Calix's jaw hung open for a few seconds before he closed the distance between them. He was practically incandescent in his outrage and shock and it made Lawton proud. It also made him want to pin Calix to the wall and bite his neck. He was stunningly gorgeous like this.

"Think of what I could do with the estate?" Calix's repetition of his words was done with the anger of an injured party, and a bit of danger whispering at the edges. "You want me to meet with the man who abandoned us the moment my mother asserted herself and wouldn't give up her family property for a small cottage in the middle of the godforsaken country? Who never once acknowledged either of our existences, and who only paid for my seat at this place because his reputation was at stake? That man? Him?"

Calix was trembling. Furious. Feeling betrayed. He'd never been more beautiful.

Lawton could only shrug. "Seems to me you have a chance to make right what your father has done wrong for so long. Most people don't get that."

Calix's nostrils flared, his lips smashed together in a tight, thin line. Lawton thought he heard Calix's teeth grinding. And he wanted Calix to touch him. Anywhere. Any way Calix wished. He would take it and ask for more. Desperate for it. For Calix's rage and his whip-smart mouth on Lawton's neck, his jaw, leaving a hot trail across his chest.

So, he edged closer. Daring. Hoping. It had been months since they'd last warmed one of their beds or sneaked off into the groundskeeper's shed to make the old workbench rattle from their efforts. They weren't meant to be celibate creatures, but Calix was more cautious in pursuing the bright-eyed young men all around them. There were plenty who sought comfort in each other, but it was a rutting, grunting kind of fumbling that was so rarely appealing. So many of the students were American, with their flat affectations and tendency to think of everything in terms of only fight or fuck.

No refinement. No stopping to stare at the beauty of a sunrise or the ripple of the stream that ran along the back of the school's vast acreage. And none of those boys would fuck him until he'd cry. None of them were Calix. Beauty personified. The same man now standing nose to nose with him, trembling in anger.

"I can take it," Lawton whispered, angling his head up a spare inch. Calix was taller only by a little, and Lawton liked it when he could lean into the other man in this way. "Give me your rage, pet. I've watched you pace all winter long, like a caged, angry animal."

Calix sucked in a sharp breath at that, and Lawton pressed his advantage. With any luck, he'd soon be pressed into the mattress, his legs open in invitation. "There's not a single man here who wouldn't put you on your back, darling. You know it. You know you're beautiful. But you know they couldn't make you feel like I do."

Lawton skimmed his lips along Calix's jaw while Calix stood stock-still, the only sound between them was Calix's hard breaths. He was an inch from breaking. The tension made Lawton's stomach knot up in anticipation. Whatever came exploding *out of Calix next would knock his knees out from underneath him; Lawton was entirely certain of it.*

"What of it?" Calix's words were whispered directly into Lawton's ear as Calix turned into his touch. "What of it, Lawton? What does anything between us have to do with my father and his money?"

When Calix gripped him by the arms, Lawton's very soul soared. Yes, please, he thought as Calix pressed a kiss below his ear. A touch so gentle, the thrill of teeth against his skin nearly made Lawton sob with relief. "You know exactly what I'm talking about," Lawton said, trying not to pant with every breath. "You could change your legacy– "

Calix reared back as if he'd been struck, dark eyes wildly alight. He was flush with anger, his cheeks ever so pink, his grip on Lawton's arms the most perfect pain. Lawton reached out to cup Calix's jaw between his hands and angle their heads just so. He wanted to see Calix's face now, during, after his friend's next words.

"A legacy?" Calix hissed. "A legacy of... what? A lineage that should have died out decades, maybe generations ago? The legacy of a man who cheated and drank and abused every moment of his godsforsaken life? A man who used my mother– "

The words slipped past Lawton's lips before he had time to think. "She chose him," he said, already bracing for the aftermath. Thrilled by the prospect of it. His Calix, so pretty all the time, but truly stunning at the height of any strong emotion. Anger, excitement, fear, lust. It didn't matter. And now anger and lust were twisted up in Calix's fine features, vibrating through him on a level that Lawton knew was too strong to ignore for long. Because he felt it, too. The anger at Calix for even thinking about throwing away his father's money; for not thinking ahead for his future, for theirs. The sheer selfishness of having all the resources you could ever want at your disposal, and turning your nose up at it because your father was a prick.

Lawton's father was a prick, and you didn't see him whining about it. No, Lawton had struck out on his own immediately, and always had several irons in the fire to keep him in fine clothes and Italian leather shoes.

The moment hung between them. Crystallized.

Then shattered.

"You absolute bastard," Calix snarled before dragging Lawton forward. Into him. Plastering their bodies together, so tightly that Lawton felt every inch of Calix's hardness against his thigh. And Lawton reveled in it.

Lawton tipped his head just so. The perfect angle. "You need a release on that pressure valve, pet," he whispered in the span of a long exhale. He knew how he looked, how he smelled, and he knew Calix. The mightiest oak in his forest, felled with one swing.

Calix's grip on his collar was crushing, but the impact of his mouth on Lawton's was divine. Lawton didn't even have the breath or space or moment to smile, to bask in his little glory, because that was Calix's tongue in his mouth. Calix's teeth in his bottom lip. Calix's hand now on the small of his back, ruthless in how his long fingers plucked Lawton's shirt from his trousers. Rough and unyielding. Exactly how Lawton liked him, in between the moments he preferred Calix to be softer, sweeter.

On some level it didn't matter. Calix tasted the same no matter his mercurial mood, but tonight, Lawton wanted to watch him unravel.

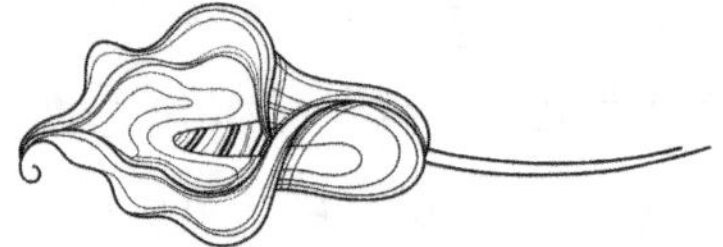

The version of Lily that had first taken up residence in his body had been a force; a gale wind pushing at him from all sides. The Lily that came to him now was tattered and winded, barely a shimmer on the edge of his periphery and even in his mind, she sounded smaller.

You were supposed to give Calix the coin, she gasped, a faded, shriveled hand going up to her throat. Lawton found himself in the strangest place, caught between wanting to help and cursing her name. This was the woman Calix had worshiped, had shown undying fealty and love to? By everything Lawton had witnessed, she was the epitome of a parent and the opposite of a mother. His mother had been like Lily in that regard, merely an adult parent responsible for his caring, but lacking in maternal love and instinct. Instead of bold and ambitious, his mother had been meek, scattering to save her own hide every time his father got into one of his moods.

"Was I? Strange that I didn't, then." Lawton twirled the pen between his fingers, admiring the way the silver glinted in the firelight. "Stranger still that you didn't make me." He thrust an arm out, as if she were mere feet away. "I bear the marks of your poison, but you seem weaker for it. I take it that coin was a vital part of your plan?"

Lily clearly bore no love for him in the moment, and Lawton wondered if she'd ever looked at Calix that way. If she'd ever cursed him once his back was turned. Calix wouldn't have survived his mother spiting him to his face, that was for certain.

You don't know what you've done, Lily rasped, her fingers scratching mercilessly at her throat. Where her skin was normally paper-white, her fingernails left behind black score marks that dripped thickly. *I would have protected him in the demimonde! I needed to be there—*

"Seems he did just fine in that regard. Protecting himself, that is. So, I wonder what it was you were hiding, and continue to hide, from your oh-so precious son even after all your promises. Because this isn't the form of a spirit with much strength left, and it, coincidentally, seemed to happen after I kept that coin here." Lawton plucked the coin from his pocket and held it up. "What does it do, Lily? Is there a bit of your soul trapped inside this *very dingy* metal? Or a bit of something you learned?"

Lawton let it drop to the floor and the thud it made on impact sent a spark of pain through him. He might as well have dropped an anchor on his head. It took the air out of him, but he still managed to gasp, "Or is there another bit of *your son* inside?"

More pain arced through him, starting near the base of his spine and following up the vertebrae. Lawton gritted his teeth to keep from crying out, but he had to drop to one knee, so intense was the shockwave.

You fool. You insipid, selfish, egotistical idiot. Lily's words were a hiss; he could practically taste the venom. *Yes, it's a soul anchor. Another little bit of me. You only had to give it to Calix and he would have found me in the demimonde and brought me back and then Talbot —*

Her torrent of words stopped so suddenly and through the noise in his head, Lawton very clearly understood. As if her very intent were coursing through him now. Memories, waves of them...

Lily at her desk, half-empty teacups scattered about bits of paper and smudges of ink, but the circle was finally *done.* She was that much closer...

...a face. But not a human one. This one had fangs for teeth, fangs that poked out from a set of fine bowed lips, and above that, ice crystals for eyes. To look at it was to see *everything* and *nothing.* Like looking at the face of God. A god.

...an angel?

No, a monster.

Pale limbs wrapped in royal purple and faded gold, a strange, skewed crown of leaves, connected to a bone-white scalp with metal brutally jabbed into its skull.

It was not human. Not of this world. And not of their reality.

Its name echoed within her, and so it echoed within him, too.

Uriel

The image flipped, split, and twisted, and Lawton's gut churned with it. Bile rose in his throat and he flung himself away from the desk to dry heave in the corner while Lily stared at him with hatred in her eyes.

He'd seen something he shouldn't have. And he could feel wrath boiling off her, reaching for him. Threatening to sweep them under. And the more she faded, the faster her memories came to him.

"I need more," she pleaded, beseeching the strange creature before her. Between them shimmered the faintest bit of golden magic, like a shield keeping her out, or it inside. "Please. The more I know, the better I can protect him."

The being hovering inside that golden column was unearthly still, so when it flashed forward to press a long, long, hand against that magic, its multi-jointed fingers bending and snapping and rapping against its cage, Lily stumbled backwards. "I take this on at great risk to myself. The other Guardians do not tolerate intrusions into their realms. So, to ask me to traverse their territories is quite costly."

Lily shook her head. "I know. I know. Anything you ask, it's yours in exchange for the stories of Oracles in other places. You already told me many of them don't suffer the way we do here. Why? Why can't their knowledge be mine?"

The creature seemed to sway before Lily, as if weighing something. Contemplating something. After a long, deathly still pause, it said, "Then we must make an accord. You will give me what I ask, and if you meet your demise before you fulfill your bargain, we will continue our agreement. In situ, even in the grave."

"You'll help me protect my son?"

The creature leered at her, those glittering ice-chip eyes vibrant even through the magical shield. "If you'll be my vessel into your world, then yes."

"You're a monster," he whispered as he spat foul bits from his mouth. What should have been the last bits of vomit were thick with a black, tar-like substance. He shrank back, horrified and confused, but as he moved, one of the black blobs moved *with him.*

"You're dying, child." Lily's voice came back to him now, her concern so saccharine, it made his stomach heave again. The blob nudged forward, moving as if in pain. It touched the toe of his shoe and he recoiled again. It strained valiantly for him, then deflated and moved no more. "The longer I stay, the more I sap from your veins. Did you think you'd survive this?"

Lawton stared at her, torn between screaming in frustration and running in utter terror. But deep down, far below the layers of armor he wore to keep his meager world afloat, was an *anger* he'd never known. He might spend a lifetime making amends, but she was already dust.

He could make her dust again.

"Perhaps not," Lawton admitted, "but I'm fairly certain you won't, either. You've lost one of these so-called soul anchors already. And you've cracked the faith of the one person you need to bring you back."

The sound she made was unearthly, inhuman. A raw-throated cross between a scream and a wail. And now she was before him, alight with fury. "You know nothing," Lily spat. Her image was wavering more now, the edges of it blurry like raindrops down a window pane. Even parts of her elegant dress and her hair were smudged. "Calix will find me and restore me—"

"This was never about him, was it? Well, I shouldn't say *never* since even the worst parents often do love their children, however deeply misguided. No, I think this was about you all along." *Because it's how I would have done it.*

Lawton's gaze went to the ceiling, to trace over fine molding covering the seams where silk wallpaper met paint. Then over to the neat bookshelves, so full of knowledge from every corner of the world. Calix's pen, still in his hand, felt heavy. It was merely a pen, but it was so tied to memories of Calix and their many years together.

With as much calm as he could muster, Lawton put the pen in his pocket and backed away from her, hands up in a warding gesture. "And I don't think I'm wrong, Lily. You and I come from the same rotten root off the tree of self-preservation. And it really is too bad we're part of the root and not the fruit. Because self-preservation can be an asset. It keeps you limber, quick, agile. Never one to be caught unawares. But at the root? Oh, no. That's paranoia. And greed. And fear. That root will wrap itself around your neck and you'll beg for more because it feels *good* to be so deferential to those dark thoughts. And you'll quickly fool yourself into thinking, *'Ah, aren't I clever, always one step ahead of everyone else?'*"

Lawton picked up the coin once more, held it up for Lily to see. "Aren't I clever? Aren't I always one step ahead? And even in death, I cannot be fooled or unseated, because I made death my fool. But then the devil found me." He closed his fist around the coin. "What deal did you *truly* make with Uriel? I'm assuming it involved Calix's life and you toying with it, beyond being some kind of... *vessel."* Lawton shuddered on that word, now knowing well what the role entailed, given his present circumstance. "I knew you were lying from the beginning, and the look on your face now tells me I'm right."

Lily's form wavered. It was if she was diminishing her energy through sheer, impotent rage. "Why would I possibly tell you anything?"

"No concern for your son, then? How very cold. And here I thought you did *everything* for him."

Lawton was very aware of how much he mirrored her; how she reflected back his worst fears and traits. And while he was no bold hero, he did have a certain level of cunning that kept him from being held down for too long. He'd never been one to shy away from a challenge. This nagging feeling, as if he were missing part of the story, wouldn't let go, either. So, he used it all to his advantage.

"Tell me," he said.

"Why?" But she hadn't turned away from him.

"Because I'll help you save Calix. I was going to no matter the scenario." He leaned in, held the coin up. "And because I won't tell him what you really did."

CHAPTER SIX

ETHANIEL

They were forced to stop walking after an untold amount of time, when Uzala and Maria rounded some invisible corner, leaving Ethaniel to crane his neck in an attempt to track them. But they disappeared, and a moment later and out of the gray mists sprung up... a *forest*. Trees of slate gray bark that chipped and flaked, like ash falling to the ground; their branches strung with dark blue vines that writhed and snaked when anyone came close and topped with leaves of dull red. The smallest of the leaves was easily twice the width of Ethaniel's palm.

"Don't touch the leaves," Maria said to him and Vincent. "They scream."

"Of course they fucking do," Vincent muttered under his breath. Ethaniel took that moment to look him over, but all his half-brother did was laugh, the sound cracked and winded. "I'm a walking bruise, brother. The kind that only time can heal."

Aubrey could heal him. Ethaniel's mind immediately fled to the corner where things were warm and safe. Where he could almost feel Aubrey at his side. He wasn't going to give Vincent any information, about Aubrey or Calix or anyone involved. He didn't *deserve it.* "Do you think it would have hurt less if it had simply killed you?"

Vincent was cut off when Uzala floated close by and said, "Sit, brothers. Please. We have many plans to make but for now... you should rest."

Ethaniel flicked his gaze over to where Maria sat on a swing made of those snaking vines. Was it his overly tired mind, or had she given him a small nod?

He turned back to the creature, whose terrifying visage was only more monstrous amidst all the trees. Trees whose trunks now oozed a black ichor that smelled of peat moss and decay. Like a fetid bog. Its wraith-like body, stark white and pulsing with those strange red lights, hovered amongst the darkness and yet it did not look out of place.

I wonder if it built this, or simply found it, Ethaniel thought. *Either way, it's all horrifying.* "He's injured," Ethaniel said, more a statement of fact than plea. "He needs care."

"Your sister can assist," Uzala said, rounding the last of the trees to point to Maria. "Go on, child. You're much more capable than I." And it held up a long hand. The sight of those multi-jointed fingers made Ethaniel's very skeleton tremble. They were beyond unnatural. *Unfathomable.* As if his mind were trying to splinter, staring at impossible angles and configurations. And then all the fingers pointed to him. "But you will come to me now, patterner. I have need of you."

Ethaniel shook his head. "Not until Vincent is healed."

Uzala grinned, all sharp fangs and strange, glinting red dots crossing its body like a map.

Like a map.

Ethaniel met Maria's eyes as her voice pushed into his mind again. *Like a map. Small and quiet, but it wears its truth on its body. It doesn't think me smart enough to know.*

Ethaniel's mind was a jumble. He heard her child's voice, her adult vocabulary, and he tried to fit the pieces together. Had she stayed the same physical age but had gained the mentality of a young woman? Was that how time passed in the *demimonde*? Did such a concept like time even exist in a place like this?

Uzala's voice became sickly sweet, spoiled candy in Ethaniel's ear. "Come to me. I need your eyes."

Ethaniel was pushed to his feet by an invisible hand, then lifted off the ground until he was floating a few feet above it. He struggled, a protest on his lips, and soon his chest was constricted as if a *hundred* hands were squeezing the life from him. He couldn't even gasp.

"You will come," Uzala said as Ethaniel was pushed to stand before its putrescence. "And you will read something for me and tell me what it means, and then I will tell you what we must do next. For my twin plans something devious, something that would break your little world in two and leave behind many, many dead."

Air. He was running out of *air*. Panic welled in his throat like a shout but nothing came. No inhale, no exhale. Just a creeping sense of cold while his vision slowly went black.

Is this how I die?

"I think the lesson is learned," Uzala crooned. Its fingers peeled back to point away from him and the world became brighter, warmer, and he could breathe once more. Ethaniel was left coughing and near to retching, unable to bend over and let the tears of pain and fear drop to the ground. They fell to his shirt instead.

Not his shirt. Aubrey's. He'd borrowed it that morning, wanting that fine cloth that smelled like his lover against his skin.

"I'll come," Ethaniel rasped before Uzala clicked its fingers and Ethaniel followed helplessly in its wake.

It walked around a pocket of these ichor-black trees to an opening where a column of black stone stood. It was twice as tall as Uzala and as thick across as a mature redwood and from what Ethaniel could see, perfectly smooth. But the black stone was dotted with tiny white specks that glinted, making the whole thing appear as if covered in stardust. It was oddly beautiful, but the sight of that stone filled Ethaniel with dread.

"What is that?" Ethaniel asked with a hand to his throat.

"Something left over from ones even older than I," Uzala replied, its voice now church bell-resonant. "A secret. The *demimonde* has many. It is why so many try to find their way here. Looking for secrets. For magic. For enlightenment." It placed two hands, fingers bent at sickening angles, on the stone. Ethaniel watched as several of the red dots on its body began to flicker, then flash. "It is a place of…

commune and power, this stone. Your kind has even found some of them in your world. They bedeck the landscapes of many planes."

Realization washed over him, his mind fitting the pieces together. This was the same kind of stone as the one in the Collectio; the one Aubrey had used to try to learn Convergence's secrets. His mind grasped for reason, for sense... and it found connections.

The stone

The book

Talbot

Calix

Oracles

"Yes," Uzala hissed, its face suddenly inches from his own. He couldn't recoil, could only stare in horror as a long, black tongue unfurled to lick across his cheek. This close, Uzala smelled of ash and rain, its tongue like sand scraping across his skin. "You assume correctly. The stone awoke something latent in Dee's soul trap; something that would have likely stayed dormant except in the fertile mind of your Oracle. With Talbot awakened, he began to seek out a way and gain back his body, and coming to the *demimonde* is a fine way of doing so. Here, anything is possible for the right sacrifice."

Ethaniel watched on as Uzala sank a fingertip into the surface of the stone; it rippled at his touch. That's when the screaming began — his and someone else's, far away and discordant and seemingly endless. He felt a red hot lance of pain in his mind and clutched at his head while tears ran down his face. Uzala paid no mind to his distress and pain, and instead forced his hand to make contact with the stone.

It came over him immediately, a wave both foul and all-encompassing.

He couldn't think. Couldn't think.

Couldn't...

think

In the darkness of his mind, a quiet lull hung low. Ethaniel was aware of nothing but the pressing black all around him. There was a dizzying lack of *anything* except that black in this space.

Was he still alive? Had that... that thing killed him?

The first pattern was nothing but a mere flash of something red.

Not red. Not like autumn leaves or cherries. Flame-hot, red and orange. Glass taken from a furnace and not yet cooled.

Another pattern, another flash. This one a brilliant emerald green, in his left periphery. The terror of the moment, of not knowing if he was alive or left in some coma-esque state, was too much for him to make sense of the patterns.

Another flash. Another pattern. Blue. Another, this one yellow, almost gold. Another. And another. And another.

Interlocking pieces of a much larger puzzle.

A sizzle of familiarity, and dread, left him stunned.

And in his mind came an echo. Soft, fuzzy, then yowling; a scream. And then a whisper, velvet-thick and dark. Distantly, Ethaniel felt his body respond. No pain or pleasure, but *ecstasy*.

His mind fully awake and open.

Ready to receive.

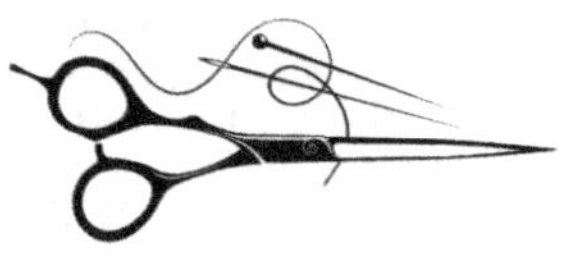

Speak to me of ascension.

Speak to me of great heights and stormy valleys, of wind curling over open land with the confidence of a known lover.

Then speak to me of the great questions, the long-hidden answers, and the way to be right in your eyes.

And in our trade, I know your world. And you mine.

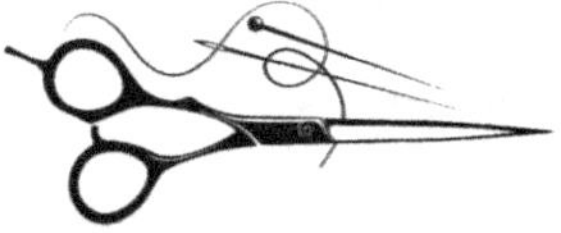

The *demimonde* was built of patterns. Overlapping, entangling. Some in languages he vaguely understood, others beyond comprehension; not human, not of Earth in any regard. Alien and lurching, veiled in slippery shadow or so bright he risked his eyesight even with the pattern in his periphery.

He could see them. *All of them.* Comprehension was a separate matter, but he could *see.* For the first time in his life. And his heart felt as if it couldn't contain it all. The utter *truth* of their world and possibly many others, floating above his head, wrapped around thick ichor trees, embedded in the ground beneath his feet.

And when he looked at Uzala, he saw its patterns. The map it wore was without a key or compass, but Ethaniel could see them. His eyes couldn't keep still, as if they were acting of their own volition, busily tracing every red line and slash over its form. Before, it made only the vaguest sense. Uzala clearly knew it was a map and had, from the scratchings in its flesh, marked the boundaries and paths itself. But they were disparate points, likely places the thing had already traveled to.

Ethaniel could read the entire map and he saw doors. He saw the golden one through which he and Calix had traveled, and noted it was shuttered and dark —

His vision was wiped away, a hand through fog, and it felt as if his very soul was slammed back into his body. And he was still floating above the ground as Uzala pried his hand from the stone and let it drop. His palm made contact with his trousers and Ethaniel cried out in pain. Clutching his hand, he looked at the mottled red and purple skin and saw a seal burned there. It mimicked many of the sketches of the solar system, but with many more rings and planets.

Uzala held up its hand and Ethaniel saw the same pattern burned into it, and while its fingers danced and bent and twitched, it said, "A little token from whoever placed these stones here. Touching the stone in my curiosity created this... ", and it gestured at the blinking red, bulbous lights on its body. "I wonder what it gave you."

Ethaniel was thrust into the air and that black tongue snaked across his cheek once more. "*Power,*" it whispered in his ear, like a delighted lover. "Yes, good. We will need it to defeat my brother."

From somewhere deep within, dragged over the jagged rocks of his soul, Ethaniel dredged up his voice. "And why do you want to do that?"

"Because he and I are twins, and we need to be made whole. Apart, we are only as strong as our respective halves. His desperation to reach your world let him make contact, but to do so, he had to make a sacrifice of the flesh. I could not talk him out of it... so he took me out of *us.*"

Horror swept over him, turned him cold. Uzala smiled at him, with a jaw of grinding, gnawing teeth that rubbed against each other. Squeaking as they moved. "He *slaughtered* us. And I think, in his orphaned state, Uriel has gone a bit mad. I need to get him back. You will help me stop him, stop his intrusion into your world."

Ethaniel wanted to vomit.

"But enough for now. I leave you to your sister and brother."

It flicked a hand at him and Ethaniel was suddenly sitting on the ground beside Vincent. Maria was at his other side, dabbing at Vincent's bruised cheek with a cloth.

"Get your bearings, brother," Vincent rasped through clenched teeth. Ethaniel noticed he was missing two, and the gums had gone black. "We'll need your magic if we're to survive this."

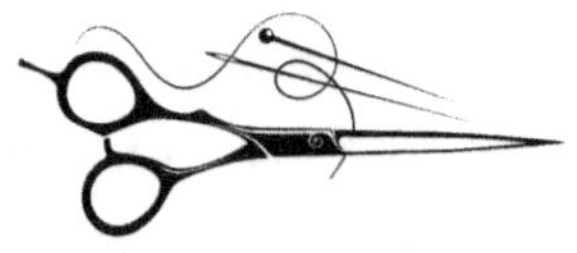

The urge to run was strong. Stronger than nearly anything he'd ever experienced. But it took only a glance at Vincent: the deep slashes in his skin, the blood caking his clothes, the broken fingers... There was nowhere to go.

And despite everything, Ethaniel couldn't leave him.

Maria drifted over to them, her hands full of ragged strips of cloth. "I cannot mend, but I can help," she whispered as she settled again at Vincent's side. "Uzala is gone for now, but it won't stay away for long."

Vincent let her wrap his fingers and bind his injuries while Ethaniel watched. Everything he wanted to say sat on his tongue, but he couldn't push it out into the air. *Were they lost forever? Was this place to be their grave?*

Maria looked up at him as the last tendrils of that dreary thought echoed in his mind. She shook her head and said, "I can get you home, but it will not be easy. You saw, didn't you? You saw through the stone."

Vincent hissed in pain as she bound two fingers together. Those hands touching Vincent were his sister's and yet, Ethaniel could almost sense a lack of something... *human* and empathetic in her. The exacting nature of her handiwork was something the tradesman in him could admire, but if this was his sister, she would have been in tears at the pain she was causing.

Instead, there were no tears. Not even a flicker of an eyelid or a slight frown. Just an emotionless mask in place of his sister's round face, and it chilled him to realize it.

Ethaniel wasn't sure if trusting this visage of his sister was the wisest thing, but it was his only choice. "How can you get us home?" It was the only thing to ask in this instance. Vincent hadn't seen what he had, and Ethaniel wasn't about to let him have that information. But if Maria had touched the stone...

Maria kept tending to Vincent, who was watching her with one bloodshot eye. His other had swollen shut. "I can find a door. I can't go through it, but I can open it."

Vincent looked sharply at him. "A door?"

What was his half-brother playing at? "The confusion in your voice is disconcerting, Vincent." Ethaniel leaned in, close enough to catch the scent of dried blood. "Did you not go through a door?"

Vincent chuckled, more wheeze of air through broken bellows than anything else. "Oh, I went through a door. One I got our cousin Isme to open, and one she happily pushed me through while she called *that thing* to her. Clever. I anticipated treachery, but not the strength of her magic. *Harkness* magic. Seems I underestimated."

Isme. He hadn't heard that name in years. Over a decade, really, when he swept aside the cobwebs of time and thought about it. They'd all been children, a big mass of them running back and forth across his mother's estate lawn, throwing petals and tufts of grass at each other. Shrieking, yelling, laughing in that way children had. This was before Maria, before Vincent. Cousin Isme was really a distant relation his mother's family claimed because of her magic — and only because of that. Because at only four years old, Isme had found a dead bird and brought it to her father. As she cried and put her hand over the bird, its heart began beating once more. It flew off, out the open window and into a balmy summer morning.

Because Isme was clearly magical. And *powerful*. And Harknesses were well-versed in spotting power in their kin.

Because the last Harkness child to show such power... that had been him. He'd been the one his mother had pinned all her hopes and dreams (but certainly not all her plans) on, and when he'd rejected that legacy, she'd tossed him to his father. They'd fled the country after sneaking Maria out of the family compound, thanks to Ethaniel's knack for patterns. Life in the States had been quiet, fairly easy, but their demons followed in a path of shadow so dark, by the time it reached them, there was nothing to do but let it swallow them whole.

Maria disappeared. His father sent him to Uncle Jeremiah. His father was found dead a few months later. Heart attack, the doctor said. His heart simply seized up, and he was gone. Ethaniel knew better. Because for all the family had exiled him, some of his cousins stayed in touch via enchanted letter. An invention of Titus, his cousin and closest in age to Ethaniel. And Titus had told him long, harrowing stories of what he'd seen happening in the compound — his mother taking Isme under her wing; strange green and blue lights flashing in the dead of night, coming from Isme's chambers; and watching a tarp-covered wagon be wheeled in on the first night of the full moon, month after month.

Ethaniel had never doubted Isme had killed his father. Hearing her name now made the back of his neck prickle and his stomach go tight with unleashed fury and fear. A heady, sickening combination.

"You've woven yourself quite the web, Vincent," Ethaniel said. He had to fight to keep his voice down, lest Uzala hear him. He wanted to be away from that creature for as long as possible, and not only because its presence evoked a singular sensation of disgust in him; one so strong, the urge to vomit whenever it was near was worse than the act itself.

"Trust me, I'm aware," Vincent bit out. His gaze never stayed on Ethaniel for long, he was starting to notice; it dipped and swung over to Maria quite often, and that made him uneasy. "We need to get out of here."

"Time. I need time," Maria said in her strange, melodic way. That, too, had Ethaniel wondering if he'd lost his mind, or was well and truly dead and being haunted by the ghost of his sister. She sounded like her but with a single, discordant note threaded through her voice. Barely off-pitch, but there all the same. "And power."

Their gazes stared him down. Hers, starved and hollow. His, curiosity-tinged wariness and delight. Both of them terribly, soul-numbingly honest. And then his sister was crawling over to him on her hands and knees, like a child playing pony. The same way Maria used to act as a pony with her dolls. It was like the voice — so close to the real thing, but with the faintest, strange edge. A single, off-pitch note in a chorus. Once he saw it, Ethaniel couldn't help but see it all the time.

The thing — his sister, a monster — crawled up on him, pressed him back into the tree, and as he watched in horror, stretched its neck to an unhuman length so her now-alien face, with all-wrong angles and eyes that had gone narrow. "I need magic to open a door," Maria said. "Blood might be better. Blood might be the only way."

"I'm sure Ethaniel can spare a little to ensure we get home," Vincent said. But his arrogant half-brother sounded scared, voice gone tremulous in a way that was hard to disguise.

"Blood and power," Maria sang. "But hush now, or we'll attract its attention."

She scrambled off him, and as she did, her face righted itself. Her spine snapped straight, bringing her to standing. And she was Maria once more. His sister. A monster.

CHAPTER SEVEN

CALIX

Dawn came with a sense of queasiness. As if his world had been upended but sleep had let him forget temporarily. The moment Calix opened his eyes, his stomach dropped. The room spun and he groaned.

The limp arm around his waist tightened. "Calix?"

"Go back to sleep," Calix whispered. The last thing he needed to do was awaken Aubrey. He'd have bet his estate and more that if he looked back now, the circles under Aubrey's eyes would have deepened overnight. He would have bet it all that Aubrey had slept one, maybe two hours.

"No, Calix… "

Calix leaned forward to press his lips to Aubrey's brow. His skin was clammy, his hands too warm. "Hush. I'm going to try to find Magnus, ask if there's more tea to be had."

He was no match for Aubrey physically, but Calix tried to gently push Aubrey back down when he attempted to rise. He'd been right; the circles under Aubrey's eyes were bruise-like, and there was a pallor to his face that made Calix's heart jump with concern. "I can help."

Calix cupped his cheek, all the easier to direct Aubrey's eyes to his, so he might stare hard into them with as much sternness as he could muster. "You *could*, but you shouldn't. Whatever is to come, it won't go well if you're not rested." *And if you are sick*, he thought.

"Calix… "

"No arguing."

Aubrey shook his head and that movement, somehow, made Calix's stomach roil. Threatening. "You're sweating, Calix. Are you feverish?"

"What?" Calix reached up, brushed his fingers across his forehead. They came back wet. "No, I'm fine."

"You're paler than normal, dove," Aubrey said. The warmth he'd come to expect from Aubrey was there, but the words were sluggish. "Let's find Magnus, inform him that —"

The door to their conjured room opened and Agrippa, now dressed in a fine three-piece pinstripe suit, burst in, tray in hand. "It set in even sooner than I'd anticipated." Agrippa set the tray down before picking up the two pewter goblets it held, then passed them over. "Drink. Get it all down."

There was nothing in the goblets. Calix was utterly confused, and from the look on his face, Aubrey was, too. "They're empty," Calix said.

Agrippa chuckled, the sound reverberating softly about the space. "They're not."

Aubrey's deep scowl was a fearsome thing, and Calix vowed right then to never be the direct cause of such an expression. All he could do was shrug before putting his lips to the goblet. Something warm and thick hit his tongue. It reminded him of the honey mead he and Lawton used to drink after exams; only one bar in Cambridge had it and they almost always overindulged. "What is this?"

Agrippa flapped their hands at him. "Drink! All of it! It won't work otherwise."

Calix and Aubrey exchanged a look before finishing their drinks, but before he could inspect the goblet, Agrippa snatched it out of his hand. "This space isn't meant for humans, magical or not. Anyone who stays here for an extended period of time winds up thinning. Think of it like a wasting disease. Stay here too long, and this place would pull you apart at the seams."

Calix saw Aubrey's brow furrow. The man likely had a million questions, many of which would be on an academic level. But all Aubrey said was, "I wish I could say I was surprised, but at this point, it feels like resignation."

Agrippa cocked their head. "Resignation to what?"

The sad smile Aubrey gave him nearly broke Calix's heart all over again. "To the fact that it's so very hard to be different and lead a normal life. All this chaos? All the danger and blood and loss of the last days? Somehow, it feels like... like I deserve it."

"Aubrey." Calix linked their fingers together and squeezed. "You don't. Not ever. None of us do."

"I wish I could see things as you do, dove."

"It'll be different once this is over."

"Speaking of," Agrippa said, "we may have a lead." They pinned Calix with a keen stare. Calix had been looked through by many a man. Usually they were wealthy and it was done with a sniff of disdain or an indifferent frown. *The pathetic earl. The orphan.* Agrippa, a creature from another place outside his own realm, his own experience, but still almost *too* human, did not look at him in such a manner.

He had seen that look once before, previously aimed at Ethaniel. *It was as if they were.... measuring my soul,* Ethaniel had said to him later, between steadying sips of tea and Aubrey half asleep beside them. *A few seconds to weigh the gristle of my being. Disturbing. Final.*

Calix now understood why Ethaniel had felt that way.

Agrippa turned to Aubrey. "Your family are healers. Bone and flesh, nerve and root. The most powerful of them can regenerate limbs. Ones like your father."

"Yes," Aubrey managed to say as he squeezed Calix's hand hard. Calix fought not to stare hard at Aubrey. *Regrowing limbs? Healers could do that?* He was so glad Aubrey could no longer hear his thoughts; they felt blasphemous, antithetical to the little he knew about Aubrey's complicated relationship with his family. As if his sudden awe might negate the history hewn there.

"But you are different." Agrippa floated closer to them. *Floated.* Hovering ever so slightly above the ground, now with their hand extended to Aubrey. "Might I see?"

A muscle in Aubrey's jaw ticked, so Calix wrapped his other hand around their joined ones. It wasn't *fear;* not completely.

They'd gone through so much unknown already.

But this was someone Magnus trusted.

"What are you looking for?" Aubrey asked, the slightest tremor of unsteadiness wavering behind his words. Aubrey wasn't afraid, but he was very uncertain, and it all had a razor-sharp edge to it.

"Power," Agrippa said. "The measure of yours."

Before Calix could even think of a reply, Aubrey put his hand in Agrippa's The channel of magic was immediate. Aubrey's power, teal-bright as an island cove, flowed *through* him and into Agrippa. It twisted and branched, the thinnest of lines and some as thick as Calix's forearm, turning blue to green to indigo.

And with it, the room changed.

The walls and floors, the simple furnishings, were gone. He and Aubrey were on the bed, Agrippa hovering before them, and all around them were scenes. Moments. Bits of time saved, as if wrapped in a handkerchief to take home.

Calix watched, stunned, as he realized these were Aubrey's memories playing out before them.

AUBREY IS A CHILD, perhaps seven or eight, and he's staring through a window at three girls with the same piercing light green eyes as his. They sit in a circle on the ground, their dresses tucked under their knees, as they hold out their hands, palms facing the earth. The oldest one, too young to marry but old enough to watch the other children, concentrates, brow drawn down but eyes open and fixed on two halves of a leaf on the ground. With naught but a moment and a flick of her wrist, her deep maroon magic extends from her palms and floats down to the leaf. The two halves are brought together, and the leaf is mended. Perfectly new.

When Aubrey turns back to the table before which he stands, there are many, many torn leaves strewn across its top, and several of which are whole, bearing only the thinnest fracture line to show a previous break. Every whole leaf was glowing with vivid teal magic.

A WOMAN WITH AUBREY'S *bearing and bone structure but not his eyes hands him a flat, white box roughly the size of a folded dress shirt. Aubrey, now older by at least half a dozen years or so, smiles brightly.*

"You've long deserved it," she says, her English beautifully accented, her voice lilting and soft. "But... "

"I know, Mother." Aubrey's smile drops but his grip on the box doesn't loosen. "He won't see it. Please know how grateful I am."

She leans in and kisses the top of his head. His hair is grown out here, longer than Calix has ever seen it, and the dense curls are a charming pairing with Aubrey's youth. The curls sway with his movement as he opens the box and stares down at a small onyx statue. Something about it sparks familiarity with Calix, but he can't recall from where or when. But he does know it is significant to Aubrey, and not only because the Aubrey in this memory holds the stone with reverence, turning it over in his hands and smoothing his fingertips across its surface.

"I'll make sure the proper one is given to you when you're of age," she says, watching Aubrey with a small smile. "Your father is a stubborn man, but he can't deny you your heritage."

AUBREY, NOW TALLER AND *broader but still carrying a gangliness of his limbs, stands over a dead body. The skin blue with cold death, the eyelids carefully glued shut. But the corpse is clean and draped for modesty, and as Aubrey looks around the small room, there are four other young people. Two men, two women, all wearing identical plain blue smocks and the type of multi-lens magnifiers Calix has seen Aubrey use before.*

"You cannot heal the living until you can knit dead flesh. Master this, and soon you will be given your own living, breathing patients. Ones with small cuts and simple conditions, but living nonetheless."

The man standing at the head of the room is clearly Aubrey's father. No one else would have the same eyes, the same hands. And no one else would capture Aubrey's attention so. Aubrey is rooted to the spot before his corpse, frozen with fear. Calix can practically taste it; a memory gone sour, like wine left out too long.

The other students have begun, but Aubrey remains as he is, staring down at a dead body, his hands empty and useless at his sides.

Aubrey's father approaches him, his own hands behind his back, one eyebrow arched. He waits to speak until he is at Aubrey's side, close enough that a whisper wouldn't carry to the others. "Is this where you finally admit it? Even after all the begging and promising you did?" He leans in closer. Calix feels his own heart rate spike at his next words.

"Leave now, Aubrey. Leave before you waste this body and take up yet another's students time, and mine. Leave now, and we can discuss your future placement after dinner tonight."

"I won't."

There is a beat of silence. It hangs between father and son, gossamer-thin.

"So be it."

Aubrey's father flicks a hand at the corpse and its skin splits from neck to navel, peeling back to reveal shriveled insides. Calix flinches even before Aubrey's father says, "Now fix it."

"You say you can heal objects? Fascinating." Magnus, his hair in a much longer queue as was fashionable roughly a decade ago, eagerly places a book on the desk between them. "I'm afraid this poor thing has seen better days. Could you give me a demonstration? I'd love to see your magic at work, Mr. Lavigne."

Aubrey, now in his twenties, wears a crisp black suit and sits with one leg crossed over the other, hands clasped about his knee. His rings sparkle in the sunlight dancing this space of dark wood and rich red rugs, but it's his smile that makes Calix gasp. This is Aubrey as he knows him, full of life and light and a power so unique it could rival miracles.

"I'd love to."

Aubrey stands, approaches the desk and pulls the book to him. "Just a moment."

And as he places his palms on the book and closes his eyes, there is a third eye that cracks open on his forehead, glowing the brightest blue-green.

WHEN REALITY SNAPPED BACK into place, it was not Agrippa before them, but Magnus. And on Aubrey's lap was a single white feather.

"I didn't know they would ask for that," Magnus said softly, his gaze stuck on the white feather. "It takes a lot out of them to do it. And they're not keen on using their full magic often. It can attract the wrong kind of attention, even here."

Calix's head was swimming and his temples throbbed, but he could feel Aubrey's clammy hand in his, so he squeezed it until Aubrey looked over at him. "Aubrey, are you all right? You look dazed."

"What... what happened?" Aubrey blinked several times, then rubbed at his eyes.

"Magnus, did Agrippa look at his memories? Is that what I was seeing all around me?" Calix could hardly believe what he was saying, but his eyes hadn't lied. And his heart ached with everything he'd witnessed, so he could only imagine how Aubrey was feeling.

Magnus did not answer him. Instead, he turned to Aubrey to ask, "How do you feel, Aubrey? I'm guessing a little winded. Take your time. It will give me a moment to explain."

Aubrey's hand gripped in his own, Calix was torn between comfort and yearning. Needing to comfort Aubrey, yearning to know more. About Aubrey and his past. All the stories he'd yet to hear, bumping up against the ones Aubrey might never tell. Boats of truth gently knocking against each other in a vast lake of dreams and disappointments.

Yearning, *desperate* for more information. His own natural curiosity was lit anew by the strange realm-between-realms they currently occupied, and about Agrippa, and their relationship with Magnus.

But all of that didn't matter if Ethaniel was never brought home. Calix needed to sate his curiosity, to feed his yearning, but not if their third, their other limb, was gone.

"I'm all right," Aubrey answered Magnus before turning to Calix. "And I'm sorry you had to see all of that. Those bits of my past are things I would have eventually shared."

"Share them with me once Ethaniel is home," Calix whispered back. He caressed the back of Aubrey's hand with his thumb, could feel the thrum of his pulse deep below. It felt good to be close like this, to comfort each other in such a state. Together, they could do this.

Aubrey huffed, more empty air than laugh, but the tiniest smile graced his features and Calix took that to heart. "And as far as how I'm feeling, Magnus," Aubrey said as he lifted his head, "I'm a tad dizzy but otherwise fine. Did Agrippa... find what they needed?"

"Of a sort!" Agrippa called from some yards away, hidden by the wall they'd conjured earlier to separate off this space for them. "When you're ready, I have a plan."

CALIX LET AUBREY GO with Magnus, the two of them side by side in companionable silence, before he flopped back onto the bed and stared at the ceiling. Or, the lack thereof. Above his head, the churning blackness now resembled more whirlpool than serene, star-studded sky, as it had before they'd fallen asleep. The ceaseless motion was too discombobulating to stare at directly, so he fixed his gaze on the northwest corner, his peripheral vision tracking the whirlpool.

Without Ethaniel here, he felt empty. It was strange to feel as though he was missing some vital part of himself. He'd been self-reliant from a young age, but he'd also had a mother on which to fall back, should things become too stressful at school or he and Lawton tripped into one of their little fights once a year or so. And even as they'd fought and run, and run and fought, cried in pain and triumph over these last several days, his mind had been quite good at filling in the missing parts.

So much of his younger years were beginning to make the kind of clear-eyed sense only dime pulp noir detectives seemed to be enlightened by. His mother had been his only real ally for so long, but with what he knew now? She had kept him safe and healthy not out of maternal bond or parental duty. No, she had kept him so in order to use him for her own ends. What her final plan had been, he could only guess at, but given her machinations... Calix could only assume it had to do with him, his magic, and potentially his youth or mortal vessel.

Perhaps he was fated to go mad and die young. Perhaps that was the fate of all Oracles. It hadn't escaped his notice that his Oracle powers had been of less use over the last days. Maybe he was broken, no longer the same brown-eyed boy, but no more powerful even with a change of eye color. Maybe his usefulness, as far as magic was concerned, had run its course.

It wouldn't matter. Because, magic or not, *he* was not useless. And he would give anything, *anything*, to have Ethaniel back.

Calix closed his eyes and breathed in, then out, slowly. Those steadying breaths were the last few seconds he'd take before throwing himself into whatever work was needed to bring Ethaniel home.

In

Out

In

Out

In...

When Calix opened his eyes, his mother's face was hovering above his own.

He bit back a scream but managed to scramble up the bed until he was stopped by the wall. "Aubrey!"

Thunderous footsteps echoed, growing louder and louder. When Aubrey threw the door open, his mother had receded into the ceiling, now only the pale, wispy oval of her face visible. Magnus and Agrippa burst in behind him, the three of them piling up on each other, but Calix couldn't look away from her face.

Her visage was pockmarked with scars and wounds alike, some stitched up in a way that would rival Mary Shelley's lab creature, others left open, the skin ragged and torn. One eye had gone milky white, like the rest of her, while the other blazed amber.

"My only chance," she gasped, "in this place between places. My only chance to fix it."

"Mother!" Calix couldn't stop from calling out to her, from reaching out to her as if he were six again and desperate to hide behind her skirts. Some part of him would always ache like that for her, for that comfort she'd once provided.

"Find Uriel. Find them." The ends of her words were wrapped in wind, snatched from her lips by the force of it. The wind was everywhere, suddenly; ruffling his hair and teasing the hems of their clothing. The room was growing colder, too, and Calix dimly wondered if his breath might show on the next exhale. "Use this. Lawton was to give it to you, but I took it back. Find Uriel. They will find their twin, and you will find Ethaniel."

A coin, roughly the size of a dollar and garishly golden, hit his knee and bounced off. Calix grabbed for it as she whispered, "I can be of no more help. Find me in the *demimonde*?"

With a final gasp too close to a death rattle, a thing that chilled Calix's very bones, she was gone. Dispersed into a whirlpool of energy that then ceased its churning and returned to velvet-inky darkness studded with the tiniest of white lights.

Calix opened his hand to stare down at the coin. On the side facing him was an impossibly complex magic circle, the lines and runes intersecting in near-microscopic ways; even peering at it from two inches away, Calix couldn't make out all the details. But the magic coming off of it was heady, and it set his own powers to sparking. Familiar, intimate, even, but rather uncomfortable in intensity.

"Flip it over, let us see," Agrippa said. Calix found himself staring up at the creature; they'd moved closer without him noticing. It was the closest he'd come to them since they'd met, and at this distance, he could sense their power, too. Ancient and vast, a deep chasm of possibility balanced with immaculate caution.

"You've suspicions?" Magnus said. His tone was light, but Calix could see the worry in his pinched brow.

"Oh, plenty, but I'm quite sure this is Uriel's coin, given her instructions," Agrippa replied.

"That's rather obvious," Magnus huffed.

His ruffled tone didn't appear to bother Agrippa. "Gaining the favor — in this case, a coin — of a creature like Uriel? It's unheard of for a mortal." Agrippa held out their hand and Calix dropped the coin into it. Carefully, Agrippa flipped the coin over and hissed at what was printed there.

A crown, elaborately decorated and filigreed, from which jagged and deadly cables ran in all directions. Monstrous to the point that Calix felt ill even looking at it. Agrippa closed their hand around it and the sensation vanished. "She traded something for this. Creatures like Uriel, made up of and from the *demimonde* itself, are horrifically powerful, but they often need a catalyst. An item of great arcane value, or other source of magic. But whatever she gave them was enough to earn her this. And she gave it to you."

Calix shook his head when Agrippa offered the coin once more. "I can't. Even being near it makes me want to vomit."

"Not surprising, given your Oracle powers are in direct conflict with the *demimonde*," Agrippa replied.

Calix gaped at him. "What? Wait, say that again."

"Your Oracle powers and the *demimonde* don't play nicely with each other. Haven't you wondered why your powers felt nonexistent and then full-throated in its proximity?"

Aubrey cut in between them, one hand on Calix's shoulder, as he said, "No, we didn't know. How could we? There's so little known about Oracles and most of it is superstition and fairy tales. We know his mother was trying to save him with what she'd learned from her research and experiments over the years, but you said Oracles are in *direct conflict* with the *demimonde*."

"Agrippa, this is... " Magnus sighed and pinched the bridge of his nose between thumb and forefinger. "What else can you tell us? Anything might be relevant to the tangle we're in."

At that, Agrippa drew themselves up, making their height even more impressive and imposing. "Not much, I'm afraid, since Oracles don't exist in any realm but your own. I've theorized the specific magic that makes an Oracle in your world likely comes from a variety of influences, but it's a deeper mystery I've yet to unravel." They blinked and refocused on Calix. Something about that gaze ripped through him, like frost-cold claws in his lungs, and he realized he'd been taking this creature for granted. For all they looked like a dawdling professor or librarian, it was still a being separately distinct from humans, and a powerful one at that.

Once we get Ethaniel back, then perhaps we can have a conversation.

Calix heard their voice in his mind; not intrusive or prying. A simple statement, an affirmation of Agrippa's commitment and their own curiosity about him. It should have been unnerving, and somewhere in the back of his mind, Calix registered the sudden, intense attention. But it wasn't anywhere near the top of his priority list.

"Questions about Oracles and my magic later," Calix said, giving Aubrey's arm a squeeze. "My mother gave me this coin. Is it part of her game— "

"To which we don't know the rules or goal," Magnus cut in.

"Or is she truly trying to help?" Calix finished. Magnus gave him a grim smile in return, more grimace than anything but he could tell the other man was trying to remain positive. They all were.

"Calix." Aubrey knelt before him, wedging himself between Calix's knees so he could rest his hands on Calix's shoulders. Aubrey was warm against his chilled skin and he shivered. Nothing sounded better than curling up in Aubrey's arms, but it wouldn't happen until they had wrested Ethaniel from the grip of the *demimonde*.

"Calix. Dove. Listen to me." Aubrey's palm slid across his jaw, his fingers tangling in Calix's hair, drawing their faces together until they could see nothing but each other. "Magnus and Agrippa have a potential lead. Throwing Convergence into the *demimonde* was the smartest thing you could have done. It's a book of magic, yes, but not from one origin. Agrippa has other writings of Dee's in this Collectio, and... do you remember how Ethaniel explained how he tracked us that night in the city?"

"When we got separated after the attack on your apartment?"

"Exactly. Maps are simply large, complex patterns. And Convergence is of a similar nature. A bevy of disparate pieces hewn together to create a whole. Not unlike how Ethaniel creates his tailored pieces. We lock onto one piece, and we find the whole. But... "

Suddenly, all the intensity left Aubrey and he deflated, the only thing keeping him upright was his iron will and the strong hands on Calix's shoulders. "None of us are patterners, so we'll need to work together to make this tracking spell work. But that coin may be an easier path forward."

Calix understood. The coin might better their chances at finding Ethaniel. It could be a gift from his mother, but that gift came with the price of interacting with the very creature with which she'd conspired. A creature possibly involved, even instrumental, in her demise. But the creature, this Uriel, was the twin of the being who held Ethaniel captive.

He had a choice: the hard road, or the treacherous one. Neither ensured victory. Neither ensured Ethaniel would return to them.

Aubrey carefully placed the coin in Calix's palm and together, they curled his fingers around it. "You know my feelings on this, and my logical thoughts. I will give anything to get Ethaniel back, and I know the same is true for you. And I trust whatever you decide, you're doing so with the care and kindness embedded into your very soul."

Aubrey leaned in to give him a kiss that was soft, sweet, and over far too quickly. Calix wanted to sink into it, into him, and never surface. Float on an endless sea of it.

The coin was warm from Aubrey's skin and even closed in his hand, he could smell the ash-smoke scent of it. "How long will this ritual take?" Calix asked.

Agrippa cleared their throat before replying. "An hour, maybe two, depending on how quickly we can tap into the right harmonies, for lack of a better word. But I'm confident I can track the book. And if I can track the book, I can follow traces of it to Ethaniel. It was in your possession long enough for some of that magic to still *likely* linger on him, influence of the *demimonde* or not."

Calix let out a long breath. It was such a risk. But could they risk interacting with Uriel? "How soon can we do the ritual?"

Agrippa gave him a short, satisfied nod. "We can do it right now. I only need to assemble the ingredients."

Aubrey got to his feet and pulled Calix up, and as soon as he did, Calix shoved the coin into his pocket. "Let's use the path of least resistance first," he said. "I'll not risk catching Uriel's attention, not if we can slip Ethaniel out of the *demimonde* under its nose."

"This is the longer, more involved way forward, but I think it's the right one," Magnus said as they left the room.

"I certainly hope so," Calix replied as he followed him into Agrippa's never-ending library of floating shelves.

INTERLUDE

Lawton

"And what is it you think I've done?"

Lily had hissed that at him right before she'd knocked the coin from his grip and disappeared into the wall, her form melting against one of the circular groupings of symbols used to open the door to the *demimonde*. He could still feel her influence, the weight of her presence deep in his soul. But she'd been right: as she diminished, so did he. The middle and ring finger on his left hand were a testament to its truth. His hand hadn't looked like that a few hours ago, and he'd been staring at it every chance he had, tracking the spread of inky blackness across his already mottled skin.

Did he know what she'd done? Not exactly. Not fully. But he could guess, and clearly Lily believed him to be distinctly more well-informed than perhaps previously suspected. He was quite good at puzzles, and well-schooled in the ways of the selfish and ambitious. And if it had been him, he would have also planned for the long-term. Would have first tried to stave off the Oracle magic-madness, such as it was. Failing that, there would have been a plan in place to come back from death to be Calix's guard and guardian once more. And once returned to the land of the living, he would have gone about gathering as much power as possible.

Well, Lily had managed to plan ahead quite well so far. Claiming power... that was merely a hunch, and he was sure Calix had something to do with it. In the deepest, darkest recesses of his mind, he wondered what Lily was fully capable of. And when he added those together, the solution came up with Calix at its crux. Namely, Calix's *magic*. He was like his mother, an Oracle. Perhaps she'd planned for him to be a receptacle for her. Perhaps she simply planned to steal his magic and take it for her own.

Perhaps there was something even darker buried beneath her maternal disguise.

But he could do bugger all about it right now, stuck in a nearly-empty house with the coin gone and a loaded revolver resting on the fireplace mantel. He never liked firearms of any kind; blades were easier, stealthier for certain, but he preferred to stay out of obvious trouble wherever possible.

The doorbell ringing made Lawton jump. *What in the actual bloody hell*?

It rang again. And again. Once more.

Sighing, Lawton strode over to the fireplace, then walked out of the room and up the hall to the front door. Revolver in hand but held at his side and pointed to the floor, he cracked the door open.

Cassandra was on the other side. Lawton tried to slam it shut but she wedged her boot in the sparse space he'd created. "Lawton, wait." On the other side, in the dim light of some time of day that could have been anywhere between noon and eight pm, he could see her eyes narrow.

"Cassandra, move," he managed to bite out despite how hard his heart was pounding. She hadn't been the one to directly torture him, but it had been done with her assistance. And to him, it didn't matter. She was still an instrument of the Order.

"No." And then she said something that took him completely off-guard. "Vincent's gone. I don't know where else to go."

Lawton stared at her, then broke out in a laugh. "*You* don't know where to go? Impossible. This from the same woman who once stared down a room full of opium dealers with nothing but a knife in her pocket and a rather... let's say *invictus* personality. Never become a spy, you're a terrible liar."

"I'm not lying," she snapped before giving the door a shove. Lawton was pushed back a few inches, which she widened with the curl of her hand around the door. "Let me in, Lawton. I can help you."

Lawton stepped back just as she shoved again, and Cassandra tumbled inside. She was graceful enough to stay upright, and with barely a stumble, she rounded on him. "Were you going to shoot me?" she asked, no trace of amusement on her face.

"Honestly, I don't know." He kept his finger off the trigger, but pointed the gun at her chest. "Should I?"

As far as Lawton was aware, Cassandra wasn't magical. He knew little about her besides that, but it was the one thing he'd have bet his yearly allowance on. When he'd gotten an allowance, anyways.

Cassandra stopped advancing on him but there was no fear in her face. "Had you the gumption, you'd have done it already."

His rage, usually not the thing he reached for under duress, was flickering to life. An old, ill-kempt pilot light for sure, but still there. Still capable of producing a flame under the right circumstances.

Lawton pulled back on the hammer, the *click* a satisfying echo through his entire body. "I wouldn't make any bets anytime soon," he said quietly. "I'm a desperate man, Cassandra. Surely you know the rule around desperate men."

She stared at him, implacable, for several long seconds. If having a gun aimed at her chest bothered Cassandra, she didn't show it. That lack of reaction made him even more worried. "Vincent is gone," she said again, "and his cousin is upending the Order from the inside-out."

Lawton could barely contain his glee. "It couldn't have happened to a more sinister group of self-involved, egotistical— "

"Surely you're talking about yourself, too—"

"— scheming group of assholes," Lawton finished, his voice raised by the time he was done. "Yes, I joined out of ambition and ego, too. And hurt pride. And I have acres and miles to go before I've made up for what I've done. Maybe I'll never pay it back. But at least I'm trying." He nudged the gun up, until it was pointed at her throat. Smaller target, but he was a decent shot, and at this distance? It wasn't an issue.

Cassandra's blank stare was becoming unnerving. *Something's wrong with her.* Lawton nearly swatted the thought away, but things were different now. He couldn't bank on luck and playing friend to power to save him from trouble anymore. "Help me find him. Isme said she sent him into the *demimonde*, and given all of his plans revolved around that fucking place, and given who his half-brother is, this is the best play. The smartest one."

Deep in, under skin and muscle, bone and tissue, his fingers began to ache. A reminder living under his flesh. Another thing he needed to pay for. "They're not here," he said. "I don't know when they'll return."

"Then I'll wait with you."

"Absolutely fucking *not*."

"I'll owe you."

Of all the things he could imagine Cassandra doing, it was this. This... odd, half-formed attempt at begging. Cassandra was cast iron, impossible to break, but that *crack* in her voice spoke of something that made his guts squirm uncomfortably.

Desperation.

Cassandra could have a million reasons for joining the Order, a million more for taking on the shit job of shepherding a flock of inept amateurs carrying out mostly low-level orders. It tugged at him, that watery mirror image of his own ambitions and wants rippling at him and shaped like a woman he'd known from the moment he'd joined the Order.

With his free hand, he tugged aside the loose neck of his tunic so Cassandra could see the circular scar on his collarbone. The skin had scabbed and flaked as it healed, but a large portion of it was still an angry red blob; one now surrounded by snaking, scraggly veins of black and red and purple. He had only vague memories of that time; swimming with pain and guilt and anger. The haze over them even now had vexed him. He couldn't be sure if the voice telling his torturer to get to work had been hers... but who else could it have been? "Did you do this?"

Lawton saw it too late. Too late to do anything but register the fist encased in a deep indigo light level itself at his face. Too late to do anything but let her knock him out —

CRACK

At first, Lawton only registered the sensation of something being pulled from inside him. As if his spine were a loom and the once loose threads had been suddenly, *violently*, pulled taut. To be yanked through his lungs, his muscle, his skin, and then *out... into Cassandra.*

Cassandra was thrown from him with such force that she fell in a heap some twenty feet from the front door, near a row of bare-branched hedges. Lawton winced through the pain and the shock, but stopped doing so when he heard the distinct snapping of bones. And then Cassandra was merely a human-shaped lump on the lawn, her face dug into the earth at such an angle she appeared as if she'd failed to land some aerobic stunt.

But her legs were snapping into place on their own, jerking the entire body to standing even as she was slumped over at the waist. Then up. Up. Up. As if someone else had control of her spine and was forcing her body to stand even as broken as it was. Blood and dirt marred her face, hair, and jacket. Part of her *visible scalp* was bleeding steadily. But it was the jagged bit of flesh that hung loose from one cheek that was the push he needed to start backing away, shoving the heavy front doors shut as Cassandra barreled toward him.

Push! Lily screamed in his head. His nose ran, hot blood gushing from it as he pushed so hard on the door he thought he might break his arms clean off his own body. The blood dripped down and down, splattering the wood floor now covered in slick mud.

The door heaved shut with a final groan a moment before Cassandra crashed into it. He'd only been able to spot — barely — the manic grin on her face before closing her out of the house. Lawton backed up at the door rattled, his heart pounding on the off-beat to her fists on the wood.

"What the fuck?" he whispered. "What in the actual hell was that?"

Are you asking me? Lily's voice sounded more distant than usual. Thready. *Weak.* A glance down told him there were more black and purple veins skittering across his skin now, and the nail on his left thumb was starting to blacken. *I weaken, so do you.*

"Slight problem with that, considering... whatever the hell that is outside," Lawton snapped as the door shook. "She's going to figure out there are plenty of windows to come through. And I can't try to save my own life from you when I'm dealing with her as well."

The wards will keep her out. Focus on our problem.

The back of his neck dripped with sweat. His hands trembled. But instead of fear, there was a hollow space carved out by rage.

He knew what to do with anger. Every fist cracked across his cheek, every night he wasn't able to win back what he'd bet, every upturned nose when Calix wasn't at his side.

Oh yes, he knew what to do with rage.

And while he wasn't a fan of idle threats (especially since if you make one too many, people stop believing you), he wasn't beyond them, either. "I've spent the last few days trying to pinpoint why I keep doing everyone else's bidding," he said slowly, calmly, as he picked up the gun that had fallen in his haste to shut the door. "And all I can come up with is that for so long, I've felt weak. Unseen. Unknown. Unloved. So, I willingly put myself in the halls and parlors and theaters where power coalesces. It was a smart plan at the time. I'm charming, good looking. Affable. The rich and powerful are smart, but there are few of them who don't enjoy being complimented or flirted with. They're shameless. It's part of why I like them."

Lawton walked through the first floor to the small washroom off the kitchen. It was more modest than the others in the house, but well equipped and had a nice, wide mirror. He'd spent a few minutes that very morning tracing the ever-growing lines of black and purple across his skin. An ill Narcissus, compelled to keep looking.

He leaned forward, into his reflection, the cold marble of the counter helping not to stem the fire flashing in his very soul. "I think you and I are terribly similar," he whispered. His cheek twitched, stretching his mouth garishly for a long, dreadful second. "We try, but we don't know how to really work in this world. We're so certain in our path forward, we feel infallible. Look at you. Safeguard after safeguard, plans A through G ready in case the one above it fails. You've hidden your true self away from the one person you loved more than anything in the world. You failed to stop your own obsessions, knowing what it might cost you. And yet you *fight*."

Somewhere, distantly in the house, the sound of glass hitting marble. But it didn't shake his focus. That twitch again, but now his thumb began to move on its own, tapping an irregular rhythm on the counter. Lily was trying to take control once more, but his guard was up too high.

Lawton punched the mirror with every bit of force in his body. It shattered, glinting bits of brilliance raining down on his head. He closed his eyes and waited for the last bits to drop off his clothing, from his hair. In the sink below, a perfect circle of glass had formed, and the largest piece was as long as his finger. Long enough to do damage.

He picked it up and held it to his throat. The kiss of tiny glass fragments across his skin made blood well to the surface. "What happens now, Lily?"

He could feel the storm build in his mind, a secondary, alien force that filled his nostrils with the scent of dying roses. Her anger was the only real power she had now; he could taste it, summer rain running through thick, black mud. Intent churning into despair and forever colored with a dearth of dying dreams.

You're a coward, she hissed in his ear, the echoes of it clarified with anger and fear. *You wouldn't.*

Lawton shrugged. He let the glass drag over his skin, digging deeper. It hurt but he'd never felt so clear-headed. Yes, this was what he should do.

Give him the power, Lily. Let him be a bank vault for your might and magic, and when it drives him to the brink, he will come and find you. He'll give it back and gladly. He'll beg you, tear his hair from his scalp, and cry while kneeling at your feet. And then, we will walk back into your world. Together.

The flash of memory, of a voice, not his own left the rest of the world dark. Lawton could see nothing of himself, could not feel the glass biting into his flesh. Couldn't feel the constant ache of dull pain roaring through his system, his nerves on fire even in sleep as he slowly lost a war against someone he had believed to be far stronger than himself.

This is what you are. There are those in this world with power, and those without. Know your place, little lamb.

A vision in white with her red hair loose about her shoulders, Lily was standing before a creature of smoke and edges. Pregnant and fearless.

It reached out to her with two right hands, with fingers long and disjointed, caressing her face. *You will raise your child with a bit of your power nestled alongside his soul, and when the time is right, you will reclaim that power. It will be plump and fresh, ripe fruit for you and I to share. He will be an Oracle no longer, and you will be unstoppable. You will save him, spare him so much pain, my darling. As a mother should.*

"Lily..." The word was torn from Lawton's throat as the image shifted, split, then reforged in his mind. Lily again, now in blue, her skin more lined but that fierce determination in her eyes that never seemed to age. He wanted to scream at her, to keep her from kneeling at the feet of a creature decked in royal purple and gold, its many-jointed fingers clasped so seriously across its bony middle.

I will give you the knowledge you seek. And in return, you will bring me to your world. Now you will save your son, and help create something new at the same time. And when you arise once more to take your power back from Calix, we will open the doors and usher in something beautiful.

The bathroom door, shut and locked, rattled in its jamb. "I know you're in there," Cassandra yelled. It was her voice and not, something multi-tonal and off-key rattling along her throat. Distantly again, he could hear her. Sense her, and the creature shoved inside her body.

He could feel the blood dripping down his hand, running rivulets over his knuckles.

When had he cut into his neck? Had he meant to cut so deeply? Surely he had....

Lily's shrieks of agony blended with the inhuman sounds from the other side of the door as something wrapped around his ankle. Through his tears, he could barely make out the damp, warm tendril, its thick skin black as midnight, now slithering up his leg.

Had he meant to cut so deeply?

Had it been an empty threat?

Lawton coughed, his mouth filling with blood. *I cut too deeply*, he thought as he crashed to the floor.

FOLIO TWO:

HOW TO PREPARE A SOUL

"*I confess that Magic teacheth many superfluous things, and curios prodigies for ostentation; leave them as empty things, yet be not ignorant of their causes.*"
— **Heinrich Cornelius Agrippa to the reader at the beginning of *Three Books of Occult Philosophy or Magic*, 1531-1533**

CHAPTER EIGHT

Late Summer 1582 – from the journals of Edward Talbot

I have been at Mortlake three days, and it only took me one to know this place was cursed. The rain never fully disperses into the ground, and the mud clings to my boots and hem and cane. My new patron, the estimable Doctor John Dee, never had the green areas around his home properly established, with stone laid wide and flat to accommodate human and horse alike, so there was no relief from the mud to be had. And inside the home, everything smelled of mold and still water. Like a pond gone stagnant, slowly eroding into itself during a drought which rain can never quench.

The first night, as John banked the fire and his wife set the table, I watched in a mix of confusion and horror at how the shadows danced along the walls. They were pockmarked by flaws in the bare bricks, but there was no mistaking the oddly bent and curved wings that grew out of John's shadow. His wife and very young son were shockingly indifferent to the thing on the wall, and then I realized that of course they would be.

They didn't see it. Neither did John.

That should have been my moment of reckoning. I should have fled that night.

One year later

I could flee still, but life on the road was not made for a man with a cane and foul temper. I have not the constitution or will to survive in the wilds. Cannot spend all hours praying no boars or bears find me. And returning to the many, many places I've called home is unthinkable. They would not have me, nor I them. We were too at odds over too many things: taxes owed, disturbed graves, the odd noises coming from my tiny home when the dead I'd raised tried to escape.

But the heart yearns for safety, and safety is what led me to John.

A mystic. A spiritualist. A fortune teller. A man gifted with prognostication in its finest form, through clay tablets and well-thumbed decks of cards. Cards the oracles of the wandering tribes still use, and somehow this man had possession of a an entire deck. The good doctor is a mystery. An enigma. A man of religion and knowledge whose spirit stagnates as his desire for more blooms deep and verdant. Once employed by the Queen herself, his fame and ego grew, and yet he still faced adversity from inside and outside the Court, thanks to his myriad strange beliefs, Dee and his wife eventually fled to Mortlake. To save Dee from a cell, yes but to chase a dream.

One night not long after I arrived at Mortlake, while I was deep in the bosom of slumber, John swore he was visited by an angel. A mighty being of gold and red glimmer, like cold winter sunrise dappled through the trees. And it told him he had so much more to give, to discover. That angel taught John his first runic circle. That was a year ago, and after many failed scribes and supposed experts, John's frustrations have left him beating his fists bloody against the walls, and this was after he had torn out what little hair he possessed.

The first angel's name had been unknown to us, a mere messenger for something greater. Perhaps I didn't understand its role, or worse... I did, and wished to remain blind to such a harbinger. When Uriel finally made its appearance, at the strike of the witching hour last night, John took it as another sign. Another portent. But this one hadn't been foretold like the others John swore by.

This one had rushed into the room on a set of golden wings and bedecked in deep indigo and soft lilac robes, and had made no effort to disguise its gruesome nature. Beautiful and terrifying, from its grey-pallored flesh to the jagged crown of metal teeth and bone and squirming black lines like ink that had come alive. And the hands... they were no human hands, nor animal. Odd and bent, they defied the laws of nature in a way that left me retching in the corner. John managed to stay upright, but only just.

And now here I am, three nights after helping to summon this creature, and I have not slept or eaten or defecated. I have not even stepped outside for a bit of fresh air. The being — the angel, John swore it was — sustained us. Nourished us. Kept us hearty and hale in a bargain made between itself and John, and I was given no chance to leave. John sliced his arm, fed the being his blood, and when I next understood what had happened, the blood compact was complete.

He was bound to it. And it to he. And I was in the middle, an unwilling purveyor and documentarian of every word spoken, every rune drawn, and every foul plan concocted in the bowels of the estate.

Chapter Nine

ETHANIEL

"Are you prepared?"

Head ringing, his hand on fire, Ethaniel didn't tear his gaze away from the figure of Maria. She and Uzala glided over the ground, her little hand wrapped in its gnarled one, and it made him sick. Distracted to the point of nearly missing Vincent's question, Ethaniel shook his head, but didn't answer.

Beside him, Vincent tensed. "Maria can help us escape, but we need to be ready for her signal."

Ethaniel focused on breathing. Through the pain, the fatigue. Through the strange, out-of-body sensation crawling under his skin.

Through the dizzying sight of so many lines of magic crisscrossing at impossible angles. And at the core of it all was a stark realization...

This is magic's birthplace.

Ethaniel wasn't one to believe in fate or destiny. He didn't see coincidences as anything more than that — the world being a funny old place sometimes. Humankind had only started to experiment with magic in the last few centuries; before that, it was seen as a type of religion. Aubrey had told him stories about the art of the Cunning Folk, the healers and apothecaries, medicine men and midwives, who took all patients. They were the ones who worked *with* the local vicar or priest, because religion and magic couldn't be separated. Because you couldn't have one with the other.

But when magic started to *expand*, to take on a life of its own in the hands of society's most intelligent people, that's when the church cried foul and when they damned the Cunning Folk and those like them for trying to displace their influence on the populace.

Except that message was framed as *Satan himself.* As *witchcraft* and *crones*, people as wicked as could be trying to snatch up children or poison the cattle. So science picked up where religion had pulled back, and it did so with aplomb, as Aubrey might say.

Gods, that voice. Still so strongly in my mind, as if he's here with me now.

And Aubrey would also say aloud the very thing I'm terrified to acknowledge: that I sit in the seat made from magic's carpentry, and I could learn so much here. But it's not what I want, even as Harkness blood beats within me. I am at war with my nature. And there is no fate or destiny or good luck to save me. I have to save myself.

Ethaniel swallowed hard and tried to refocus. His innate knack for patterns would serve him well if he could just bloody *concentrate*, but his head was ringing and his hand was slowly throbbing in time with every heartbeat.

"Brother," Vincent snapped, jostling him with a shoulder. "Are you listening?"

"You're planning something with Maria, and not including me in that discussion," Ethaniel hissed back. It was taking everything in him not to clock Vincent in the jaw, damaged hand be damned.

"I would if you would fucking *listen*," Vincent whispered. "Maria can find us door, and while she's dealing with that... thing, we can perform the incantation to open it."

"You mean I will," Ethaniel said. "I'm the one with family magic."

Vincent grinned at him, all bloodied teeth and blackened gums. He looked terrible. He looked like he was *dying*, and that thought made Ethaniel's stomach lurch. "But of course. Lucky you."

Ethaniel closed his eyes and took a deep breath. He'd fallen into the same old trap with Vincent and now his half-brother believed he had some kind of upper hand.

"Lucky me," Ethaniel whispered, dropping his voice as Uzala and Maria began to turn in their direction. They were doing some kind of strange loop, and the withered trees bowed as they passed. "Lucky me, in fact, that I got the family magic and some kind of conscience at the same time."

"Oh, what a terrible blow you've dealt me." Vincent's tone was like gravel scraped over concrete. "And our bickering means nothing if we don't get out of here alive to continue the argument."

Ethaniel let his gaze scrape over Vincent, lingering on the bruises and cuts and makeshift bandages. Up close, it was hard to ignore their resemblance. The same tilt to their mouths, the same nose, but Vincent's eyes were dark while Ethaniel took after his father's hazel ones. But what he hated the most was what Vincent represented: Harkness in name and deed and ambition.

The path not chosen. What might have happened to him had fate or luck or destiny intervened merely a few degrees off, a few minutes later.

Something snapped inside him. He lashed out with a fist, and the moment his knuckles impacted Vincent's chin, he found himself frozen in place. It was another strange thing on top of so many other strange, frightening moments over the last few days, but this one came with a dash of déjà vu.

Aubrey lashing out at Lawton in the hot springs, and Ethaniel throwing out a haphazard pattern to stop them both in their tracks.

Whispered threats for them to both behave. Aubrey backing down, then Lawton, before Calix came over to confront them.

It felt and smelled and *tasted* like his power, but he hadn't created this pattern. It hung in the air, in Ethaniel's periphery, before it was all blotted out by the dense, looming shadow of Uzala.

"You are not setting a good example for your sister," it whispered as it slunk around them. One black claw tapped Vincent on the shoulder and he instantly slumped forward. A noise of protest left Ethaniel but he didn't — couldn't — form words. Uzala had frozen everything, including his voice. "I was going to heal your brother, as an apology for the wounds I caused, but now I think pain must be part of the lesson."

Uzala's lower left arm shot forward and it wrapped all of its blisteringly cold, disjointed fingers around Ethaniel's damaged hand. The pain was blinding. It wiped out all thought, all function, until he was a ball of incandescent agony.

"I return your sister to you, little patterner," Uzala whispered in his ear. "Dream now, and when you wake, I will ask you what you saw in your slumber. For it is my, and our, next step."

Darkness took him.

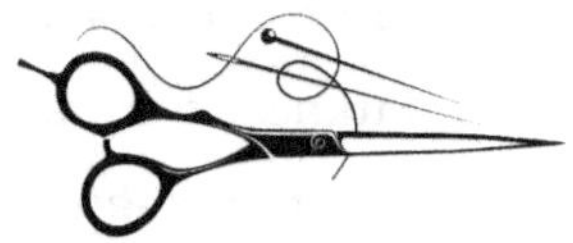

The warm hand on his face knocked the last bit of sleep loose from his brain, and without opening his eyes, Ethaniel turned into Aubrey's waiting arms. "You certainly know how to wake a man up," he said into Aubrey's neck. Aubrey was delightful in many ways, and as the weeks together passed, Ethaniel found more and more things to be enamored by.

Those glass green eyes, so sharp and calculating, and how they went heavy-lidded when Ethaniel did something clever with his hand or mouth.

His rings, heavy silver things that Ethaniel liked to touch in their quiet moments; the quiet was rushed too often, since being in public together meant crowded spaces and sticky floors. But in the dark, in the heavy-moon silence of Aubrey's apartment, Ethaniel would touch those rings and feel more in tune with the man beside him.

The way Aubrey's skin smelled. The bite of iron and ink, the musk of finely-tooled leather, and the sugar cubes he placed in every cup of tea or coffee. There was comfort in it, and desire, and right now Ethaniel felt the early stirrings of lust walk fingers down his spine. He shifted into Aubrey, who tightened his hold and whispered, "Is there something you want, Ethaniel?"

Ethaniel huffed and sat up. Aubrey's gaze was already darkening, sharpening, honed into a thing more than capable of finding Ethaniel's weak spots and attacking them with such precision. Aubrey would make him sigh and tremble and shake loose from his staid, rigid foundations to become something new. Something freer. Unburdened by the past and the present, and only belonging to Aubrey.

"I'd call you cruel for teasing me, but I know you'll hold it over my head," Ethaniel said even as he leaned in to cup Aubrey's cheek. "So come up here and kiss me already."

Laughing, delighted, Aubrey acquiesced and kissed him. Softly at first, then with nipping teeth and slick tongue and Ethaniel fell down down down, head first into need. A few touches, a few kisses, and he was Aubrey's to command. It had been this way from the beginning, and Ethaniel had to admit to himself that he liked being held tight and safe.

He'd never felt so safe. So seen.

And now as he floated somewhere between memory and fantasy, Ethaniel felt Aubrey's arms tighten once more.

Too tight, now, with cold fingertips pressed into his skin.

It was not Aubrey staring down at him when Ethaniel shifted, restless, feeling suddenly so alone and so cold. It was the creature, that monster Uzala, and even without eyes, it bore into him.

"I care not for your human connections," it purred. The black tongue that had already graced his flesh a few times now snaked out once more, twitching and writhing, the tip flicking against his cheek. All to make Ethaniel shudder. Uzala seemed to gorge on his pain and fear, and here he was feeding the slavering beast.

"Then why.... why infiltrate?" Ethaniel bit out. He could feel his anger rising, beating back the terror. "Why not let me have him in my dreams?"

"Because you're dreaming wrong," Uzala hissed. Its claws sank into his arms, his ribs, and Ethaniel cried out in agony. "Focus, little patterner. Connect your mind to the magic around you, and find me my twin."

Ethaniel struggled, cried out, hot tears running down his cheeks while his blood dripped to the sheets below. Uzala had him pinned, pressed down, and with every twist of his body, Ethaniel only dug its claws deeper. Pain ricocheted through him, made black spots dance in his vision.

"FOCUS!" Uzala screamed. "BRING ME MY OTHER HALF."

Desperate, panicked, Ethaniel dug his own fingers into his damaged palm. Everything dropped away.

"You found your way back. Very good. But will you let me be right in your eyes? Will you let me follow you back to your home?"

Whatever waited for him on the other side of the mass weaving of magic flashing before his eyes... it spoke through the stones. And it wanted him.

Can you save me? he thought, his vision going blurry now. Tears and snot and blood. So much blood. A veritable downpour of it. And if he waited too long, there'd be nothing left but his shriveled husk.

"I can, and I will. The creature who holds your leash will want more after you find its twin. It cannot help its nature, as malformed as it has become. So, listen closely."

When Ethaniel awoke, he did so on soft black moss, and the first thing he saw was a pattern drawn into the sand-like texture of the ground between he and a sleeping Vincent. And in the middle of those intersecting lines and runes, was an arch.

Like a doorway.

And when Ethaniel touched it, he could *feel* the power within. Could feel his hand throb and his eyes water and his heart race. "It's our way out," he whispered.

CHAPTER TEN

AUBREY

The circle of bones — some twice as long as he was tall, others small enough to be the wing of a songbird — on the floor didn't halt Aubrey in his tracks. In fact, it spurred him on. And he started talking before either Magnus or Agrippa had the chance.

"That's Cunning Folk magic," he said, footsteps echoing in the cavernous space Agrippa called home. Above their heads, the shelves floated lazily, undisturbed by his outburst. He doubted much could cause a ruckus here, let alone the slightly raised voice of a single human.

Agrippa smiled, quite grim. The expression pulled at their face, made the feathers around their eyes tighten too much. "To you, it is. But the first Folk pulled the knowledge from the *demimonde*. Largely on accident, but the point remains."

Aubrey shook his head, ready to object, but reason stayed his hand. *Of course* it came from the *demimonde*. That simply made sense, once he took a moment to let that information sink in. Oracle magic, visions, patterning... why would Cunning Folk magic and rituals be any different? It seemed terribly obvious now. And Agrippa had no reason to lie.

Acceptance was another turn of the screw, and not one he was ready for. But arguing over what had come from where didn't matter right now.

"You'll have to pardon me," Aubrey said as he pinched the aching space between his eyes. The headache starting there was only the beginning. "I know this ritual because it was one of the first my mother taught us. My sisters and I. We used it to summon little things. Flowers, leaves, a rock. It was the start of my arcane education."

But even as the words left him, the memories that rushed to the surface kept him from saying more. He'd learned to hate those summoning circles after his eighth birthday, when his schooling passed from his mother to his father.

"It's what all healers in our line must do," his father had said, wiping out Aubrey's protestations with a flinty glare and steel in his voice. "You leave the bones to your mother, she's the town Visionary for a reason. But you.... you will follow me and keep our family known, both in name and deed."

But Aubrey hadn't wanted to leave the bones behind. He hadn't understood it then, but what called out to him in the bones wasn't some inkling of power that resembled his mother's. But it also hadn't been the faint green, almost medicinal sting of his father's magic, either. What had spoken to him were the cracks and crevices, chips and fractures in the bones. Some from careless handling, others the only evidence left of what had killed the creatures. His palms had itched, like fire ants across his skin, and there was a tug in his chest, right below his sternum.

A tightness. A beckoning.

His habit of sneaking out at night to play with the bone bags in his mother's study had lasted for months, until he'd been too loud, the shock of not merely mending, but fully repairing the shattered eye socket on a hawk skull, had drawn his father's attention.

And after that, no more bones. No more witching hour experiments. No more reckless, rampant joy at slowly coming to understand what he could do. Shouldn't his father have been elated? Shouldn't he have seen Aubrey's unique talent and risen to the challenge, both as a scholar and a parent?

Wasn't a healer just that... someone who healed? Why was it so awful Aubrey couldn't heal people, but objects instead?

Whywhywhywhy... burned into his tongue and his brain and all the spaces laced with acrid memories and even more acrid words.

Whywhywhywhy...

"Apologies," Aubrey said, voice rough as he shook out of the haze of memory. "Agrippa, I let my ego get in the way. An old reflex, one I should have long grown out of."

It didn't surprise him to feel Calix gently touch his arm, then slide his fingers down to squeeze Aubrey's hand. What did shock him was the careful, considerate way Agrippa approached him now, then put a feathered hand on his shoulder. Their flighty, brusque energy bled into something a tad softer. "You humans do love your burdens. A conversation I have with Magnus every fortnight or so, when things are weighing him down."

Aubrey glanced past Agrippa to see Magnus shift in his chair, then fuss with his sleeve. Magnus was the most fastidious person he'd ever met; there was no way he'd muss those perfect press lines unless nervous.

Was Magnus nervous? What on earth for?

"I'm not going to cause you undue grief, Aubrey," Agrippa continued. "I might not fully know the weight on your shoulders, but I sympathize." The grip on his shoulders tightened, and something like a spark lit behind Agrippa's strange galaxy eyes. Aubrey feared if he stared for much longer, he could easily fall in and never surface. "Hold onto that weight for just a bit longer. Use it to help find Ethaniel." Agrippa stepped away, then waved them over to the bone circle.

"Shall I give them the theory?" Magnus asked as he rose to join the three of them.

"I'd love to hear it," Calix said as they followed Agrippa's directions to take up one of the points of a simple cross drawn across the center of the circle. "I've always done better with instructions. Magic feels too unwieldy without something to ground me."

Aubrey suddenly realized how true that was for Calix. The slowed, timed breaths, the touch he'd established when helping Aubrey during the attack from the Golden Order on his apartment, and all the other little notes and doodles and the very *categorized* way Calix had about him. Undoubtedly his mother's doing, helping a brain that seemed to never stop slow down, organize, *think*. He was ever so curious what Calix had been like as a boy, if his theory was true.

Aubrey wished he could take Calix's hand, but they were easily five feet apart. "What can we do to help Calix with that?"

Magnus tsked at him but it carried no heat. "Now, now, let's not get ahead of ourselves. Agrippa?"

With slow, methodical movements that reminded Aubrey of a stage magician (if the magician were caught in a time bubble), Agrippa began to draw runes in the air. The moment the first character was completed, Aubrey felt a buzz begin in the back of his mind. There was no pain, no nausea, only a *tingle* but in his bloody *brain*. It was deeply uncomfortable, to say the least.

Calix hissed and pushed the heel of his palm into his forehead. "Oh, that's.... very strange."

"It would be much worse if you hadn't drank that concoction Agrippa gave you," Magnus said, but he came over to them, his hands fluttering over Aubrey's shoulders, then Calix's. Immediately the buzzing was softened, as if the bees in his brain had their stingers pushed into butter. "Agrippa claimed this domain long ago and cleared it of the worst of the *demimonde's* tendrils, but once it became part of the Collectio, we had to ward it for security. Think of your presence like putting bone buttons on a fine wool coat. The buttons do their job by keeping the coat closed, but they're not supposed to be on that kind of coat. When you're here, your presence provides the wards with energy, but on some level, the wards know you don't belong here."

Aubrey paused, watched Calix do the same, and finally said, "The wards feed off magical energy?"

"A safeguard, and one harmless to you," Agrippa said to them, without looking at them. "Not so much to those who wish to intrude where they're not welcome. But even with permission, your existence here is against the laws of the domain. Your magic is in direct violation of the ground rule, which is to keep out anything of the *demimonde,* even if it's tangential."

"What would happen to us if we overstayed our welcome?" Calix asked. Aubrey noticed he'd moved even closer and it was such an easy thing to wrap his arm around Calix's shoulders. The fabric of his simple shirt, warm from his body, was grounding under Aubrey's fingertips; a reminder, a promise, an oath.

"You'd be excised. Like a tumor."

"My God," Calix breathed, his grip on Aubrey's hand tightening.

Aubrey cut his gaze over to Magnus, saw the man's little nod, and via that strange, silent way of communicating they'd had for years, Aubrey *understood.* "Your magic feeds the wards," he said, his tone far shakier than his reasoning. They'd just awoken and already, the world had been turned on its head a few times.

"Indeed." The runes Agrippa continued to sketch began to move, some breaking off to join another group, while a third group tailed closely behind a fourth. It was like a school of magical fish following each other somewhere deep in the ocean. And the magic on the air was setting his hair on end, goosebumps rising in their wake and covering his arms, his legs. "It is a mutually beneficial, if parasitic, relationship between Magnus and I. And this space provides the quiet I need to continue my work."

"I know you have questions," Magnus said as he slipped over to Aubrey's left. "It's a very long story. A moment in my youthful folly that turned into something rather different."

There was pain in Magnus's voice, but it was pain etched with more pleasant memories. Aubrey wanted to know, of course, but already he was forming a hypothesis in his mind about Magnus and Agrippa, and the use of "folly" added a more personal aspect to it. He'd not been expecting it, but he knew Magnus well enough by now and trusted in the man's entirely steady personality and quirks. It didn't matter how Magnus and Agrippa navigated around one another, but that they did so well.

"Tell me once we get Ethaniel back," Aubrey murmured.

"You have a deal, my friend." When Magnus smiled, a bit of his usual warm mirth returned, and it soothed Aubrey's soul a little.

Once Agrippa stopped drawing runes, the strange buzzing stopped as well. "The theory is this," they said, the feathers around their eyes slowly changing color, from white to a deep, rich black. But Aubrey didn't hear their next words. It sounded like water in his ears, an echoing roar that then turned to deathly silence.

Then a void. In his ears, behind his eyes, in his *mind*.

Time slowed. Stopped. Hung there, cold starlight in an endless black.

And with the power of a slap to the face, Aubrey was slammed into his body once more, where he only heard a voice. It was far off in the distance, as the black of Agrippa's feathers twisted and lurched and became...

... the onyx stone in the Collection...

... then flashed to a copse of trees sluggishly bleeding black ichor...

... then once more to feathers, then again to trees...

The onyx stone, the trees, the feathers. Another stone, somewhere deep in those trees.

His vision filled with these things while his mouth filled with an awful taste, the bitterest of medicines mixed with mud and tepid rainwater. He was nowhere, he was alone, he was —

The onyx stone, the trees, the feathers. Another stone, somewhere deep in those trees. The outline of a creature at least twelve, thirteen feet tall, with multiple arms and tattered robes, but no other details —

The tight squeeze of Calix's hand on his arm shook Aubrey loose, and he immediately caught Calix as the other man stumbled into him. "There's... something... " Calix managed. Aubrey held him close, smoothed back his hair, and let Calix hang off him, as it seemed he couldn't stand on his own.

"I think it's working, Agrippa," Magnus said, his voice tight. "Be quick, we can't leave them like this!"

"A moment," Agrippa replied, and then the world snapped back into place. But the images were burned into Aubrey's eyes and, terrified he'd lose the details, he asked Magnus for something with which to draw.

"Give Agrippa your hands," Magnus instructed, leading them over to the circle of bones. "Let them see what you did. You were given pieces of the puzzle they need to complete the tracking spell for the book. Which should lead us to Ethaniel, or at the very least, get us in the right direction."

The words coming from Magnus didn't make any sense, but together, they formed an emotion. A promise of safety away from the dark, toward the light Ethaniel had become in his life. No more tendrils of *demimonde*, eager to wiggle inside his brain and take what wasn't theirs. No more fear.

Only power.

Magic.

Ethaniel.

The combination of warm flesh and cooler feathers gripping his wrist should have been jarring. Aubrey understood on some level, like distance understanding a horizon on the ocean. But the gentle prodding of Agrippa's magic against his was less odd. Not unnatural but not the intimate embrace of Calix's magic brushing up against him or the steady blaze that was Ethaniel.

This was a question. Magic against magic, mind against mind.

Will you show me?

Aubrey's only reply was, "Yes."

When reality snapped back into place, bumping his teeth together, making his spine shake, Aubrey was kneeling on the floor and Magnus had a hand on his shoulder. "Calix?" Aubrey rasped when he realized Calix wasn't at his side.

Aubrey's head was too heavy on his neck, but he rolled his eyes over to see Calix standing before the floating runes, his hands out as the magic cast him in a deep purple glow. He was so beautiful, so *powerful*, and the magic that poured off him nearly stole Aubrey's breath.

Agrippa stood before him, a bit more distance like normal between them, and pointed to the rune circle. "I think your Oracle understands. You showed me what you saw, and now we can keep working. I needed an anchor to Ethaniel, and your connection with him was vital to the spell. Thank you." When Magnus prodded them with an elbow, they haltingly continued. "I apologize for not telling you beforehand what I was doing. I've found that most humans tend to flinch when they're informed that they'll be used to channel magic."

Aubrey's head was still ringing, but he couldn't fault Agrippa. It sounded like their history with the human species was tense at best, outside their close relationship with Magnus. "Not a worry," he managed to say. "Though, a little warning might have sufficed."

"I will take that under advisement," Agrippa said. They redirected Aubrey's attention to Calix. "Your Oracle is a natural, it seems."

Magnus nodded. "We still don't know so much about Oracles, about the *demimonde*, but Agrippa knows they're linked. The *demimonde* is like bone-marrow to an Oracle's sheer existence, and from what I can gather, his mother was relying on that tie to save Calix, and save herself if she got in over her head."

"She didn't get in over her head! Lily *experimented on her son*," Aubrey said, his tone harsher than he meant even as anger rose up in him. Anger at Lily, not at Magnus. "Put him at risk over and over again. Hid so much from him. *Stole his memories*." Then he shook his head, the anger so quickly dissipating into exhaustion that he feared collapse. "Because of her, Ethaniel is trapped there. You're telling me a lot, Magnus, without giving me many answers."

A bit of flint sparked in Magnus's eyes, and Aubrey wondered if he'd waved the proverbial red flag at the bull. But it was reeled in immediately, and Magnus replied in a smaller, softer voice. "I know. Some of it is because... I truly don't understand it all. I'm mainly acting as translator. Agrippa is the one who knows what they're doing. But I don't want it to sound as though I'm shirking responsibility, Aubrey. I will do everything in my power to keep you and Calix safe now, and all three of you safe once Ethaniel is back home. But we are playing with forces far beyond our ken here, and... "

When Magnus hung his head and sighed, Aubrey couldn't stop himself from reaching out, curling an arm around Magnus's shoulders, and pulling him close. Magnus had been the one to teach him that affection between men, platonic or romantic, was a good thing. Kind and empathetic and wise. His father had been the opposite, and Magnus had always been the mentor and the parental figure. The dual natures combined into something Aubrey had, from their first day's meeting, found incredibly endearing.

Magnus had never steered him wrong. And he wouldn't do so now, either.

"My friend," Aubrey said as he helped Magnus to his feet, "what do we need to do?"

"No harm done, you know that." Magnus gestured to where Calix had stepped back from the runes and bones and was still glowing, but the purple had faded into a soft lilac. With his gold eyes flashing and his body radiating magic, Calix looked like a deity come to bless them with gifts and coin. He was radiant.

"I saw what you did, Aubrey," Calix said. "The stone, the trees, that creature. And I felt Ethaniel's magic, but it was weak." He turned to Agrippa, who was back to adding more runes, closing off some lines and starting new ones. "Is that where Ethaniel is?"

"Likely, since your vision was fairly clear. But I have no way to pinpoint the location. It could be anywhere in the *demimonde*, and I can't aim at a borderless target. This is why we're tracking the book. It has a magical signature that doesn't change. People's magic can change from day to day based on thousands, perhaps tens of thousands of reasons. Weather, mood, location, proximity to a leyline, and on and on. Also keep in mind, we have no idea how the *demimonde* is affecting your patterner. So we track the book and use it to find Ethaniel."

Calix closed his hands into fists and let his arms drop to his sides. "I should have held onto it."

Agrippa paused in their work, a gruff but not unkind look on their face. "No, you did precisely what you should have. Had you not, and the book had come back, we would have lost much time trying to find another way to locate Ethaniel."

Aubrey reached out for Calix, who came willingly into his arms. "Excellent work, dove," he whispered into Calix's hair. "We'll find him. We will."

"But that creature…" Calix's words wandered off and became lost in a shudder that wracked his thin frame. "It felt familiar, somehow."

"Another theory we're fairly certain about," Magnus said. He had walked over to stand opposite Agrippa, across from the circle of bones. "I think it and Uriel, our star of your mother's mishaps, are linked. How, I'm not certain, but those are the kinds of ties we can trace. So this Uriel is a backup plan to tracking Ethaniel."

"I'd prefer we use your nonmagical guest at your estate," Agrippa said. "He's more closely tied to the book, but Magnus said it could bring him to harm. It sounds as though he's due a little bit, given what he's done."

Calix was very quiet, either too stunned to respond to Agrippa, or too conflicted. Either way, Aubrey understood. It was a potentially vile suggestion, using a living human being as a source of magical experimentation. And they'd seen the damage the Golden Order had wrought. Seen how they'd charred Lawton's flesh. How they used people for their own gain. How *Vincent* did.

And yet, the thought flared in his mind. Only the shortest glimpse of a moment in another timeline, where Lawton paid back his debt in his own blood. Not enough to cause death, never that. The guilt of such a thought pushed out his anger, made Aubrey grip Calix tighter.

"Magnus told me no to that, so this is the plan." Agrippa etched a final rune into the circle, then stepped back to review their work. "And it's complete. Magnus, could you... "

Magnus motioned them over, then instructed Calix and Aubrey to stand opposite each other, putting them at exact East and West points with the help of a compass. With all of them gathered around the circle, Magnus said, "Both of you are deeply tied to Ethaniel, but also to Convergence. We're going to rely on that connection to track the book. Agrippa and I will keep the channel open, and you will need to provide your own energy as well, but first... I need you both to think of Ethaniel."

Aubrey was beginning to understand. He and Calix had ties to Ethaniel, but in very different ways. They'd been together, then fallen apart, and put back as a whole, but the latter wouldn't have happened without Calix. And Calix met Ethaniel because of Convergence.

"We're the center," Calix said.

"Precisely," Magnus replied. "Aubrey, do you remember that first time in the museum's topiary garden? Do you remember what I told you?"

Dear gods, did he. It was one of his fondest memories of Magnus. "The night you told me to take the blinders off my magic and stop being so afraid of it,"

Aubrey said. He saw Calix swallow hard and put a hand to his chest. "You stood out there with me for hours, showing me how the pieces could come off and be put back together. You made me stronger."

Magnus's smile was small but so full of pride. "You did that last part all on your own. I simply... played magical tour guide, if you will. I need you to do that again. Your control is honed now, refined into a perfect tool. Use it, then let it go. And as you do, think of Ethaniel. Whatever that tie to him means to you."

When Magnus turned his attention to Calix, the fondness didn't drop from his expression. But what he said was delivered the weight of gravity down upon them. "Calix, open your mind and *channel*. Reach for the deepest parts of your magic and remember every detail you can about the moment you and Convergence met Ethaniel. You are the catalyst here. Magic isn't merely a strong will or focus and some fancy words. It is raw power channeled through a lens."

The idea struck Aubrey so suddenly, he was reaching for his pocket before his brain and mouth had caught up to each other. "A lens for you, one Ethaniel and I have both used," he said as he passed his monocle over. Calix's poor fingers were freezing, so Aubrey curled Calix's hand between his own and stared down at him. "Are you ready, Calix?"

"Yes," Calix said, voice hoarse. "Let's do this now. I can't stand the thought of Ethaniel all alone in that place."

Agrippa motioned them back into place. "Brace yourselves, and don't believe everything you see on this side of the circle. We're *trespassing*, I suppose you could say, and the *demimonde* doesn't like having things taken from its domain. Your patterner would be a mighty prize in that place," they said before they drew a final rune in the air. Aubrey knew it was no joke to them, but their tone was so dry, so clinical, that he almost laughed. The nerves were clearly getting to him.

The breath he took died halfway on its exhale as the ground beneath their feet began to crack and splinter. But it did so with no sound, no fury. Only silence as it split and split; some cracks were as long as his arm and as thick, other lines slight enough to compete with the finest spider silk.

"Stay steady," Magnus said, his hands now out in front of him, palms facing the center of the circle. Lances of clear light shot out from his fingertips, hitting the slowly churning column of magic Agrippa was forming. It was a dazzling display, one that made Aubrey's heart beat harder. Watching Magnus become the amplifier to such a strange magical force was something he felt deep in his bones.

He spared a glance over at Calix, who was staring hard into the circle's center, his chest also rising and falling rapidly. The knuckles of one hand were balled into a tight fist and this close, Aubrey could see that hand tremble.

Only a little longer, Ethaniel, Aubrey thought as he refocused.

"Steady," Magnus warned. "Wait for my signal."

More fractured ground appeared beneath their feet. More light from Magnus's hands, which now fractured into angles; some not so normal, seeming to defy the laws of their world. More magic into the column while a sudden, harsh wind ruffled Agrippa's long white hair. The wind didn't touch him, but Aubrey could feel its awful pressure, its unbearable *presence*.

Not wind, something in him howled, feral and angry and frightened. *Not wind. Something rising.*

Aubrey put his hand into his pocket, where he'd put one of Ethaniel's ascots. The touch of silk on his skin, cool and slippery, was grounding. Reassuring. Immediately, he felt that awful pressure begin to vent, slowly leaking out of some space deep between his lungs and his heart. A sense of relief washed over him, and in that moment, he was able to focus on Ethaniel.

Ethaniel. His essence wrapped around Aubrey's spine, tugging at every nerve, every fiber. Ethaniel had slotted so neatly into his life so quickly. It was the fate of all queer relationships, to some degree: burn bright and hot and fast and hope the connection didn't fade.

It hadn't with them, even after they'd fought. Even after Ethaniel had turned his back on him, told him to get out, to never come back. Even after ignoring Aubrey's letters. Even after Aubrey himself had admitted defeat and spent a long, dark weekend slumped in his favorite chair and reading terribly romantic poetry until he wept. He'd felt connected to Ethaniel even then, and could only hope the universe would push them back together.

The room slapped itself back into view as something howled, and Aubrey swore he felt teeth at his throat.

Agrippa was solely focused on the whirlwind of magic in the center of the bone circle but Aubrey saw the edges of their feathers greying. Saw that long white hair start to droop; no longer vibrant but dingy. The power in the room was *choking*, and it took everything in him to keep upright, keep focused.

The howling grew louder. They all knew this sound.

Hellhounds.

His mind was a mire of thoughts now, stuck between recollection and memory, love and fear. Aubrey felt split in two, cleanly down the center.

You've always been of two natures, Aubrey. The family power and obligation, and the duty you have to yourself. You don't have to be.

Ethaniel's words, whispered in his ear after their first night together. A night that had been weeks in the making, spread across outings splashed with flickering lights and the scents of good wine and heady perfume. Nights spent huddled together at rickety tables, knees and elbows touching, while they talked in ways other people couldn't. There were only so many like them in the city, and many had variations on the same story: grief, loss, abandonment, loneliness. Ethaniel had been a kindred soul from the start, even though they'd come from wildly different backgrounds.

It had always been Ethaniel. And because of him, they both had Calix.

Calix.

Aubrey felt his mind snap back into place and he craned his head, desperate to see...

The hand that reached for him was glowing gently, gold backed with indigo. Calix's magic was rising to meet his own, meet the channel Agrippa and Magnus had ripped open with their own brands of arcane power.

"I see him!" Calix gasped as another howl echoed around them. "It's faint, but he's.... he's not alone."

"The book! Focus!" Agrippa's voice was a boom of thunder now, and Aubrey saw clouds appear overhead, dark and looming. "I don't have enough to locate Ethaniel properly— "

Out of the funnel of magic between them, something lashed out at Agrippa. They didn't flinch, didn't move a single inch, but dark blue blood welled on their cheek and across their lips.

Calix surged forward, one hand outstretched, grasping, reaching, scrabbling for the magic Agrippa was using. "I can see it!" Calix cried as he pushed forward.

"Keep him back, Aubrey!" Magnus yelled "We need only a few more moments."

Heedless of the wind and howling, Aubrey ran to Calix. He grabbed the slighter man by the waist, making sure they were still both outside the bone circle. But Calix was straining so hard, sweating with exertion, and nearly toppled them both across the circle and into the maelstrom, howls all around them. He pulled as hard as he dared just as another shape, this one sword-sharp and as long as he was tall, aimed right for Calix. Aubrey had a single moment to block Calix with his body.

It caught him across the back, shoulder blade to hip, and he cried out in pain but held firm. The consequences if he didn't.... he couldn't think about that. He couldn't think about much more than the strength of Calix's grip and the sizzle of his own blood against his torn skin as magic pulsed and pounded and throbbed all around them.

Aubrey remembered so much in that moment, his mind tumbling down a hill of recollections that brought him such joy and such pain. Ethaniel and Calix, Calix and Ethaniel. The book. The city. His own fears and worries knocking at the doors of his consciousness on the worst of those nights, between the last night Ethaniel had been in his bed and the next time they'd seen each other.

A flood, a torrent...

...down to a single thread, the one connecting him and Ethaniel and Calix and that fucking *book*...

There was another awful sound now, like the slap of flesh against stone combined with the squeaking of teeth against ice, and a language Aubrey had only ever heard Magnus speak, and it had only happened once. And now that language rose again, somehow both musical and harsh, lilting bells and harmonies of Agrippa's voice with the infernal fires of something not of their world.

Magnus's warning after one-time incident, which had nearly burnt down the Collectio's library: "If you ever hear me speak that language again, you run. Promise me."

He couldn't run, not with Calix wrapped up in his arms and fighting with every fiber of his being, but he could get them both to safety. The instinct to protect was so strong... he had no choice. Aubrey pushed them both to the ground and only caught a glimpse of the arcane portal snapping shut and something dark falling to the floor before his vision went fuzzy and his brain began to hum with another, more discordant wave of magic. It jarred against his own, against the pulsing energy of Calix's magic. It was utterly alien and terrifying. He felt out of his mind, out of his body, with it, in a way no words could possibly describe.

When the room fell silent and the magic dropped, his mind scraped raw with confusion and stress and terror, Aubrey realized there were five beings, not four, in the room. In the middle of the circle of bones, which was still intact, was a hellhound the size of a small horse, and its leash was made of fire and wrapped around Agrippa's left forearm.

"It seems my trap worked," Agrippa said, a note of pride in their voice. "A backup, in case the tracking failed. But you two did well." They motioned to the bones on the floor, which began to shudder, tapping in a strange rhythm against the floor, until they slid into place one after the other. Even from his distance, with sweat and blood in his eyes, Aubrey could tell the bones were forming some kind of map. "Power points, anchor points, and doors," Agrippa said, pointing first to four star shapes, then to three bird skulls, and finally to a single dried rose closer to their side of the circle. "Power points we can influence from here, and... " Agrippa trailed off. "Well, we'll talk about it later. This is a very good start."

He should have felt elated, but in his arms, Calix was shivering, and Aubrey winced. Between the pain of his wound and Calix's trembling, he was barely holding together. "Calix," he said softly, the question unasked.

"I saw him," Calix whispered back. "I saw Ethaniel. All that power... it *opened* something in my mind. Or maybe pried open was what already ajar from all my mother's meddling. But I saw him." The gold of his eyes seemed to dim. "And that man... his brother? Vincent."

A wave of nausea hit him. Maybe it was the wound, maybe it was the thought of Vincent anywhere near Ethaniel. Aubrey tried to curl closer around Calix, willing his spine to bend despite the pain. Calix was *trembling* in his arms and he couldn't do anything about it.

He couldn't focus past the pain. Someone made a noise — soft, wounded, fragile — and whether it was him or Calix, it didn't matter. *They* were hurt, wounded, scattered, and they needed *Ethaniel*.

He needed Ethaniel.

"Get them out of here, Magnus," Agrippa snapped, their voice full of fire and fury, the bells deep in their tone now clanging. The hellhound's snarls were slowly turning into whimpers and Aubrey's head began to ache anew, like an icepick behind his eyes and a vise around his temples.

The world was starting to blur. Panic wormed its way into his gut.

"We need to get that seen to," Magnus said, suddenly at their side and hauling him up. "Calix, help me."

Calix clearly hadn't seen Aubrey's back, because he put a hand on the small of it to guide Aubrey to his feet, and Aubrey damn near *shouted*. The agony was exquisite, unlike anything he'd ever felt.

And then the world went blissfully black.

CHAPTER ELEVEN

CALIX

While Aubrey gently emanated soft blue light, his eyes shut as he focused on thoughts of Ethaniel, Calix let himself drift. Or, rather, he tried to. He was so out of his mind with worry and pain and fatigue that it took everything in him to stand on his own two feet.

But Ethaniel needed them. And he wasn't about to fail at this. At bringing him back home.

The moment the thought crossed his mind, Calix was thrust into a memory.

No, *the* memory.

Of that day.

The book in his ear, wriggling through his mind. The panic in his chest, the harsh breathing, the sweat down his back. The feel of the people he pushed past, their faces blurring together like watercolors.

Back to the tailor's shop.

Back to *Ethaniel*. Who he'd tried to flirt with but couldn't because he was both too in awe of the man's skill and his looks. He remembered going home that afternoon, stripping to the skin, and laying on his bed, a hazy sort of arousal coursing through him, almost out of thin air.

The cold of the room on his bare flesh, despite the fire in the hearth and the thick blankets all around him.

The smell of the shop, leather and beeswax and warm, worn wood floors gleaming in the sunlight. How sure Ethaniel's hands were, how strong they looked. He wondered how they'd feel on his body, and Calix let himself sink into that feeling. He was soon wrapped up in a daydream of thick arms and gentle smiles.

Ethaniel had saved him. More than once.

His life had changed completely, irrevocably, because of Ethaniel's kindness.

Ethaniel's eyes stared back into his. A flicker of truth was pounded into Calix's brain because he was suddenly seeing *through* Ethaniel's eyes.

An enormous creature, spindly and bone-white, scuttling across the ground like a spider out of a keyhole, and on its back was a girl who bore Ethaniel's dark hair and hazel eyes, but her shadow was all wrong. It jittered and jolted and made him ill to look upon.

And beside Ethaniel was Vincent. The half-brother. The man to blame.

The brothers were shoulder to shoulder, Vincent badly bruised and scraped, one eye nearly swollen shut. And he was saying something to Ethaniel...

"We can't overpower him," Vincent whispered into his shoulder as they both watched Uzala climb a tree. Then its head spun around to face them even as its body faced forward. "But it has a weakness."

"Trust you to go for the jugular," Calix-as-Ethaniel muttered. "Fine. What's the weakness?"

The fingers clutching his arm tightened, the strength in them painful. Bruises throbbed under that touch, but Calix and Ethaniel both held still under the flash-heat of it.

"What gets us all in the end. Us unrepentant souls, anyways." Vincent lifted his head and smiled, teeth still bloody. "Pride, brother. Always pride."

And then Vincent cocked his head and leaned in, a curious look on his face. "Are you—"

Ethaniel pushed Calix out, the panic fluttering in his lover's chest cold as ice. *He can't know you're there.* That was the only thing Ethaniel managed to say before the connection was severed.

And then he was in Aubrey's arms and the world was spinning, and Magnus was making them *float* into the other room. Magnus lowered his arms and they gently landed on the bed. "Calix, can you help me?" Magnus asked with real fear in his voice. "A void touched Aubrey, and he needs seen to."

Calix's head spun, but he managed to get to his feet. "A void?"

Magnus was already tearing through a chest of drawers, ripping cloth with his hands and teeth. He looked frantic. *Terrified.*

Fear wasn't merely a stone in his stomach. It became an anchor in his heart. *Not Aubrey, too. I can't lose either of them.*

"Tear these while I heat water and get Agrippa's lab kit," Magnus said before shoving the cloth into his hands. "And I'll need you to help me get Aubrey out of his shirt. We have to get rid of anything the void touched."

He dashed off, leaving Calix with a pile of tattered shirts pulled from the ether of Agrippa's little bubble realm, and an unconscious Aubrey. Calix immediately put a hand to Aubrey's chest, feeling the thump of his heart and the even rhythm of his breath. He looked fine, a little wan, but that was understandable given the strain of the last days.

He wasn't in any way prepared for the third eye on Aubrey's forehead to flash to life, then train its sight on him. Somewhere deep inside himself — his body, his soul, his essence — Calix felt something *widen*. Pried open, cracked and tunneled out like a shell. A carapace, perhaps. A shield built for him by his mother, crafted by her loving, scheming hands and she'd known exactly how to help and hurt him.

She might have built him into a tool for her own use, but that wasn't what he wanted to be any longer.

He stared back at the third eye and instead of hiding, instead of holding back, he let it in. And once it slipped inside, there was no reeling it back. Calix welcomed it, welcomed a part of *Aubrey* into himself...

...and he *saw*. He *knew*.

He knew it as well as he knew himself. Like knowing where those secret, soft spots on his body that, when touched, made him shiver. Like every scar and bump, every ache, every bruise, every wound he'd ever been given.

The backhand his father had dealt once, then perfected. The careful embrace of his mother. The distance of his sisters. The wounds were worse on the soul. A bruise faded, a split lip healed. No, those slights that manifested into something larger, something bigger than Aubrey himself, were reforged. Made into ambition and drive, powered him through long nights of study, training that drained him of everything he had.

He didn't hate his father anymore than he could hate a bird for flying. Some people were made in a mold that could not and would not break.

And Calix felt all of it. All of Aubrey inside him, beating like a second heart, and he knew. *He knew he knew he knew.* They didn't need a mental connection anymore, not with the way their magic was so intertwined.

That third eye flickered, shuttered, and faded. For a brief moment, Calix swore he felt it retreat into Aubrey, as if giving him a chance to awaken on his own. To be himself once more.

Aubrey opened his eyes as Magnus ran back into the room. The pain was evident on Aubrey's face, but Calix didn't know if it was malingering from their minds and magic touching, or from the wound. "Calix."

Aubrey grasped for his hand and Calix held it between his own as Magnus said, "Oh, thank God. You're awake. But that almost makes this worse."

Aubrey heaved a laugh, mostly air and sound so faint Calix nearly missed it. "You worry too much," he rasped.

"Perhaps, but not in this case. Calix, help me roll him to his front."

Aubrey was weak, his limbs limp and of no assistance, but they managed to get him splayed on his stomach. Calix bit back a curse when he saw the wound on Aubrey's back. It oozed with black ichor, not unlike the ichor he'd seen when he'd shared Ethaniel's sight moments ago. He took the proffered gloves and scissors from Magnus and carefully cut away Aubrey's shirt, the ichor clinging to the silver blades, dulling them. A bit of something bubbled on the handle and Calix nearly dropped them. But Aubrey's shirt was now in tatters and they could more easily reach his wound.

"Agrippa calls it the void," Magnus said as he set about dipping strips of cloth into steaming water, then handing them to Calix along with a small clear bottle. "Put exactly three drops of that oil onto each cloth, and we should be able to neutralize the poison."

Calix was quiet for a moment, intent on following Magnus's instructions to the letter. "What is it?" he finally asked in a soft voice. Aubrey was still breathing, still shifting every now and then and hissing in pain when Magnus wiped away the excess ichor. He wasn't fully conscious; drifting in and out of their reality, perhaps, and Calix could only hope to help soothe the pain.

"Honestly, I don't know. Agrippa says it's everywhere in the *demimonde*. It flows like rivers and hangs from trees like moss. Sometimes... things come out of it, like a terrible birthing process." Calix swallowed hard at that, his fear and disgust compounding, but it couldn't distract him from his task.

"Hold his hands," Magnus said, now armed with several soaked bits of fabric. "The oil neutralizes the void's acid, but it's a wound like any other. It certainly won't be... comfortable."

"Do it," Aubrey slurred. He reached out again and Calix took his hand. "We... need to find him. Ethaniel."

The desperation and pain in Aubrey's voice made Calix suck in a sharp breath. *How was he supposed to hold them all together when everything was falling apart? Could he even...*

"Hold his hands," Magnus repeated, so Calix did. He held onto those hands, caressing Aubrey's knuckles with his thumbs, his fingertips rubbing the insides of Aubrey's wrists. Aubrey's pulse was fast but strong, his breathing steady. It was all Calix could hope for right now.

The first cloth was laid down and Aubrey arched away from it with a pained groan, but Calix gently whispered to him — about how good and kind and strong he was and how this would all be over soon. How they'd fix it, all of it, and find a new normal. He wanted to believe his words, wanted to feel the truth of them nestle somewhere deep beneath his ribs.

Once Ethaniel's back. Once we're together again.

Magnus was silent as he applied the cloth to Aubrey's back. "There's just so much we don't know," he muttered. "And we keep running headlong into trouble. I simply don't know... "

Calix didn't know what to say. Didn't know what to do other than anchor himself with the feel of Aubrey's hands in his and continue whispering that they'd be all right, it would all be all right in the end...

"He'll sleep for a long while, I think," Magnus said as he sat back and moved the bowls to the side after a few minutes. Calix saw the water was now murky-grey and had to swallow against the way his stomach revolted. Something about that sight was vile, on a level he couldn't quite explain. "The poison is neutralized, thankfully. And he should heal just fine. I'm no... well, I'm no Lavigne, but I've dealt with void in the past."

Calix glanced at the wound and yes, it had already begun to knit. And Aubrey was breathing more evenly, as if he was asleep.

When Magnus got to his feet, he held a hand out for Calix. "Come on. Staying in here won't make him heal any quicker, my young friend."

Calix hesitated. He didn't want to leave Aubrey's bedside, but there was an urgency — no, *expectation* — in Magnus's eyes and Calix felt its pull. "Not for long," he acquiesced, and Magnus nodded, mollified.

Outside the room, Agrippa was kneeling beside the hellhound, one hand hovering over the orb in which it had been encased. Calix saw that golden light and was reminded of when they'd done something similar to Convergence. It felt like an age ago.

"It's part of the pack that came after you in the *demimonde*," Agrippa said. Calix still wasn't quite used to how abruptly they jumped into conversation, and the pain and fear of the last several minutes was fading to a shakiness, a fog in his brain that he had to push against to find any kind of clarity. He wouldn't have been shocked if someone told him Agrippa could hear his thoughts, but even that potential revelation left him dizzy. "I had a feeling if we cracked open the door, they'd rush for the chance to get their teeth into you."

The hound, a creature of fire and ash and rock, was snarling and snapping at its magical cage, for all the good it did. Calix still kept his distance. "You can use it?"

"Indeed. What we did before was triangulation. Focusing on your companion made it easier to pick up the book's magical signature, since you and he spent the longest in its... estimable company." Agrippa pointed at the hellhound, who was now foaming pink at the mouth and scraping its fangs against the magic cage. "I knew there was also a chance the hellhounds that attacked you would wait for their opportunity, so I had this at the ready." They tapped on the cage. "I've found the best approach when dealing with the *demimonde* is to trick it. So we're going to make it think the hound is seeking a way back in. With any luck, a door opens."

Calix's very *soul* shuddered at the thought of going back to that place, but he would do it. He'd never doubted that. Ethaniel needed him. "Tell me what I need to do."

Agrippa and Magnus exchanged a look. Calix had the damndest feeling it was one they exchanged a fair amount, but he was absolutely certain the trust between them was reaffirmed with that one glance. "You and I are going in," Magnus said. "I'm going to borrow a bit of Agrippa's magic and we'll use it to track the book. The book will get us to Ethaniel."

There was an odd drop in Magnus's tone and Calix was surprised to see the man's sculpted, emotive face replaced by a blank mask. He ran his startled gaze over Magnus, then Agrippa, who looked a bit more twisted up about this plan, their feathers rustling audibly. It was still a beautiful sound, but not one Calix had heard them make before.

"So, we're following Ethaniel's... magical signature, once we find Convergence?" Calix asked, questions swirling in his mind.

"No," Magnus said as Agrippa replied the opposite. The stare that passed between them made Calix feel like an intruder in some very private scene and it made his insides squirm.

"That plan is not acceptable," Agrippa finally snapped, their galaxy-deep eyes going pitch black. "Magnus, you cannot — "

"I can, and I will, because it is the plan that will *work*, Agrippa." Magnus's voice was blisteringly cold and as sharp as the icicles that hung from Rosehill's eaves in the dead of winter. "You cannot change my mind on this."

Magnus's tone was raised only a little, but that seemed to set Agrippa off. They strode toward Magnus, power crackling in the air around them, eyes like gaping portals to somewhere truly dark and dire, white hair billowing up behind them. Calix could feel himself being pulled in against his will, toward the being whose energy was unlike anything he'd ever experienced.

It all stopped when Magnus put a hand on Agrippa's face.

No more waves of magic, no more threats in the room. Magnus had stopped it all with a careful, gentle touch.

Calix had to cover his gasp with his hand and turn away. *This* was far too intimate a moment —

"Stay, please," Magnus said, an order punctuating his words. "We'll only be a moment."

Calix was frozen in place, torn between the urge to flee and check on Aubrey and the worst of his own curious impulses. What lay between Magnus and Agrippa was deep and wide, a trench filled with stories and longing, and that knowledge alone had him sucking in a deep breath and rolling his eyes skyward so he didn't look. And so he didn't cry.

"They need me," Magnus said softly. "I've been on the sidelines this entire time, Agrippa. But no more. I did as you asked, but please. Hear me."

"You're a fool," Agrippa whispered back. The pain was so horribly clear in their words and Calix wanted to curl into a ball at the sound. He had to look, but regretted it instantly.

Calix ripped his gaze away right after Agrippa pressed their forehead to Magnus's. "You're a fool if you think the *demimonde* won't sink its teeth into you."

"I'm counting on it," Magnus whispered back. "It won't give anything up willingly, and the hound will be helpful for opening a door only."

A long beat of silence followed. Eventually, Agrippa said, "I do not approve of this plan, Magnus. But I know I can't stop you."

"You can't."

"You... you must come back." Was that fear, held like a pristine note, in Agrippa's voice? He felt empathy rattle through him, the few last coins in his cup. Agrippa was *afraid* of Magnus going into the *demimonde*.

"I've no desire to stay in such a place." The soft sound of a hand against cloth (*or feathers*, Calix thought with another stifled gasp), and then Magnus whispered something that didn't quite meet his ears. All the better for it. They deserved to have something only for themselves.

When Magnus put a hand on Calix's shoulder and turned him, it was no surprise the man's deep brown eyes looked pained, his expression pinched. But he shook it off and said, "Quite simply, we're opening the door with the hellhound, and then I'll help you amplify your Oracle powers to finish tracking the book. The book leads us to Ethaniel."

Calix's head spun. It seemed far too easy, especially after all their struggles. "That's it?"

Magnus chuckled. "Not quite so much, but that's the plan. I have a backup, just in case Talbot is angry about being left to...well, fend for himself, as it were. But yes, that's the plan. Once Aubrey is awake, that is. Agrippa will need his help keeping the portal open, so we're on a bit of a timer. Speaking of, do you still have Aubrey's monocle?"

Calix reached into his pocket and pulled it out. "Yes, but why?"

"Because we'll use it in the *demimonde* as a way to connect back to Aubrey via the portal."

Calix looked to Agrippa, who nodded. Magnus continued. "Strictly speaking, the monocle is a focus and it tethers you to someone on this side of reality while in the *demimonde*, and that tether connects to the portal, which we keep open by tapping into a power point. And those on this side will guide you through from there, via anchor points, so I hope you have a strong stomach."

Calix wanted to go now. He bit down on the urge to voice his desire and waited Magnus out while the other man paused.

"It's a bit... dizzying to jump through anchor points, and the closer we get to a door, the worse it could get. But Uzala, the creature holding Ethaniel and his half-brother, will be close to a door. At least, that's how Agrippa explained it to me," Magnus finished. "Honestly, it all gets a bit hypothetical and far too deep into the realm of arcane physics for me to understand. But I've jumped anchor points before, and I am very clear on how to do so again. I wouldn't think too much on how the *demimonde* is akin to a minotaur's labyrinth or you'll lose some marbles up there."

The shuffle of footsteps had them all turning to find Aubrey slowly walking toward them. Deep purple-black circles under his eyes drained them of color and spark, and he looked an inch away from needing a sick bed, but when Calix rushed over to him, Aubrey didn't hesitate in putting an arm over his shoulders and letting Calix take the weight. "This is madness," Aubrey said, "but I'm guessing it's the only way?"

Another look passed between Magnus and Agrippa. "That either of us know of," Agrippa replied, their tone a tad terse still. Calix could easily imagine the maelstrom of emotions rolling through them, because that's how he'd felt when Ethaniel had taken control of the hellhound situation back at the house, and how easily he'd sacrificed a part of himself to keep them safe. It was also how he'd felt when Aubrey had stayed behind to give them both a chance to escape while the Golden Order set fire to his apartment.

It *was* madness. And he would do the same for them any day.

Calix looked up at Aubrey. "Magnus and I can do this. I'm not coming back unless Ethaniel is with us."

"That's not really — "

"Agrippa," Magnus whispered, "shush."

Calix let it go. All he needed, right now, was Aubrey's arm over his shoulders, his warmth pressed up against his side, and the understanding written all over his face. Aubrey understood. He didn't have to say a single word for Calix to feel it.

"Before we have no time left," Aubrey whispered to him. Calix looked up, and Aubrey kissed him softly, sweetly. The curl of warmth that settled in his belly tugged him in two directions, two halves of himself warring for the space between them.

"I'm coming back."

"I know."

Following Agrippa's instructions was like swimming underwater. Hazy, dream-like, but strangely comforting. Calix had always loved the ritual of magic, had been desperate to learn all he could at his mother's feet, and now, in this strange place with this being standing across from him, and one of their feathers in his pocket, Calix wasn't fully sure this was at all real. Perhaps it was the stress, the strain and exhaustion making him feel so unmoored. Perhaps it was the grief.

Perhaps magic was a little strange. A little hazy. A little bit like a dream.

But reality had to seep back in, and did. Just a few moments later and Agrippa, now surrounded by blinding white energy, the wind in their space buffeting them from all sides, picked the snarling, snapping hellhound up with one hand and crushed its skull.

"It's not a loss," Agrippa said as they stared. The hellhound's body had gone limp, the lava-like fire under its crackling skin now gone, its flesh turning into even more ash and dust, the smell of sulfur on the air. "The *demimonde* will want it back in any form and it wasn't practical to let that thing go in through the same door as the two of you."

Magnus rubbed his hand over his face and Calix almost laughed out loud at the resignation written there. Clearly, he was losing it a little, too. They all were. "Oh, Agrippa," Magnus said as he held out his hand to begin channeling.

He said it again once the door to the *demimonde* cracked open, but it was all either of them could say in the moment. Calix could see Aubrey's focused, determined expression and Agrippa's almost placid one across the circle from them. He had no room for fear right now. He had Aubrey's monocle in his pocket, Agrippa's feather in his other one, and Magnus had the rest of their supplies.

They were going to find Ethaniel. And they wouldn't come back until they did.

The body of the hellhound was tossed into the golden doorway the moment it opened fully, and then Magnus pulled Calix in after him, and then they were back.

Back in that place. That horrid, godawful place that had taken Ethaniel from him, from them.

Everything was grey and shrouded in mist, and the ash of the hellhound lay at their feet.

"Oh, Agrippa." Magnus gave Calix a rueful smile. "Here's the thing, Calix. I couldn't tell Agrippa everything, or they would have never let me do this. Not even for you all." From out of his pocket came a mother-of-pearl snuffbox they'd found amongst his mother's things. "But Agrippa's plan was never going to work. They are a lot of things, my friend, but understanding of the folly of humans.... not exactly in their purview. So I let them make a logical conclusion and get a tad angry with me, because that's what they expected me to do." Magnus gestured at their surroundings, then gave the snuffbox a little shake. "And here we are. But that's just the first step."

Calix leaned forward to peer inside and saw fine red dust. "That's the red divine we found at the estate," he said. Magnus only gave him an expectant look. "We should use this while here, shouldn't we?"

Magnus nodded. "You'll have to forgive me if I've.... well, spiked it a bit. Red divine, on its own, can help with focus and concentration, but in this place, we need something a tad stronger. And no, you don't want to know."

Calix huffed out a shocked laugh, heard it echo around them in this strange space. "I'm so glad you're here," he said before pulling Magnus in for a hug. "So glad."

Chapter Twelve

LAWTON

Lawton's entire body was one massive bruise. Or so it felt, since thrumming pain tinged with nausea was the first thing he noticed when he opened his eyes.

"What a sweet thing you are. Wherever did you come from?"

The pain immediately morphed into fear. Real fear, the kind that would make a man sweat and turn his hands to ice, set his heart racing.

Thin fingers, as cold as a gravestone, curled into his hair and yanked his head up. He scrabbled at the hand, but the grip was iron-tight. "Oh. How unexpected."

Lawton's head was yanked back again and now he was on his knees, back arched as they held him at bay. He felt like an insect pinned to a board as a woman with long, dark red hair, blood and ash smeared around her thin, fox-like face, stared down at him. He tried to raise his left arm, but it flopped at his side, all dying fish on a dock.

"Be still," she said through a pouting frown. "You cut awfully deeply and when I saw your sparkling soul flutter in here, I had to reach out and snatch you up." Then her other hand shot forward and there were nails, sharp and ragged, digging into the scar at his collarbone. Lawton screamed as her nails sank in, five knives right through his flesh.

And then she dropped him and when his knees hit the ground, the pain was gone. Lawton pressed a hand to the scar, which was as whole as it had been a moment ago, and watched as her long red dress trailed behind her, the hem clumped with mud and a thick black ichor whose smell burned his nose.

"You're welcome to stay there," she said over her shoulder, "or if you follow me, I'll get rid of that nasty scar for you. A shame Vincent couldn't put that brutal nature of his to better use. Such a waste of potential."

She flicked her hand at the air and a churning portal appeared. Looking at it made Lawton sick to his stomach.

She glanced back again. "You want him back, yes? You've done an admirable job of pushing your jealousy down. Squashing it like an annoying fly. But you are jealous. Because now that you've had time to truly think about it... they took him away, didn't they? Those men with their magic and their charm and their kindness. Their selflessness. I'd tell you sweet little lies, tell you it won't last between the three of them. But we both know that's not true."

Her words snapped in his ears, in his mind, unsettling all the doubts he thought he'd laid to rest. And then she was back in his face again, looming. Up close, she was older than he originally would have guessed, but she was the cold kind of beautiful that made Lawton ache. It wasn't attraction... or maybe it was. It was insane to even think that way, but impossible to ignore when she was so close. It was a cruel seduction. One that was pervasive, persistent. The kind that made him want to chase.

Somehow, she knew him.

"Those men," she said again, a harsh whisper of breath against his cheek. "The healer. With his suits and cane and rings. Rings on big hands with long fingers. A manly man, if a beautiful one. Poised. Elegant. Smart. Wealthy. Magic seeping out of his pores. And when he was pressed up against Calix, those big hands with their silver rings touching his skin, you didn't look away. You watched. You watched when they thought you asleep, and if you couldn't watch, you listened and thought of those hands."

The hand that cupped his jaw was warm and Lawton leaned into it. He was cold all over, down to his bones and nearly mad with it. The cold and the pain and the loneliness and yes, the jealousy.

"And the other one. So selfless, the patterner. Hard to be that in a family like his, but he managed it." She was on his other side now, a hand pressed into his scar, and

Lawton felt every pulse of his heart under her palm. For a long, terrifying moment, his heartbeat was the only thing he heard.

"Your mind betrays you," she crooned into his ear. "Because even now, as frightened as you are, you can't keep from thinking about that man's power. How it tasted on your tongue, how it felt prickling your skin. Power you'd kill to have, even now. After everything. Jealous. So broken and jealous and desperate, this little bird I found."

She slipped around him again, looming once more. But there was a curious spark in her depthless eyes, and her finger pushed up under his chin so their gazes could meet. "You cannot help your nature. But I saved your life, and if you wish to go back to your body and your world, I'll send you on your way."

Lawton licked his lips. More than mere thoughts, whole diaries' worth of emotions bubbled up to sit on his tongue, lean against his lips, and beg to be aired out like laundry.

What did he want?

And why did she care?

"What do you want in exchange?" he asked, and she threw her head back, laughing with delight. "I know how this works. Tell me what you want."

"Oh, this little bird. I like him." She leaned forward and pressed her forehead to his, her hair tumbling down around them like a curtain. "Nothing except if we ever see each other again, you give me a chance. It's good to have friends."

He didn't dare move. Dare breathe too hard, lest she change her mind. He knew everything had a price, and even his price tag wasn't out of reach of this strange, electric woman who smelled like death and magic. "And if I want more?"

"You can have it."

"It's never that simple."

"Of course it is. And as a little gift, a sign of my sincerity, I'll take care of your trespasser."

Lawton woke up on the cold bathroom floor, his fingernails ripped and bloody from where he'd dragged himself across the tiles. He managed to push up against the wall, and only once he was sitting up did he allow himself to suck in sharp breaths. Everything *hurt*.

But he was alive.

It took several attempts, but Lawton got to his feet and stumbled over to the mirror. There was no evidence of the mirror shard he'd pressed to his own skin, and though his brand from the Golden Order remained, he thought it looked a tad more dull. Or perhaps he was truly losing his mind... and maybe that was the case, as full of questions and doubts as it was now.

Who was that woman? And what did she want?

And why should he even care, because it was, quite simply, someone who wanted to use him. Like Lily.

His thought flitted to Calix and a burn of shame flared to life in his chest. Yes, in the few spare moments he'd had between pain and danger, he'd been quietly jealous. He and Calix had been each other's for so long. It hadn't stopped him from flirting, dancing with, and bedding those who caught his fancy, and Calix had been free to do the same (though they both knew Calix rarely did).

He knew everything about Calix. And by the gods did it *burn* to see him in the arms of not one, but two capable, beautiful men.

Lawton pressed his palm to the brand, hissing when the pressure slipped to the side of *too much*. And when he dug his ragged nails into his skin, he remembered pain like knives and eyes like a hunting ground. It shook something in him; nameless, without real form or function but it left a sharp sense of loneliness in its wake.

A noise came from outside the closed bathroom door. *Cassandra*, he thought, his heart immediately pounding against his ribs. She'd been... crazed, almost feral. And that was not Cassandra at all. She'd been his handler from the first day with the Order and no charm or smiles could make her do anything but stare flatly at him. When the charm and the smiles didn't work, he tried to prove himself, ingratiate himself into her sphere. Make a commodity of himself. Be valuable. Useful. An endless well they could tap again and again, whenever he could find the chance to slip away. He met clients in bars while Calix was in a booth around the corner, or slipped away when Calix had finally fallen asleep to swap plain envelopes with some singer or dancer or man in a tweed jacket.

No, that hadn't been Cassandra at the door.

I'll take care of your trespasser, she'd said. He never assumed she'd meant Lily. That would have been too lucky.

Lawton closed his eyes, and with the threat of hope sticking in the back of his throat, reached for Lily. Not one second later, his gut clenched in pain and he thought he might actually vomit, but was left leaning against the sink, sweating and aching.

"Fuck," Lawton bit out as he stumbled, then straightened. "Well, nice to see you're still there. I knew fortune wasn't in my favor there."

What he got back was wordless. But who needed words when Calix's mother was screaming like a banshee inside his chest and the indigo and black-stained veins traced over his skin felt like they could pop at any minute.

And now he wondered if the house was actually empty, noise not withstanding, or if this strange woman had been toying with him. Lawton picked up the gun, checked the chamber, and eased the hammer back. He hated guns, awful things, but *something* had grabbed him, had left a thick, oily black substance across part of the bathroom floor to disappear under the door.

Lawton pressed his ear to the door and waited. Held his breath, felt his heart thud with each passing second. Still nothing.

Carefully, he pushed the door open enough so he could look out without fully exposing his head or body.

Nothing other than smashed glass on the floor and a mirror frame hanging crookedly, and more of that disgusting black sludge dragged across the wallpaper, but there was no trail he could see.

By the time he'd edged out of the door, his breathing had calmed a little. Not enough to let him relax, but he was fairly certain Cassandra was gone. Which meant he needed to check on the rest of the house. This wasn't a penny dreadful, where he could follow a trail of bloody footprints or handprints to the culprit. He needed to actually investigate, room by room.

"I am going to get killed this way," Lawton muttered to himself as he slowly, quietly took the hall down to the parlor where Calix had disappeared through a portal with the others. Where Aubrey had threatened him and then handed him a weapon.

As he passed Calix's study on the left, the parlor just up ahead to the right, there was a noise again. Lawton paused, and when no other sound came through the cracked door, he pressed himself into the wall opposite, gun aimed at chest level. His hand was steady despite the strange, roaming numbness that accompanied Lily's occupation in his body, and before he could lose his nerve, he pushed off the wall and swung the door open wide.

All the furniture had been pushed against the far wall, and not merely moved. *Stacked.* Two chairs on top of the loveseat, Calix's desk flat against the wall (but standing up, somehow, on two legs). Even the books were pinned to the wall like butterflies. It was a horrible sight, but not nearly as awful as what was in the middle of the room.

Anchored to the rug with forearm-length jagged spikes of iron and glinting glass was Cassandra. A spike in both shoulders, both ankles, both thighs. One through the neck. Her clothes and skin were dotted with that black ichor, and around her waist was something shiny, like brass or gold.

That was all he managed to take in before the shock of it settled in his ears and his mind like a high-pitched whine. He didn't want to get any closer.

She's wearing something, Lily hissed in his ear. *Some artifact. I can feel it, even from here, even as weak as I am. It tastes like something I'd found when Calix was a boy...*

Her voice faded, and with it she did as well, reduced to a shiver down his spine and the taste of blood on his lip. He'd bitten it hard while staring at Cassandra's corpse, and the pain shook him loose, pushing him into the room.

"Christ," he whispered as he edged closer to her. There was no expression on her face; no pain, no shock. As placid a death mask as you could find outside a funeral parlor. She almost looked like she was sleeping from a distance, but the closer he got... her eyes were open. Staring directly up at the ceiling, and they were pitch black.

He was wrong. She had no eyes. They'd been plucked from her head as neatly as one would pop a snail from its shell.

Behind him, a desk drawer shot open, and it spat out a little black box with a tag attached. A demented gift from an unwanted suitor.

He instantly regretted picking up the box. Something *squished* against the insides.

You can vomit after you look, he told himself.

Lawton opened the box and immediately knew he'd have nightmares for weeks, if not months.

Cassandra's eyes stared up at him, the tag in his hand stating they were "valuable" and "in case you want to reach me".

Lawton made it to the planted ficus in the corner, one of the few things in the room not shoved out of place, before throwing up stomach acid into the poor thing's soil.

He sat on the cold floor, only vaguely aware of his body. He couldn't drag his gaze away from Cassandra. The brutality of it. Nothing he'd ever done had been close to something so awful. Some numb part of him wondered if she was truly dead. But she must be. No one could survive such torture.

Her eyes are in a box beside you, you bloody fool, he thought, pulling his knees up to his chin just to feel some kind of warmth. *Of course she's dead.*

The clouds outside parted for a moment, and the thin, pale beams of sunlight weren't enough to help. But they did draw his gaze back to the shining thing at Cassandra's waist. And the longer he stared, the more his curiosity started banging about.

He crawled across the floor, avoiding the small pools of blood underneath each spike as best he could, and reached out to the body. If he didn't look at her face, he could do this. And he had nothing left to vomit up.

"What is it?" he asked as he brushed his fingers across leather that felt like metal. Some kind of belt, but the sensation was completely *wrong*.

Take it, Lily said, her voice distant and strangely calm. *We may need it.*

"You mean you need it," he snapped as he flipped open the gold buckle. The *sheink* of a chain rattling to the hard floor sent his heart into his throat, flinching against the unexpected noise. *Calm down, you fool.*

I won't know until you hold it with both hands, Lily said, her tone going steely.

Lawton bit down on the inside of his cheek to keep from screaming at her. All his pain and rage and confusion and loneliness were starting to ball up inside him; a snowball rolling downhill, picking up anything in its wake and carrying it along for the journey. He was weak from the lack of restful sleep and lack of appetite. He was exhausted, cold, and... and...

Defeated.

He was defeated. He was tired of having to scheme twice as smarter and harder just to stay afloat. Tired of his apologies falling on deaf ears. Tired of being told he was on Calix's time. Their relationship hadn't always been so... competitive and shallow. They'd only had each other for so long at boarding school, bedding down beside each other between walls as unforgiving and harsh as the winters that seemed to last half the year. And when it hadn't snowed, it had rained, and the rare sunny days had been some of the best moments of his life.

Because Calix's hair had shone like copper in the sunlight, and he'd looked so *alive.*

Calix at eleven, still small for his age and having nightmares that sent him into Lawton's bed simply because Lawton would stay awake until he fell asleep.

Then fourteen and finally catching up to all the other boys in height, he was still slim. So thin that Lawton could wrap his hands around bony wrists and touch his thumb and forefinger together. Then he'd become caught up in the way Calix had gasped when he'd done that one night as they'd argued over an assignment. He'd meant it as a tease, as a way to shake Calix from his adamant arguments... but that gasp. It had gone right through him, hot and slick. And then Calix had blushed and looked away, and Lawton let the matter drop like Calix's hands.

Then they're seventeen and Calix is heading to Cambridge ahead of him. His extra months spent studying in some dusty library is not what Lawton envies. It's that Calix will experience something new without him. That he will be untethered from Calix for longer than a holiday home. That once Lawton arrived, Calix may not want him anymore. Suave, older boys and young men, mostly of Calix's caliber in breeding and wealth, would roam the halls and green lawns. How could any of them resist such beauty? Would Calix still want him after that?

Then they're twenty and Calix is outside and Lawton is yelling at him from an open window to get his arse upstairs to warm up. Then Calix wraps his body around Lawton's, drawing the ouroboros of need and want and loathing tighter and tighter still. Until Lawton doesn't know the end or the start of either of them and even when Calix leaves for his own apartment and bed, Lawton can still smell him, still feel him. And the pain is so delicious, he wraps a hand around himself. Closes his eyes and presses the sheets to his nose while he comes.

You're a pathetic fool, but you don't have to keep being one.

Very carefully, Lawton picked up the belt with both hands, but wound up watching in awe as the leather faded away into gleaming gold. "What is it?" he asked as the magic hummed and buzzed under his skin once more.

I don't know, but you should keep it. Wear it, even.

"That seems highly dangerous, if not monumentally stupid," he snapped.

Then give it to Calix and his curator and let them sort it out.

"Generous of you."

Hardly. I simply don't want to waste energy arguing with you, Lawton.

"And on that, we can agree," he said.

Lawton managed to stumble back to the parlor, gun and belt in hand. He left the eyeball box by Cassandra's body. And then he waited, and waited, and waited, staring at the wall and watching the hazy grey daylight slip across it into twilight shadow.

He was jostled awake by a heavy *pop* in the air, and the appearance of not three, but five, men in the room, the air itself *smoking* around them. Smoke also curled off their clothes and Calix and Magnus were covered in soot and blood, but seemingly whole.

Lawton got to his feet to greet them and then locked eyes with Vincent de Laine.

Chapter Thirteen

MAGNUS

I'm going to have the worst headache tomorrow, Magnus thought as he pressed the pad of his thumb into the red divine and held it up to Calix. "You only need a bit, like this. Then rub it over your gums." When Calix made a face, Magnus nearly laughed. The young Earl was so expressive despite his delicate appearance. It wasn't difficult to understand why Aubrey and Ethaniel were so taken with him.

Or maybe you do understand because of another, he thought as his mind flitted back to the anguish on Agrippa's face once they realized he wouldn't back down. After so many years, their minds were linked by a fragile connection; not mind-reading, per se, but something along the lines of sensing each other's emotions. And Agrippa had been within a hair's breadth away of shackling him to a wall to keep him from journeying into the depths of the *demimonde*. He'd felt it; crystalline and perfect and it pierced his heart in the way it had Agrippa's.

They were inarguably the most grouchy being he'd ever met, and he adored them for it. And they were hardly ever grouchy at him. Agrippa was truly a curmudgeon, often annoying in their exactness and inexhaustible (mostly because they didn't sleep, they didn't need it). But from the day they'd grabbed him by the collar and hauled him into a pocket portal of their own making to better suss out his intentions and his magic, Magnus had been utterly charmed. Their silent swiftness, their scoffing, the little smiles they hid and the ones they didn't. He had no name for their bond, and as far as the Collectio went, they treated Agrippa like any other curator... because Agrippa had been involved in its work from the start. Agrippa was why the Collectio had multiple pockets of storage and safekeeping across leylines. A secret so well kept that Magnus could count on one hand the number of people who knew.

A sharp pain in his palm shocked him out of the groove of his thoughts, and Magnus withdrew his hand from the pocket of his jacket. He'd grabbed the dagger at the same time as he'd swiped the snuffbox of red divine from Agrippa's office. And now staring at the endless grey void of the *demimonde*, he was glad to have it. The dagger was made of this place, forged from a mixture of magical reagents and the strange black sap, or void, that one would find growing — *thriving* — in the company of one of the many Guardians that walked here. According to Agrippa, that specific mixture could only be shaped by a Guardian's hands in the swirling grey miasmas of the *demimonde*, honed with intention rather than steel.

Agrippa had crafted the one he was holding, but he didn't like Magnus handling it, and rightfully so; an amplifier's magic on a tool of the *demimonde* was unpredictable at best. So of course he'd grabbed it. It could very well save their hides in a place like this. And Agrippa had been so long removed from the *demimonde's* sphere that it should no longer recognize their magic as displaced. Agrippa's word, not his.

"But that's all theoretical," Agrippa had told him before tightly shutting the lid on the knife's box, "because you have no place in the demimonde." The look that stole over their face was lined with old aches and worries. It was a shockingly human expression despite the depths of their galaxy eyes.

As the red divine flashed hot through his system, Magnus sighed. "Coming out of it is... unpleasant," he said as Calix gingerly rubbed the pad of his index finger over his gums and winced at the strange tingling. "But with any luck, you'll have two wonderful men to tend to you."

Calix laughed, the sound thick and wet with some unknown sorrow. "Gods, that sounds truly incredible. Don't get my hopes up, Magnus."

The doubt in Calix's voice might as well have reopened the cut on his palm the dagger had made. Or, worse yet, some invisible one on his heart. "We'll find

Ethaniel, I swear it," Magnus said as he put a hand on Calix's shoulder. "We will. Now, give that a minute to settle in your system. You may see... well, *strange* isn't exactly the word for it. You'll be seeing the *demimonde* through your magic. It's the best way I have to describe what you're—"

He cut off as Calix's eyes went wide, his pupils blown open until only the thinnest ring of gold remained. He envied Calix that first moment with real sight. For him, it had been a life-altering experience.

Calix grabbed Magnus by the arm and squeezed tight, his cheeks going pink rather quickly. "Easy, easy," Magnus said as he rubbed his own hands over Calix's shoulders. "Once it settles, we can start tracking Convergence. Talbot?" He shook his head. "That damn book."

Calix snorted. "You sound like Aubrey."

"And that, my friend, is a lovely compliment." He tried to keep his tone even, despite where they were standing. Despite what he knew was coming.

Despite the fact that no, he couldn't guarantee they'd find Ethaniel. But he was going to try.

He watched Calix shut his eyes and squeeze his hands into fists, as if sheer willpower could stop what he was seeing and experiencing. Under the influence of red divine, the *demimonde* looked a little cockeyed; ground and sides and sky (or lack thereof) all sliding together until he was convinced he was standing at an angle gravity would never allow. It was a trick, one he knew how to rationalize his way around, but poor Calix was probably seeing all sorts of mad things.

"How do you feel?" Magnus asked, keeping his voice soft so as not to startle the man.

It took a moment, but Calix finally replied. He kept his hands balled up but opened his eyes, and they were gold once more. "It's like a river of that black sludge, the void," he whispered, pointing to nothing in particular that Magnus could see. "It's pulling me to it, I think."

Magnus nodded, not surprised. Agrippa had spoken at length to him on how the void touched everything in this place between places, between realms, and how dangerous it was. But to an Oracle like Calix, it would be more of a beacon.

He held out his hand and said, "Now I need you to trust me again. Can you do that, Calix?"

Calix didn't hesitate to nod, and it should have made Magnus feel grateful. And he did. But it was colored with a shade of dread so dark, he didn't dare think more on it. "What do you need me to do?" Calix asked as he placed his hand in Magnus's.

"Keep looking. Keep focusing. And if you can… " Calix's expression turned curious and Magnus sighed. There was no way around it, and he was wasting time trying to be cautious. "Let it in, Calix. If you really want to find Ethaniel, and I know you do, I need you to let the *demimonde* in. Because this is a place of secrets and locks, and every Guardian who walks here has their own domain, for lack of a better word. We can't get into Uzala's without some kind of a key. And these keys aren't something we can craft. We need to steal one, or lure it here."

Calix narrowed his eyes and Magnus could almost see the gears churning. "This was never about Convergence," he said slowly, as if finishing the final pieces of the puzzle.

Despite where they were standing, Magnus felt rather proud. "No, it was not. But I couldn't tell Agrippa what I was going to do. None of it. And they weren't *wrong*. The book itself is a powerful tool, but it doesn't matter whose hands hold it. All that power is dangerous. It's better lost to these lands, if you can call them that."

He squeezed Calix's hand tight, then let go. He had no right to hold it, even though the simple warmth of another person would ease his nerves. Admissions were always the utter worst. "I'm deeply sorry for the subterfuge, Calix. But Agrippa… " He couldn't do it. It felt too much, too big of a truth to speak aloud. Despite his life and his work, this was the one thing that felt sacrosanct.

I care for them. Adore them, even. Our physical forms, our origins, our lineages…. they don't matter. Not when I'm with them.

"They care for you," Calix said, his voice so soft a simple breeze would have swallowed it up. "And you for them."

It wasn't pain, but damn near enough, the prickle behind his eyes. Suddenly his throat was too dry to do anything but whisper back, "Yes."

Seconds. Minutes. They were losing time. Time they didn't have. And the itch behind his teeth, where the red divine had long dissolved, wasn't the only thing setting his nerves on fire. Anxiety swirled about him so densely, it might as well have been his own fog cloud.

"Tell me the plan." Calix wasn't demanding, but Magnus was no fool. He'd watched something spark behind the young Earl's eyes more than once. That was a man used to getting what he wanted, after all, good intentions and charitable donations aside. Still powerful, still rich, still titled. Magnus was grateful Calix used his power and influence for good. Someone like him with ill intent... well, look what happened to his home country of India.

Magnus considered what exactly to say, then threw it all out the window. "You and I are going to merge our magics, not unlike how you helped Aubrey when his apartment was attacked. But we're not after the book. We're after Uriel. He's tied to you through your mother. It's a more direct route than trying to locate Convergence."

Calix stared at him for a moment that felt infinite, stretched taffy-thin and yet impossible to break. Magnus held his breath and waited, too. "Agrippa wouldn't let you do that," he said, voice still soft but Magnus heard the steel there, too.

"They would not."

"But Uriel's powerful."

"He is." Magnus gave him a short, sharp grin. "We're going to build a cage, lure him here, trap him, and use him as bait for Uzala. So we can get Ethaniel back."

He expected a look of dismay or doubt, but the grim reality settled into Calix's expression like it was meant to be there. Perhaps it was Aubrey's influence. Perhaps it was a steel will Calix was learning to hone all on his own. He felt oddly *proud.*

"Are you ready to hear the rest?" Magnus finally asked after Calix had taken a few slow breaths.

"I am." And by the gods, Calix did appear to be more steady now.

Magnus smiled, felt the pull of it on his face. It wasn't a *nice* expression, but he did mean it wholeheartedly. "I'll make this simple. You'll give me your hands and focus on the *demimonde*. All those things you've held at bay by sheer will? I need you to open yourself to them, Calix." A note of fear in Calix's eyes made Magnus hurriedly continue. "I'll be here the whole time. The moment you open that door, I'll know. And we'll use everything we know about Uriel to lure him here. Your magic may be enough as is, but I'm not willing to take that chance. This is our only shot."

He reached into his jacket pocket and pulled out the dagger. The handle was alabaster bone splattered with void but the blade itself was an ugly thing, jagged and vicious.

The fusing of the blade to his body was a process Magnus hated with every inch of his being, but it was necessary. In anyone else's hands, it was simply an odd-looking dagger. The blade's edges were brittle-looking, but Magnus knew how sharp they were. Flesh was a mere suggestion to this blade. It was meant to cut something far more difficult — reality itself.

Calix leaned forward, eyes wide. "What is that?"

"A... a thing of this place," he replied. "It's complicated and we've not the time for stories. I'll tell you when we get back. I swear." Magnus could only smile fondly at the evident concern on Calix's face. "Trust me now, Calix."

"I do."

"Good." Magnus hissed as the blade's handle, now flat against his forearm, began to merge with his skin. His flesh smoked and bubbled and the pain was *magnificent*, but only for a moment. The merging itself never took long, but the after-effects of having it tied to his body would be.... well, best not think on that.

Magnus carefully threw his magic at the blade, waiting with bated breath that it would recognize him after so many years. The energy of the thing made his arm quiver as if he'd been holding up a boulder for hours, but he held firm, waiting for its response.

It's... not sentient, but something like it. Less intelligent but still aware.

Magnus repeated Agrippa's words to Calix as the pain started. Anything to distract him from the way it felt to have bone merge with bone; worse than any healing magic or graft he'd ever had applied to his body. It made him feel brittle and worn. But as Calix watched in mild horror, the blade finally finished its merging and now Magnus only had to flick a hand out to unsheathe it.

"I've no idea how quickly Uriel will show themself, so we'll need to move fast. You, my young friend, get the hard part." Magnus curled his wrist slightly and the blade disappeared into his arm. "I'll get us somewhere safely with this, and when the moment is right, I'll spring the trap."

When he pulled a small bell out of his pocket and held it up, Calix's eyes went right to it. "I've seen something like that before," he said, leaning in to better read the fine script inscribed on the faintly iridescent silver metal. "My mother had one. I tried to play with it when I was just a boy and she… " He trailed off, gaze dropping to their feet, and Magnus felt a pang of heartache. "Well, let's just say it disappeared and I'm sure it's down in her strange vault of half-alive artifacts."

Magnus wanted to hug him. Instead, he could provide Calix comfort by making this plan work and getting him home safely. "I doubt hers was made from the bone of a Guardian," he said, feeling the heft of the bell in his palm. "A little gift from Agrippa. This and the knife." The knife now melded with his flesh seemed to *pop*, a strange sensation that kicked up bile in his gut. *It's not sentient*, he reminded himself. "But all you need to do after the hard part is to stay hidden. Do you understand, Calix?"

Calix's gaze narrowed and Magnus could feel the brush of his power. A sticky, sickly sort of fear suddenly clogged his throat and for the briefest moment, he was eleven again, tiny and undignified, staring up at an older boy who emanated magic. But it disappeared and he was *Magnus* again.

"And yes," Magnus said, managing to steel his voice into something close to normal, "it's as much of a check on your understanding as it is a warning. These Guardians? You've seen them through a lens, in a way. Through your mother, through Talbot, through Ethaniel. But to look at one directly for more than a few seconds is not advisable."

Calix immediately blanched. "But Ethaniel's been staring at one for gods know how long."

He'd been afraid Calix would say that. "And that is a bridge we will have to cross if it comes up. But the fact that he seemed cogent in your vision speaks well. I wouldn't be surprised if his bloodline or the magic tied to it was helping keep him— "

Sane

" —rooted," Magnus finished. "I wish I had a better answer for you."

Calix was silent, still, for a beat, and then he sucked in a deep breath, squared his shoulders, and said, "Then let's find him."

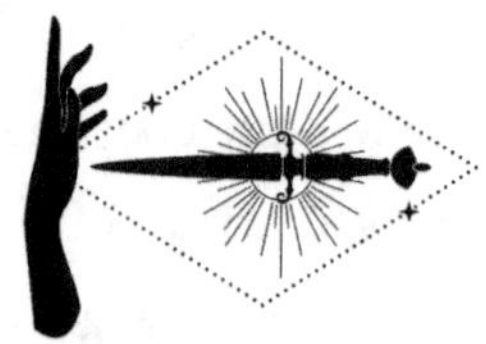

There was no fancy circle of bone. No runes. No words or chanting or even sound. The *demimonde* was a roiling silence filled with grey mist, but at least no one or thing had found them yet. Magnus was aware of the time ticking by as much as he was aware of the sweat dripping down his back while he watched Calix close his eyes. Waiting for Calix to cast out his magic, seeking a response in return, was a study in patient fear.

He was fucking terrified of what was about to happen. But given no other good options, this was what needed to be. He wasn't going to leave anyone in the *demimonde*. Not even the head of the Golden Order, a place trying to bury the Collectio in enough legal paperwork to drown the city. He hadn't told Aubrey any of that, of course, but it didn't matter now.

Magnus shook his head and waited.

Calix wasn't the first Oracle he'd ever met, but he was the only one with whom he'd been in extended contact. Amplifiers like him could feel magical energies more clearly than most, just like Ethaniel could see patterns more easily. Magnus had always theorized that patterns were the essential veins and capillaries of magic, but that some, like Ethaniel, were simply more sensitive and thus could see and manipulate them. Others, like Calix, experienced them differently. And some, like him, could *feel* them more astutely, more keenly. Colored harmonies and hearing were now reported on in the medical journals, with papers discussing those who experienced sound or letters as color. It made sense; if the brain could cross two senses in a typical human, why not in someone with magic?

Watching Calix let down his guards and take in the *demimonde* made him want to toss all his magic theory books out a window.

It was the first time in a long while he felt something like *elation* sizzling under his skin. Because Calix wasn't simply absorbing the *demimonde*, he was *reflecting* it. Like the lead and velvet inside the onyx stone room at the Collectio, the magic of this strange place sunk into him, and Magnus could feel Calix's powers turning it around, shining it back.

Oracles are mirrors, he realized as he stared. He was still deeply aware of the strained wait before him, of that pivotal moment he needed to act on, but his scholarly brain was doing cartwheels trying to compartmentalize what he was witnessing. He watched Calix glow a soft, shimmery gold, and as he gasped and opened his eyes, the magic churning around him began to solidify.

"I think this place could be beautiful," Calix whispered, "if it was molded the right way."

A theory for another day, Magnus thought. "Calix, are you all right?"

"Yes," the man hissed immediately, his hands coming up to rest on his cheeks. The shimmers around him began to bend, growing angles and edges where it had been a cloud a moment ago. The shapes hurt to look at, making his head throb, but Magnus hung on. Watching.

"Calix... " Magnus said after a long moment. "Are you close?"

Calix opened his mouth but no sound came out. Magnus edged closer. Closer. Palms up, silver energy crackling between them. A warding spell he'd prepared beforehand, just in case. Enough to keep them from harm so they could get back to Agrippa and Aubrey. To survive and try again another day.

"Calix?" He tried again, now within a foot or so of the other man.

Calix's head snapped down with a sickening *crunch*, and those gold eyes were now black and bleeding. Dripping void tears down Calix's cheeks. He opened his mouth and screamed.

"HE'SCOMINGHE'SCOMINGHE'SCOMINGHE'SCOMINGHE'SCOMING—"

Magnus grabbed Calix by the back of the head, pressed their foreheads together, and let him in.

A red-haired woman in white, a little hand clutched around her fingers as she walked Calix through a field of lavender. She turned to him, bright and shining, and gold tears ran down her face as she whispered, "Oh, my son. You are my most precious. And because of your magic, I will live long enough to find a cure for what will befall you, and move us to somewhere your father can never hurt you again."

Calix looked up at her, confused. "But... "

"But what? You can ask anything. It's important I tell you everything, before you lose... well, before I tuck something very special away. Just for a while. Until you come of age. So ask, my love."

Frustration welled in the little boy's chest. His thoughts were too loud, too blinding, for words. He made a noise of distress, which drew Lily closer, and he managed to say, "Will it hurt?"

She froze, her face dropping into horror. "No. No, I would never do that to you. And the time isn't now, Calix. It's years away, once you start coming into your magic. And then, you'll simply be fine."

Somehow, that little boy knew she was lying.

Magnus gasped. Dropped to his knees. Felt immense loss and shame and guilt all bundled up into an agonizing group of emotions that burned. He saw Lily's betrayals, her lies, her schemes. He saw Calix reclaim his memories, but there was still something...

"Whatever you do, Lawton, don't let him take red divine."

A pause, and then Lawton's voice. Different from what Magnus has heard at the estate. That man was beaten, broken. Discarded. This one sounded exactly like the kind of pampered, monied Earl he'd expected Calix to be.

"A high demand coming from a woman who keeps her son at arm's length. And is now talking to me in my dressing mirror. You'll have to forgive me if I don't immediately bend to your will, my lady."

A crackle of laughter, like canned sound from a phonograph. "I always liked you, Lawton. And liked you for him."

"Ah, now the complimenting begins. And once that doesn't win me to your side, you'll use threats."

"My, my. You've got it all figured out. Aren't you the smart one? But in this case, it's not a threat. It's blackmail. Keep him away from red divine, and I won't let him know about the money you've stolen from him over the years. How do you think he'll feel about that?"

"Interesting. I won't say I'm not tempted, since we both know I'm going to stay in Calix's good graces for many years to come, and that's just through sheer personality and charm alone. But if I'm doing this, I want something in return."

Lily gasped, then laughed again. The sound was mocking this time, edged with a coldness that chilled Magnus's bones. "Quid pro quo is fine by me if it gets me what I want. So, by all means."

"Pay my expenses. For the year."

"I'll ensure the money gets into your account, though it won't come directly from me."

"See? That wasn't so hard, was it."

And through Calix's eyes and ears, Magnus felt his heart kick up a notch. He, as Calix, knew he shouldn't have been eavesdropping, but he'd learned long ago that a little innocent spying often saved him a mound of grief and headaches. Especially where Lawton was involved. He should have been shocked. At least a little stunned. But he'd known Lawton was taking money from his wallet and off his dresser. Slipping the bills into his pockets as he pulled on the pants he'd dropped at Calix's bedside or had draped over a chair in their haste to taste each other.

Calix had no taste for red divine, whatever it truly was. Someone like him, already too sensitive to the world, didn't need his brain driven to such heights. His mother shouldn't have worried, but now he wondered why she wanted him to stay away from it.

What was she scared of him seeing? For the longest time now, years, he'd felt as if something was missing. Not all the time, not even some of the time. Only a sensation now and again, usually upon waking with the sun, that he'd sit up in bed and gasp for air and clutch his throat. Calming down took too long, but he was useless until he could breathe again. And then he'd remember a nightmare — a void, a yawning portal swirling with black ichor, a stretch of white skin pulled tight over impossible formations of joints.

Dread. Fear. Emptiness.

Magnus's mind saw Calix's entire life. Reveled in his successes and took in his agony, his pain. He saw what had made the man. The woman he'd worshipped even when he knew she was lying. He loved her, adored her, saw her as the only one who understood him. Because for so long, it had been the two of them.

And then a boy his age but with red-orange hair and a crooked smile stuck out his hand and said, "I'm Lawton. Lawton Adler," and a part of him was ripped away from her. Given to this bright boy with pain behind his eyes, and he made Calix want to protect him. Love him. Hold him close to fill up that strange hole near his heart, the one that always itched after a thunderstorm and ached when he saw roses.

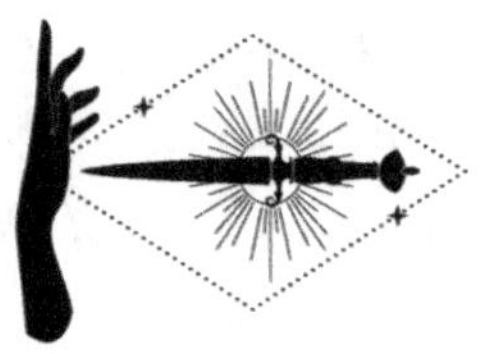

Magnus could feel something coming. Darkness, a vortex of it, aimed directly at them. Distant still, but coming.

A hand clutched his shoulder and he clung to it, desperate for anything real. But Calix's mind, his magic, were impossibly strong. His memories potent.

"You called me," a voice boomed out, making Calix look up. The angel before them was beautiful, all purple and gold and shining like a beacon. Like the sun.

But Mother didn't seem happy. She was frowning and pacing, her arms crossed tightly over her chest. "I did as you asked! And yet you deny me? Why, Uriel? Why?"

"Such demands," Uriel said, disapproval strong in a voice that rolled like thunder. Calix felt his skin blossom with pinpricks, felt the pressure in his head, and expected to see lightning behind the angel. Expected to feel rain on his face.

He met the creature's eyes and saw... nothing. And the magic it emanated made him want to curl up in a ball and cover his face with his hands. It was too much.

He started to rock back and forth. Overwhelmed. His stomach in knots. But he couldn't look away from the endlessness staring down at him.

"You told me —" Lily began.

Uriel held up a hand and Calix saw fingers. So many fingers, all bent in strange angles. But his mother didn't seem repulsed by the creature, and she abhorred even the simplest of beetles. He didn't understand why they weren't running away from the horror hovering above their heads, and he felt guilty, as if he was seeing something he shouldn't.

Then in his head he heard, "Ah, so you can see me. The part of me I hide from your mother. How fascinating. Be a good boy and keep quiet."

When Calix snapped out of the vision and back into his own mind, Uriel was scolding his mother for calling him for, "...such trivial matters. I told you he would live and yet you bring him before me. The boy breathes. My promise is upheld. He won't come to harm unless you fail me."

"I would never fail you," Lily spat, and Calix hunched away from her. He didn't like that tone, and she rarely used it, but it scared him. He didn't want to watch anymore, so he hid his face and drew his knees to his chest.

Somewhere around them, darkness coiled. *So close. So close. Not quite but so close.* He could feel the thickness in the air, how it clogged his throat and made him pull at his collar. Calix was no longer screaming, thank the gods, but he was radiating power. Beautiful synergy. Magnus's senses were flooded with pleasantness — the scent of fresh dirt and herbs; jasmine tea on a terrace overlooking a park; the sound of river water and rain; the sweetness of a fresh blueberry scone. It nearly ripped him from his task, so delightful was Calix's power rubbing up against his own.

And then the screaming again. From Calix? From him? He didn't know anymore.

HE'SCOMINGHE'SCOMINGHE'SCOMINGHE'SCOMINGHE'SCOMING

And then he – it, Uriel – was fast approaching, scuttling out of the grey mist on eight, ten, no *sixteen* legs, with horror as its face. Magnus tossed the bell, then unsheathed his knife and split the air in two. He shoved Calix inside the gap made in reality, slapped a hand over his mouth, and cast them into darkness with another flick of his hand.

Calix. If you can hear me. We're in a little pocket of reality, one I made from the demimonde. I'll know when the trap is sprung, and then we can be free. But until then... do not fight me.

Calix's voice came to him. It was small but strong, and he heard truth in it as Calix replied in his mind. *I understand. But don't let me move, Magnus. I don't know what I might do until that... thing is captured.*

Magnus's heart broke all over again for this poor boy. He sounded so tired, so sick of always being afraid.

I'm here, Calix.

CHAPTER FOURTEEN

ETHANIEL

Something in the *demimonde* shuddered, and it rippled through him. It shook him awake. He wanted to open his eyes, but Ethaniel was also terrified of what he might see. He'd been visited by enough horrors lately, and the sight of disjointed, multi-fingered hands or Vincent's red-purple wounds or Maria half floating, half skittering was enough to send him reeling all over again.

The door. That voice.

Carefully, Ethaniel took the chance to peer out of one eye, keeping it open just enough. The grey, roiling mists of this strange place were now pockmarked with odd lights, like orbs floating in the fog. He was fairly certain they weren't the source of the sensation that had awoken him.

And when he chanced a glance at Vincent, his half-brother was propped up against the same tree as he was, his head lolled to one side at an angle that made his own neck ache sympathetically. His wounds had stopped bleeding thanks to Maria's ministrations, but he looked haggard.. Pale and worn, as he'd been rubbed down with turpentine.

Ethaniel chanced another look around, this time with both eyes, and saw they were alone. Or seemed to be. And the drawing he had made in the sand nearby was gone, wiped away with no trace left. He didn't remember destroying it. It was tempting to draw it out again, as if the mere image of the arch surrounded by all manner of runes and glyphs could be comforting.

Instead, he decided on a different action.

Caution might have stayed his hand in the past. He had no good or even mediocre choices now, and wasn't it ironic that given low odds of success, he was willing to risk more. Aubrey would be proud of him.

He would. Because Ethaniel was going to do everything in his power to get back to him and Calix.

No more caution. He wasn't willing to die a strange death at the hands of a creature not of his world. He was in a land that followed no rules. There were no civil or social constraints here. No one was holding him back. And Harkness magic slithered in his veins.

Ethaniel reached up and began to pry off a hunk of brittle black tree bark. Beside him, Vincent stirred, so Ethaniel nudged him with his shoulder. One Harkness was powerful. Two would be a force to be reckoned with. And Vincent might not have his mother's arcane power, but he still had Harkness blood.

Vincent shifted, groaned, then slowly opened his eyes to catch Ethaniel slicing the outside of his forearm with the bark. "What the hell?" he asked groggily.

"I need blood. Yours, and mine," Ethaniel said. He held up the bark for Vincent to see. "If our power is bound to this place, and this was the place to curse our line, then it seems right I could unravel some of it."

Vincent blinked a few times, and despite the bloodshot veins in his eyes, there was a brightness. A *keenness* for anything magical. Like an ever-hungry mouth. "I don't have the magic you do," Vincent snapped. "And what you're doing is against your own doctrine."

"Doesn't matter," Ethaniel said, but his mind was only half-listening to Vincent. Some other part of him, quiet and distant but absolutely humming with power, held him to the side. Like a fly on the wall of his own conversation. And that voice again, the one from the stone...

"You found your way back yet again. Even better. But do you promise? That you WILL let me be right in your eyes? That I could follow you back, and find a home of my own in YOUR world?"

Ethaniel shuddered. It was like having rough cotton rubbed inside his ears and behind his eyes, but some part of him *responded*. It banged away inside of him, clanged with the sound of discordant bells and smelled like iron-rust and bitter cold. Another sense. An extra beat of his heart. That somehow under flesh and muscle, vein and bone, teeth and jaw, there was another *him*. A being made of pure magic.

That was the voice. The one from the stone, the one now not so-distant-or-quiet.

It was creaking open a little door in his mind to say, **"I said I would save you. Not all of us are mad or angry or lonely. Some of us do not wish to use you, like Uriel. Like Uzala, who would never admit they also hunger like their twin. Some of us do not mean harm. We are merely curious about the world wrought with our essence and made more beautiful. The *demimonde* could be like your world. We wish to know yours, so we might recreate it here."**

He was a stranger on the horizon of his own mind, but it was *his* hand that slashed out, dragged the tip of the bark shard across Vincent's upper arm. The skin was already bruised and bloodied, his shirt long torn past any salvage. It took a moment, but then Vincent cried out and as he did, Ethaniel dragged the bark against his own flesh. His right arm to Vincent's left.

Twins. Brothers. In some ways, the word was the same for either, or both. Him and Vincent. Uzala and Uriel. The worst kind of contrived foils, but still able to blind each other.

He didn't want Vincent blind. He wanted his half-brother *bound* to him. An easy feat when they shared blood. Blood that was so closely tied to the *demimonde* and the horrors in the gray mists.

And on that horizon, Ethaniel distantly watched himself make a promise to the entity from the stone that he would take them along. That in return for their knowledge, Ethaniel would carry them over the realm barrier. Not feasible for any magic wielder, but for a Harkness? Simple.

Vincent made to push him away, anger and fear written in every line of his face, but Ethaniel grabbed his hands. "Do not fight me," he whispered. "We have one chance. Uzala won't let their guard down like this again."

He gave Vincent no chance to respond. Warnings didn't need replies. And even if he could, Ethaniel didn't know if he *wanted* to. The power in him wasn't a flicker of warmth; it swept him under, ripped him from his moorings and tossed him into a stormy sea.

He felt *strong*. He felt *alive*. And the voice inside his mind crowed with triumph.

Vincent made another sluggish move to swat at Ethaniel, but he knocked those bloodied hands away. "Enough," Ethaniel bit out with a snap of his fingers. The moss under them lashed out at Vincent, lassoing him to the tree. The tendrils of it wrapped around Vincent's body until he was covered from mouth to knees. He slashed at Vincent again, this time on the other arm, then gave himself the mirroring wound. The lack of pain was... odd. Maybe the entity was helping, masking the pain so Ethaniel could do what was needed to get them all out.

So Ethaniel set to work. The precise hand needed for recreating the runes and arch in the black sand around them still took focus, but it wasn't as difficult as he'd expected. The warm rush of extra vigor was welcome, even if the source was suspect.

Every time his mind started to slip too deeply into the task, the entity now housed in him sent a crackle of alertness though his veins. It helped Ethaniel keep an eye on their surroundings, but in those sweeps of his gaze, he also caught Vincent staring at him with a mix of horror and wonder. As if no part of him could believe quite what was happening, but his fragile jealousy and deep fears about unchecked magic sang to a new tune of discordant, ringing melodies.

And when he was done, he held up the bark, now crusted with black sand and sticky, drying blood, and held the tip of it against his tongue.

"Mother always liked that story," came Maria's voice, carried on the wind that darted between the trees and slapped at his face. "The one about the blood never drying when kin kills kin. She said it was written about us."

A memory flickered to life in Ethaniel's mind. "The one about a boy killing a crane in the river, and his brother slaying him for the crime," he said slowly, his mouth tacky. "I remember that."

"She told all of us. All the siblings and cousins, even the halves like Vincent." Maria was beside him now, hand out. Waiting. Carefully, he put the bark on her palm and watched her smile that awful thing so full of teeth. Some part of him... *liked it*. Like the frightening visage, this wraith, who had his little sister's memories.

Deeper inside his chest, Ethaniel felt cold. This wasn't him. He abhorred blood and violence, and yet felt called to it. He knew it was luring him in as best it could, beckoning with a hand bearing too many fingers, too loose joints.

Some part of him wanted to take it. To link his fingers with it and follow it into the mists and become like Maria. And the rest of him wanted to vomit at the thought.

So, who was he really?

Could he be part monster and stay true?

"You can take his," Maria said as she edged closer to Vincent. Vincent was watching them with narrowed eyes. Ethaniel swore he could feel the man's heartbeat, kicking like a terrified rabbit's.

Inside his mind, Ethaniel heard Maria say, "His magic is still there. Down deep. Use it to fuel the ritual, maybe, instead of spilling more of your blood."

Ethaniel blinked slowly. His head suddenly felt heavy, a warship anchor hung from thread. "I can't, he...Vincent doesn't have magic. Not like mine."

"He did, at one time," Maria whispered mentally to him as she floated closer still. At her proximity, Vincent's eyes widened and he began to struggle against his bonds. Ethaniel watched him for a moment, but he wasn't remotely tempted to assist. "Mother took it. She gave him money and new memories in return, but only because he was almost too old to take from. A soft spot for him, she always had." She cocked her head and part of her cheek twitched.

Not twitched. Ripped open, sprouting thin black legs. The wound sealed up and on her cheek now rested a bloated spider.

"You remembered one way, then the other," she whispered. "You were always the strongest of us. Mother knew it. She didn't want you to remember Vincent having magic, but some part of you did. Or managed to remember again."

"What are you saying?" he whispered.

But some part of him knew.

"She was going to do the same to me," Maria said, her voice normal again, but that twitch under her cheek moved, slithering up to under her eye. "Drain me, and if I survived, I'd be like Vincent. Powerless. Human. Worthless."

Reality reasserted itself and the horrible reality of what Maria was saying — and not — made him freeze in place. Calix hadn't been the only one betrayed over and over again by a mother. "Maria."

When she turned back to him, his sister was no longer there. In place of her sweet cherubic face was a death mask; stark white bisected by lines that crisscrossed at odd angles, and dotting those lines were small red orbs. At a distance, they were the size and shape of junebugs, and like the insects, they slowly moved across her face. There were no eyes but a slash of garish red across the space where a mouth would be.

"It's what would have happened to me if Carmen hadn't brought me here," Maria said.

That's not your sister. You know it isn't. And you've known for nearly the entire time.

Ethaniel wasn't sure if it was his own conscience or Vincent's he was listening to, but the fear on his half-brother's face had him reaching out to put a hand on Maria's shoulder. "Is Carmen Uzala?" he asked, voice low in case the Guardian was nearby. He had no idea how much time had passed since Uzala had left, or if time even mattered in a place like this. "Did it save you? Bring you here?"

She nodded, her mouth turned down but the sadness it mimicked didn't spread to the rest of her pale, blank face. "They saved me. It's why I can't break away from them. I want to. But it is... part of me." Maria touched one, then another of the little red orbs. "He molded me after him. Sometimes I... I forget who I am."

Ethaniel didn't hesitate to gather her up in his arms, hold her close. She smelled like nothing, and it was like having a bundle of clothes in his arms. Nearly weightless. No breath. No heartbeat. Merely a shell stuffed with some semblance of his sister. And any joy that had made his heart swell upon seeing her again was doused in the coldest of water. She couldn't leave this place, and there was no place for the little bit left of her in his world.

She'd been dead all those years, just not in the way he'd thought.

Ethaniel pulled back from her. "You're still my sister," he said, mustering as much emotion as he could without letting fear color his tone. She was half-human, half-creature, and had been in the *demimonde* far too long. He knew that. But some part of him wondered if Aubrey or Magnus could —

"You can't," she said, with far too many years weighing down her words. "You know you can't save me. Not deep down. Where it counts." The finger she poked him in the chest with was bent like a gnarled tree branch and as sharp as one.

Ethaniel didn't quite know what to say. What *could* he say? It was all wrong, in that mind-tilting way this whole place had on him, but it also made his entire body prickle with awareness. Sweat gathered behind his knees, in the bends of his elbows, along his temples, and with that sensation, Ethaniel was made painfully aware of his own fragile mortality. How tired and worn he was; his skin stinging from a dozen small cuts; the bruises pressing hot into the deeper layers of his joints.

What could he say? Other than, "I know."

The death mask that was her face seemed to smile. "Then it's time."

Then all the lights on her mask went dark, as did the space around them. Ethaniel whirled, eyes darting about in the thick darkness. He yanked on the cord in his mind that would release the moss from around Vincent's mouth and harshly whispered, "Do you see anything?"

Vincent answered with a wet cough and a sharp, "Bit hard to do that, tied to a tree and all and in the pitch black."

Maria snapped her fingers and cold flame sparked there, giving off a small circle of pale blue light. "Just for a moment," she said. "The magic will attract him if I linger too long. But he's not too far away. We need to hurry." And when she stared up at Ethaniel, that death mask showed nothing as she said, "He's coming."

Everything in Ethaniel's body went cold. "Uzala?"

"No. The twin."

Chapter Fifteen

CALIX

Part of his mind knew the danger they were in. It was a heavy thing that sat on his chest, pinning him in place. Leaving Calix only able to watch Magnus, who was peering out of the tiniest crack between their pocket reality and the rest of the *demimonde*. To Calix, it looked a bit like an envelope, if held vertically and opened with only the sharpest of letter openers.

The rest of him was fighting tooth and nail to get to Uriel.

He didn't need to see the Guardian to know how close it was. He could smell the heat of it; hot sun on dry earth, cracking it into a tapestry of ever smaller crooks and crevices. And he could sense it moving, skittering about on too many legs. He had a vague image of it in his mind, but it wasn't enough.

He wanted to *see it*.

"Oh no," Magnus whispered, slightly panicked, as Calix reached toward the slit between realities. "Sorry, my friend, no going to your certain doom under my watch. Aubrey would absolutely murder me, and I'd probably let him." Magnus gave him a weak smile. "And don't think I'm taking my hand off your mouth. You'll call right to him."

Calix tensed, then looked down to see his own hand reaching out, past Magnus, fingers clawing the air. When had he done that? There was grime under his nails. Blood, too.

Magnus followed the path of his gaze, to the scratches all over his hand. "You weren't in your right mind," he whispered. "Hell of a dirty fighter, though. I apologize for the bands, but it was the only way to keep you still."

He wasn't merely pinned to the nonexistent wall by suggestion and Magnus's hand. There were thick iron bands around his ankles, his waist, and he could not *move*. Not an inch. But for whatever reason, Magnus had left his hands free, and he must have scratched the man in his haste to... to...

"Don't think on it, Calix. Not now. Torture yourself later if you must but... " Magnus let his words fade as he peered out of the pocket again. When he turned back, his face was carefully blank. The distinct lack of expression a funeral home director might wear when talking to family members of the recently deceased. "Do not move. Not a bit."

But Calix burned to know *why*. It was some odd tug inside him, up from the stomach and through the heart; someone yanking on an invisible string, pulling him forward toward the faint opening.

Magnus's eyes widened, and he quickly snapped the opening shut. "Tricky bastard," he muttered, glaring at the space where the opening had been. "Not today. You don't get to influence him like you did his mother."

He pressed his hand against Calix's neck, muttering something low, the consonants slipping against vowels. He'd heard something like it from Agrippa not a few hours before. Magnus was speaking the language of this place, but also using the magic of it.

"Focus on that clarity," Magnus said, his fingers tapping out a quick rhythm on Calix's shoulder. With each tap, a few thready strands of magic spooled out from his fingers to spread out wide across Calix's body. It was warm and smelled a bit like down, that strange animal musk mixed with the taste of light on his tongue. "Focus on your goal in this place, Calix."

Calix let his mind drift to thoughts of Ethaniel. How good it would be to have him back. How long had it been since he'd felt those arms around him, those lips on his. How it felt to be watched by deep hazel eyes that drank in details most others would miss or ignore. As his thoughts of Ethaniel cast out, Calix felt something *spark* in his chest. It was a strangely sweet sensation, one that left him tingling all over.

"Very good," Magnus said as he pulled back. Calix didn't miss how he shook out his hand, how the tips of his fingers were now a dusty blue. "Just a strange little side effect of borrowing some of Agrippa's magic."

"You cleared my mind," Calix said.

"I did."

He was *himself* once more. But it still lurked on the edges, with the scent of dry earth and the prickle of a thunderstorm at his nape. And it was making a sound, like a large animal snuffling outside a wall made of linen. Even as closed in as they were, Calix could still sense it. Might have been able to touch Uriel if Magnus hadn't been blocking his way forward.

The mere fact that this creature drove him out of his mind, had made him injure Magnus, was enough to chill Calix's blood. But on its heels were questions. He couldn't believe any version of any story his mother told him. But he didn't doubt his mother had dealt with this creature, maybe even bargained with it. But to what end? The memory was there, but he couldn't access it, and frustration welled inside him.

"Is it the Oracle in me?" Calix asked, his voice soft even though the snuffling sound had faded. "Is that why I'm... drawn to that thing?" He caught Magnus's gaze, held it, and tried not to burn the other man with his ferocity. "Or is it because my mother had dealings with it?"

There was an answer bubbling on Magnus's lips, but the other man stoppered whatever words threatened to spill out. "I'll give you my best guess, but only if we get out of this alive."

"Hell of a bargain."

Magnus smiled. "It's all I have right now. Bargains and dealings with the devil and others like him. At least until we're back home. But my answer is simply *yes*. All of it." He turned back to where the opening was, then his smile turned shark-like. It was a shocking look on a man so polished and yet so full of good humor and verve, and Calix could see his darkness for the very first time. Like with most good people, there were urges or feelings or thoughts, or a mix of all three, that were never indulged. And in Magnus, Calix could see a layer of *something* under the wit and soul of a good man.

He felt strangely proud that Magnus trusted him to show it.

"The bell," Magnus whispered suddenly.

Outside, in the grey void that was the *demimonde*, the sound of a bell became clear. Followed up by a horrible noise which Calix could only equate to all the musical instruments of an orchestra being dropped from several stories overhead. It grated through every bone in his body, set his teeth and hair on edge, and even Magnus flinched back from it.

But once the noise stopped, the grin Magnus gave him was brilliant. "If there's one thing a Guardian can't resist," he said as he carefully reopened the thin gap between their realities, "it's a silver bell. Agrippa refuses to tell me why." His grin dropped, and something pensive flickered over his face. "I don't think I want to know why, to be honest. We should all be able to have our secrets from time to time."

Magnus pried open their exit and stepped out, motioning for Calix to follow. "Be ready," Magnus said as he pointed to a strange tangle of what looked like thick, black tree branches forming a dome as twice as tall as him. "Just because it looks trapped doesn't mean it's not capable of getting free."

"Have you seen a Guardian before?" Calix whispered as they inched closer to the dome. "Aside from Agrippa, I mean."

He was surprised when Magnus frowned, looking all the more like a very disappointed headmaster Calix had once had. He'd only been the naive witness to more than one of Lawton's childhood schemes, so he hadn't been on the receiving end of the man's full power. But if he had, he guessed it would have felt something like the way Magnus was staring him down now.

"It's not a conversation for here," Magnus said as he adjusted the collar of his jacket. "Perhaps later. Once we're back home." Then Magnus put an arm out in front of Calix once they came within a few feet of the cage. "Stay back, and be ready," Magnus said quietly.

Calix could feel his heartbeat in his ears, his throat, in his fingertips. A fast but steady *thump thump thump* of life in his veins, but it felt otherworldly, too. As if that odd axis on which he'd been standing since entering the *demimonde* had added some impenetrable, utterly foreign extra angle that his mind couldn't decipher. He could only *experience* it.

But when he let his magic rise, prickling against and over his skin, the air around them seemed to still.

The void remained.

The mists of the *demimonde* stopped moving.

And from the cage before them, thick emerald green moss sprouted, crawling and scraping along the branches. It wrapped the entire thing with snaking tendrils that slithered along, and a moment later, tiny flowers sprouted. Tiny petals that looked soft to the touch and were a bright red, almost carnelian.

Here in the *demimonde*, Calix felt strong. Impossibly so. His magic wasn't some *thing* he dealt with, but part of him. It was the first time he'd ever felt like that. Whole. Complete. As he did, a wind picked up and something like the word *more* carried itself along the drifts.

Magnus stared at the moss and flowers for a long beat, then gave Calix a nod. "Ready?"

"Very much so," Calix said, and more than that, *felt* it in his bones.

Instead of whispering a spell or drawing runes, Magnus held out his hands, palms facing each other a mere foot apart, and power sizzled and snapped between them. It was like silver lightning between Magnus's palms and it was mesmerizing. Calix felt as if he could stare at it all day and never be bored.

And then Magnus shoved both of his hands into the tangle of branch, moss, and flowers, pulling in opposite directions as if forcing his way in. The dome began to creak warningly, and as Magnus strained against it all, Calix felt the wind shift. Now it pulled against his clothes and slapped at his cheeks, so sharp he thought blood had been drawn. But he didn't dare check.

Because Magnus needed help and wasn't going to ask for it. Calix saw the vein bulging in his forehead, the redness creeping into his eyes, and a pallor to his face more like that of someone in a sick bed than the robust, healthy man who had willingly walked into this place with him.

Calix didn't hesitate. His power was already crackling under his skin, begging to be used. He rushed up to Magnus and put a hand on his back.

Instead of his mother's words about magic and balance, Calix found his version as he wrapped Magnus's power into the tangle of his own. Instantly the landscape shifted; gone were the gray mists and in its place, something else entirely.

A stone building. The bite and snap of cold autumn winds whipping along the cliffs. Cliffs he knew well. Cliffs he swore he'd never come back to after taking up in London some months ago. His apartment was extremely small but clean. His job at the Collectio was new. Exciting. Something different every day, some new challenge or discovery to dig into.

But he was back home on the cliffs of Tenby, inside an old ruin that had once been some kind of outbuilding for a farm, because this is where Agrippa had taken them. Not back to the Collectio, where Magnus could figure out what in the hell was going on.

He'd taken Magnus home.

The word *connection* was whispered into his mind. Maybe carried on the wind, or put there by his own conscience. But *connection* was what held him to Magnus now. A shared curiosity about the world. A keen desperation to understand magic in a way no one else had yet to understand. That longing for a link to someone else who might understand *him*.

Magnus had first felt that with Agrippa. And it was what Calix latched onto as he pushed his magic forward. Magnus's power was a thunderstorm, a torrent, but tightly controlled. A weapon and a tool, depending on the use and the target; and it was held by the finest control Calix had ever encountered.

Magnus was a maelstrom kept bottled and hidden away.

We need this, Magnus. Not all of it. A fraction.

Magnus's thoughts shook with their strength, their ferocity, but his aim was true. *I'm terrified of that, Calix.*

I know. As am I.

A chuckle rippled through Magnus. He actually hunched with it as together, slowly, they pulled the branches apart. Somewhere in the distance there was a howling; a thing wounded and so very angry. But underneath the howl was a hunger, and Calix could see that maw coming directly for them.

We must hurry, Magnus! It is trying to find a way out of your trap.

Then we hurry.

In his mind, it was like a shutter being thrown open after a rainstorm.

Clarity.

The cork came out of the bottle, and Magnus's maelstrom rushed at him. Not the full force. Calix had half a worry before Magnus let him in, but he needn't. Magnus all but wrestled his magic into a funnel and let Calix have the other end.

A moment later, the branches cracked, then split, like a giant's ribcage, and below the tangle of thorns and moss was a face so lovely Calix thought he might weep.

Don't let it fool you, Magnus's voice came to him. *This is a greater Guardian. We're lucky it even fell for the trap.*

Resplendent in purple and gold robes, the greater Guardian known as Uriel stared up at them, thick black tears running down its perfect, golden, sculpted face.

"Have mercy," Uriel said, its voice like dove song and morning light. "Please."

Magnus shot him a look so terribly loaded, Calix felt its strain through his entire body. "I think not," Magnus snapped at it before clapping once and then pushing Calix back with a gentle hand. "No closer. They're terribly tricky things and nothing about them is stagnant." Some of the fire bled out of his stare, but Calix could still feel its heat. "Not even their magic."

"Please," Uriel whispered as Calix slowly backed away.

Five feet. "Please. I felt your call."

Ten feet. "Calix."

A shudder rippled through Calix and he had to clamp an arm over his middle, the spike of sudden pain a ricochet through him.

Twenty feet. "Your mother. She's here. Part of her."

Calix's backwards steps slowed, and soon Magnus was crowding against him, physically propelling him back. He didn't fight. He didn't want to. He was so tired of fighting. That's what this creature – Uriel – couldn't understand. It came to him because Calix had let in the *demimonde* and had become a lighthouse in the gray mists. Uriel was called. Now it was trapped and desperate.

Well, Calix was feeling rather desperate, too.

"Seal it back up," he told Magnus, whose eyes went wide for a flash, and then a steely resolve took over. "Even if it's not lying, I can't trust it."

"I would," Magnus said with a grimace, "but we have to leave the trap open. It blocks out anything from the *demimonde*. Its twin won't be able to find it if we cut it off completely."

So many things could go wrong. So many ways this creature might try to lure Calix in, hooking him with the promise of his mother. And Calix knew it stood a chance of working. His own resolve was honed but still brittle from everything his mother had concealed from him, and now he had to wonder what had been her point all along.

His gaze slid over to Uriel and the thick dome keeping it trapped. "We're luring the twin here?"

Magnus shook his head. "We're going to it."

From inside the dome, Uriel said, "They won't come. They won't. They rarely leave their domain."

With a snap of Magnus's fingers, a thin silver sheet covered the crack in the dome and Calix watched it run, as thick as molasses, over the entire thing to drip to the ground.

"That will buy us a few minutes," Magnus said.

Calix had to wait until the tingle of magic on his tongue died down. But a flash of memory, of vivid déjà vu complete with sounds, sights, and smells, took him back to the night at the Minotaur Baths and the privacy veil that Aubrey had controlled with the press of a button and a tendril of his own magic. It was the exact same sensation, down to the way the tip of his tongue was numb and his whole body felt warm and safe.

He wondered how many things across the city Magnus had touched with his magic. A thought for another, safer time, but it only made him more curious about the man and his brand of magic. Maybe the *demimonde* changed his, too.

"You need to be ready," Magnus said. He put his hands on Calix's shoulders, his grip urgent, tight. "That cage won't hold Uriel long. We need to bait Uzala into leaving its domain for... wherever we are now. Uriel was right. They're territorial creatures by nature, these Guardians, and even the promise of Uriel might not be enough."

Calix frowned. "I thought that was the point. Use Uriel to bait Uzala into coming, then we trade for Ethaniel."

Magnus held his gaze, and somewhere beneath the focused calm on his face, he was hiding something else. It wasn't quite fear. Calix now knew how fear looked on the faces of his nearest and dearest quite well, and Magnus's stare didn't dance with nerves. He was *frighteningly* calm.

It was the face of a man who knew what came next.

Calix felt the bottom drop out of his stomach.

"What are you planning?" Calix managed to say.

"The rules of this place are... wild. Feral," Magnus replied as he looked around at the swirling gray mists. "It exists for reasons unknown to humans or, according to Agrippa, anyone, really. But something they told me many years ago has always stuck in my mind. Like a splinter, really. Annoying. Dug in just under the skin."

When Magnus met his eyes once more, that calm had spread, a placid lake in place of a true expression. "I think it was always going to come to this," Magnus whispered. With a neat step backwards, he pointed past Calix's shoulders. "You need to be ready, Calix. You need to grab Ethaniel the moment he appears— "

"Magnus."

Magnus continued. "Grab anyone Uzala brings through, and use Aubrey's monocle to get the door back open. Make sure you're at least fifty, maybe one hundred feet away from Uzala before you do it."

Calix could feel the unsteady *thumpTHUMPthump* of his heart. His palms began to sweat. He wanted this to stop. They just needed to think, then —

"Do you understand me?" Magnus raised his voice and it drew Calix's attention. "Calix! Hear me, damn you!"

Calix shook free of his stupor, but his hands were still trembling. "Magnus, whatever you're doing, or planning to do, you can't."

Magnus gave him a small smile as he put a hand over his heart. From underneath the arch of his fingers, a soft yellow light began to shine, cutting through mist. "It's already done." Magnus's face betrayed nothing, but Calix swore the grey streaks at his temples were longer now, pushing deep into Magnus's thick black hair. Had more fine lines had gathered at the corners of his eyes? It was impossible to know for certain.

The words fell from his lips before he fully understood them. "What did you give up?"

"It's only temporary, Calix— "

A noise, like trees cracking in an ice storm, made them both whirl around. There was no waiting like with Uriel. Off in the distance, beyond some space they couldn't see but could *feel*, came a primal scream. A shadow formed, long and lean and multi-limbed, the joints all bent in strange ways that defied the rules of their world.

"The monsters make the rules here," Calix whispered as he backed away, his hand going into his pocket for the surety of glass and metal and the whisper of *Aubrey* against his fingertips. It happened without thought behind it; more on instinct did Calix begin to channel that connection running between his magic and Aubrey. It rose up in him sweetly, a gentle tide measured with the promise of *home.*

But he wasn't going to leave Magnus to fend for himself.

Calix thrust out his other hand and immediately, a ball of light sat in his palm. It was the first spell his mother had taught him, one that condensed magic into a tool to be shaped by the one holding it. She would give him that ball of light, the scent of roses all around them, and then ask for it back. Sometimes she'd let him hold it, roll it between his palms to feel the way it made him shiver. But he never liked to hold it for long. It hadn't felt *right* to touch it for more than a few minutes, and the relief that had washed over him once she'd taken it back had left him nauseated.

He'd known something wasn't right, all those years ago. Every time he asked, his mother had dodged the questions skillfully, but that only worked until his world-class education shoved logic and reasoning into his mind, and then he questioned *everything*. And she couldn't dodge his inquiries any more, so she'd refused to talk about those nights when they passed a ball of light — a ball of her own magic — back and forth until her invisible metric was met.

That's when he'd taught himself how to shape his own ball of light, using his own magic. He was his mother's son, after all, and all her power was no match for his keen eye and his own growing arcane skills. But where hers had been finely honed, masterful, his had been a spherical storm between his palms. She'd taught him control over everything and yet here was proof that something in his Oracle magic still ran wild.

But standing here in bitter panic, waiting for the monster to emerge from the mist, that storm was his once more.

Magnus knew immediately what that little sphere was. Magic was a gift that had to be given freely, and now Calix was letting Magnus have a piece of him. His mother had imparted upon him how important magical gifts were, and how rare. Calix didn't even have to think about it in this case.

"I'm never one to turn down a gift. Especially not one so generous," Magnus said as he turned back to Calix, hand out. "Do you mind if I— "

Confused, Calix tipped the ball into his waiting palm, and Magnus smiled with too many teeth. "I won't forget this," Magnus said. "It's more than what that... *thing* deserves."

Another shriek, this time closer. Calix's heart was rabbiting too fast now, forcing him to breathe more quickly. There was sweat on the back of his neck, at his temples, and the grey mists around their legs felt too heavy, like walking through muddy marshland. The entire void around them felt *thick*, like the worst humidity of the deepest day in July. Summer in the city, in all its glory; but here, no sun shone, let alone beat down to bake bricks until they were too hot to touch.

No, the entire *demimonde* around them was simply *too much*. The urge to take the sphere back from Magnus roared within him, but Calix bit it back, smacking it away with the power of fear and anticipation. If this worked... gods, if this *worked*... Ethaniel would be back home.

They could be together again. Start anew. Really take the time to discover each other, in all the ways mundane and not. It was a yearning rooted deep in him, to the point that Calix wondered if he'd ever wanted anything so much before.

Magnus was manipulating the sphere of borrowed power into some kind of platform, and it was hypnotic, watching him bend and shape Calix's magic into something else entirely.

"Is that meant to protect us or harm Uzala?" Calix asked as he eyed the ballista Magnus had molded from his magic.

Magnus gave him a grim smile. "Both, I think in this case. It's a precaution, since I think they'll be too concerned about each other to pay us much mind. I hope."

But what Magnus loaded into the ballista he'd constructed wasn't a bolt or arrow, but a single bright red bead no bigger than a quarter. "As much as I'd love to explain," Magnus said, "I think we're out of time." He jerked his head toward the cage holding Uriel. "On my mark, break the seal."

"What?" Calix could hardly believe what he was hearing. "Break the seal?"

"Break the damn seal, Calix. But wait for my signal."

More shrieking. The air grew tighter still, until it felt like a hand on Calix's throat. "I'll keep them at bay in case they turn on us, but your goal is to grab Ethaniel and *run*."

From somewhere deep in the distance, a shadow grew. Shifted. Grew again. And repeated that pattern until it loomed over them and nothing but utter *dread* filled Calix's entire body. He was locked in place by his own fears and nothing came out of his mouth when he tried to yell for Magnus.

It all happened so fucking fast.

There was Uzala, their strange body draped in torn white cloth dotted with glowing red orbs. No eyes. Too many teeth. Deep onyx skulls on its shoulders, their broken teeth clattering as the creature shifted closer. Cold with sweat and nerves, Calix fumbled for the monocle and thrust out his other hand, grasping for the magic sealing Uriel away.

When that silver sheet dropped away and Uriel spiraled up into the air, the accompanying *crack* of thunder shook the ground, the mist, *everything*.

Magnus was yelling, his words an earthly roar in Calix's ears. The two creatures — *twins, siblings* — dashed at each other, many arms slashing out like knives, so many teeth bared and an inhuman scream filled the air. Their clash was impossible to track with the smell of sulfur and rot in his nose, coating his throat, and their frenzied movements.

Calix knew he had no time to decide on what to do.

The decision was made for him the moment Ethaniel and his brother stumbled out of a gap that opened in the space thirty or so feet to his left. The power released with their appearance was overwhelming, making Calix's ears pop, but he didn't care.

All he saw was Ethaniel.

Ethaniel noticed him immediately and the sweetest smile stole over his face. And that's when Calix saw the pockmarked and flaking skin, the deep red of muscle and tendon just below it. A burn, a bad one along Ethaniel's jaw. And the man behind him, that dark haired one Ethaniel had called *brother*, looked terrible; bruised and bloodied, his hands wrapped in ragged cloth bandages. But he was following in Ethaniel's wake, despite everything Vincent had done to them.

To Lawton.

Calix stumbled over to them, monocle in hand and the image of Aubrey forming in his mind. "Ethaniel, you're... how?"

Ethaniel shook his head. "No time." But for the shortest second in the world, he put a hand on Calix's cheek and whispered, "I'm so glad you're here."

Ethaniel reached into the gap they'd stumbled out from and pulled a girl out of it. She had his eyes and nose and hair, but her pallor was deathly and her dark blue dress was several seasons out of fashion. And underneath the dress, her legs – six, no, eight of them, like a spider – scurried along as Ethaniel tugged her forward.

Calix gaped as Ethaniel rasped, "Vincent, we have to go. Now." He turned to Calix, a hand on his shoulder; a reminder he was alive, he was real, he was *here*. "You have a way back home?"

Calix nodded and pulled out the monocle. "Aubrey and Agrippa are on the other side."

"You have excellent timing, dove." Ethaniel cast a glance over his shoulder at the creatures clawing and ripping at each other, at the way their blood dripped to the ground and turned into black ichor. "Magnus, let's go!"

But Magnus stayed on the ballista's pedestal, aiming right for the Guardians who were flying above their heads, their bodies blurry with movements that made Calix's head ache. "I'm buying you time! Go!"

Ethaniel grasped Calix's hand in his so they were both holding the monocle. "So we go. Maria, is this the right place?"

The little girl – *Maria, dear god, truly*? – began drawing figures in the air. Runes and calculations in a language that Calix couldn't read but somehow *understood*. The figures pulsed with magic but it was a foreign kind that wormed its way under his skin and set his teeth on edge.

"We're close," she whispered, pointing to the left. Closer to Uzala and Uriel, who were now ripping into each other with arms that ended in knives and jagged swords. Several of Uzala's orbs were floating around their body, occasionally darting in to strike at Uriel, who was fighting back with blobs of purple, brackish energy that made Calix feel as if his fingernails were being peeled back one at a time.

It was horrific, monstrous, and Calix wanted to never see anything like it again.

Vincent and Ethaniel exchanged a look that Calix couldn't read, and then Vincent said, "Take us there. I want out of this hellhole now."

Maria's narrowed eyes and jut of her chin made Calix think she wanted to argue. Then she was... gone and suddenly standing near Magnus, pointing off to a golden shimmer in the distance. Magnus, for his part, looked confused and mildly horrified at Maria's sudden appearance (or horrified because of her less than human form), and he was still aiming the ballista at the war waging in front of their very eyes.

Ethaniel was practically dragging Vincent by the collar toward that light, his other hand tightly wrapped around Calix's. "We're going, Magnus."

Something like grief passed over his face; a flickering, fleeting thing that Calix barely caught. There was a weight there, solid and heavy and so very real, resting on his lover's soul, and it wasn't hard to parse that it was due to Maria. His little sister who had disappeared all those years ago. Ethaniel's mind must have been crawling with questions.

Calix hoped Maria had been able to answer some of them while Ethaniel had been trapped.

Magnus took one hand off the ballist but didn't step away. Maria crowded in beside him, her spider legs extending until she was as tall as he. That made Magnus step back, shock written all over his face.

"I will hold them off," she said with a swipe of her hand. All at once, the crossbow was gone, Magnus was holding the small red bead and Maria was holding the orb of magic Calix had freely given.

When she stared hard at Calix, he knew she was the right being to wield that power. He nodded and she looked relieved. The relief didn't last long.

Both Uzala and Uriel turned their heads to stare down at their little party, and Calix felt real *dread* overtake him. They were both oozing black ichor from a dozen wounds, but still somehow beautiful in a way that set his hair on end.

He knew then what it felt like to be *prey*.

Immediately, both Guardians were coming toward them, their motivations entirely as opposite as they were in form.

"He's mine!" Uriel roared, its hands stretching out, aimed right for Calix's throat.

Uzala rushed up behind their twin and wrapped two of its arms around Uriel's body, yanking them both backwards. Without turning around, Uriel clawed at Uzala with two arms, but two more were still reaching for Calix.

And not out loud, but in his head, he heard Maria scream, "GO!"

They ran into the mists.

A mad dash toward that golden glimmer. The panic welling in his chest, his breathing too fast, his heart pounding *toohardtoomuch*, and Ethaniel's grip even tighter now. Painful. Calix welcomed the pain, because it meant Ethaniel was at his side.

Vincent was hobbling along with them, managing to snag Magnus's arm as they ran past.

The air around them began to sizzle and pop. Grease on flames, or fireworks in Acadia Gardens. And as the air ripped open to rain down fire and ash on their heads, a fierce wind kicked up, carrying with it the scent of sulfur and death and Maria's screams echoed as several heavy *thumps* sounded around them. Calix felt the sound like a physical blow at his back, forcing him to stumble forward as they ran for their very lives.

Beside him, Ethaniel's breath hitched. Tears were running down his face, but when Calix started to ask, he said, "She's saving us. She made me promise I wouldn't stop her."

What exactly could Calix say that wouldn't be lost to the chaos and madness of the moment, or whipped away from him by the wind buffeting them on all sides. Now was not the time for comfort. They merely had to *survive*.

Up ahead, Magnus had yanked Vincent into a run and Calix and Ethaniel followed in their wake, ducking as pieces of what was once grey mist became whole and tried to crash down on their heads. There was no fire blazing around them, but whatever Uzala and Uriel were doing...

"Fuck!" Vincent screamed as an impossibly sharp piece of *something* pierced his right calf. He crumpled to the ground, pulling Magnus with him, and when they caught up to the pair, Magnus was frantically surveying the destruction and hellfire all around them.

Ethaniel let Calix go to rush to Vincent's side, and with Magnus's help, they pulled Vincent to his feet. But there was no running now, only a painful hobbling that cut their speed by at least half. And Vincent was leaving a trail of blood behind them.

Calix felt it before he saw or heard it; another chunk of the *demimonde*, blazing with fire hot enough to take hair off skin.

Every breath burned.

And the monocle in his hand shattered.

The pain was exquisite, glass embedded in the meat of his palm. A dozen or so of the thinnest cuts into his skin, the glass glinting softly as he stared down at the mess. Deep inside his chest, Calix felt warmth begin, then balloon, pushing against his organs and threatening his sight with specks of black.

Shock, maybe. Fear definitely.

But he'd never felt so powerful.

Without thinking, Calix dropped to his knees, pushed his hands into the ground that wasn't ground but was also somehow *sand*, the fine black granules running between his fingers. Dug into the belly of the *demimonde*, surrounded by strange magic, Calix felt a calling, soul-deep and inexplicable.

The pain of his hand, the confusion, the fear, fell from him as his blood dripped into the sand. Calix pushed all that emotion into it, let it run from him as a tributary dumps into a river, and let the *demimonde* eat it.

A sacrifice, then, Calix thought before a wall of thick black ichor slammed up behind him. Panel after panel, denser than a bank vault's walls, appeared until they were fully out of sight of the Guardians and Maria. He hadn't been able to look up. Some part of him hadn't wanted to see, fearful of what the image might do to his sanity.

Calix stayed there until a warm hand landed on his shoulder and squeezed. "Come on," Ethaniel said as he pulled Calix to standing. His hazel eyes were red, the wound on his face garish and awful, and there were tracks carved through the dust on his cheeks. And Calix remembered himself again, became himself again; brought home by having Ethaniel near once more.

They hobbled to that golden glimmer in the distance, the fire and wind fading behind them. And once they reached it, Ethaniel only said, "Give me a moment," before kneeling and beginning to draw. Carve was actually the better word for it, as Ethaniel took a thin piece of stone or bark from his pocket to use as a tool. But every character he drew glowed a soft green, and soon Calix was staring at a series of rune-esque shapes that again felt so familiar

"What is that?" Magnus asked, leaning closer.

Vincent scoffed but Ethaniel ignored him. "It's the language of this place. Our runes come from them, like so much of English is rooted in Latin and Greek."

"Progenitors," Magnus mumbled. "It makes sense."

All Calix could see past the glowing runes was the strength of Ethaniel's back, the muscles at play under his filthy shirt, and how the tendons of his bared arms flexed as he drew. He fell head over heels all over again, and swore he'd never let either of his lovers out of his sight for a good long while. He had money, he could give them whatever they wanted. Take them anywhere. Treat them like royalty.

The softest, sweetest tide of adoration had Calix kneeling at Ethaniel's side and gently whispering, "How do I help?"

Ethaniel smiled at him. "You do simply by being here with me. And it won't be long now. Aubrey's probably beside himself."

The teasing note in Ethaniel's voice was laced with a gentle fondness and it made Calix smile back. "How close are we?"

But it wasn't Ethaniel who answered. "I'd say *very*," Magnus said. Calix looked back to see Magnus and Vincent stepping as the amorphous golden glimmer they'd followed started to take on the shape of a doorway.

"Nearly there," Ethaniel said before pressing the sharp edge of that black thing in his hand to his arm. Calix reached out to stop him, but Ethaniel shook his head. "This is a place of blood. There's a lot of my family floating around here, and they and everything they've ever angered that lives here all want the same thing." He nodded to Calix's injured hand. "I'm afraid yours was merely the first course. You need to let Aubrey see that, Calix. It looks painful."

Calix reached out but didn't touch the wound on Ethaniel's face. "I could say the same to you."

"Then we'll let Aubrey kiss our wounds and make them better."

Calix let out a pained laugh. "I doubt that's all he'll do."

"I can guarantee it. He practically hovered over me the one time I got a cold while we were... " Ethaniel shook his head. "Never mind. And done."

He carefully pulled Calix back and watched as the runes all lit up at once and the sight alone made Calix dizzy. The magic of the *demimonde* was strange enough, but this felt very different. Whatever Ethaniel had drawn, it was pulling on some unseen well of arcane power, but it *worked*. A door suddenly snapped into place not twenty feet from Vincent.

"Thank fuck," Vincent said as Magnus and Ethaniel got him to standing.

"Well said, *brother*," Ethaniel snapped out, but Calix didn't care.

Ethaniel's hand was in his once more, and they were going *home*.

FOLIO THREE:

STRIFE & FINALITY

With hair up-staring – then like reeds, not hair –
Was the first man that leaped; cried 'Hell is empty
And all the devils are here.'
The Tempest, Act 1, Scene 2 by William Shakespeare

Chapter Sixteen

Documenting all this seems like an idea fraught with nothing but sorrow and empty memories. But I fear if I do not, she will not let me have them ever again. And I need to document, because my suspicions of her run deeper than what the strange, animalistic sounds that echo from the woods late at night can shake loose. And that is a primal kind of fear, the sort that runs deeper than the roots of a tooth.

There are half a dozen of us, and all of them my half-siblings save Celeste. The twins stick to each other, glued at the hip and wary of the rest of the brood. Two of them have left the ancestral home; Ethaniel vacated some years ago, when his father stole him and the youngest, Maria, in the dead of night. Celeste has stayed but has turned the eastern turret into her sanctuary and rarely is seen in the main home, choosing to walk the grounds late at night and duck into shadows when anyone approaches.

Maria had been something of a bright light for all of us, but with that light came a power that Mother clearly envied. The family blood was strong in that little body, and Mother knew it immediately. I tried, in my own ways, to shelter Maria from Mother's... inclinations, but every effort failed in the end. And now she is gone, squirreled away somewhere in the vast expanse of the Americas.

Mother says it may be my turn next, to try to tame the whispers and screams at the edge of the woods. We are not allowed to cross the boundary of the estate without her permission, and I dread to think that the day I'm to do so is near. What purpose do I have in such a dark, foreboding place? Ethaniel was snatched away before it was his turn, and in two years it will be Celeste's. I have no time left to waste.

She says I will go into the woods in three months. I have been trying and trying to access Mother's vast library. The books she keeps hidden are not protected by metal lock and key. No, that would be too easy. And if it were a simple blood spell, I could open the door in her study with a few drops from my finger. That has failed, too.

All I know is I have three months to uncover her secrets and find a way to protect us all. I will not admit this to anyone but this little journal, but I am terrified. I am caught between so many spaces; between youth and adulthood, between my mother's blood and my father's familial name; between old loyalties to a brother who willingly abandoned me, and the new ones I have built for the siblings left.

Tonight, I will try an old ritual to make the blood Speak. I want to hear the song that sometimes I feel thrumming under my skin, usually when in close proximity of one Mother's odd artifacts. She says we are called not to earthly concerns, but the ones of the Old Realms. Sometimes I've wondered if she was a bit mad.

But she's not. Nor am I. And I am a far sight more clever than she will ever give me credit for. Tonight, I make the blood Speak.

—From the journal of Vincent de Laine, 1874, Spain

Chapter Seventeen

Calix and Magnus were gone for roughly forty-five seconds when the long cord of magic Aubrey had looped around his forearm went taut. He was yanked forward a few feet before he managed to catch his balance, both hands now on the cord, the corners of his mouth pulled back in a grimace. "Shit."

Across from him, Agrippa's galaxy eyes narrowed. "Well, that's not good."

Aubrey gritted his teeth and dumped more energy into his hold on the door. He and Agrippa were holding it open by "tethers", as Agrippa called them. Aubrey's tether was connected to his monocle, which Calix had on his person. He didn't know what item of Agrippa's Magnus had with him in the *demimonde*, but he could chance a few guesses. (A feather, a silk handkerchief, or one of Agrippa's undoubtedly *many* patterned ascots. They seemed the type to enjoy a good pattern, given the splash of peach and sage green at their throat, pastel-spring bright against their deep navy suit.)

And up until now, the tether had been warm, almost comfortable against Aubrey's skin. Slightly tingly, like the heady buzzy he got when he kissed Calix's mouth (or other wonderful areas across that lithe body). But now it was sparking and popping, bits of it flaking and fraying.

"A terrible understatement," he bit out as he struggled against the tether's pull. "What do we do?"

One moment, he was staring at Agrippa and hoping for an answer. The next, he *felt* their voice in his head, large and powerful, brimming with possibility and a stiff kind of encouragement that bordered on fervent. "WE HOLD," Agrippa said, voice ringing with authority, making Aubrey's guts shrink into a tight little ball. "WE DO NOT LET GO. WE HOLD UNTIL THEY ARE BACK SAFE."

Aubrey nodded. What else could he do but respond in the affirmative? "Of course. We hold."

"WE HOLD."

Surety bled into his mind, changing his framing of the situation. Of course. Absolutely. They would hold. *No matter what.*

Aubrey let his magic gently release, like bathwater lapping at the edge of a tub but not spilling over. A threatening. A regathering, a regrouping. A second chance, and at the back of it, a guiding hand; invisible, but Aubrey swore he felt the brush of feathers.

"VERY GOOD," Agrippa said, their sternness melting slightly. "WE HOLD."

Somewhere, distantly, something snapped. It was a pop deep down inside his chest. A sliver of coldness jabbed into the soft meat around his heart.

Panic. Fear. Claws like serrated knives slashing through grey mist and stone-like skin, until black ichor flowed. A droning buzz. A scream. Pain, bright and burning, until everything was reduced to ash.

And then light. Shadows emerging from the dark. One, then two. Then three. Three of them returning from the demimonde, a land of nothing but darkness.

But a fourth? Who...

Features like Ethaniel's, but slightly more pointed. A deeper golden complexion now marred by blood and dirt and ichor and many, many wounds and the plum-black of bruises.

No. It couldn't be.

Across the circle of bones, Agrippa began to tremble. Aubrey blinked and looked again. Not trembling. *Vibrating,* faster than Aubrey's eye could track, until their entire willowy form was a blur.

"They come," Agrippa said, their words smaller but their tone still commanding. "Aubrey, you must hold."

At his temples and on the back of his neck, Aubrey felt sweat gather. He reached up to wipe it off his face and his palm came back red.

"The price of the *demimonde*," Agrippa said right before they stopped blurring. "They're nearly here... "

Again came another yank on the tether, but this time, Aubrey felt heat instead of cold, and under his fingers, the tether began to *smoke*. Thick, black, roiling clouds filtered away from the tether, and Aubrey could hardly hold onto it for how hot it burned. But he didn't care. He would flay the skin from his hands if it meant bringing them back *home*.

"Hold!" Agrippa yelled over the sudden wind that kicked up. Aubrey gave it everything he had, thinking only of Ethaniel and Calix and Magnus, knowing the three people most important to him could be gone in a blink if he didn't *hold fast*. The scent of burning hair reached him, the smoke billowing, roiling.

They stumbled out of the doorway coughing and wheezing, clutching at each other as ash and dirt rose in clouds from their clothing and hair. He saw Ethaniel first, and when their eyes met, Ethaniel sucked in a deep breath, but he didn't run over. He couldn't, as he had an arm around another man.

That man. The one bearing the same Harkness family resemblance. The one who'd started this all. Some tucked-away part of Aubrey *seethed*. But then he saw Calix and Magnus and his fury dwindled to embers.

Aubrey was on them in three long strides, shouldering the half-brother aside to wrap Ethaniel and Calix up in his arms. But while he gathered them close, Aubrey also tried to reach out to Magnus and instead found his mentor and friend trailing after Agrippa, who was briskly walking away. Their turned back spoke louder than any words, and he didn't need to see the aggrieved look on Magnus's face to fill in the blanks.

Aubrey shut his eyes as he held them close and pressed his face to Ethaniel's temple. Calix was smashed between them but clearly didn't care, for all the tighter he gripped Aubrey's shirt.

In the chilly quiet of the room, the magic still sparking and smoking off their bodies, their clothes, Aubrey finally felt *whole* again.

Calix was the first to stir, but Aubrey didn't bother to look up until he heard the other man gasp. "Lawton, my god. What happened?"

His head felt too heavy for his neck, but Aubrey had to look. Calix wasn't one to react like that without good reason. Lawton was seated about ten feet away, which was already odd, because Aubrey and Agrippa had opened the doorway in the secondary Collectio, but somehow they were back in Rosehill.

But the mystery of their swift and sudden shift was shoved aside for how sickly Lawton looked. The purple and black veins that had been visible but not prominent under the man's pale skin were now standing out in stark relief, as if someone had painted them on his body. Lawton's face, neck, and bared forearms pulsed with nauseating magic; so much that Aubrey's gut churned just to look upon him.

Calix slid away from them with an apologetic look, only to pause a few feet from them when Lawton held Aubrey's gun up, the barrel pointing to the ceiling. "Turns out I didn't need it," Lawton rasped. "Though we did have a visitor while you all were gone." His gaze flitted over to Ethaniel, then to the stranger Aubrey knew was Vincent de Laine. The look on Lawton's face was a mixture of stark terror and scheming contemplation; as if he were considering pointing the gun at Vincent. Aubrey wouldn't have blamed him in the least.

Vincent looked more sallow than when Aubrey last saw him, resplendent in black and gold and standing on a stage in front of a crowd of magic scholars, and historians. Nearly two years ago, and it felt like yesterday.

The speech Vincent had given at that time was memorable only because of how sincere he'd sounded. From anyone else, it would have been the work of someone addled by magic addiction (a thing healers were only now admitting existed in some magic users who turned livelihood or hobby into obsession). But Vincent de Laine hadn't introduced himself as the head of the Golden Order. He'd introduced himself as a Harkness. Had even used the last name on his registration papers; Aubrey had checked immediately afterwards, which helped him avoid the crowds of skeptics and the crowds of all-too-willing magical scofflaws. But he hadn't connected him to Ethaniel outside of the name recognition. There were plenty of non-related Harknesses dotted across America and England, so it wasn't something Aubrey had lingered on.

And now here Vincent stood: burned, bloodied, and bruised. Pale and trembling. Stinking of mud and ichor and foul *demimonde*. Taking stock of everyone in the room, but barely lingering on Lawton or the gun. No, he seemed much more interested in *Calix*.

For that alone, Aubrey wanted to rip him to shreds. But whatever he'd put Ethaniel through.... Aubrey would *destroy* him.

"Not now," Ethaniel said as Aubrey stared daggers into an oblivious Vincent. "Please, Aubrey."

Aubrey took a few deep breaths, ending on a long gust of air while he pressed his forehead against Ethaniel's. Questions swirled in his mind, but Ethaniel was in no state to answer them. Except one. "What happened?" Aubrey asked, using the palm of his hand to frame, but not touch, the deep, ugly burn on Ethaniel's jaw.

"I don't... it's all such a blur," Ethaniel whispered as he leaned in, pressing against Aubrey despite what must have been terrible pain where his wound was touched.

"Let me take care of it, then, and when you can tell me when you're ready." He framed it with a gentle voice, but it wasn't a question.

Ethaniel pressed their lips together, his entire body sagging the moment they kissed. He didn't answer Aubrey, and it left him with a terrible feeling.

And behind them were enemies and allies and questions compounding with even more confusion and mystery. Agrippa was gone, stalked off to some other part of the estate, or perhaps even flitted back to their domain. Magnus was drained to the point of dangerous depletion, and even Aubrey could feel his energy waning.

And Lawton and Vincent were in the room, too.

One arm around Ethaniel's shoulders, Aubrey turned to face everyone else. He caught Magnus coming back into the room, his head held high despite the evident pain on his face. He took stock of the way Vincent's gaze skittered about, how steady Lawton's hands were despite how they gripped the arms of the chair in which he sat.

Aubrey held out his hand to Calix, who eagerly took it, and when he reeled the slighter man in, Calix sighed. "Lawton, give Magnus the gun," Aubrey said, mustering as much steel in his voice as he could. He didn't like anything about the way Lawton was curled up in the chair, how dark his eyes had gone, or how thin his lips were as he straddled some border between fear and rage.

Never was he more grateful for Magnus than these moments, where the other man seemed to understand exactly what was going on. He strode over to Lawton, his face devoid of anything but neutrality, and said, "There's been enough horror and violence for a lifetime over these last days. The gun, Lawton."

But Lawton didn't move, and neither did Vincent. They were now staring at each other with shock and outrage, but behind Vincent's eyes was a cold calculation. It made Aubrey bristle, wind up what was left of his energy into crackling sparks that danced between his fingers as he held his left hand aloft.

No one in the room seemed to breathe. The moment spun aimlessly, fruitlessly, while everyone stared at each other.

"I do appreciate the heft of a fine weapon," Lawton finally said as he lowered his feet to the floor and sat up in the chair. "And I do appreciate you leaving it for me, Aubrey, despite our... disagreements."

Lawton didn't try to aim the gun at Vincent, but the weapon sitting in his lap felt like enough of a threat. Aubrey looked to Calix, who immediately slipped away from them to stand beside Lawton's chair.

"I know," Calix said as he hovered close to Lawton without touching him. "Lawton. I know."

"You don't, actually," Lawton said in a cold tone. "See, while you were gone, Vincent's little lackey, my former handler, knocked on the door, barged her way in, and chased me through the house— "

Vincent recoiled as if struck. "Cassandra?"

Lawton kept going. " —trapped me in the bathroom, the one with the lovely wallpaper, and then... " His voice faded and his left hand went to his neck, pulled away the tightly buttoned collar of a shirt Aubrey recognized as Calix's. With a vicious yank that sent buttons flying, he bared his throat to the room. Under the deep purple and black veins skittering across his skin, above the brand the Order had seared into his flesh, was a jagged, ugly line across his throat.

Everyone moved at once.

Calix went for the gun as Lawton started to raise it. Ethaniel rushed to Vincent's side. Magnus moved between them all, with Aubrey coming at the little group from the other side.

All Aubrey could see was the gun and the steady aim of Lawton's hand and Ethaniel moving in the path of the barrel. Fear was a pit in his stomach, a burn in his lungs, and he flung his hands out, hoping there was time—

The gun went flying across the room. Vincent and Ethaniel were pulled back against the bookshelves, while Calix and Lawton's legs were bound in thick green vines. Aubrey was frozen in place, left to stare at Agrippa, who had come back in from gods knew where and was radiating magic and power.

But everything around Agrippa was hazy, their visage warped by something akin to how the air simmered above the concrete sidewalks during a city summer. The heat boiling everything under the mighty power of the sun. And through the haze, white feathers and galaxy eyes were an overlay, somewhat obscuring whatever lay beneath. Aubrey squinted, trying to make out the details.

It's a mystery you cannot be privy to. Agrippa's voice echoed in his mind now, every syllable laden with a command. *Magnus trusts you, so I am willing to set you free, but only if you use that freedom wisely.*

Aubrey swallowed hard. Sweat was gathering at his temples again and he felt far too warm, as if a mere touch to his skin might burn someone. And Agrippa was waiting for an answer.

I'll pull Ethaniel and Calix away.

As you should, Agrippa responded.

Time restarted, but only for Aubrey. He dashed toward Calix and moved him across the room with a simple pull; his fingers around that thin wrist. Ethaniel he also shifted, left to stand shoulder to shoulder with Calix. And then Aubrey took up a place in front of them and watched Agrippa wave a hand and bring the gun to them. It disappeared into their suit jacket, and as Agrippa gently maneuvered

Magnus to stand by the fireplace, on the wall across from them and also away from the fray, Aubrey saw no telltale bump in their pocket. The gun had been... well, probably whisked away to their little domain.

On his next blink, time restarted, but Lawton and Vincent were still unable to move. But they could talk.

"You fucking wanker," Lawton spat at Vincent he strained against his bindings. Fury thinned his features, turned them lupine, and behind Aubrey, Calix sucked in a deep breath. Theirs was a bond so old and so worn, and yet Calix's heart couldn't handle such strife.

Vincent's stare had gone imperious. Despite the blood and injuries, he managed to nudge his expression into something that betrayed arrogance. Aubrey wasn't surprised. "Why was Cassandra here?" Vincent asked.

Lawton scoffed. "As if you didn't send her."

"I didn't." Vincent's brow dipped and that little flicker of doubt had Aubrey worried as well.

Aubrey turned his attention back to his lovers, looking over his shoulder at them. There was so much to say and yet right now, none of it was fitting.

Ethaniel was hunched over, his hands on thighs, his gaze on the ground. "It's a... being of that place. Agrippa," he said thickly, digging his fingers into the muscle. "Its magic has the same taste." He lifted his head, confusion sunk deep into his hazel eyes. "Did you know?"

Aubrey knew that was for him and only him. He could barely begin to understand what Ethaniel had gone through, but the implication wasn't so unclear. "Yes and no. It's not a concern right now. You need rest, Ethaniel, not more worries."

"We all do," Calix said while getting Ethaniel to standing. They both stared at Aubrey, faces awash in relief and pain at the same time.

All Aubrey could think was how badly he wished to take them home. Though, that word had a very different meaning now, one that was shattered on the very foundations of their entire journey together. His apartment was gone. Ethaniel's was marred by illness and the ghosts of old wounds. And Rosehill, all Calix's, had only been the birthplace of new terrors and the keeper of old ones.

"Take them away." Magnus's words broke through the fog in his head. "Aubrey. As far as this blasted house will take you. But do not go outside. We don't know what state the wards are in."

Aubrey couldn't tear his gaze away from Ethaniel and Calix. Magnus's words were a distant echo, reverberating somewhere deep inside his body but unable to penetrate his mind.

"Aubrey." Magnus was in front of him now, worn and soot-covered, the very air around him rippling with fractured magic. Dimly, Aubrey picked up the brush of Magnus's magic mixed with Agrippa's; the dark of the *demimonde* had breached even here, it seemed.

"Let Agrippa and I handle this for the moment," Magnus said softly, his hands braced on Aubrey's shoulders as if he meant to make his words seep in. "There are questions still. But for now, take solace in the fact that they're here with you. You won't want to miss a single chance to show them the affection you keep so tightly bottled up, afraid to let others see it."

Aubrey tried to scoff at that, but it came out a weak shudder of air. He *had* shown them.... hadn't he?

Hadn't he?

Doubt was an insidious thing wriggling through him, so all he could do was nod and say, "Thank you, Magnus," before taking Calix's hand in his left, Ethaniel's in his right, and guiding them toward the stairs and up to one of the several guest rooms on the second floor.

No one spoke on the way up the stairs, or even once Aubrey shut the door of the guest room and leaned against it. He let the deep forest green, sage, and cream color scheme soothe his eyes and his weary mind for a long moment. Let his mouth and brain catch up to each other, but the words wouldn't come.

He wanted to hold them close. Or maybe simply look at them, reassure himself that they *were* here. Alive and mostly unharmed. And he wanted to rub his cheek against Calix's, press his lips to Ethaniel's, and remember their scent, their taste, how their skin felt against his own.

Ethaniel was the first to break. "Help me out of these?" he asked, his fingers paused on the buttons of his shirt. "I don't want the smell of that place anywhere near me ever again."

"Of course, but your wound, Ethaniel... " Calix replied, instantly slipping in front of Ethaniel with a quick glance to Aubrey, as if to say, *Well, you heard the man*.

"It looks far worse than it is," Ethaniel replied quickly. "It's... odd. Here, it doesn't hurt anymore, and I only now realized it."

Aubrey pushed off the door finally, his body heavier than any anvil or anchor, but he managed to stumble over to them. He pressed himself against them just to feel their warmth, hoping it might chase the chill from his body.

He'd almost lost them both.

The next thought came unbidden, shocking a sharp breath from him. *We need to finish this.*

A thought for later, when bodies and minds were more hale and hearty. Not for right now. In this moment, in a room darkened by velvet drapes and the slap of rain against thick windowpanes, he wanted to imprint both of them on his very soul.

"I was terrified," Aubrey admitted only after gathering them close, his words a whisper into Ethaniel's hair. "So goddamn afraid I'd lost you both."

"You didn't," Calix replied, his words muffled into Aubrey's shoulder. He was tracing Aubrey's spine with his fingers, sending little soothing ripples across Aubrey's entire body. It was a grounding thing, that touch, but it wasn't enough.

Ethaniel was so quiet and Aubrey had to fight against every urge to fuss over him. Make him bathe, change, then lay down and simply *sleep*. But Aubrey's fussing, or perhaps his particular brand of it, had been what started their past arguments. Now was not the time for any kind of strife, but especially not that.

Aubrey settled for kissing Ethaniel's temple and waiting him out. It was all he could do right now. But Ethaniel merely fumbled for the buttons of his trousers and when his fingers couldn't perform the motions, he looked up at Aubrey, his eyes far too bright.

"Help. Please," Ethaniel whispered.

"Of course."

He and Calix pried fabric stiffened by blood and dirt and unnamable grime from Ethaniel's body; their touches careful, almost hesitant. Only their soft breaths sounded in the room and the only light from a few candles Calix had lit by flicking a hand at them. Aubrey had a feeling anything that was *too much* (too bright, too loud, too fast) would rattle Ethaniel down to his marrow.

Ethaniel deserved softness. Now. Always.

They didn't let Ethaniel be bared to the room for long. Calix wrapped him in a blanket, shrugging away Ethaniel's protestations about getting filth on the fine wool. But the smile Ethaniel gave Calix was honest, even if it was merely a suggestion playing about his lips.

"The bath down the hall has a large tub," Calix said. "I'll get it ready."

But Ethaniel reached out to snag his wrist. "Please stay."

Calix looked to Aubrey, a question on his face. Aubrey only had one answer.

He thought about water heated along copper pipes, a novelty in any home, but here the pipes heated quickly thanks to a marvelously magic fire starter in the boiler. Calix had told him of it their first night at Rosehill, and he was never more grateful for such a contraption. His father would have *hated* such a thing in his home, but in his medical theater, it would have been welcomed with open arms and wallet.

His father also would have hated that Aubrey used the last spark of his magic to wake the boiler to life, to push hot water along those pipes and up into the faucet, which began to stream. And he could do it because it was in the name of *healing*. It was pure intent refocused in a way that wasn't completely alien to him but had long been pushed to the back of his mind.

He'd convinced himself not that he couldn't do it, but that he *shouldn't*. Because it wasn't "true" magic, but some mutant offspring that didn't deserve to exist. But magic was intent and theory and prop put together to create a desired outcome. His brand of it wasn't lavish or fancy; it was rooted in his family's culture, yes, but he'd only understood it fully once he'd *embraced* it.

"It's done," Aubrey said, trying not to huff with the effort of speaking.

When Ethaniel looked up at him, it was with wonder on his face. But he didn't ask *how*, a thing the Ethaniel he knew would have already tripped over on his way to even more questions. This Ethaniel was still his, but he was also *theirs*. A dance they were only beginning to figure out. And whatever mark the *demimonde* had left on him... it was a question for later. So many questions needed to be answered, but now was the most terrible timing. Clarity wasn't a thing easily won, and in the aftermath of everything heaped upon them, Aubrey both feared and yearned for it.

Not now. Not right now. Let us have peace in the long, rainy night and tomorrow we can begin again.

Aubrey took Ethaniel's hand in his, rubbed his thumb over the scratches on his knuckles, and said, "Let us take care of you."

Once they hobbled to the bathroom, Calix was quick to close the shutters on the windows, save for one over the tub, and he only did so because Ethaniel asked for it to be left open. Aubrey helped him lower into the steaming tub while Calix darted about collecting various bottles with soft *clinks* of cut crystal and thick glass.

Aubrey bit down on his amused smile when Calix returned, and at Ethaniel's raised eyebrows, he said, "I can't help it. I like scented things, usually because they remind me of someone or somewhere. I thought one might catch your attention."

"You're sweet," Ethaniel said, letting his head loll back against the rolled porcelain edge of the tub. "Why are you always so sweet?"

There was a flush creeping up Calix's neck, but Aubrey didn't need to point it out. The poor man was fidgeting the moment he sat down on the other stool Aubrey had swiped from the large oak vanity on the far side of the bathroom. But his hands were steady as he held up two small, stoppered bottles, the amber and dark blue liquids sloshing against the inside.

"I got this one in Paris last spring," Calix said as he held one bottle up to Ethaniel's nose. "It's juniper and orange and something else the perfumer wouldn't tell me. Some secret ingredient." But Ethaniel wrinkled his nose at the smell and Calix held up the bottle with blue liquid inside. "And this one is grapefruit, chamomile, and spruce, and what I swear is sugar, but I'm not sure... "

As Calix described each scent and let Ethaniel sniff to his heart's content, their conversation became a gentle lap of sound in Aubrey's ears; like sitting out on the beach and listening to the tide slowly roll in. It lulled him into somewhere safe and warm in his mind, as his body was already feeling the draining effects of the day and the unending stress of losing Ethaniel to the maw of the *demimonde*. Aubrey let himself sink into it, fully, instead of holding back. He let their proximity, their voices, their very presence weigh him down while he drifted on a current of their words.

And somewhere in that cozy darkness, a flame flickered to life. It was a gentle spring green. Harmless, really, even though its presence wasn't asked for. As Aubrey locked his eyes on it, the spark neither dwindled or roared to life. It simply *existed*; constant and alive.

When Aubrey came back to himself, on the lingering echo of Ethaniel's soft groan of relief as he sank up to his chin into the water, everything under him felt like wet sand. That unsteadiness was a rarity for him, and it was already forcing magic along the tunnels of his wrists, into the channels of his fingers. Readying for a fight.

He was tired, exhausted, even. Being paranoid wouldn't help anyone.

But was that all it was?

It took effort and patience, but Aubrey clamped down on his magic. He could feel Ethaniel's eyes on him, curious but not prying, and all he could do was inhale and shake his head. Ethaniel's wet fingers squeezed his, and Aubrey returned to ground once more.

"I know I owe you both the truth of what happened," Ethaniel said softly, cracking the silence around them. "I know I do. But can it wait?"

"Oh, darling," Calix said, leaning in to brace his forearm on the tub and put his other hand on Ethaniel's knee, which was bent and poking out of the water. "In your own time."

Aubrey had to unjumble his thoughts enough to say, "We only wanted you home, Ethaniel," and it seemed to satisfy. But Aubrey could feel the hollowness deep down, a little pit of doubt and worry that platitudes couldn't fill. He knew Calix's words, his intent, were honest and pure, and in his heart, he was, too. Having Ethaniel back was a weight lifted off his shoulders. A sense of relief that made his limbs heavy, his head foggy.

And yet that doubt lingered. He needed to shake it off completely. Healing, caring... that he could do.

"Do you still have that lovely jasmine hair wash, Calix?" Aubrey asked as he slid his stool to the back of the tub, so he could sit behind Ethaniel. Calix brought the bottle down from a little shelf beside one of the shuttered windows, and Aubrey spent a moment cleaning his hands in the large basin sink before settling back down and pouring a generous amount of the slick liquid into his palm. He'd used the stuff the other day and had been entranced by the scent. Aubrey hoped it would help relax Ethaniel, too.

"Lean back for me?" Aubrey asked, his words curling softly into Ethaniel's ear.

Ethaniel shifted back, putting his head in Aubrey's hands. The sight got caught in his throat and when he glanced over at Calix, the younger man had on a brave face, but the cracks in the facade were evident. The furrowed brow, the chewed-on bottom lip; how Calix danged his fingers in the water, their wake leaving behind little swirls of deep blue that seemed to glitter; the intensity caged in his lithe frame, as if he wanted nothing more than to hide Ethaniel in a nest of blankets and pillows and never let him leave.

It broke Aubrey's heart.

The moment he dug his fingers into the soft place under Ethaniel's skull, Ethaniel groaned. The hand he had on the edge of the tub clenched then released while Aubrey did the same for the pressure on his head. It was an old technique to release tension, one his mother had taught him, and it worked on everything from headaches induced by squinting at some absurd text to a sudden shift in the weather, and everything in-between. It was the very least he could do to help Ethaniel find equilibrium again.

The soothing rhythm of washing Ethaniel's hair, the scrubbing and rinsing, massaging and simply *touching*, felt like an indulgence. But mere earthly pleasures had *never* felt so good, and as Aubrey watched Calix's eyes drift shut, he said, "Calix. Dove."

"Hmmm?" But Calix didn't lift his head from where he'd pillowed it on his arms.

Ethaniel let out a chuckle. "You look as tired as I feel, pet."

Calix gave them a dreamy smile. "It's okay. I don't want to leave yet."

Ethaniel reached back to squeeze Aubrey's wrist. "Neither do I. But this lovely man is doing all the work, and I think he deserves some sleep, too."

Calix's eyes shot open at that. "No, I didn't mean— "

Aubrey waved him off. "You're fine, dove. Come on, everyone up."

Calix darted into the bedroom to turn down the covers, leaving Aubrey to help Ethaniel dry off. Ethaniel tried to protest at first, but Aubrey stopped him with a look, then rewarded him with a gentle kiss.

"You had me so worried," Aubrey whispered against his lips.

Ethaniel twined his arms around Aubrey's shoulders, his fingers warm and damp against Aubrey's neck. "It was no one's fault but those *things*." Ethaniel pulled back to stare hard at Aubrey. "Agrippa is one of them. A Guardian. I can feel it."

Aubrey frowned. "We knew they were from the *demimonde*, but it's a place completely undocumented— "

Something flashed in Ethaniel's eyes, but it was gone just as quickly. "I can *feel* it," he said, his gaze dark. "While I was there, something... talked to me. I don't know who or what, but it wasn't the same as the Guardians I met. Uriel, Uzala."

Aubrey's breath caught. "Ethaniel. We don't need to do this right now."

Ethaniel kept talking. "I can still feel *us*, too," he whispered as he leaned in, smelling of jasmine and sea salt and spruce, and it made Aubrey's head spin. "That connection we shared so briefly."

"What are you saying, Ethaniel?" Aubrey whispered back. *What had the demimonde done to his Ethaniel?*

"When I'm ready, I think I can share what happened. With both of you, through that connection. Whatever that thing was that spoke to me through the stone Uzala made me touch... it wasn't angry. Wasn't terrifying, not really. It was *curious*. It helped me. And I don't trust it, not even close to completely... but I think it opened something in my mind. Let me tap into... "

"Your potential," Aubrey said. And then he understood all at once.

Ethaniel was a Harkness. That would never change. Could never change. But Ethaniel could dictate what that meant for him, and for the longest time, that had meant being the one to hold the center in a crisis. To be stable, reliable. To use his magic and natural skill at patterning to others' advantage.

Now he had a chance to take something for himself. The ache in Ethaniel's voice was evident, but Aubrey heard the fear, too.

"You don't have to make any decisions now," Aubrey said soothingly.

"But what if I do?" Ethaniel slid his fingers up Aubrey's head, pulling them together until their foreheads touched. "What if I don't get a choice?" The silence was short, sharp. "I saw her, you know."

"Who?"

"Maria."

For the first time in a very long while, Aubrey didn't know what to say. He only held Ethaniel tighter and kept holding even after Calix rejoined them and wrapped around them both.

Chapter Eighteen

ETHANIEL

Ethaniel couldn't stop shivering. He was firmly held on all sides, the warmth of Aubrey and Calix penning him in, pinning him down. It was the most delightful sensation. But it was all blasted to bits because he *couldn't stop shivering.* If he drew his hands into fists as tight as he could manage, it helped. After waking Aubrey and Calix up multiple times, he finally found a way to make the worst of it narrow into a wobbly kind of tremble; as if one were shaking the sleep out of a limb.

But it never *stopped.*

Ethaniel closed his eyes for the twentieth time in what had been surely no more than an hour and yet as long as eternity.

In the dark, it spoke. A single green flame distant, but present.

You remember.

Rather difficult to forget, Ethaniel thought not without bitterness. His foul mood didn't seem to bother the being, as it neither retreated nor burned brighter. *I'm not sure how this is possible, since we never made a proper agreement.*

You made one when you listened to me.

Ethaniel bit down on a sharp retort. But it burst out anyways, not caring of his deep concern for what angering such a creature might cause.

Deals have contracts. Terms negotiated on. I was forced to put my hands on that blasted stone. You're a... stowaway. Like Lawton's, but worse.

I am not worse. And I am not human.

You certainly have intent, like humans. Selfish need and ego. Ethaniel let his hands uncurl; his shaking had stopped the moment they'd begun talking. Not possibly a coincidence. *Is that a threat, the shaking?*

No. It is your frail vessel's latent reaction to the exposure of pure magic combined with the potency of your blood. It will not last. I thought to use my sole chance to learn, and to warn you.

Ethaniel wanted to SCREAM. He barely got the heel of his palm to his mouth and bit down before one escaped, all impotent whimper that still made something inside his chest release.

Why are you surprised?

Behind him, Aubrey shifted closer, sighed into his neck. Calix didn't move from how he'd wrapped around Ethaniel, octopus-like, and Ethaniel couldn't shift at all. Couldn't risk waking either of them. Stuck with an interloper he had no reason to trust.

It is your blood, Harkness. You cannot help what pumps in your veins, shakes life into your limbs, and makes you capable of such great things. You are your mother's child, no matter the weight of your father's blood. And We are attracted to you so easily.

Ethaniel's heart began to pound. He needed to stop this creature from talking. He couldn't stand to hear what it was saying, didn't want to hear it. He'd already embraced more than he'd ever wanted to, sending those hellhounds back to their conjurer, opening his veins in the *demimonde*.

He was so terrifying close to treading a line he swore he'd never come within leagues of. To protect two people he cared more than the world for. Perhaps even loved, as mad as it was. For them, he'd walked right up to the line and dared himself to cross it. Dared himself and the *demimonde* and now this thing hovering in the back of his mind.

I am not the ones you met. Uriel. Uzala. They are a broken thing, halves of a whole that can never be put back together. Uzala will walk through the realms themself to recombine with their half. Uriel is their splicer, splitter, detonation and salvation. They will slowly go more mad the longer they

are apart, but Uriel strives for a way to your world. Saw it through the woman, both security and vessel.

Ethaniel bit back the words that wanted to tumble out, and had to squash the urge to wake Calix. They knew Lily had been in contact with Uriel, in either some misguided attempt at saving Calix, or at restoring her own sanity. But he'd always had this niggling suspicion that they'd missed something. If Lily had planned on returning, as they suspected, then it made sense why she'd split herself into pieces. The little he knew of the necromantic arts was that a human who dies whole rarely returns in such a way. The process of rebirth wasn't merely some ritual done during the witching hour over a freshly dug grave or caged in by the dusty innards of a mausoleum. It involved weeks, even months, of careful craft, patterning, and tracking down enough parts of a soul to forge anew.

But Harkness family secrets remained a mystery to him, and rightfully so. He'd never been one to dive into that ugly business, and being more curious than smart would only erode himself further. He'd done enough damage.

What was she trying to do? Ethaniel asked, mindful of how tightly he was gripping Calix.

Strong-willed, but foolish. The woman. The Oracle's mother. He has paths before him, choices, she was never given. Her bond with Uriel erased many of them, because as Uriel was using her, she was carrying out her own plans. Bits of herself locked away in the *demimonde*; hoarded and hidden. I do not fully know her intent, but I know Uriel has been seeking the boy since his mother's passing.

A new vessel. A new chance.

Ethaniel wasn't going to let that happen.

He felt the pressure in his chest lessen some, and when he searched for the entity, only a trace remained. It had faded away like morning mist, eradicated by sun's glow.

I will keep watch here. Uriel and Uzala both live, but they are wounded. And something disturbs the order of things here. It is only a ripple now, and it could be any number of things. It is a ripple of arrival, much like

when you entered the *demimonde*. The energy was disturbed, the magic flipped over onto its head, and in that wake came a storm.

Tell Agrippa about me. They'll know.

He felt it leave all at once, and despite being hemmed in on all sides by real human warmth, Ethaniel felt cold.

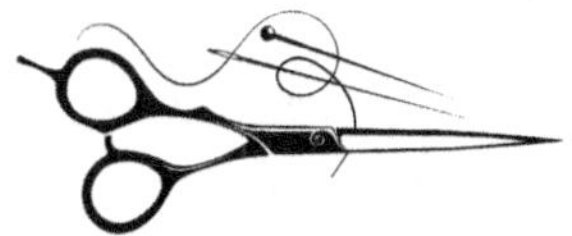

The fingers carefully running through his hair was the thing that brought him to waking; the soft words were the second thing he noticed. Still too fuzzy-minded to fully comprehend, Ethaniel flickered his eyes open and was met with a honey-gold stare.

"Oh!" Calix smiled at him, all sunshine and loveliness, a balm to Ethaniel's weary soul and bruised body. "Aubrey."

"I know," Aubrey said, his words tripping over a chuckle, an undercurrent of slightly darkened amusement that curled into Ethaniel's ear. "I felt his breathing change."

"And I'm right here," Ethaniel groused, and of course they both made amused noises. "Did I... " He raised his head, but the shutters were drawn tight. "Did I sleep through the night?"

"And then some," Calix said as he sat up and stretched. "It's after ten in the morning." With his arms above his head and his hair sticking up at all angles, he looked ethereal and at least ten years younger. For some reason, the sight made Ethaniel ache in a way that defied description.

"I checked on our... *guests* about an hour ago," Aubrey said, the bed dipping as he shifted closer to Ethaniel. "Magnus said Lawton was no trouble, but Vincent got on Agrippa's last nerve and has been... ahem, *pacified*." The hand on Ethaniel's hip slipped lower, down his thigh. Right over a nasty bruise. Aubrey didn't press, hovering his hand in silent question.

"Save your energy," Ethaniel said softly. "We don't know what comes next." Aubrey withdrew his hand, opting to instead wrap his arm around Ethaniel's chest. Ethaniel pressed back against him. He was so glad to have them both here. "And I don't object to Vincent being *pacified*. But, should we trust Agrippa?"

He watched Calix's gaze shoot over his head to Aubrey. "Magnus trusts them," Aubrey replied slowly. "And they were instrumental in returning you to us. They're different, Ethaniel. Different from the ones you met in the *demimonde*."

Ethaniel felt the chastisement somewhere deep down in his chest, then sighed and squeezed Aubrey's hand on his middle. "I'm being paranoid," he said, ducking his head.

"You're not. And even if you were, it would be warranted. Agrippa just wants to help," Calix said as he leaned in.

Ethaniel watched the play of golden-amber lashes across his cheek as Calix looked down. The swell of affection he felt was eroding the panic and terror and fear he'd experienced. It would be a long time before he'd be able to sleep soundly, but he didn't doubt it would be much worse without both of them.

Slowly, gently, Ethaniel reached out to touch Calix's hip. He needed grounding. Touch made up a large portion of his life, through slippery silks and velvety-soft damasks, to the rough but light feeling of cotton. The supple leather of a finely crafted belt, no longer a blank template but a canvas on which to apply his magic.

Sight and touch. His best senses. How he observed, measured, and judged the world. Right now, his world consisted of Calix and Aubrey and the large bed in which they all now sprawled.

He reached up toward Calix's face, and the other man quickly obliged by tipping his chin up until their lips met.

"Better?" Calix asked, no more than a murmur against his lips.

Ethaniel wanted those lips again and again. "No. Kiss me properly."

Calix made a wounded noise but was immediately there, warm and real and alive in the very best way. Ethaniel kept it sweet but firm. If Calix opened to him too much, he knew he'd want to *take*.

To let himself go in one more way.

He'd already crossed so many lines. He'd felt power — *real* power, there in the *demimonde* — and nothing had ever terrified him so badly.

Because it had felt so fucking *good*.

But even with his thoughts swirling, it was impossible to ignore the long, warm line of Aubrey at his back, so he didn't; he shifted his hips back, his hand going to curl over the top of Aubrey's where it sat on his hip. Aubrey's fingers tightened under his own and it sent a flare of *need* through him. Yearning mixed with a bolt of lust.

Was it so awful, these sensations? The pining, the desire? Why shouldn't he reunite with his lovers like they could part again at any minute, and let that urgency drive them headlong into blissful oblivion?

Maybe it's too much, being so cautious all the time.

Ethaniel dragged Calix close and kissed him again, swallowing up the younger man's surprised moan, letting it roll over his tongue to slide down his throat. He wanted to cage those sounds inside himself, bank their fire into one he could share back with them.

Aubrey's lips against the back of his neck made Ethaniel shiver. "Let it go for now," Aubrey whispered. "We're here. And the next person or thing who tries to take you will have to go through me first."

Already Calix was pushing up the hem of his simple shirt, warm fingers spanning across Ethaniel's skin. And his mouth moved in tandem with Ethaniel's, the slick slide of his tongue bold enough to have Ethaniel twitching with desire. He let them do as they pleased, those honey-soaked moments only spiraling his need higher, and the blood that ran hot in his veins helped Ethaniel push aside any reservations.

He had two willing partners and a lifetime of repression and caution to unravel. *So why not?*

"Be careful. You're injured," Aubrey whispered into his skin.

"I'll tell you if it hurts."

Aubrey's fingers dragged down his sternum, until he was pulling Ethaniel's shirt up by the hem and with Calix's help, got it off and thrown to the side. Bare from the waist up, his soft linen trousers already sagging from where some set of clever fingers had loosened their closures, Ethaniel reached back for Aubrey and out for Calix. He needed their skin under his hands, the taste of their lips on his.

Gods, did he ever *want*.

"So gorgeous," Calix murmured between kisses. "And absurdly brave."

"I promise from now on, nothing but boring," Ethaniel said. "I really do prefer boring."

Aubrey's hand slid up his chest, until it spanned wide across his collarbone.

"Fuck," Ethaniel bit out, making Aubrey nip at his neck. It drove a sparking, shuddering spike of pleasure into the base of Ethaniel's spine, that simple thing. Ethaniel tightened his grip on Aubrey, slid the hand he had on Aubrey's thigh up until his fingers could dent flesh with more give. Aubrey inhaled sharply but didn't moan, and that only made Ethaniel want him more.

"Ethaniel." Calix smeared his name into his jaw, his lips slick, soft.

All that bottled desire. All the years of repression. The fear, the hiding. Knowing the name he carried, and the responsibilities that came with it. But he'd stood in a realm of grey mist and monsters and had come out the other side with his sanity intact. His magic still beat like a second heart in his chest. He was still a Harkness, but he'd found his own ground to stand on.

And these two men made him feel *invincible*.

"I need one of you to fuck me," he managed to gasp out. "And I need the other one down my throat."

"Fucking Christ, Ethaniel." Words he expected from Aubrey, but it was Calix staring up at him, his devilish tongue swiping over his bottom lip. Ethaniel wanted to bite that lip, so he leaned in and did so, sending Calix toppling into him, breathless and whining.

Instead of answering, Aubrey slid his hand over Ethaniel's hip, then clever fingers dipped into the crease at his thigh and groin before Aubrey ran his index finger up Ethaniel's cock. He chased the sensation with his hips, back bowed slightly while Aubrey ran his tongue over the shell of Ethaniel's ear.

The pulsing ache of desire in his body went taut. Waiting for the next uptick in urgency, until their soft moans filled the air and the sheets beneath their bodies grew damp with sweat.

"Where do you want me?" Aubrey said in his ear.

"I was going to ask that," Calix said with a pout, so Ethaniel nipped his lip again. The flesh dented beneath his teeth and he pulled oh so gently, loving how that tiny spark of pain made Calix writhe and grip him harder. There were hands all over his body, warm and seeking for any sensitive areas. Trailing over his chest, down his back and sides. And there were two mouths dragging hotly over his skin. At any other time, he might have been overwhelmed by the dueling sensations; he often preferred to follow in a lover's wake, letting their passion — or their words — command him. Aubrey was a master of both, and Calix had shown to be less verbose and more physical in bed.

And right now, he wanted all of it. He wanted their delightful sounds, the glide of their bodies, the taste of their skin.

He didn't want safety or security. He didn't want to slow down or pause. He wanted to watch them take and let him take in return.

And he wanted all of them inside him.

Ethaniel tugged Calix on top of him while rolling to his back. Aubrey got to his knees behind Calix, who had gone bright pink about the cheeks, the color cascading down his fine throat.

Aubrey didn't waste time pulling Calix up until Calix's back was flush with his chest. His silver rings glowed in the soft light of a damp spring morning, and those *eyes* watched him closely.

"Isn't he lovely?" Aubrey said.

Ethaniel nodded. "Always," he replied softly, reaching up to undo the last few buttons on Calix's shirt, while Aubrey worked on the collar. With shaking hands, Calix gripped Aubrey's wrists but didn't get in the way of those long fingers plucking away at his clothing.

Ethaniel reached up to both of them, but Calix stopped him. "Put your hands on your thighs," Calix purred. He leaned back into Aubrey's touch, almost preening, and Ethaniel grew breathless at the sight. Calix was always pretty, especially when he was caught in the throes of lust, but a confident, smirking Calix was a sight to behold.

"I'll do anything you want," Ethaniel told him. "My fierce, fiery Oracle who rescued me from the pits of that place." He dug his fingers into his thighs, the temptation to *touch* so strong. But he had to watch as Aubrey slowly opened Calix's shirt, and each bit of skin revealed left Ethaniel squirming. Seeking any kind of friction, against any part of his body. *Anything* to rub against, rut against, if he couldn't have them right now.

"Tell me what he looked like," Aubrey said, voice gone low and tight. Those glass green eyes were hooded and dark, swirling with thick emotion and desire, and they were only focused on Ethaniel. "What did you see when Calix came for you, Ethaniel? Tell me."

"Like a dream," Ethaniel said. He didn't hesitate to dig the heel of his palm into his thigh; a poor substitute for how he wanted to touch his cock, but it was *something*. "Like a bright, golden dream."

Calix gasped, eyes fluttering shut, as Aubrey pushed his shirt away and set his lips to the soft spot under Calix's ear. Now Aubrey's hands roamed, and he left no bit of skin untouched, unteased. Fingers ran up and down Calix's arms, across his shoulders to sweep down his chest. Thumbs lingered over pink nipples, and when Calix groaned his pleasure, Aubrey smiled into his neck.

Ethaniel barely caught how Aubrey's hips shifted before he had an armful of warm Calix. "Such a cocktease," Ethaniel growled at him.

"Me.... or him?" Aubrey bit back, grinning fiercely. His hips were now pressed into Calix's backside and Calix arched into it. Caught between them. Perfect and lovely.

But Ethaniel wanted his Earl *under* him.

He kissed Calix hard, not stopping when Calix whimpered. But Calix kissed him back just as fiercely, and only when Calix ripped away to snap, "Fucking hell, Aubrey", did Ethaniel manage to suck in a lungful of air.

Aubrey looked pleased as punch, smug little smile and all. He leaned over Calix's back, getting into Ethaniel's face as much as he could to whisper, "Say please, Ethaniel, and we'll put you where you really want to be."

Any other night, he would have teased or distracted them. Anything to play up a bit of resistance. To watch them play along, of course, but to also tighten the tension a bit more. He might have traded sweet words or sharp swears or a mix of both to give them enough to soothe, but not satiate. He might have gotten to his knees as well, wedging Calix between them, and put his lips and tongue to all that skin. His hands would have wandered, taking in every dip and curve and bump of bone, and he would have kissed Aubrey over Calix's shoulder, fingers dug into Calix's hair.

Any other night, Aubrey and Calix would have earned his *please*.

But not tonight. They'd earned it already ten times over by saving him.

Ethaniel raised his arms over his head and stretched up until he could brace his palms on the cool wood of the headboard and simply said, "Please".

The moment Aubrey let Calix go, the younger man was hurriedly pulling Ethaniel's trousers from him. Ethaniel moved and lifted as Calix needed, and his clothes were tossed aside with everyone else's, and then Aubrey was pulling him up, leaving Calix to roll under them until he was splayed in the spot Ethaniel had abandoned.

The frantic energy between them continued to simmer, though all Ethaniel needed to feel was the trembling in Aubrey's fingers to know what bubbled under the surface. It was the same thing that would likely plague his dreams for many nights to come.

How were they all alive, and how close had they come to ruin?

Aubrey grabbed and pulled and Ethaniel went willingly, until they were face to face and Calix's hands were running up his backside, thin fingers gripping tight enough to leave red marks.

"I missed you both so much," Ethaniel said before Aubrey hauled him in for a blistering kiss. He groaned and leaned into it, into *Aubrey*, unable to stop the tidal wave of emotion and fierce need that swept through him. Aubrey's plush lips rendered him silent, but the moment that mouth left his to bite and lick the skin of his throat, Ethaniel couldn't help but moan Aubrey's name.

Aubrey kept moving — kissing, touching, licking, teeth grazing and forcing Ethaniel's frayed nerves to completely unravel. Every touch wound up him a little more, until he was weak-kneed, his cock throbbing.

"Get him ready," Aubrey said over Ethaniel's shoulder. Ethaniel glanced back to see Calix, already so pink about the face and neck, shudder and light up even more.

Calix got to his knees behind Ethaniel, leaned in, and whispered, "How do you want me?"

Ethaniel's mind went completely blank. He was no stranger to the more *illicit* of acts; the kind usually reserved for partners. It took quite a bit of trust and mutual adoration to use anything but one's fingers. But Calix was his, and he Calix's, and both of them Aubrey's and he simply *wanted*.

Ethaniel swallowed hard. "Your choice," he said, voice choked with all the tension in his body.

Calix smiled, then leaned in to kiss Ethaniel's shoulder. "So sweet for me. You come back from hell and still trust us."

He turned at that, and even Aubrey's touches slowed at Calix's words. "You brought me back," Ethaniel said, his mind spinning. "I... I would give you both anything, and I want you to know that for certain." The weight of Aubrey's gaze was like a second set of hands on him, so he looked back to find those eyes hooded and a little sad. "I would give you both anything. Everything. For all time."

Then he smiled, grinning even now with the stress and grief of everything leaching out into a desire to be held and touched and fucked in a way that reminded him of *everything* he'd fought for. "Can we save the emotions for later? I'm in quite a mood to be— "

"Taken?" Calix supplied.

Aubrey snickered at that, and the sound was light enough to make Ethaniel chuckle, too. "Taken. Claimed." He felt teeth in his shoulder; gentle, but persistent. Ethaniel arched into it and Aubrey moaned with appreciation and a heady dose of his own desire. "Plowed into the mattress works, too."

Calix collapsed against him, laughing. "We are hopeless."

Aubrey's voice had gone dark once more. Tempting. "Hmmm. Perhaps." Aubrey gripped Ethaniel's chin, forced him to meet that all-seeing gaze that always knew exactly what he needed. What he wanted. And right now, he knew Aubrey saw how desperate he was for both of them. "But if this is hopelessness, I know we only have better days ahead. The universe can't take so much and not give back."

Whether it was Aubrey's words of assurance or Calix's own need rising to the surface, something in the way Calix breathed out against Ethaniel's skin felt like a turning point. And the hands sliding down his back, light-fingered but with intent, told him a story written with the musk of warm skin and the press of soft sheets.

Ethaniel let Calix arrange his limbs as he pleased. And Calix *did* look pleased to have Ethaniel at his command, but it wasn't a hardship. Because from this vantage, on his back, Calix looked like a towering angel. He was beautiful in a way many men weren't; lithe and limber but quietly proud. Too proud to wear his beauty like a set of armor, even though it would have been simple and expected. But behind that beauty was a keen mind, sharp as any needle in Ethaniel's shop and twice as deadly.

He reached up for Calix, who fell into his arms and kissed him like they'd been parted for years and not a few days. Calix took up nearly all his attention, but he didn't miss how Aubrey, as nude as the day he was born, strode off into the attached washroom and came back with intent steps and a fire in his eyes, a small bottle in his hand.

"Go on," Aubrey softly commanded as he handed Calix the bottle. "He's waiting for you." Aubrey's voice was a sinful thing, slipping down Ethaniel's spine like it had never left for all those months they'd been apart.

"Don't leave Calix without the promise of your touch," Ethaniel said, reaching for Aubrey.

Aubrey easily interlaced their fingers, the warm metal of those rings smooth on Ethaniel's skin. "Trust me, I wasn't going to." His other hand now free of the bottle, Aubrey put his palm on Calix's ribs and slowly, gently slid it down. The touch made Calix pause in opening the vial, teeth sunk into his lower lip, eyes fluttering shut. Utterly rapturous, ensorcelled by Aubrey's warmth.

They looked like a painting. Lovers entwined. It made Ethaniel wish for artistic skill outside of cloth and pattern. Some way to capture it. His memory would have to serve, and if fate was kind, he'd have many more chances to watch Aubrey and Calix touch like this, kiss like this.

When Calix broke the kiss, he swooped down immediately to claim Ethaniel's mouth and whisper against his lips, "Spread your legs for me?"

"As my Earl commands," Ethaniel whispered back.

Calix's touch was tentative, but it took nothing to light Ethaniel's nerves on fire by this point. He watched Aubrey lay a line of kisses across Calix's shoulder and run an oil-slick palm down Calix's cock. With every twist of Aubrey's hand, Calix shivered and then pressed a little harder. They were a strange machine bound and run by a connection deeper than mutual attraction.

There was an echo of them in him, and he in them. Ethaniel felt the latent spark of it in the furthest recesses of his mind; a flicker of flame, the ghost of an old touch. If their mental connection was truly gone forever, that didn't mean the spark that birthed it was gone, too.

Ethaniel's breath hitched as Calix pressed inside his body with a finger, his hips twitching up, seeking more. Somewhere above him, Aubrey groaned and said, "How dare you be so pretty like that, Ethaniel."

Ethaniel tried to scoff at him but the noise caught in his throat as Calix nudged at him with a second finger. "Is this all right?" Calix asked. His big gold eyes were even bigger now and Ethaniel felt like falling into them, enraptured by the sight.

"Yes," Ethaniel hissed. It felt *so* good like this. He was warm and pliant, a liquid sense to his bones that felt *right*, and he wanted more.

Whatever Aubrey did next had Calix shuddering in his arms, that resonance traveling up through Ethaniel, too. "Is he torturing you?" Ethaniel teased between hard breaths.

"Only in the sweetest way," Calix breathed back. Behind him, Aubrey grinned into Calix's shoulder.

"You're sweet," Aubrey said as he pressed kisses to Calix's face. "Both of you."

Inside him, a sense of urgency built all over again. Calix's touch was sure now, steady, too, and quickly driving Ethaniel mad. He wasn't beyond begging. "Please," he said, tugging Calix back down into a kiss. It forced the angle of Calix's touch to shift and somewhere behind his eyes, the world went *white*.

The bed dipped and suddenly Aubrey was beside him, kissing him so fiercely, Ethaniel wondered if his lips would be bruised. He welcomed it; the rush of slight pain, the way Aubrey whispered, "Let me have you now, Ethaniel", and how his entire body ached to be filled.

Together, they got Calix down on his back and Aubrey behind him. Ethaniel took a moment to admire the flush in Calix's cheeks. "Gorgeous," he breathed before leaning forward and taking Calix's cock into his mouth.

Calix immediately tensed and let out a shocked, stuttering curse, but Ethaniel only felt *him*. He was surrounded by them now; Calix filling his senses, and Aubrey pushing two fingers inside him, a pleased sound escaping him while Ethaniel groaned around Calix's cock.

Careful, cautious hands made it into his hair, and another set of larger, more steady hands found his hips. There were lips on his spine and thighs clamped around his ears and Ethaniel finally, *finally* let himself be convinced he was home. He couldn't possibly hallucinate something like this.

No ichor. No blood. No Guardians or gates. No sentient book. Only them.

In the pass of a minute that could have been ten but maybe was five, the fingers in his hair tightened and the knot of pleasure at the base of his spine became a wash of heat. Aubrey was touching him everywhere, from his throat to his cock and back up, blazing a path over his skin as if he meant to memorize it.

Calix below him, panting and restless, said his name over and over again. Ethaniel let his eyes shut and let himself *feel*.

He felt when Calix went tight all over, his body locking up, then his breath releasing in one gust as he tipped over the edge. It nearly sent him toppling, too; to know he'd done that, had brought someone such pleasure. But his body was far too focused on the way Aubrey took him and took him apart, the thick weight of him inside nearly too much.

"You gave him that," Aubrey purred in his ear. "Gave our Earl so much pleasure. The sweat on his skin. How he smiles." Calix touched his cheek and Ethaniel felt something inside him *crack*. "Kiss him for me?"

Ethaniel tried not to collapse on top of a pink-cheeked, grinning Calix, and Aubrey gripped him all the more roughly to help him. It was just enough and it *wasn't* enough, those lips against his and the hands in his hair and how deep Aubrey was inside him.

He teetered. Caught between them. Desperate. Wanting.

"We have you," Aubrey said.

"Let it go, love," Calix murmured against his lips.

Ethaniel wept as he was plunged into a deep well of pleasure. He let it pull him under. Let it make him forget. And when the world returned and he was wedged between them with Calix's head on his chest and Aubrey's hand on his hip, Ethaniel managed to say, "I won't forget you saved me."

"There's not a version of us where we don't," came Calix's steady reply. "I don't think either of us works without you, Ethaniel." He held up his hand and Ethaniel saw that old silver band of his on Calix's thumb. "For luck, remember?"

Ethaniel could only smile and kiss him and whisper, "Keep it" in Calix's ear.

Aubrey was quiet for a long moment, but it gave Ethaniel a chance to untangle his thoughts. "Is it mad if I tell you both how much I care for you?" he asked. The lump in his throat made the words stiffer than he'd meant them. "Because I do."

Aubrey turned Ethaniel's head so they might look each other in the eyes. The pressure of those two points on his chin from Aubrey's thumb and forefinger *burned*. And that spark of familiarity came back, its blaze a little brighter now.

"As do I," Aubrey said. That gaze was so intent, so *open*, Ethaniel could not mistake the truth in those words.

Calix raised his head. "It's not mad," he said softly. "Who gets to dictate that other than us? If we all agree, and I do, by the way... I mean, feel that for you both. Intensely. It's truly more than I... " He broke away, looked down. When he raised his head again, there was a brightness in those gold eyes, but he seemed unable to keep speaking.

Neither he nor Aubrey needed Calix to. They all understood.

Chapter Nineteen

It wasn't until he was face to face with the strangest thing he'd ever seen did Lawton realize it. He should have been marveling at this Agrippa's human face surrounded by bright white feathers, or the neatly pressed green velvet suit, or their ankle-length white hair, or the eyes that looked like a conglomerate of stars in the inky blackness of space.

But looking at those eyes only reminded him of the darkness he felt slithering through his veins, so Lawton averted his gaze even as he proclaimed, "She's gone."

"She's not gone," Agrippa replied in that melodic voice that still somehow came across as clipped. "I'm suppressing her for the time being. At this rate, your body has two weeks left. Probably less."

Mortality rushed up to greet him with open arms, the shock of it lancing him. "What?"

Agrippa looked over, then down at him over half-moon glasses, one feathery hand heavy on an open book. "You'll need to clarify, I'm afraid. Are you surprised at my admission about the guest sharing your soul, or my statement on your physical decay?"

"Agrippa. Goodness." Magnus strode into the parlor where Lawton was still bound to the chair. "He's... well, not a guest, but you shouldn't abandon your manners."

"My understanding of the situation may not be complete, so I'm acting on information you've given me, Magnus. Manners have nothing to do with it, and the truth is rarely cognizant or caring of someone's *feelings*." They cocked their head at him, exactly like a bird might. A large bird, like a barn owl or some other bird of prey.

Lawton only raised an eyebrow at Magnus. In truth, the vines that held him fast to the chair weren't uncomfortable, but slung somewhere low in his body was a deepening ache, one that had been building to some massive crescendo since Lily had taken up residence. "Well, the shuttering of her undue influence is greatly appreciated," Lawton said while giving Agrippa a nod. "It's more than anyone else has managed so far."

Magnus shot him a look of utter loathing and he nearly laughed. It wasn't hard to play the object of ire even now, and annoying Magnus felt, in some small way, to be a little jab at Aubrey. One of the men who had swept Calix off his feet.

Welcome back, old friend, he thought bitterly. Jealousy was an ugly animal, but it was better than the loss of all hope. At least jealousy let him feel *something*.

Magnus placed a chair in front of Lawton but kept out of reach by a few more feet than the zero Lawton could currently manage. "You said you were attacked. By one of Vincent's agents."

"So someone *was* listening." Lawton choked back harsher words, but it was a near thing. His head felt blissfully empty for the first time in days, and while the marks across his skin had yet to shift in any noticeable way, the silence in his mind was enough to have him feeling charitable. "And her body is just down the hall. It's an ugly scene, so I wouldn't go in there after eating."

Magnus's face flickered through a few emotions: shock, confusion, then grim reality made him frown. He was a handsome man and his face did all sorts of interesting things as he stared at Lawton. "Did you kill her?"

"Of course not."

"And I'm to believe you."

Lawton gave an impotent shrug. "I'm covered in soot and ichor and what little blood is on me is on my trousers and shoes. The scene isn't exactly neat and tidy. I'd be covered in blood if I'd killed her."

Magnus turned to Agrippa. "Is he telling the truth?"

A pick of ice lodged in his stomach. Agrippa wasn't human, that much was clear, and stranger things had certainly happened of late. But the thought of someone other than Lily being able to *read his bloody mind* terrified him. He'd only gotten adjusted to her constant interference.

But Agrippa was another thing entirely. Was he going to feel the creature rustling about in his brain, searching for secrets? Would it seek out the ugly truths he'd spent so long burying? *Would it know what had happened in the bathroom, see his moment of weakness? Would it see him as he truly was, lowly and unrepentant?*

Lawton drew in a deep breath, then let himself look at Agrippa. And now instead of a bird of prey, he was staring at an impassable blank wall. Not a flicker of expression or emotion on their face. And he felt... *nothing*.

"Hmm." There was such a *human* quality to the way Agrippa flipped their hair over their shoulder; it was almost startling. "Well, he's certainly not the worst I've encountered. Petty schemes, mostly. A reputation for swindling." Their eyes flashed and the feathers around their face began to quiver and Lawton felt *something* alien inside his mind.

Lawton was completely certain in that moment, as he fell into Agrippa's endless gaze, that they were seeing everything he'd done to lead up to this point. The pain he'd caused. The people he'd fucked, ones he'd toyed with and the ones he'd let do the same with him. Eavesdropping at parties for secrets, or blackmail, or both. The burn of jealousy and what he'd thought, at the time, was righteous anger. Anger at losing what should have been his. *Who* should have been his.

And Agrippa could see it all, pulling down memories with the practice of a washerwoman at the laundry line. He was exposed, completely, and that vulnerability should have had him shrinking back. Instead, he felt a clinical eye overseeing the jigsaw pieces of his memory and piecing them together to find an entire picture. An entire *person*. Flawed, sometimes deeply, but still a person.

As quickly as it had come on, it was gone again, and he felt as if someone had forced him to look at the world upside down. "What a fascinating boy," Agrippa murmured as they leaned in. This close, Lawton expected a scent or a feeling of some sort, some way for him to categorize such a strange creature in a more human way. But there was nothing, only the void in their eyes and the slight rustle of feathers around their jaw.

And this close, he could see the teeth and by everything holy, he should have been afraid. Instead, he was enraptured.

"But yes," Agrippa said to Magnus, who was hovering in the background. "He's telling the truth. There's a dead woman down the hall. He didn't kill her but he certainly has a sordid past."

Fear should have glued his words to the sides of his throat. Whatever this creature was, whatever shock he was experiencing... something had shifted. It was a sensation he couldn't explain, new and somehow laced with dreadful, bloody *hope*.

Agrippa leaned in closer, now a few inches from Lawton's face. "A possession like this should have killed you within a day or so of exposure. How did this happen?"

Lawton could only stare and say, "Didn't you just raid my mind, like a thief in the night after the family jewels?"

His feebly mocking tone didn't rattle Agrippa in the least. "It was a rhetorical question, Mr. Adler, and nothing you need to worry about."

What in the hell was he supposed to say to that? "So, I'm supposed to be dead," he said, shifting in his bonds. He wanted free but didn't want to make Agrippa angry. "Do you know why I'm not?"

"I have a few theories," Agrippa said. Then, with no warning or ask, they ran their fingers through Lawton's greasy, soot-covered hair. A cloud of the stuff had settled in the room, thick as sawdust on a lumber mill's floor, and only Agrippa had kept away from it.

"Excuse you," Lawton snapped, only a mote of his energy behind the tone. He was too exhausted for any and all of this nonsense.

Agrippa held up their hand, their snow white palm a mess of black soot and.... red orange. The exact shade of his hair. "The void from the *demimonde* has a number of strange properties. I noticed a few months ago, during another experiment, that it also had a tendency to leach. You are the latest victim. It won't last long. Your hair may even get its color back."

Now fear settled in his bones like an old friend. "Care to explain?"

Agrippa smiled slightly, but it was less smile and more a corner of their mouth shifting up a touch. It certainly wasn't a *nice* expression. "Not yet. Magnus?"

When the other man didn't answer, Agrippa frowned, shifting out of Lawton's eyeline enough for him to see Magnus staring blankly at the bookshelf to the left of the fireplace. It was where Calix kept all his mother's journals and sketchbooks along with various tomes on art and architecture. But Magnus was glassy-eyed, staring up at the top shelf, hands limp at his sides.

Something about the entire tableau unsettled Lawton. "Could you untie me?" he asked Agrippa.

Agrippa answered him by waving a hand at him while approaching Magnus. "Magnus?" Concern slowly dripped into their voice; another, much more human behavior. "Magnus?"

The moment Agrippa touched his shoulder, Magnus startled and spun around. "Agrippa?"

Agrippa turned his back to Lawton, blocking Magnus from view, leaving Lawton to wriggle inside his bonds. "Nothing visibly wrong," Agrippa muttered, barely louder than the pop of wood in the fireplace. "Stay here."

They waved a feathered hand, there was the *snap* of what Lawton recognized as their magic on the air, and then Agrippa disappeared inside a slowly spinning silver portal to gods knew where.

Magnus sighed, then came over to Lawton. "I can free you, but if you cause trouble, Agrippa will put you back here."

"Understood." Lawton sat very still while Magnus coaxed the vines to fall limply from his body with a flicker of fingers and a brief burst of wind that smelled like burnt sugar.

Lawton made to stand but paused. When did magic ever have a smell? Sometimes there was a sensation, like champagne bubbles on the tongue, or a general feeling of warmth... but scent?

Magnus narrowed his eyes, his entire face now a mask of curiosity. "Admittedly we don't know each other well, but you strike me as someone who speaks your mind, Lawton. Yet right now, you withhold."

He tried to scoff. He did. But it came out stuttering and weak. "Hard to think with that being in the room," he snapped, twisting against the slowly loosening vines until he was able to rip himself free of their hold. "Bloody things. That really was inhospitable, you know. Tying me down like that."

Magnus didn't feed his complaint with a response. Not a curt word or even a raised eyebrow. It was such a *polite* slight and he almost laughed. Instead, he said, "Well, it's true. I could have done damage with that gun. The one *Aubrey* left me with, I'll remind you."

More silence. More staring. Expressionless, but not dazed like a moment ago. Lawton couldn't tell if Magnus was studying him, doing complicated sums in his head, or playing some mind game, but it was starting to grate. "Hello? Anyone there?"

After a few more long seconds that had Lawton considering slapping Magnus to shock him back to reality, Magnus finally said, "How odd. Agrippa? Could you come back, please?"

That same silver, swirling portal popped into place, and Agrippa stepped out. They were now wearing a deep plum vest and trousers, their shirt the perfect gray of a rainy London afternoon. The deep colors were shocking against their skin, hair, and feathers, and Lawton caught himself staring.

"You felt it, too?" Magnus nodded, and Agrippa rubbed their chin, gaze intent once more on Lawton. It sat there, heavy and *very* present. A strange albatross.

"Would either of you like to inform me of the specifics? I feel as if I'm an insect under a microscope," Lawton groused. He hadn't moved from his chair, not with how Magnus and Agrippa were staring at him, but now he forced himself to his feet, only to stand before them and say, "Well?"

Agrippa smoothed back the feathers around their face. "To put it bluntly, I think you're a magnet for magic. I think the reason you didn't perish in the hours after Lily's possession is because of this… strange type of absorption. *You* are not arcane in any way, but you've been exposed to very strong powers of prognostication over the course of a few decades. Oracle magic is arcane power in a raw, unfiltered form, and it has slowly seeped into you. It guarded you, however incidentally, simply by its nature."

"So not sympathy, but… adaptation?" Magnus asked. What he said meant nothing to Lawton, but the concern on Magnus's face was enough to make him worry. "That would be remarkable. And would open up all new fields of arcane study."

"I would classify it as a kind of confluent sympathy, made up of disparate parts that somehow become whole. Meaning if any one piece was missing, the end result would have never happened. Whether it is a byproduct of bad luck or some other influence, I can't say."

While Lawton silently begged his mind to catch up with the new reality laid before him, he watched Agrippa hold up a thin disc in front of his face. The disc itself was made of some deep gray, hammered metal and was etched with symbols that made Lawton's head swim just by looking at them.

"An invention of my namesake," Agrippa said.

While they stared at the disc expectantly, Magnus said, "Like a dowsing rod for magic. It's not terribly accurate after all these centuries, but it— "

He was cut off by a sound like metal squeaking against glass, and Magnus and Lawton both shrunk back from the disc, which was now glowing a deep orange. Or, rather, a few runes on the disc were glowing, but so brightly they engulfed the entire thing.

"Though it can be accurate in the face of very strong arcane energy," Magnus finished quietly.

"Like I said. He's a magical sponge, if you will, and even more so now that he's been branded like that." They motioned to Lawton's chest.

Lawton was too warm, and he pulled at his soot-covered collar. Anything to relieve the mounting, horribly hot pressure building inside his chest. *Was this what real fear felt like*? "So… what do I do?"

"For now, we suppress Lily. We resolve the outstanding issues. And then you will come with me to my end of the Collectio for further study." Agrippa crossed their arms over their chest and then delivered the fatal blow. "She's too deeply embedded now, and it will take precision and careful extraction to ensure you return to yourself."

Lawton blinked. "So, I'm a prisoner?"

Agrippa shrugged and Magnus looked aggrieved. "No. Prisoners cannot leave. You can. But you know the consequences if you do."

He couldn't stop himself. "Which are?"

The stare he got in reply could have scalded geysers. "An ugly, very painful death in roughly three to seven days, starting the second I stop suppressing your possessor."

Death? Lawton nearly laughed. He'd nearly missed an appointment with Lady Death many times, from the fever that had swarmed their household when he was six to the time a bolting stallion charged him to the few close calls he had while sneaking out of windows at least two stories off the ground. Mostly cheap thrills, since he'd been very sure, until very recently, that he wasn't capable of dying young. But looking back on them now? So many little brushes with death that only Luck had kept him from the worst of.

And now, the good Lady Death was staring him in the face, taunting him to cross over to her.

He was, if nothing else, supremely defiant.

"Can you get rid of her?" Lawton asked, even as his throat closed up with some beautiful, horrible amalgamation of dread and stubbornness, laced with righteous anger.

"I make no guarantees," Agrippa said. "My magic isn't what it used to be. But she is weak and clinging to you by the tips of her fingernails. That was the only reason I was able to suppress her to begin with. Though... " They broke off and glanced toward Magnus. "You may wish to have a conversation with her son before too much else occurs. We're not free of the things grasping for our necks, at least not yet."

Lawton watched them go to Magnus, whisper something in his ear, then turn and disappear into the adjoining hall, leaving Magnus looking worried. "Was it something I said?" Lawton asked.

Magnus startled, then chuckled. "Hardly. Trust me when I say you are not the one causing them all manner of vexations. To Agrippa, you are a problem to solve. An equation, if you don't mind me putting it so bluntly. Things aren't so simple with others." And he gestured toward himself.

Lawton couldn't say he was surprised, given the strange frequency he'd sensed between Magnus and Agrippa. Not lovers, but more than friends. And quite like he and Calix had been for so long; strung together with the thinnest of threads, but able to withstand so much.

With a sigh so faint, Lawton almost swore he was hallucinating, Magnus picked up a nearby chair and set it down in front of where Lawton was seated. "Now, I need you to tell me what happened with Vincent's lackey, and leave nothing out." Lawton made to speak, but Magnus held up a finger. "There are beings in this house far more powerful than I, but I'm the only one who can separate the chaff from the wheat, so to speak. So don't lie, Lawton."

Oh, how he wanted to lie. How he wanted to leave some things out of his line of truth, abandoned like an irksome dog on the side of the road. But the fever pitch of the last few days, coupled with the brightness in Magnus's eyes, made him realize how dire the situation could yet be.

He wasn't interested in further suffering, particularly not his own.

"She's been in my mind," Lawton began, "and I can't shake her loose."

Chapter Twenty

MAGNUS

An hour later, Magnus's heart was heavier than it had been in some time. Perhaps in the entirety of his life, though it was a close call between this and the death of his brother. But, a member of his chosen family was in grave danger and Magnus didn't have the heart for that conversation right now. Even though every instinct in his body screamed with urgency, with the need to run to Aubrey and shake him awake and make him listen to every detail.

A complicated web was woven between them all, and Magnus needed only to pluck a single strand to cause ripples in every line. But he couldn't do that without rest. And if he was being completely honest, delaying the inevitable was something he could do with only one hard conversation at a time.

His choices were between waking Aubrey or facing Agrippa. Agrippa's wrath was a blow he deserved; none of the men on the second floor deserved what he needed to tell them.

All Magnus had to do was follow the tingling trail of Agrippa's magic down the hall, to the glass observatory on the back of the estate. It was a lovely sight, even in the gloom of a rainy spring afternoon and pockmarked by deep blue and red pots of plants that had long dried up. A few dead leaves were scattered across the dark gray tile floor.

Standing in the middle of the room, Agrippa had their back to Magnus, their hands loose at their sides. He took the time to admire the perfectly straight line of their spine, the exacting fit of the suit, and marvel in how very *human* Agrippa so often appeared. It was hard not to admire them, but that was his modus operandi when around Agrippa most days.

Right now, though, that admiration had teeth and they were sunk, muscle-deep, into his heart. There was a charge in the air between them, and it wasn't only because of the storm outside. No, he'd had Agrippa's magic *inside* him, and even though he'd returned it, there was still a nest for it inside his chest.

Magnus took a few steps forward at the same time he let out a breath. "I'm afraid this little adventure isn't over yet."

Agrippa didn't move. Didn't turn to look at him. Simply said, "The boy talked, then?"

"He did." The longer Magnus stared at it, the more the straight line of Agrippa's back bothered him. Agrippa was a creature of rigidity and focus doused with a hefty serving of stubbornness. They were not unyielding, however; and yet, that proud, stiff profile sat like a hot coal in the vicinity of his stomach.

Agrippa's silence was heavy between them, and it felt so terribly like dread. Like waiting for the other shoe to drop. Magnus was beginning to edge into the territory of impatience when they finally said, "Did he tell you he tried to take his own life? Or, rather, threatened it and then made a grave error."

Magnus couldn't help but flinch. He wasn't sure if it was the act itself, or the methodology used, that bothered him more. "He did. A rather vulnerable admission. He also said something or someone stopped him, likely Lily, since she had the most to lose if Lawton died."

Agrippa's refusal to look at him bored a hole between his lungs. The pain curled with an edge of sweetness. Of denial. But it was wielded with a secondary bitterness, from years of denying themselves what they truly wanted. And in this moment, Magnus felt delirious with it: with anger, with fear, with dread, yes, but mostly with the utter foolish adoration he felt for Agrippa.

Adoration. Admiration. Affection.
Utterly and wholly enamored.

But they'd traded nothing more than bottles of wine by the fire, stories, and a handful of exhilarating experiences tracking down rare magical artifacts. Or so the lie he told himself every fortnight or so went. Because in the dark, quiet moments between breaths, between the lands of waking and sleeping, Magnus knew how deep his adoration was dug. He *knew*.

Maybe that knowing was the propellant for him walking up to Agrippa's right side to stare at their profile and say, "You're angry with me."

Agrippa's nostrils flared. Some part of him was giddy at the thought of being in Agrippa's line of fire. All that bottled fury was far better than the dispassionate countenance they'd been clinging to these last several minutes.

"I'm furious," Agrippa whispered as they clenched their fists at their sides. Perhaps he was imagining it, or it was the haze from the small woodstove nearby, but Magnus swore their form flickered, rippling with energy.

"Care to tell me— "

"You know why," Agrippa snapped, jerking their head to the right to stare at him. "You *know* why."

He could joke. Tease Agrippa on how they groused about Magnus vexing them on the regular. About that low-slung, but constant, simmering tension between them.

He didn't have the heart for it. Not now.

"What you did reverberated across the *demimonde*," Agrippa said in that angry whisper. "You were reckless. You disregarded my concerns about you going in the first place, and then you took that dagger into the place of its creation and... what? Simply hoped it would all work out?" Now they whirled on him, so fiercely beautiful. Radiating power. "You gave the *demimonde* something."

He couldn't lie, even if he wanted to. "I did."

"Do you care so little about your own mortality?"

Gods, those galaxy eyes were *endless* and Magnus was quickly losing himself in the slow swirl of power. But their question slapped him across the cheek. Magnus had to press a palm there; his skin was feverish even though Agrippa hadn't laid a finger on him. "You know that's not it," he said softly.

"Don't I?" Agrippa was close now. Close enough to touch. Close enough that Magnus need only reach up to brush his fingers across the feathers at their jaw. "Why, then? Why risk yourself— "

"You and I both know that place has no rules but the ones made by the monsters. You knew our chances were slim."

"They weren't zero."

Magnus smiled a little at that. Even now, this close, Agrippa vibrated with annoyance, but he had enough experience with their moods to see the warmth at their edges. It was irritated, maybe even angry warmth; fuel on a fire, instead of a cozy blaze. "I did what was needed to ensure the right outcome. Surely you see the wisdom in that."

Agrippa sucked in a sharp breath. "This line of rationale is fractured, Magnus. You took too many chances."

Magnus edged closer. The very air between them *burned*. It made his chest heavy, made him aware of *everything* about Agrippa. "I did what was needed. I couldn't leave a Harkness inside that place." Agrippa reared back as if struck, so he pressed on. "I couldn't — and wouldn't — walk away from that scenario any more than I could not help Aubrey. You know how much affection I hold for him. But no, ultimately I didn't do it even for Aubrey alone." He wanted to touch. "I couldn't let the *demimonde* have a Harkness," Magnus repeated.

Agrippa looked away, and the thread of tension between them snapped. He felt it reverberate down his spine. "You cannot logic your way out of this, Magnus."

The aching, yearning need to *touch* won out over caution or worry. Magnus stroked two fingers down Agrippa's jaw, from sharp corner to chin, watching the white feathers there bend to his touch. They looked down at him, eyes slightly wide, brow furrowed.

What Magnus wouldn't give to stare into those eyes for the rest of his days. The *demimonde* had been given some of his mind in exchange for their escape; a sliver, but enough. He could feel it immediately upon their return, in how reality flickered at its edges. And maybe, as he grew older, his mind would slip even further into fog. He could only hope Agrippa would be there for him, stubbornly badgering him into drinking different tonics and undergoing little tests to find new solutions. He'd bear it all with a smile and with the way love curled sweet and hot in his chest at their mere presence.

It shouldn't be this easy or simple to feel these things for a being far removed from humanity, but in truth, they weren't. Agrippa *loved* humans and chose isolation to help keep the *demimonde* at bay, to keep it from bleeding into the human world. A human very likely wouldn't choose the self-sacrificing path. In fact, he didn't know anyone outside of Ethaniel who would, and he only knew that about the tailor because he'd already made a similar choice in tossing aside his arcane heritage. Humans were ugly, vain, selfish creatures. Agrippa was a curious being, and not immune to self-interest (or self-aggrandizement), but their very nature was predominantly antithesis to what made people so utterly *human*.

And because the *demimonde* was a constantly ravenous beast, and it consumed all in its path, and because Agrippa felt a responsibility toward it and to the few humans they knew, they stood in its way day in and day out. The feast the *demimonde* wanted was contained by Agrippa and a handful of others across the globe. Their mission had purpose, had meaning, but like with so many good deeds, it was done in secret.

Magnus had a similar edict, as part of his role as the head curator of the Collectio. Working with Agrippa was part of the job. But the affection? That had grown over the years. And now he had them in the palm of his hand, transfixed.

"I did what I thought was best," Magnus repeated, voice spring wind-soft. "I did what was needed. I can only hope you'll be willing to help me, but I'll understand if not. I know it's not fair of me to ask that of you, but— "

Agrippa turned into his touch and said, "You are the most stubborn human I know."

"And how many humans do you know?"

They nuzzled into his hand, some human-bird combination of trust and closeness. His heart swelled at the sight. "I think you're being very stubborn right now," they huffed, their breath warm on his palm.

Magnus slipped an arm around their waist, but he did so with his heart pounding in his ears. "You're the most stubborn person or being I know, so that must be quite a lot."

Galaxy eyes slowly blinked open, boring into him. Into his soul. His very *essence*. He was drowning in it. "Why must you vex me so?"

He had no answer other than to push up and press his mouth against theirs. And he was home.

Their kiss was brief. Soft and warm with a buzzing undercurrent of electricity that made Magnus aware of every atom of his body. It tasted a little like his magic and Agrippa's; mint and tea and small, cautious hope.

"I know this is how humans show affection," Agrippa said once they parted. They had one feathery hand on Magnus's shoulder, the other loose at their side before those fingers trailed up his arm. "I understand it to be possibly a sign of more."

Magnus raised an eyebrow, trying not to chuckle. Granted, his heart was still attempting to burst free from his chest, but Agrippa looked so baffled, he couldn't stand to tease them. "It's a sign of affection from me, to you," he replied, "and I'm leaving the door open for you, so to speak." Agrippa's galaxy eyes were so enchanting and he felt dizzy at the slowly churning sight of them.

"I will need to... understand more," Agrippa said slowly, as if every word needed to be weighed before spoken aloud. "Love is a universal language for humans. I've seen this displayed over and over again, written in the basest and most florid of terms in all the books and plays and poems. I've come to..."

They looked away and the swell of affection Magnus felt was almost too much. He had wondered if Agrippa, an exiled Guardian of the *demimonde*, was able to feel anything in the equivalent. Or if, perhaps, Guardians had their own form of affection, and if so, how it might translate to the intricate web that was human emotion.

The pained expression on Agrippa's face spoke of confusion, yes, but also a need to understand. Maybe to even experience something like that emotion roiling through him.

Magnus took their feathery hand in his and interlaced their fingers, one at a time, timed one by one to his breaths. To give them a chance to pull away, to object. But they watched their hands link in silence, as placid and still as stone.

"I can't tell what you're thinking," Magnus whispered. If he spoke too loudly, he was afraid he'd rattle the very windows with the force of his yearning.

"And you wish me to say it aloud?"

They were curious, not upset, and the realization helped Magnus breathe a bit easier. "Only if *you* wish to," he replied. "I seek nothing but the promise of your company from time to time, Agrippa. And perhaps, some of those times, we are... physically close. No more than you wish to be."

Their gaze drifted up, a dreamy quality to it. Or maybe it was simply how much his head was spinning at what had just happened. *Dizzy like a child in a dandelion field.*

"I think I am so different from you. From any human. And then I try to reckon that with what just happened, and the math is incomplete," Agrippa said quietly. "So that makes me question if the equation is wrong to begin with." They looked down, frowning. "This metaphor is needless. I am confused but glad, Magnus. You made something I have questioned myself on many times a reality, and you did it without so much as a 'By your leave'."

Magnus grinned. "Good to know you still like that phrase."

"I haven't used it in nearly a week. You speak as if I say it daily."

"You did. For a while."

Agrippa huffed but didn't pull away. Instead, they reached out to his face. The softest, gentlest brush of feathers against his cheek made Magnus feel all wobbly about the knees. There was something like wonder written across Agrippa's face, and he might have marveled at it, but that expression only made him want them more. Carnality was a distant thought (never mind the mechanics involved or the difficulty therein if their parts didn't *interlock*). He'd thought of it as a yearning for so long, and standing here with Agrippa's fingers tracing his jaw, a sense of completion washed over him.

Magnus had always been the odd one out. Brilliant, affable, but more comfortable in the corners than in the center or on the edges. It was why he had asked Aubrey to be the face of the Collectio. Why he'd been at the top of all his classes but largely unknown by most other students. Why he'd faded into the grey middle of a pack of siblings all vying for Mummy and Daddy's attention and money.

Here, now, he could take up space. That space Agrippa had offered the moment they'd met, twenty-eight years ago in the belly of the Collectio. Agrippa had never once made him feel inconsequential or membrane-thin. Of course, those he managed at the Collectio never made him feel that way, either, but this was *different.*

Effulgent.

An electric rhapsody.

And in the thick cloud of his mind, as he tumbled all this over and over again in that space, Agrippa watched him. Magnus was aware of their attention, of the deep pull of their gaze, and yet all the while, they were so utterly patient.

"I'm sorry," Magnus finally said, voice a little rough. "I seem to have gotten a bit lost."

"Every human I have ever met needs that time and space in different ways," Agrippa replied. Their hand had drifted down to rest on his shoulder and Magnus felt the warm weight of it sink into him, obliterating any cushion his jacket and shirt might have offered.

"I need more than most, I think."

Agrippa made a noise; a tonal thing, soft and low and like agreement. Their version of a hum, Magnus had come to learn over the years, when long stretches of time bent over the same table or artifact or even book had coaxed that noise out. It also usually signaled when Agrippa was about to say something rather bluntly. It wasn't difficult to guess what it would be about this time.

"You shouldn't have done what you did," Agrippa said as they gripped his upper arms. A claiming, not a bruising, hold. "You should have come back, reassessed."

He had at least five arguments on the tip of his tongue, but what fell out was, "Do you think your siblings would have allowed for that? Truly?"

Agrippa drew back a little bit, any trace of softness now gone from their face. They looked stern. Sad. "I would have found a way. It wouldn't have been the first time I snuck someone in under Uzala's notice."

Magnus frowned at that. "Only Uzala?"

Agrippa nodded. "They are the Mapmaker of that place, writing their wandering paths through the mists on their body. They count and track; occupants, unwanted guests, the branches on the ichor trees Uriel built long ago. Or they did, until Uriel forced their split. It has made them fractured, which I could have used to our advantage."

Magnus couldn't help but pull them closer. They went without protest, but the center of their eyes started to spin more quickly, and the feathers around Agrippa's jaw were puffed up. Magnus let his previous words rest for a moment longer before saying, "And in that same time, we could have lost one, or some, or all of them. A risk I was not willing to take, when the cost on my part was so low."

With a strength not belied by their willowy frame, Agrippa closed the distance between them, drawing Magnus tight against their body. They said nothing, nor did they need to.

Magnus felt the same way.

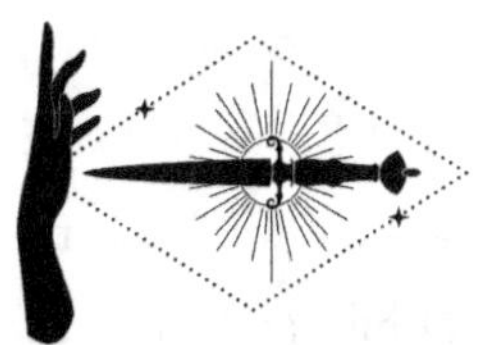

Magnus carried a tray into the small bedroom at the back of the estate and set it down to the side, then pulled the desk chair next to the bedside. With a flick of his hand, the tray floated from the table to hover in front of Vincent.

"It turns out, being besieged in a home like this means a full pantry and a well-appointed kitchen. So, we were never at risk of starving. You're lucky. Desperation begets... well, rather ugly things."

Vincent was sitting up on the bed, back against the headboard. His bruised face decorated with cuts still managed to bear a look of faint contempt. Magnus almost laughed. "You know, I'm not surprised you're in the middle of this, head of the Collectio and all."

Magnus gave Vincent a thin smile. "I'm afraid we haven't properly met, even after all these years of your *silent* reign at the Golden Order," he said, voice calm and flat like a frozen lake. He wasn't easily rattled from his moorings, but knowing Vincent couldn't break free from the manacles Agrippa had manifested was a relief. But the imperious way Vincent held himself made it clear: he also wasn't a man easily rattled, even after what he'd been through.

Agrippa had helped Magnus patch Vincent up and had now gone to deal with the unfortunate soul pinned to Calix's floors. He thought they'd argue against him interrogating Vincent alone. Agrippa's mind and talents were better suited for dealing with the body, which they both knew; what neither of them had to say aloud was that the promise of a magical mystery was like catnip to them. Which left him to weigh Lawton's story against anything he could get from the head of the Golden Order. A tall hurdle, but not an impossible one.

"This looks a bit dodgy," Vincent said as he poked the bread roll with a finger. "How do I know you're not trying to poison me?"

Magnus almost laughed but then considered things from Vincent's point of view. Killing him might truly be to their advantage, since they had a full-blooded Harkness in their ranks and that man was Vincent's half-brother. Necromancy was a lucrative hobby for that family, and while Ethaniel hadn't shown any aptitude for such dark magic, it wouldn't have been *completely* out of line with recent events.

"Honestly, you don't," Magnus said as he finally took his seat. "The only person here you have any close knowledge of is Ethaniel, and he's a full Harkness, not half of one."

The scowl on Vincent's face was directed at his tray, but it radiated with a hot whip of anger and self-righteousness. And Magnus actually *felt* Vincent's anger, which was startling in itself, since Ethaniel had said the man had no magic to speak of. But this was magic; like a distant echo of a fire in a cave long ago, forgotten to the winds of time, but existing in a thin space of memory buried deep in Vincent's skin.

The back of Magnus's neck prickled with awareness. Something was off about this entire thing, and he was rather sick of surprises. Magnus decided directness was a better route, so he leaned forward and said, "Do you resent him? Ethaniel, I mean. I've wondered that since the moment we found out about the relation. If it was me, I would feel slighted, certainly. Maybe I'd even question the reputation my family had built around their power, because surely the great and mighty and feared Harknesses had enough magical blood to spare. Surely they could make up for such a loss in other ways."

Vincent set down the roll, leaned back once more, and crossed his arms over his chest. "I let myself be angry as a child and teenager. I'm far removed from such concerns. My work with the Order is paramount now."

The steely gaze, the defensive posture, the clipped tone. Magnus would have bet Vincent was as uncrackable as one of the Collectio's vaults, but he was an injured thing now — physically, mentally, emotionally. And had it been anyone else, he might have not done this. Might have refused the interrogation entirely.

But Vincent was the cause behind all this chaos and pain and blood. Magnus couldn't fill a broken cup with the sandy remains of his empathy. Not for this man.

From his jacket pocket, Magnus pulled out a small marble the color of moss and palmed it. Aside from Agrippa, no one else knew he had it, knew it existed, and even if they'd been privy to all that, they would have no idea what it was. But Parsimonious's Sphere was an incredible tool made by a wizard of foul heritage and intent. It had lived in Agrippa's section of the Collectio since 1624, one year to the day after its invention.

The Occult Hunters, led by Parsimonious Appel, had begun in Hungary. Appel, a minor English lord, had certainly taken after the definition of his first name and been so terribly stingy that his estate collapsed. Appel blamed his misfortunes on a woman who had spurned his advances, called her a witch, and had been the propellant of her demise (which involved a field of cows sickened by rotten hay, a mob, and a short run of rope). Once the villagers had come to their senses and understood what Appel had done — a miracle in and of itself, such introspection — they ran him out of town, and eventually the man made his way across Europe, selling his "witch and occult mage hunting services" to any unfortunate with ill family or rotting crops.

The Occult Hunters had been blamed for dozens of deaths, some only loosely connected to the group and others the direct cause. But while the Occult Hunters were only occasionally successful in finding a witch or mage, they always used dark magic to do so. Oh, the unsubtle, unsurprising irony of it all. And Appel was the most prolific user, to the point that historians suspected a dormant ember of magical talent inside himself was ignited, and it was off to the races. Appel, or Parsimonious as he preferred to be called, invented all sorts of nasty little tools to help him interrogate alleged witches, mages, connected family or friends, or even his own witnesses and sources.

Magnus held the marble up for Vincent to see. *Desperate times*, he thought. *Because I know this isn't over.* "Your right hand, Cassandra, is indeed dead in another part of the house. I want to know why, and who did it."

Vincent's gaze searched his for a moment, and Magnus read a flurry of emotions there: surprise, confusion, mistrust, denial. And then like a snake's, that gaze flattened. Magnus, from a young age, was no stranger to such looks, but this oddly wasn't aimed at him. It was the locking of a door that had already been firmly wedged shut.

"Ask the con man friend of your Oracle," Vincent said calmly. "He was here when it happened, apparently. I was not." He gestured with a bandaged hand, then smiled and showed off his missing teeth. "But I think you know that already. Try asking me something more interesting."

Magnus choked down another laugh. This was the feared head of the Golden Order? He was a cult leader in a fancy suit; a lion tamer with no lion. No one had ever been sure if Vincent de Laine was magically talented or not, but he was known for a steadfast, iron will and a sharp mind (and tongue). What he had in front of him was the broken, bitter remnants of that man. It was a fascinating paradox.

"All right, we both agree on Lawton's, er... typical nature. Then, do you know why would Cassandra be here?"

"I have no idea. She was supposed to be on another assignment."

"Did she know the estate's location?"

Vincent almost smiled at that. "She did not. She didn't need to. Cassandra was Lawton's handler until she wasn't. Once ties are broken in the Order, they stay that way."

He'd take one more stab at this, and then let the sphere do its work. "How ruthless of you. We'll skip over Cassandra for now." Magnus conjured up a ghostly replica of the description of the red-haired woman Lawton had provided. It was a watery thing, but enough to go by. "Who is this?"

All pretense from Vincent's face dropped and he stared at the conjured image. The shock written there felt like a victory. "I don't know."

"I'm afraid I don't believe that. One, because your face says otherwise, and two, because she was able to do things I've only ever heard connected to a single word: Dreamwalker."

"What does it matter?" Vincent asked, suddenly arrogant and downright rude. "Dreamwalkers aren't unheard of in magic communities. They're far more common than Oracles."

"I'll concede that point, but here's where I don't care about those little facts." Magnus stood, moved the chair back and then sat on the edge of the bed. Vincent tensed against his bonds and Magnus wasted no time in flicking a hand out. The manacles were snapped taut instantly and Vincent's arms and legs were pinned flat to the bed, leaving him on his back, vulnerable. Vincent yelled out in pain and shock, giving Magnus a chance to hold his other hand out so the marble could lift off his palm.

Now fear sparked in Vincent's eyes. "Whether you know what this little thing is or not, it doesn't matter," Magnus said as the sphere slowly spun. "If you won't answer truthfully, then I'll extract the truth from you. My line in the sand, my good man, is when those I care about are harmed. I'm no role model, but I do have a creed." He gave the sphere a little mental flick and a moment later, it hovered right above Vincent's nose. "But even decent men with a decent set of rules to live by get pushed to their limits. And you are no better angel, I'm afraid."

He didn't give Vincent a moment to object or yell. With a final push, the sphere entered Vincent's left eye and Magnus was given answers to every one of his questions.

Chapter Twenty-One

The fingertips tracing over his arm were warm but worn. Aubrey felt the small, raised bumps and ridges skip over his skin, the sensation pleasant enough to have him burrowing deeper into the pillows.

And then his mind caught up with his reality.

The body beside him was undeniably Ethaniel's; broad of shoulder, smelling like lavender and salt and sex. And those fingertips were broad, too, and steady. But aside from a few old nicks and burns, Ethaniel's fingertips had never been so heavily scarred.

Slowly, Aubrey opened his eyes to see Ethaniel, face bandaged and bruised, staring at him with a gentle smile. "You must truly be tired," Ethaniel said, voice rough from sleep, "because you let me stroke your arm for a few minutes before you woke up."

"I'm not that light of a sleeper," Aubrey said.

Ethaniel only grinned. The expression made his lips stretch and Aubrey waited for him to hiss and pull back in pain. Ethaniel did nothing of the sort.

"And now I'm curious why that makes you grouchy," Ethaniel said.

Aubrey just shook his head, but it was impossible not to smile. Ethaniel was home. Whole. Safe. And they had so much to figure out, so much to do, but Aubrey was intent on showing Ethaniel how much he cared. A silent promise that he wouldn't let anyone come between them, and this time, they had a perfect, beautiful, kindhearted third in the form of Calix.

It shouldn't work. But it would. Who better than the three of them to come to terms with their sudden, incredible arrangement? To make it new in the face of surviving horrible dangers and terrors? They could now figure out who they were *together*. How to balance their lives, their interests with one another's. It would be a wholly new experience for all of them. What started at the auction house had metamorphosed into something drawn with bright colors but painted wholly outside the lines. Now, they had time for lines, and boundaries, and anything else they desired.

And with all those thoughts rattling about his mind, Aubrey still noticed the scars on Ethaniel's fingertips.

When Ethaniel passed his fingers up Aubrey's arm, Aubrey gently wrapped his hand around Ethaniel's wrist and brought that hand closer to his face so he could get a better look. There were indeed ridges and pockmarks of scar tissue across Ethaniel's fingers, many of the marks white with age. But there were also more scars: down his fingers, across his palms, even into the soft, thin skin on the inside of Ethaniel's wrists.

Aubrey's heart was stuck in his throat, but he managed to say, "Ethaniel? What are these from?"

Ethaniel had gone rather sallow in the face while Aubrey had investigated the marks, and neither one of them noticed Calix enter the room. "Is something wrong?"

Ethaniel let Aubrey shift them until they were both sitting up against the headboard, staring at Calix. The poor man's eyes were sunken with exhaustion, the dark circles under them stark against pale, freckled skin, and now, Calix was staring at them with apprehension.

"Nothing quite so bad," Aubrey reassured them both. "But Ethaniel... did these come from the *demimonde*?"

Ethaniel let Calix look his fill, then pulled the younger man down with them until they could sit in a triangle. "It's not from the *demimonde*, not directly maybe," Ethaniel said. "Both of you can stop worrying. I'm not going anywhere."

Calix turned to Aubrey, a sad smile gracing his fine features. "I don't know about you, but I'm tempted to tie him to us somehow."

The pain in Calix's words was so terribly evident. All Aubrey wanted was for their safety. All he could hope for was their affection. And all he desired was to have them against him, in the dark nocturnal hours and during sunlit winter days and every moment in-between.

Aubrey knew it then, as sure as he knew his name and his heritage, that they were fated for each other.

"As promising as that sounds from a carnal perspective," Aubrey said, making Calix chuckle and Ethaniel give a rusty laugh, "I don't think we need to, dove. He's here."

Ethaniel picked up Calix's hand and kissed the back of it. "I'm not going anywhere." Then he sighed, carefully put Calix's hand down, and turned over both of his. "They're old scars. Somehow, they've come back. If I had to guess, it's some strange effect of the *demimonde*. The energy of that place is... beyond any words we have, I think."

Aubrey caught Calix give the bandaged wound on Ethaniel's face a look before he ran a fingertip over a long scar across Ethaniel's left palm. Ethaniel shivered. "Where did you get them?" Calix asked.

Something like *hesitation* flickered across Ethaniel's face. "If you don't want to tell us, we'd never force you," Aubrey said, wrapping Ethaniel's big hand between his two. "Recent events have proven to be a significant source of adventure and drama. An old story of yours isn't something we need to feed that fire."

Ethaniel paused for a moment, then gave a laugh that sounded as though it had been wedged between two parts of a sob. He tipped his head to Aubrey, and Aubrey didn't hesitate to capture Ethaniel's lips. His lover was as sweet and pliable as always, but there was a thick undercurrent of nerves from him that Aubrey wanted to calm. He'd been through so much lately, an ugly story from his past was nothing that needed airing right now, or perhaps ever.

Aubrey kept the kiss gentle, more reassurance than anything else, and after a few seconds he pulled away. Ethaniel blinked up at him and whatever hesitation had been there had faded.

"It's part of learning patterning," Ethaniel said as he rubbed his fingers together. "We're taught to pattern first with pencil, tracing patterns over and over again, each one a little more complicated than the last. Then we spend months memorizing, so we can redraw them from memory. The first few years of my apprenticeship were grueling, I won't lie. But there were times when I felt as if the whole thing was more difficult for me, next to everyone else."

Ethaniel shook his head, his hair falling into his face, and Aubrey brushed it back. Ethaniel's grateful smile quivered at the edges. "It didn't take long after I started my studies. I began dreaming in patterns," Ethaniel continued, "and I was told that was normal. Fine, even. 'The sign of someone meant to be a patterner.'" Here, he paused and Aubrey didn't hesitate to edge closer. He saw Calix do the same, but if Ethaniel noticed, he did so at a distant horizon.

"But every now and then, there was this darkness that crept in. Like the periphery would suddenly grow black and I could feel the weight of it, pressing and pushing down, until I would wake up gasping for air and clawing at my throat."

Whatever lay unspoken between Ethaniel and the end of this story, of how the scars came to be, made Aubrey's stomach tighten. He didn't think for a moment that it would be any kind of happy revelation. "Ethaniel, you don't have to go on."

"No, I very much do. If only for selfish reasons. If only because I hope that saying all this out loud, to you two, will help." Ethaniel wiped his palms on his trousers, sighed, and said, "I started waking up to shallow cuts on my fingers. They'd heal within hours, often by midday. And they didn't appear every night. So I took to wearing gloves all the time, even to sleep."

"Did that help?" Calix asked.

"No." A single word from Ethaniel, dropped like a stone from a wild height. "Because in the morning the gloves were off, and the wounds were back. I didn't say anything to anyone. I was too ashamed, too confused." He turned sad eyes to

Aubrey. "Gods, I wish I had known one or both of you back then. You would have helped me." Then he straightened, cleared his throat, and said, "But eventually the cuts got in the way of my work, so I told Uncle Jeremiah. He had me come home more during the week, instead of staying in the dorms. And one night, after I simply couldn't take it any longer, he stayed awake by my bedside. He watched over me all night."

Ethaniel balled his hands into fists, squeezed until his knuckles turned white, and whispered, "I was doing it to myself. Like a sleepwalker might wander about the house, except I was doing everything with intention. I'd get up, go to my kit, take out one of the three-inch tracing needles, and carve into my skin."

All the air left Ethaniel in a gust, and he took some of Aubrey's breath with him. Aubrey could scarcely believe what he was hearing, and from the look on Calix's face, he felt the same way. But despite the shock and pain, Aubrey's mind immediately went to work, treating this like a problem to be solved, a mystery to be unraveled.

Stop. It isn't your place. Ethaniel needs you.

Ethaniel took one of Aubrey's hands and one of Calix's into his own and held them against his chest. "It's not... a moment in my life I enjoy reliving. And after some time it simply *stopped*. It terrified poor Uncle Jeremiah, whose magic was only ever meant for patterning, and small patterns at that. We tried a few things — tonics, a handful of 'peaceful mind' spells — but eventually it just petered out. And it hasn't happened since." He held his hands up for them to see. "It's not painful. More like a dull ache than anything. The same with my face, oddly enough."

Aubrey weighed his words, his intention, then said, "Did that wound on your face happen when you were trying to get free of Uzala?"

Ethaniel nodded. "Maria was able to lure it away long enough for me to draw the pattern to open a door. I thought it was a door leading us out of the *demimonde*, but it led to you, instead. The blowback of magic was merely a side effect." The look he gave Calix was shot through with honey and gratefulness. "I knew neither of you would leave me there."

But Aubrey noticed the way Ethaniel avoided further explanation about *how* the wound happened. It was an easy thing to assume it had been Uzala to leave that mark, but the *demimonde* was full of strange things.

And even deeper-set into his mind was a question that filled him with dread: what happened when someone with a true heart but Harkness blood in his veins tried to leave that place?

Aubrey pushed it all aside to focus on Ethaniel. He was a healer, *demimonde* or not, and he wanted to help. Carefully, slowly, he ran his fingertips over Ethaniel's undamaged cheek, and when a smile graced Ethaniel's features, Aubrey finally said, "Would you let me try to heal it? At least to keep the chance of infection at bay. We don't know nearly enough about what lingers in that place."

Ethaniel was quiet for a long, still moment, then nodded. "All right. But Aubrey, please don't… " He looked away. "Don't take any risks. You're right. We don't know enough."

Aubrey knew exactly what Ethaniel was saying. *Don't push too far or too deep. Even I don't know what darkness still lingers, embedded in my skin like so much glass.* "Heard and understood. I absolutely won't put any of us in any more peril. We've had a lifetime of it these last few days."

He had Ethaniel lay flat on the bed, Calix on his left and holding Ethaniel's hand while Aubrey took up the spot on the right. Aubrey chose a chair over sitting directly on the bed, both to give him room to work and to provide a modicum of space for Ethaniel. And moments before he reached down to help Ethaniel remove his bandage, he asked Ethaniel a very simple question.

"Would it be all right if I let Magnus know what's going on?"

Ethaniel paused, then nodded. "Understandable. But… don't tell him about the scars on my hands, Aubrey. It's not connected to the wound on my cheek other than exposure to the *demimonde*."

Aubrey had to bite his tongue, an instinct fortified by the starkly worried expression on Calix's face. "I won't," he said.

Aubrey stuck his head out the door and called for Magnus. When his mentor and friend appeared in the hall, Aubrey slipped out to join him, closing the bedroom door behind him.

Aubrey quickly explained that he was going to try to heal the wound on Ethaniel's face, but Magnus interrupted him before he could explain *how* he would do so. "All I ask is that you be careful. More than you ever have been in the past." And then he gripped Aubrey by the shoulders. "I've never been more serious in my life, Aubrey. If anything *at all* seems off, yell my name. And after you're done, because I'm choosing success here, find me anyways. We have things to discuss."

The weight on Magnus's shoulders, the heavy droop of his eyes, told Aubrey everything. He would bet his entire life savings that it had something to do with Lawton or Vincent. Perhaps both.

"I will," Aubrey promised.

He and Ethaniel might still be working on healing and renewing their connection and relationship, but Magnus was as steady as the stones of the pyramids. If he said he'd be there to help, Aubrey would never doubt it.

Aubrey returned to the room to find Calix sitting against the headboard, Ethaniel's head in his lap. He was rubbing Ethaniel's temples with careful, sure motions and only looked up once Aubrey closed the door. Then he noticed the light in the room had been reduced to a few candles and one golden orb floating directly above the bed. It made the space feel warmer, more welcoming, and even Aubrey's tired eyes appreciated the sight and lack of stimulation.

The appreciative smile he gave Calix was mirrored by Ethaniel, and that sweet man lit up like the sun. Calix gave a little shrug and went right back to massaging Ethaniel's scalp, but he didn't hide his shy grin.

"Back to where we were," Aubrey said as he sat. "Ethaniel, I'm going to try to do something similar as I did with Richard, and with Lawton. I'm looking for any source of infection, anything that might have come along from the *demimonde*. If I find nothing, we'll move on to attempting to knit the skin back together. It won't hurt, but it may feel strange."

"And if you do find something?" Ethaniel asked. Panic began to settle on his face, so Aubrey leaned closer; a sad attempt at comfort, at intimacy, at reassurance that everything would work out.

"I'll try to neutralize it. If I can't, I'll call for Magnus."

"Perhaps I should do that? Who's to say you'll be able to if you're battling something that latched onto Ethaniel from that place." Calix waved his free hand in the air. "What about some kind of signal?"

"Sharp as ever," Aubrey said.

They settled on a quick set of three taps on the bed if Aubrey needed assistance. And then Aubrey poured all his focus and energy into centering himself, then reached for that place deep within.

A thick slab of pure onyx stone formed in his mind's eye. Aubrey pictured his hands sliding over the perfectly smooth surface. When his magic sparked to life, the space between him and the stone narrowed, focused, and snapped into place. That's when he felt it.

That *rush*. Pure adrenaline and arcane power. In his mind, Aubrey pushed his fingers deep into the stone. Every crevice, every divot, every crack and imperfection were filled with magic, with *life*.

Aubrey turned that third eye toward Ethaniel and even though his vision swam with effort and sweat beaded on his brow, he did not hold back. Ethaniel deserved to be *whole*. To be untouched by that place, so that even if the memory and the trauma lingered, he wouldn't have to see a reminder of that experience in the mirror every day.

What Aubrey saw beneath the bandage wasn't a garish, vicious slash from claws dripping with ichor. Instead, it was a pattern. His mind put it together like a puzzle, the pieces interlocking before he could stop himself. Part protection, part warning, those runes were carved on Ethaniel's jaw and the arch of his cheekbone.

They couldn't be removed.

The power that had etched them was far, far beyond Aubrey's capability. But there was no malice he could sense, only a desire to keep Ethaniel safe, from a being that had the same strange presence as Agrippa but was as corporeal as a shadow. It didn't malinger like Lily, and other than to protect Ethaniel, it seemed to have no real intent. It was all he could glean from the entity before he snapped back into his body, gasping and panting from the effort.

Immediately, Ethaniel sat up and he and Calix crowded around Aubrey. "What the hell happened?" Ethaniel asked, a hand to the bandage on his cheek. "It felt... strange. That's the best word I have for it."

"Well," Aubrey managed between heavy breaths. He looked down to see his hands shaking, but this wasn't from fear's icy grip. This was red-hot adrenaline; touching a live wire or the wild laughter let out by a lover who just escaped out the window of their paramour's bedroom.

There was a spark of *life* to that shadow, and whatever it was, it wanted to keep Ethaniel safe. Aubrey would have doubted it, had he not experienced it firsthand.

"You encountered something else in the *demimonde*," Aubrey said, no accusation in his tone. "Whatever it is, it seeks to protect you."

Ethaniel's head hung, his messy brown waves blocking his face. "I did," he whispered. "I... I didn't want to trust it. Uzala forced me to touch this stone, said it would awaken my magic, and it did." He lifted his head and Aubrey swore there was a flicker of emerald green in those hazel eyes. A flash, then gone. "I could see *everything*, Aubrey. The patterns that make up the *demimonde*. Even now, I feel as though I can see deeper into our world. Like I'm staring at our realm's bones and every bump, every fracture is there. Distant, but it's there."

Silence hung around them. Aubrey wasn't sure what to even say, and it was clear Ethaniel was both distressed and confused.

"We'll sort this out," Aubrey said as he gathered Ethaniel close. Calix curled up beside them and rubbed circles into Ethaniel's chest as his breath came faster and his eyes squeezed shut. "We will. We have Magnus and Agrippa now, both with knowledge far greater than mine."

It was on the tip of his tongue to ask about the wound, and yet Aubrey was afraid to say what he suspected. If true, it meant Ethaniel had done something desperate in an attempt to come back home. He could never fault the man for his actions in that moment, but if true... gods, then that meant the *demimonde* had a piece of him. Blood was the obvious answer, as there were plenty of miraculous and nasty things you could do with a few drops of blood from an arcane practitioner.

But Harkness blood, in the *demimonde*? A frightening thought for certain.

Calix was the one to finally speak up, and Aubrey was grateful for it. "We should change your bandage," he said after Ethaniel was able to get his breathing under control. "To keep the wound clean."

Ethaniel nodded and Calix went off in search of supplies. When he came back after a few minutes, Magnus trailed behind him. "I'm here as emotional support," Magnus said as he entered, wielding a tea tray, "and in my world, support comes in the form of sustenance."

Aubrey gave him a grateful look, to which Magnus shrugged. As if to say *it's not even a worry.* He helped Calix gently peel away the bandages on Ethaniel's face, noting how Ethaniel didn't even flinch at the pull of skin.

"Well, that's something," Magnus said as he leaned in over Aubrey's shoulder.

"How bad is it?" Ethaniel asked, his hand going up as if to touch his face. "Should I avoid mirrors for the foreseeable future?"

Aubrey felt all eyes on him. He was the healer, after all, even if people weren't his ideal patients. "There's no wound left. But..."

"But?" Ethaniel's face bore a slightly panicked expression. "You know I hate it when you do that."

"Sorry, love." Aubrey reached up to run his fingers over Ethaniel's jaw. "Your skin is whole again. No wound is visible. You're back to your handsome self." He turned to Calix. "Can you see it?"

When Calix nodded, he posed the same question to Magnus. "I get the feeling anyone with decent magic might," Magnus finally said after taking a deep breath. He strode across the room, rummaged through a few drawers, and came back with a pewter hand mirror. "Best you look, Ethaniel."

Ethaniel let Aubrey hold the mirror up so he could look for himself. "What in the hell... " He turned his face this way and that, at different angles, but it never made the runes along the skin of his jaw change. They were faint but visible, in a language they all now recognized as that of the *demimonde.*

The same runes that had been carved into his bone were now etched on his flesh. "Something in the *demimonde* seeks to protect you, but that's all I could glean," Aubrey said. "It seems we're not rid of that place quite yet."

Ethaniel slowly shook his head. There was a finality in his eyes and it made Aubrey's stomach clench. "I don't know that I ever will be," he said. "It has its claws in me. I let it in. Now I have to live with it."

Chapter Twenty-Two

CALIX

When Aubrey gathered all of them – including Lawton and Vincent – in the parlor, Calix could have picked any seat.

Closer to the fire might help him chase away the cold that seemed affixed to his bones in this cursed place.

Between Aubrey and Ethaniel was probably the most natural choice.

But he took the seat to Lawton's right, instead. Lawton was once again tied to the chair; likely for Vincent's safety more than anything. Vincent was far across the room, directly beside Agrippa. So there was no need for Lawton to be bound anymore. Before he sat, Calix said, "Agrippa, could you free Lawton?"

One white, slightly feathery eyebrow went up. Calix tried not to shrink under the former Guardian's imperious gaze. "Manners will get you everywhere, Earl Batherton. Even with a being such as myself."

Calix didn't dare look to Ethaniel or Aubrey for assistance; they were probably trying not to chuckle at the consternation he felt and the frown he knew he was wearing. But Magnus he could clearly see, as the curator was sitting directly across from him and had a fist pressed against his lips, eyes dancing with mirth.

"My apologies," Calix said. "Could you *please* release Lawton?"

"Much better." Agrippa snapped their fingers and the bonds melted into nothing but air. "Behave yourself, Mr. Adler."

"I'll be nothing but a paragon of obedience," Lawton said as he stood and stretched his hands over his head. Gone was his usual snark, though that had been fading for some time now. And as he reached above his head, Calix saw bare skin

- at his wrists and waist - and how deep indigo veins skittered about every inch of his friend's flesh.

The anger, betrayal, and resentment he'd been holding onto began to melt. And when their gazes met, the small, sad smile Lawton gave him pierced the very center of Calix's heart. Perhaps he'd been *too* angry, *too* hurt by Lawton's actions and not reflective enough on his own behavior.

Calix went to Lawton's side. "Could we have a moment?"

Lawton blinked at him, then slowly lowered his arms. As he crossed them over his chest, the neck of his tunic dipped and Calix saw the brand; the ugly red, ropey scar permanently etched into Lawton's body. If he focused his arcane senses, Calix swore he could *feel* the void the brand's magic had left behind. No one deserved such treatment.

"All right," Lawton said warily.

Calix motioned him to the door, then said to Magnus, "Give us a few minutes?"

Magnus looked around at the others, then nodded. "We'll need it anyways, as Agrippa is finishing something to help keep Vincent in order." For their part, Agrippa didn't look away from the silver mechanism in their hands.

Calix gave Aubrey and Ethaniel a small smile. "We'll be in the hall."

He followed Lawton out the door and down the hall a bit, until they were standing outside the kitchen. Lawton leaned against the wall, arms still over his chest, and Calix took the other wall. Physical proximity was something he could control, and being too close to Lawton right now felt like strumming a raw nerve with a piece of rusted iron. Too much all at once.

"Well, here we are," Lawton said. "And what a mess."

"I couldn't agree more, actually," Calix replied, trying not to wince at how quickly the words tumbled from his mouth. There was a gnawing, swirling pit in his stomach; a strange blend of worry, apprehension, and regret, and it left him feeling all the more unmoored. In the few moments he'd had to spare since this had all started, Lawton had never been far from his mind.

But now, face to face with his oldest friend, Calix didn't know what to say. Every thought crumbled, every word turned to ash. The haunting melody of an apology lingered, but he didn't have the notes practiced.

"I'll make this easy on both of us," Lawton said as he uncrossed his arms. The sleeves of his tunic hung loose, down to his fingertips, so he pushed them up and rolled them into a bunch at his elbows. Calix watched, stricken ill with how deathly pale Lawton's skin looked under all those indigo and black veins.

"I'll be staying with Agrippa for the time being," Lawton continued. "Your mother is contained for now, and will hopefully stay that way until they can... disconnect us." He looked down, flame-orange hair falling into his face. Calix hated that he couldn't see Lawton's eyes. "She doesn't have long, Calix. You may want to speak with her before my relocation."

Suddenly, Lawton was before him, the space between them eaten up by two big strides, and he had a grip on Calix's shoulders. "For what it's worth, I am sorry. I know I can keep apologizing until the end of time, but I hope you know I'm being sincere."

Lawton's words were cut with desperation and sadness, and it was a knife that got lodged deep in Calix's heart. "I know," Calix whispered. "None of this should have happened. I'm so sorry that it did."

When he pulled Lawton into a hug, his friend sucked in a sharp breath and froze. Calix kissed his cheek and slowly Lawton relaxed, trusting Calix would hold him up one more time.

Once they parted, Lawton gave him a weak smile. "Things must be dire if you're embracing me."

Calix tried to laugh, but it was only pained breath. "Honestly, I'm not sure. There are too many unanswered questions, and even if those are resolved... gods, this place is cursed. I should have never set foot back here."

Lawton gave a half-hearted shrug. "You could sell it. I wouldn't use the word 'cursed' in the description, though." Then he frowned. "The room where Cassandra is, or was, might need to be completely redone."

Calix felt a pang of empathy for a woman he didn't know, someone who didn't deserve to die like that. No one did; it was inhuman and horrifying. And it wasn't what he wanted to think about right now. "So, Agrippa can help you?"

"They seem quite certain," Lawton replied quickly. "And truthfully, they terrify me on a level I didn't know was possible, so if they can put that power to use on the extra passenger using my body as a puppet, I'm perfectly fine with that. It beats dying, which will definitely happen if I don't let Agrippa work their strange magic." He sighed. "I will miss the city, though."

Distantly, Calix heard Lawton's words. Heard the reason, the logic, in them. But he couldn't shove his way past the thought of *Lawton* dying. "Lawton, you're not… " He couldn't say it.

"Not yet." Lawton's smile was small, gentle. "Agrippa is willing to help me, mostly because I'm some kind of oddity they've not seen before and will likely make me do strange things in their laboratory or wherever they reside. But if I stay with them, I stay alive."

Calix slumped forward, all the air forced from his lungs. He could only pull Lawton close, press their foreheads together, and say, "You do enjoy causing me grief, don't you?"

"It's what I live for, Calix." Lawton pulled back, then cupped Calix's face in his hands, gaze deadly serious. "The shreds of your mother are just that now. Bits and pieces. The longer she has residence in me, the more of her is lost. And there's not much left, darling. I know you must feel all sorts of ways about her and the things she did. I'm not saying you should forgive her, or me. But I don't want you to miss what might be the last chance to talk to her before this is all said and done."

"I don't know how to do that without making you even more ill," Calix replied.

"I do. Or Agrippa does. He has your mother sectioned off into some kind of… well, honestly, I wasn't fully listening because I was mildly hysterical in the moment. But if a being like them can exist, they must be able to section off someone like her." Lawton blew out a sigh. "Otherwise, I have completely lost my mind and this is all some grand hallucination."

Calix's smile was just as watery as Lawton's had been. "Better than the one you had after you tried opium the first time?"

Lawton let out a shocked laugh. "I nearly forgot about that. Ah, the follies of youth."

The urge to hug Lawton was strong, so Calix leaned into it. Lawton melted against him for a few precious seconds, with only a murmured, "I'm so terribly jealous, you know," before pulling away completely.

Soon, his friend's warmth was gone, replaced by chilly, stale air. Only now, it didn't feel much like a canyon, but something resembling a proper New York City sidewalk. Wide enough for the two of them, with a little bit of space between.

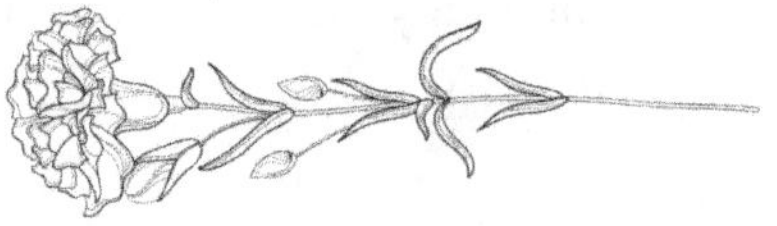

Calix gave himself a moment of quiet after Lawton returned to the room. He spent those moments with his hands on the wall, his head hanging low between his shoulders, as he focused on his breathing.

None of this was easy. It was all, quite honestly, rather terrible with a few exceptions. He knew Lawton was jealous of Ethaniel and Aubrey. It had been evident all along, because Lawton had never been good at hiding his emotions. And he was especially terrible at it when it involved Calix and other lovers. Oh, he'd never *stopped* Calix from pursuing someone or letting him be pursued, but the undercurrent rippled around him.

But this time was different. This time, Calix knew Lawton was also jealous of *him*, because of the two men he'd fallen in with. Because Lawton had always chased delight and pleasure and pretty things that shone under chandeliers. But he'd also never been afraid of shadows or darkness, and Ethaniel and Aubrey had both; buried under layers of dry humor and propriety and talent. And Calix needed to be all right with all of that. There was no changing how Lawton felt, and if anyone had a right to feel some certain way about the current state of affairs, it was the man who had been tortured and maimed and possessed.

No, he owed Lawton. Not in recompense for what had recently occurred, but for a million little slights they'd traded like friendly jabs. For the nights he'd ignored that specific three-rap knock. For the plays he'd left at intermission and never returned to, waiting outside for the performance to end and for Lawton to come out with some pretty thing on his arm.

For all the wrongs he'd done a friend. For all the times he'd never spoken up about those slights or hurts. For all the love they'd given each other and circled back to themselves; vain, selfish, sad creatures looking for something different instead of holding tight to the thing in front of their faces.

Eventually, Calix returned to the room, gave Lawton a nod, and took the chair to his right once more. It wasn't all settled, not yet, but they had a decent start to mending old wounds.

"I thought we might clear up some things," Magnus said as Calix sat. "See, young master Adler here had a fascinating story to tell about the attack Cassandra made on him and the house. And since Cassandra was under the command of the Golden Order, I figured I'd go to the source." Magnus snapped his fingers near Vincent's ear. "Do you want to tell the story, or shall I?"

"You should make him do it, and punish him when he lies," Lawton said primly. "And he will lie."

"Punish him how?" Ethaniel asked. "He's been attacked plenty."

"I was thinking more creatively, like filling his head with the sound of mosquitoes buzzing. Something truly... *annoying*." Lawton's tone was as placid as a lake, but Calix saw the fire in his eyes.

"I don't think that's necessary," Ethaniel huffed. "Vincent's been through an ordeal as well. We barely made it out of the *demimonde* alive."

"And to that point," Magnus cut in, "Vincent... care to share who the woman Lawton saw in his vision is? I think Ethaniel would be very interested in that information."

Vincent worked his jaw back and forth and Calix realized Magnus must have magically bound his mouth as well, and the release of that invisible bond was what had caused a tiny *pop* of magic. "I didn't know she was going to do any of this," he muttered. "This wasn't the plan."

Vincent sounded weak. Defeated, even.

Calix's mouth nearly dropped to the floor. This was the head of the Golden Order? The same man who had stood outside Aubrey's apartment building as it burned, as nonchalant as could be? Things in the *demimonde* must have been more dire than they'd realized. It looked like life itself had been drained from the man and he had no fight left.

"Then I'll do it for you," Magnus said. He nodded to Agrippa, who gestured with a feathery hand to the space in the middle of their chairs. From thin air, a wispy figure began to coalesce.

Calix stared hard at the figure. Agrippa's conjured image was slowly forming from the bottom; a long, tattered dress that dragged behind a tall, willowy, female-presenting human. Hair down to her waist, her arms bare but decorated with what looked like paint, and a thin face with a pointed chin and sharp eyebrows and nose.

Across from him, Ethaniel froze. "That's cousin Isme," he whispered. All the color had drained from his face and he looked like he might vomit. "Vincent. You didn't."

Vincent had a similar expression on his face, but he was also twisting in his bonds. "She's extremely powerful," he bit out. "So much so that she was the one who dragged me into the *demimonde*."

Beside Calix, Lawton jolted to life. "That's the woman who saved me," he said. "The one who came to me after... " Lawton touched the pinkish scar across his throat.

A heavy weight settled across the room, choking every word and thought. Calix felt trapped, as if he'd been shoved between two walls with no space to move or even breathe.

Aubrey pointed at the illusory figure of Isme. "That's a family member, Ethaniel?" Ethaniel nodded, still too shocked to speak, so Aubrey stood and crossed the space to loom over Vincent. "What did you have her do?"

Vincent's laugh was grating; an ugly thing tipped with poisoned daggers. Some of the man's attitude was surfacing and it made Calix want to slap him. "What all Harknesses do: use their magic. Look at my *poor* half-brother, who denied himself for so long that holding back was all the more painful. You could have had everything, Ethaniel. Mother would have given you *everything*."

Beside him, Lawton shook his head but kept quiet. Calix thought he understood the sentiment. Vincent was a goddamn fool too used to wearing expensive suits and giving orders.

"All well and good," Magnus cut in smoothly, "but we're not nearly done." He gestured to the figure, then to Lawton. "That's the woman, then? You said she was rather conciliatory."

"She healed my wound and then pinned Cassandra to the floor and took her eyes. 'Conciliatory' is a bit strong," Lawton said. "But she also struck me as the type not to turn the other cheek, as it were. So I wonder what Vincent did to her to make her so wrathful— "

"I did nothing!" Vincent bellowed, straining once again against his bonds. "She broke the single most important rule in our family."

Calix immediately looked to Ethaniel, who shut his eyes and dug the heels of his palms into them. "We don't betray family," Ethaniel said softly.

"What?" Calix was out of his seat now and charging toward Vincent, fury powering his steps. "You've done nothing but betray Ethaniel."

Aubrey put a hand on Calix's arm. "Ethaniel may wish to explain, dove."

He immediately deflated. "Yes, of course."

Vincent snorted. "And that's one of the many, many reasons why Ethaniel isn't family. Harknesses take. It's our nature. If Ethaniel were really a Harkness, he would have made husks out of all of you." He gave Ethaniel a desperate look. "I know you can feel it. Even I can. The power they have. Imagine what you could do— "

Vincent didn't finish the sentence. Ethaniel, calmly and with great purpose, punched his half-brother directly in the face, then marched over to Calix's chair and sat down.

"Magnus, what else did you learn?" Ethaniel asked as he cradled his now reddened knuckles.

Calix knew it was wrong of him. He *knew* it; it wasn't terribly modern thinking. But seeing someone defend him and Aubrey, and do it with no hesitation, made some part of him flush with pleasure. Watching Aubrey silently, gently, press a hand to the torn skin on Ethaniel's knuckles and release a small swirl of healing power was an extra benefit. The care, the consideration... it made him proud and weak in the knees.

"We can't get blood from a stone, no matter how much the stone deserves a good wallop," Agrippa said from their post against the bookshelf. "If you break his jaw, I'll be the one to put it back together." Then they shot Vincent a dark look, a thing that sent a shiver down Calix's spine. "I've never really studied human anatomy. It could be interesting, results-wise."

Magnus looked pained by all the commotion and Calix felt for him. They were like a bunch of exhausted, angry cats. "I guess we're keeping this quick, then. This woman, Isme, is indeed a Harkness. One of many cousins to both Ethaniel and Vincent. She's a Dreamwalker."

Aubrey sat down beside Ethaniel with a heavy sigh. "Well, shit."

"Is that bad?" Calix asked. "I've heard the term before but never any explanation as to what it meant."

"Very," Ethaniel and Magnus said at the same time.

"She's always been a little... odd," Ethaniel replied. "Talking to random trees or rocks. I know her father was worried because she insisted the things she spoke to weren't her imaginary friends, but her *dream friends*. But she fell in line with the family training and when she was about twelve or so, she disappeared."

Ethaniel's face went tight and Calix immediately could guess the reason: Maria had disappeared as a child, though a younger one. And now she was likely gone for good, having held off two Guardians so they could make their escape. Calix wanted badly to reach out to him, so he knelt in front of Ethaniel and took his hand.

A few moments passed while Ethaniel gathered his thoughts, then he looked up and continued. But as he talked, he rubbed his thumb over the back of Calix's hand and that little touch meant everything.

"Isme eventually came back, almost a year later. And she was... off. Much worse. Secretive. Skulking about the compound at night. Stealing supplies. Disappearing for days or even weeks, and coming back with some strange new knowledge. And by that point, I was dislodging myself from the family, so I lost track of her. But I know Mother took her in."

"She got worse. Much worse," Vincent said, his voice muffled a little by the swelling in his cheek. "She's in full control of her powers. Which is why I hired her."

Aubrey turned to Magnus and Agrippa. "How do we find her? If she can move between dreams, we're all in danger."

Vincent laughed. "She never cared about any of you. She got what she wanted."

"Which was access to the *demimonde*," Magnus said. "She trapped Vincent there. I don't think it's a far leap to figure we're not the next target, at least from what I gleaned of her intent from Vincent."

"You mean stole from my memories," Vincent snapped. "Magic users. You're all the same. You take and take and take. Just empty vessels to be filled with resources from others."

Calix nearly snorted but held back. Could Vincent not hear himself? The bell of hypocrisy rang loud and clear, but a glance at the man told Calix plenty. Vincent was still straining at his bonds but the movements were growing weaker by the second, and the swelling in his face would bruise spectacularly. And yet here he was, still fighting, still cursing them.

Still so, so jealous of Ethaniel.

Calix could tell Magnus's patience, which usually seemed infinite, was nearing its end. The man barely bit back what Calix figured were pretty harsh words, pinched the bridge of his nose, swore, then said, "Right, let's just cut to it, then.

She's in the *demimonde*. If she comes back, Agrippa will know. There's no other way I know of to keep tabs on her unless we go back into the *demimonde*."

"Which is *not* happening. Ever," Aubrey snapped.

"Agreed," Calix said as he squeezed Ethaniel's hand. Their eyes met and Ethaniel gave him a tiny smile. Calix couldn't help but whisper, "We're here. We're not going anywhere."

Agrippa moved Vincent to another room and put him behind some kind of magical lock, then retired to their portal. Once they departed, the five of them scrounged in the pantry and managed to come up with a half-decent dinner. Lawton left them soon afterwards, and despite Calix's protests that his wounds needed to be looked at, he eventually let his friend go off to a room to sleep.

And then it was the four of them in a warm kitchen, the large counter in the middle of the room holding them all up. Calix could feel his very *will* draining away as the day wore on.

"There's one more thing," Magnus said while he pushed potatoes around his plate. "And it's not pretty."

"None of this has been," Aubrey said before draining his wine. Calix leaned against him and Aubrey smiled. They were all a little red in the face, slightly sloppy from a bit too much wine and not enough sleep. Hopefully they'd sleep like the dead tonight.

"True enough. And all of this is aside from losing track of Convergence and a Harkness Dreamwalker in the *demimonde*." Magnus waved a hand, then dropped it in his lap. "Those are problems for another day. The pressing issue concerns your half-brother, Ethaniel."

Ethaniel slumped in his chair and Magnus patted his shoulder. "My fucking family," he groaned. "All right. Tell us."

Magnus opened his mouth, closed it, then shifted his gaze away as if in thought. Seeing the always-controlled Magnus off-kilter made Calix feel uneasy. Beside him, Aubrey shifted and a warm hand wrapped around Calix's knee. He covered it with his own hand; silent, solid reassurance.

"Vincent says he never had magic. Not real magic, as he calls it. Just a spark because of his blood. But... " Magnus dug around in his jacket for a moment and came up with a bit of chalk. Using the wood slab counter as a canvas, he carefully drew what looked like a backwards P, then extended two lines out from the bottom to curve up and around the symbol, then brought those lines down once more into shapes that looked vaguely like wings.

"Have you ever seen this before?" Magnus asked Ethaniel.

"I... yes," Ethaniel replied slowly. "It's part of the family crest. We're all taught it as a 'point of pride'. There are more shapes and lines to it, but this is the part we learn to draw first. But... Maria."

Calix felt unease build in his belly. "What about her?"

"She told me the same. That Vincent had some bit of magic and that my mother took it. Used it for something profane, I'm sure. But I thought she was wrong, or the memory she had was broken or spliced in some way."

Magnus tapped the symbol. "I don't think she was wrong, Ethaniel. This came up quite a bit in Vincent's memories. Specifically as part of a spell."

For whatever reason, dread filled Calix's lungs. It felt *alive*, pulsing with malcontent as it fed on such ugly parts of all their pasts.

Ethaniel closed his eyes. "Tell me. Don't mince words, Magnus. I can't take any more of that from anyone right now."

"And you aren't questioning how I know this."

"Not at all." Ethaniel opened his eyes, raked his gaze over Aubrey and Calix. Appreciative in so many ways, and Calix felt that, too. "You've protected us from the minute Aubrey contacted you. I trust you, Magnus. And Vincent seems no worse for the wear."

"Very well." Magnus rolled the chalk between his fingers and the dust floated on the air. "Vincent and that symbol are tied together because, from what I can tell, the symbol was part of a spell to strip magic from your half-brother's blood, then replace any memory of said magic with a new one. One where he was born without arcane power."

A pin could have dropped in the room and it would have sounded like crashing glass. Calix stared at Magnus, stunned. The second thing he felt was a pang of empathy for Vincent. If what Magnus said was true, the man had something ripped from him; something intrinsic to his body and mind, but also to his identity. Calix could understand that specific kind of violation.

Ethaniel was the one to eventually find his voice. "Does Vincent know any of this?"

Magnus shook his head. "The memories of his magic were *replaced* but not erased. A limitation of the spell, perhaps, or some other variable I wasn't able to glean. The memories are there, tucked away in a little part of Vincent's mind, and it wouldn't be terribly hard to unlock that particular box."

"Keep it locked. Don't tell him." Ethaniel's words were as solid as steel.

"Are you sure, Ethaniel?" Aubrey asked. "That's... Vincent knowing that information could change his mind about this Golden Order nonsense. It could change his *life*."

"No." Ethaniel's eyes flashed and Calix saw the pain and anger buried there, and he understood. "It stays the way it is. He stays the way he is. Besides, with those memories, he could do even more damage. Think of how angry any of you might be if this was part of your past."

Calix reached out for Ethaniel's hand, and when Ethaniel linked their fingers together, he said, "Right now, I think the only person able to make that call is you, Ethaniel. But it wouldn't be healthy for you or Vincent to cling to these ideas for too long. All I'm asking is that once we're clear of this mess, you give it some real thought. And you can come to us if you need to talk or work things out."

Ethaniel swallowed hard. "I know. And I'm grateful. Right now, I'm so angry with Vincent for causing all these problems. I admit I can't separate my anger from what's right or moral. It's an ugly thing, this fear and hate. I feel as if it's growing inside me and if I'm not careful, it could strip away everything I know about myself. That terrifies me."

"We're always here for you," Calix said. "Always."

"Then I'm a lucky fool," Ethaniel replied softly.

INTERLUDE

This will be the last time I put ink to parchment. The final time I document the strange journey that has been my life. I do not doubt that John will squirrel this away somewhere, meant to be discovered by scholars dozens or hundreds of years later.

Or perhaps a fire will find it. A single spark in this mountain of paper would decimate everything and everyone inside.

Or perhaps time will be unkind once more. It would be very much like her to spit in my eye even after my flesh has sloughed off and my bones have been made into little pockets for the many things that crawl beneath the earth.

Perhaps... it doesn't matter what becomes of this writing. I will be dead tomorrow. Physically erased from this realm, a bit of my spirit captured within the pages of a book an angel handed to my colleague and once friend, Doctor John Dee.

An angel.

No, a demon.

A thing of gold and purple wearing a crown of crooked, ugly metal spikes. A demon that offered John the very thing his heart desired most: knowledge. And the more it offered, the more it hungered. A beast with tongue lolling and saliva dripping. It was no longer content with the tiny sparks of magic within all sentient creatures of this realm.

It was not content with the birds or rabbits. Nor the goats or cows, dogs or cats. It wanted and craved and cried out to John in desperation, and he eventually caved. He did so at first under cover of dark, so neither myself nor his wife would know. When the maid disappeared, I said nothing. My regret for that mistake is great.

I thought there was no possible avenue for proving what John had done. Household staff did not last long at Mortlake, and even the old cook, who had served John's parents, eventually left after complaints of strange noises in the dark. A missing maid was of no concern.

When John asked his son to help him in the study, Arthur did not hesitate to comply. The boy adored his father and would have done anything for him. That blind love cost the child his life. John sacrificed his own son to the creature, this Guardian.

Uriel.

Had John been in his right mind, none of this would have occurred. That was the argument I made for many months after the nightly sessions began. John was a man of science and faith and fully believed the two were not separate, but parts of a greater, grander plan. I could have stopped him. But I wanted to believe it, too.

Call me a cozener. Call me a thief. Accuse me of witchcraft and necromancy and many more black arts even the strongest magic wielders have barely heard whispers of... and it would all be true.

But my last word will be this, and it is as honest as I can be. The book sits mere feet away, shielded by a gently glimmering, lavender-hued cage, and it might as well be an executioner's axe. Tomorrow, John will feed me to Uriel, stripping my body of life and splintering my soul in two. One part of it will be laid into the paper and binding of a book which will hold all of John's secrets. The other half will die with my mortal flesh.

The creature outside the sphere, our Uriel, has taken on an even more monstrous form. Its true form, apparently; a thing of bone and sinew, antler and hair, a horrifying conglomerate only vaguely humanoid but with far too many ears and eyes and mouths.

Uriel.

Lundrumguffa.

Its real name, its real form. All revealed to me because my demise is imminent. I do not know if such a creature can feel joy, but I saw it smile as it filled my head with this forbidden knowledge.

When I asked it why, Uriel showed me its many teeth, crooked several fingers at me, and said, "Because I still wait for the one who comes. You are inconsequential, but John loves you. And I love John's pain."

Tomorrow, I die.

Tomorrow, Uriel and John live on.

After I am gone, what happens to the book becomes a mystery. It is my hope it stays locked away in John's library, because I will be of no help to anyone who finds it. I will not be me any longer.

I will be a part of it. Merged. Converged.

CHAPTER TWENTY-THREE

ETHANIEL

"Are you certain?" Calix asked him.

Calix's sweet face stared up at Ethaniel and it made what he needed to say even more difficult. "I am. Whatever it was that ran roughshod over my mind in the *demimonde* seems to know Agrippa. And Agrippa helped you all save me. I owe it to them, and to myself."

Ethaniel didn't want to be dependent on anyone outside of Aubrey and Calix, and even then, that willful loss of autonomy still rubbed salt in a wound that would never heal. He'd prided himself on reliance and steadfastness from a young age. He wouldn't have survived his family otherwise. But Agrippa had proven themself a steady hand, despite their origin; and after all, it was only a message.

"I'll be quick, I promise," Ethaniel said as he kissed Calix's cheek. "You'd both better be resting when I come up."

"Well, let me take that threat *very* seriously," Aubrey teased with a glint in his eye. All it took was a look from the man and Ethaniel felt his face grow hot. Aubrey could have been talking about using a wash basin or about giving Calix the kind of bath he'd received when tumbling back through to their realm. It didn't matter, because Aubrey's sensuality was a living, breathing thing and he drove Ethaniel *wild*.

Ethaniel left the room and followed the hall, then the stairs to the first floor. He'd barely been in any mindset to admire the estate, but here he paused to look around. Everything was done in the utmost of taste and could have been from the early 19th century or the present. It all fit seamlessly into a flowing of lines and delicate patterns, softer pastels forcing the bold jewel tones to yield somewhat. Tile and wood and fabric all matching or complimentary, and it would have cost quite a bit of money.

Ethaniel tensed when he realized what he was doing: falling back into old habits, sizing up anyone wealthy with a gimlet eye. An observation of detail to grasp some higher, more defined meaning. *Who were they? Did they come to wealth through family or business? How finely are they dressed compared to what the new department stores were selling? Were their clothes properly tailored?*

And on and on. It was how he based his prices and work estimates. This netting of details was nestled into notes he kept on every client, even the errant thoughts. And he remembered what he'd written about Calix after their first meeting: "Wealthy but too proper to fully show it off. Kind, polite. Inquisitive about patterning, shows a heightened intellect and understanding of magic. Felt something in me stir at his approach; it's never happened quite like that before."

Aubrey's note was somewhat similar, but Ethaniel had also written: "The most handsome man I've ever seen in my life."

Yes, he'd been smitten instantly with both.

Rosehill was both genius and mildly haphazard. Many of the colors and patterns shouldn't work together, but Lily had balanced the house with just the right amount of understated gilt and quality pieces. With as much as they knew about Calix's mother, Ethaniel now sensed something else in the house.

Chaos. The slanting of a slowly unwinding mind.

To anyone else, it would look like money troubles. The hasty seams of wallpaper in a few corners. The cracked leg of a side table, the line of glue hardened into small bubbles. The wall sconce with the candles placed upside down. It wasn't carelessness. It was a lack of *caring*, because she had been obsessed with Uriel and Calix and the *demimonde*.

Before stepping into the parlor, Ethaniel laid a hand on the rich red wallpaper and whispered, "You deserved better."

The room was empty save the steady blaze of fire and Agrippa, who was sitting in a chair by the window, watching the spring wind whip bare branches together in a discordant melody.

"I was hoping you'd be here," Ethaniel said as he carefully shut the door.

"You knew I'd be here," Agrippa said in a tone much like a stuffy schoolteacher's.

"Yes. I did."

"And how did you know?"

Ethaniel shoved his hands into his pockets and rocked back on his heels. Agrippa already had him flat-footed, didn't they? "I... I simply knew. I can't explain it."

"I can." Agrippa got to their feet and *floated* over to him. They were already a full head taller, but now he had to crane his neck to look in their eyes. "You brought something back from the *demimonde*. A small spark, the manifestation of a voice that helped save you."

Ethaniel had the sudden, mad urge to flee. He was alone with Agrippa, and not all of his reservations about them had been dismissed. He could see his earlier panic around their presence as shock and stress, but his distrust wasn't so easily won over.

"You don't need to fret so much. Or so loudly," Agrippa said, stern tone still firmly in place. "I felt that spark the moment you came back. I wanted to see how long it would take for you to seek me out on your own."

Ethaniel dropped back to sit on the sofa and gestured toward the one facing him. Agrippa didn't so much as sit as they did settle onto the velvet cushions, looking all the more like a feathery statue. "It said it knew you," Ethaniel said after a long moment. "It helped me find my magic again when I thought it had been lost in the noise of that place."

Those galaxy eyes narrowing at him did not help his slowly rising pulse. Ethaniel felt like caged prey waiting to be devoured. "Did it say anything else?" Agrippa asked.

"To let you know about them."

Agrippa slowly let themselves relax, but there was still a rigidity to their posture that made Ethaniel's back ache. "I was the Bridge Builder," they said. "A joiner of separate paths. A repairer of ones broken. I was dedicated to my work, and it was work I was destined to do from the moment I became part of a realm. We Guardians know only our work and each other. We're meant to stay out of the way and not meddle. But whoever or whatever created us or pulled us from some primordial muck never gave us any real clue as to *who* we are."

Ethaniel frowned. "That sounds very... well, human."

Agrippa chuckled, the bells of their voice lower but still ringing. "Every being has a purpose. For most, it's to reproduce, spread its genetics, then die. Spawn, perish." They flicked a hand at the fire, which roared to a higher, brighter blaze. "Now imagine if a creature with great magic but a singular purpose started to wonder what *else* it might be capable of."

Ethaniel's head swam. "But you aren't in the *demimonde* anymore. So, did you find your purpose?"

The abyss of their eyes darkened, and while Ethaniel was wondering if that was even possible, Agrippa was suddenly looming over him, one hand on the back of the sofa and the other in front of his face. Gone were the feathery, but still rather human, fingers. It was now a clawed appendage, wickedly sharp and inches from his cheek. Delicate tendrils of magic, pulsing with energy that made Ethaniel's head throb, curled around their claws.

"I left. On purpose. I wasn't the first, and I doubt I will be the final one. But it takes a great deal of effort, research, and sacrifice to jump realms. Even more if the intent is to settle somewhere else permanently. How does one make a home when they had none to begin with?"

Ethaniel blinked and Agrippa was back on their sofa as if nothing had happened. What sat tight and hot in his chest wasn't the threat of their claws, but the larger question of finding purpose and meaning. He didn't know a single human not chasing after those things, and more often than not, they filled that hole with pleasure or dramatics or pain, alcohol or opium or sex. Few used that need for purpose to do something greater than themselves.

"I think I understand," Ethaniel said slowly, much quieter now that Agrippa's many layers of meaning had sunk in and stuck between his ribs.

"On some level, perhaps. But it's an argument for another time. The piece of this being you carry is quite small. But like we've seen with Calix's mother, a soul can be broken apart in the hope of reforging it at a point later on in time. But Guardians do not split apart the way humans do." From their pocket, Agrippa pulled out a pane of glass. At their touch, the glass *shivered*, then split, separating into six even smaller square pieces. These hovered over their palm for a moment, then snapped together with several clicks. And the cube now in their palm seemed to *sigh*.

Something inside Ethaniel's chest, near the bottom of his left lung, quivered in response.

"I can take it from here," Agrippa said, finality the only note in their voice.

For all the trouble they'd seen and been through, all the pain and blood and panic-sweat, Ethaniel still paused. He didn't want this thing taking his body for a ride like Lily had done to Lawton. It was a thing of the *demimonde*, this being. A Guardian, perhaps, or some lesser entity. And the Guardians he'd seen were strange beyond definition. Even Agrippa, as civilized as they were, still scared the living daylights out of Ethaniel.

So why was he hesitating?

Agrippa must have sensed his uncertainty. "The spark you carry is of another Builder. Their purpose has long been forgotten by most, since they've been fractured for so long. Because you have been congenial, I can share a small piece." Agrippa motioned to the room. "What do you see when you look at this room?" They tapped their forehead, which Ethaniel took to mean *what do you see with your magic senses*, or something like it.

Ethaniel pulled on the thread of his magic; a difficult thing, between the many stressors over the last days, the lack of proper rest or food, and the shock of what he experienced in the *demimonde*. But once he made himself and his intent known, it swirled up to meet him. When Ethaniel turned his on sight, he saw it once more.

The lines and shapes, jagged and curving, swooping and dropping. All manner of runes and magic language covering various surfaces - the sofa Agrippa sat on was protected against stains and general wear, the rug under their feet similarly patterned and spelled, and even the candles and lights were graced with extension charms. Fairly household stuff, if one's home was a wealthy estate in upper New York.

A glance at the walls made Ethaniel instantly nauseated. The patterns here, ground into rock and wood and plaster, were thick with old, strong magic. They immediately reminded Ethaniel of the vault on the grounds, just below Lily's tomb and where this adventure had taken a turn into truly wild territory.

Where their lives had changed forever.

"Now you see the magic running through this world, don't you, little patterner?"

Little patterner

Little patterner

Only Guardians had ever called him that.

Across from him, Agrippa was *glowing*, their eyes endless pools of black, and Ethaniel could only stare. *This* was the Guardian underneath the suit and well-combed hair and stuffy demeanor. *This* was the being who had chosen to make the human world their home. It was a shocking, beautiful sight.

"Is there magic in everything?" Ethaniel managed to ask.

"No, and yes. As you open your sight more in this world, the more you'll see, and the more you'll learn. I am willing to assist, but everything you have to learn is in your power and your control, Ethaniel."

He could barely stand it anymore. It felt as though he was being pulled in sixty different directions and none of it was natural, so he let his magic dwindle to the ever-constant flame.

"If you were to hang onto that spark of a Guardian, it would be your ruin. Yes, it would provide you power for some time, but it would make you an addict. This is a lesson few in your family have ever learned. But I know this Builder well. It is a burden I will gladly carry, and one you should not have to."

All he wanted was a life with Aubrey and Calix. Ethaniel didn't think that was too much to ask.

Finally, Ethaniel put his hand out and said, "What should I do?"

"Merely take this." And Agrippa tipped the cube into his hand. "And wait."

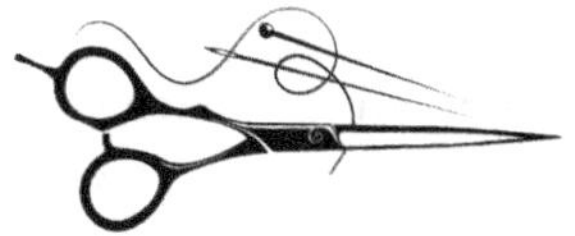

The Guardian hadn't been part of him long, but now with it gone, there was a small void. Ethaniel was certain it would heal over time; scab, then scar, until age eroded red and pink into silvery-white. And here he was about to create another void within himself, but this one would be far more painful.

Though, if he was truly honest with himself, Vincent had always left a void near his heart. He'd thought they could be brothers, but jealousy and power and the twisted roots of their family tree, gnarled and battered by striving for things not meant for mortals, had left them on opposite sides of a chasm.

Of a war.

He needed to put it to rest.

Agrippa waited until Ethaniel was seated across from a sleeping Vincent before putting a feathery hand on his shoulder. "I will remove myself from view, but I am monitoring this space. While I do not think anything will happen, I cannot promise it." Galaxy eyes flicked over him before softening. "Keep it brief."

Ethaniel planned on it.

Once Agrippa had vanished, Vincent inhaled sharply; the only warning Ethaniel would get that he was coming to consciousness. Agrippa had given Vincent a proper bed but if Ethaniel focused, he could barely see the faint lines of purple hued magic encircling it. The buzz of energy under his skin and tapping at the back of his teeth told him enough. It was a powerful containment spell, and one even he couldn't break. Vincent wasn't going anywhere anytime soon.

"Brother," Ethaniel said as Vincent sat up, frowning.

"Why are you here?" Vincent asked. "That creature said I could sleep."

Ethaniel had to bite down on the immediate reply that surfaced, a remnant of snarky rejoinders and arguments left open like festering wounds. But he didn't have to do any of that, say any of that. Not anymore.

"And you will get as much rest as your body needs, but I wanted one last chance."

Dark eyebrows went up despite Vincent's frown. "Why? What's done is done. You won."

"To some degree." Ethaniel thought about Aubrey and Calix and a warm bedroom and soft sheets and real sleep. He wanted all of it. But he needed to do this. "But cousin Isme is still loose. At some point, she'll need to be stopped. And you've never told me what became of Uncle Jeremiah."

Vincent laughed. "Well, godspeed, brother. Enjoy chasing that traitorous bitch. She couldn't even stay loyal to our family. She's worthless." Then he paused and what looked like regret flashed over his face. "Jeremiah is lost to the city, I assume. Living up his final days."

The anger flared in him once more. Ethaniel had so few people left in his life, and his uncle had been a close confidant for so long. "So that's it? You don't know where he is?"

Vincent shook his head. "It's all I know."

Ethaniel closed his eyes, a poor attempt to shove that anger and pain down deep where it couldn't easily resurface. "And Isme? You truly think she's gone, too?"

"What do you want, Ethaniel?" Vincent asked, spite forming at the edges of his words. "Get it over with."

His questions had been long shots. Wide and far guesses based on hunches built on the rocky foundations of their relationship. He could find Jeremiah on his own, but Isme was an entirely different issue. "Are you really telling me, once and for all, that her 'betrayal' wasn't part of your plan?"

To his credit, Vincent looked incredulous. "You aren't that stupid, Ethaniel. What do you think?" He gestured to his bandages and bruises. "You think I wanted this?"

Anger simmering, but not yet boiling, Ethaniel leaned forward and said, "I think you would do almost anything to get into the *demimonde* and access magic our ancestors only ever brushed up against."

"You're insane," Vincent bit out. "Our cousin isn't my charge. She was hired to do a job, she went rogue. I had nothing to do with her plans."

It was as if a wall had come down over Vincent's face, and Ethaniel knew he wasn't getting any further tonight. Well, he'd let Vincent stew in isolation, locked behind barriers and spells Agrippa would keep in place for as long as needed. And the reckoning with what Magnus had told them about the violent theft of Vincent's magic would come. But not tonight.

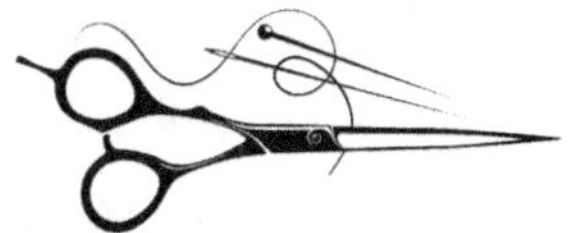

When Ethaniel returned to the bedroom, Aubrey was already asleep, but Calix was lightly dozing and woke when he entered. As Calix sat up, rubbing his eyes, Ethaniel put a finger to his lips, then pointed at Aubrey. Calix nodded, content to wait while Ethaniel changed and slipped in behind him.

"Did it go as you thought? Your conversation with Agrippa?" Calix whispered over his shoulder.

"That is a complicated answer," Ethaniel whispered back. "But yes. And I finally feel like we might all be free of that place for a time." He kissed the back of Calix's head, then settled into the thick, firm mattress and let sleep claim him.

CHAPTER TWENTY-FOUR

CALIX

In his dream, it is raining. Calix would only need to turn his face up to feel its soft spray. But he didn't need to worry, because he was sheltered under a large black umbrella, the beautifully polished handle held tightly by Aubrey.

"You're quiet, dove," Aubrey said as they came around a corner.

The sidewalk, new only a few months ago, was firm under Calix's feet. Aubrey's arm was around his shoulder, warm and heavy but so, so welcome. "It's simply one of those days, I suppose," he said. "The rain doesn't usually bother me, but today I feel it more."

Aubrey nodded. "It's been what... months, now, since you had a headache?"

"Almost four months exactly." He gave Aubrey a tired smile. "I think this is merely a ripple, not a wave."

Gloved fingers trailed down Calix's neck and he shivered. Whenever he was like this, overstimulated and too sensitive to the world around him, Aubrey and Ethaniel could bring him back down with a few touches. And Calix would never turn down the opportunity for more contact; he soaked it up like a plant dying of thirst.

"Let me know if it becomes too much, and we'll pop back home," Aubrey said.

Calix tried to glare at him. He might not have been entirely successful, from the way Aubrey's lips twitched. "You shouldn't use the blink device for a headache, Aubrey."

Aubrey now pressed his fingers in the soft spot behind Calix's left ear. The spot he knew started to ache when a headache became something much more violent and nausea-inducing. (And in Calix's case, actually violent, since sometimes his magic

*flares would rattle doorknobs and window sashes or shake the floor.)
Immediately, that touch made Calix pull his shoulders away from his ears.
Aubrey had gotten very good at infusing his touch with the smallest spark of
healing energy, and it was a boon for both of them. Calix would get relief and
Aubrey would get to practice his craft over and over again, which was something
he wanted to do every chance provided.*

*"I think this rain and chill plus you waking up with a bit of a headache all
necessitate us going back home, but only if you want," Aubrey said. "The blink
device is a tool, yes, and not to be abused. But Ethaniel and I made it for you,
dove."*

*"I know. Thank you." He curled even closer under Aubrey's arm as they
turned another corner.*

Aubrey's pale green eyes were full of warmth as he said, "Of course, Calix."

*And then everything shifted, like the world splintered in two and swallowed
him up, only to spit him back out on a sun-drenched street, the white span of
little shops and cafes stretching out to the ocean. Beside him, Ethaniel had his
face tilted toward the sun, all that brown, wavy hair loose about his shoulders
and so honey-soft against his all-white outfit.*

*Here, everything moved slower. The sun seemed to take its time moving from
east to west, and the ocean only became cold once it had returned to its horizon
home. It was a beautiful landscape, thriving at all hours until tranquility set
in, replacing the sun with an indigo stillness bathed in moonlight.*

*Calix had never seen any place like it, and he can scarcely believe Ethaniel
was sharing it with them. His home country. His first real love. The land, the
people, the twists of deep green leaves on trees that gnarled like grapevines and
grew against houses as if they were trying to retake such precious space.*

*"I'm turning red, aren't I? This sun is hotter than I remembered." Ethaniel
said when he caught Calix staring. Gaping at him, more like.*

*"What?" Calix didn't jump three feet into the air, but it was a near thing.
"No, not at all." He slipped closer to Ethaniel, grinning. "You're so pretty, I can
hardly stand it."*

Ethaniel scoffed, but Calix caught the pleased little smile and how red his ears turned. If he teased Ethaniel too much, the man might combust on the spot. And they were already pushing it, having left Aubrey back at the villa while they ran out for more wine and food. Aubrey alone, in a big bed meant for the three of them, his skin glistening against white sheets, had nearly kept them from leaving at all.

"And you're still being sweet." Ethaniel's smile turned into a wicked grin. "I'm trying to figure out how that's possible after everything we did this afternoon."

This Ethaniel, still the same one he met all those months ago, had an edge to him that was more willing to playfully banter, or even flirt, out in public. Calix never missed a chance to flirt back. "You mean after what you both did?"

They moved up the line queueing for fresh citrus, the final item on their hurriedly written list. And they were both antsy to return home to Aubrey. But Ethaniel was feeling feisty, apparently, because he leaned in and whispered, "You mean after you begged us to plough you into the mattress?"

Calix gave an overly scandalized gasp. "You cad, how dare you."

A gentle, but firm, finger poked him in the ribs. "No, how dare you, dove."

They spent the rest of the wait playfully bickering, then hurried back to their little oceanside villa with the bright teal door and a walkway that led out to the sea.

When Calix woke up, he was covered in sweat and his body felt cold, as if he'd been through a nightmare. Beside him, Aubrey stirred, but Ethaniel was the one to roll over and whisper his name, a question in his voice.

"I'm not entirely sure," Calix said, reaching out to touch Ethaniel's shoulder. To ground himself, remind himself what was real. *This is real. This is real. This isn't a dream or...* "I think it was a vision. From the future," Calix said. "It felt too real, too right, to be anything else."

Ethaniel frowned at that. "Your magic has been a tad sporadic for several days now. If it was a vision, I wonder what brought your magic to the surface."

Calix shrugged, but the movement seemed more aloof than he felt. Inside, he was a tumultuous riot of panic, anxiety, and gnawing worry. It had been such a short span of time, and they'd been fighting tooth and nail to simply survive, but for the first time since then, Calix felt *normal*.

Ethaniel searched his face for several long breaths, then leaned over Calix to gently shove at Aubrey's shoulder. "Aubrey, wake up."

Calix tried to bat him away while fiercely whispering, "Ethaniel, no! Let him sleep. I'm sure it's nothing."

"What's nothing," Aubrey mumbled as he rolled into Calix's back and immediately spooned up behind him.

Calix sighed, feeling frustrated that Ethaniel would wake that poor man up for some random dream he had. But some part of him was grateful, and feeling rather smug about the whole thing; mostly because Ethaniel was right. It hadn't been a dream. It hadn't been some subconscious wish of Calix's brought to the surface by a night of decent rest after so much pain and drama.

It had been a vision. He knew that.

When Aubrey managed to sit up and shake himself awake, Calix told them everything. His visions weren't always cryptic or haunting or dire; sometimes they were banal or even completely normal. This had felt normal. Good. *Right*.

"A glimpse at our future, perhaps," Aubrey hedged, and Calix had to admit the idea was compelling. "And we were in Spain together? I've always wanted to go there."

Ethaniel shook his head. "I'm afraid I have to be the pessimist here, because under no circumstances will I return to that place. I miss it horribly, that is true, but while my family resides there, it is forbidden for me. To even set foot on the opposite side of the country from them would be disastrous. At best."

Calix's imagination was already running away with itself. "And if they weren't there?"

Ethaniel shook his head. "Even then, it might be too risky."

Aubrey curled around Calix, his hand rubbing Calix's arm, but he could tell Aubrey was only looking at Ethaniel. Ethaniel was locked in with Aubrey in that way they had sometimes; that shared history, a bond forged through strife and passionate love. Calix could have watched them stare at each other for hours.

"There's no reason at all, even a wild one, for you to return home?" Aubrey asked.

That seemed to bring Ethaniel up short. He looked away and rubbed the blanket between his thumb and forefinger. "So many impossible things would have to fall into place but yes. Maybe one." When he looked up this time, he stared directly at Calix. "Maria would have to return, whole and alive and human. That would get me on a boat immediately."

In the bubble of silent space around them, Calix heard so many variants of the question: *what if?*

He reached out to reassure Ethaniel once more, when a loud sound, like a rock smacking into the house, rattled the nearby window. They all turned toward the sound only to be stopped by another; this one at the opposite window and that shook the closed shutters.

"What in the actual hell?" Aubrey said as he got out of bed, Ethaniel and Calix on his heels.

The sounds came faster now, picking up in speed *and* volume, all the windows reverberating and the roof above seeming to quiver in tandem. Calix heard commotion downstairs, so he took off down the hallway, then descended the stairs, but was met with Magnus halfway.

For the first time since they'd met, Magnus looked practically disheveled. Oxblood-red smoking jacket open and missing its sash, black wavy hair sticking up at a few angles, a bit of something like a burn or a rash on his neck.

"Are you all right?" Calix and Magnus asked at the same time. They both had to yell to be heard over the constant, horrendously loud, *wet* smacking sounds.

"I'm fine," Magnus said, a steadying hand now on Calix's shoulder. "Are you all well?"

Ethaniel and Aubrey came down the stairs to flank Calix, and once they both responded affirmatively, Magnus turned back to Calix. "Agrippa is checking on Vincent, and Lawton is already in the parlor. I ran there first, since that's where the door from the *demimonde* had opened, but I only saw him."

Calix glanced at the wide oak front doors. "Should we check outside?"

The sounds stopped. No more shaking. The world grew horribly still.

The suddenness of it only put Calix more on edge.

Lawton wandered out into the hall, his distant shape a welcome one, and Calix motioned him forward. They all met at the long, black tiled table set up as an accent piece between the curving double staircase. Somewhere between the stairs and the table, Agrippa appeared.

"The prisoner is accounted for and unharmed," Agrippa said. "You all appear to be in fine health."

Magnus nodded. "We're all fine, Agrippa. But what in the bloody hells was that?"

Lawton, who was staring at the ceiling, pointed. "Not anything pretty."

The ceiling above them wasn't entirely closed off, as a series of glass panels had been strategically placed to welcome the late afternoon sun, since the house faced west. But those glass panels were now covered in strange, shadowy shapes and dark streaks of... something. It was too dark outside to see more than that.

Calix felt odd, as if the world had slid sideways a few inches. He had no other way to explain it, and standing underneath those glass panels, he simply *knew*. Knew in the way he'd known about the fire at Aubrey's and his mother and Lawton, and every other little pinprick of precognition to the nightmares that felt like rip currents.

He *knew*.

"They're birds," Calix said as they all stared up. "Hundreds of them, I'd guess."

Agrippa wasted no time marching to the front door and yanking it open. They were already crackling with energy as they pushed past everyone; to the point that it made Calix's hair stand on end, but once the door was open, they flared with magic, wide and white and brilliant against the deep indigo of night. Their flare helped chase that darkness away, until they could see the steps of the estate and the gravel path beyond. It was littered with small, winged corpses.

"My god," Magnus said.

Calix didn't need to say anything. He'd been right. He felt sick.

"I need to get back to the Collectio," Agrippa said as they closed the door.

The telltale tingle was at the back of Calix's skull now. An ache, just behind his ears and leading down to his neck. The onslaught of a vision. His magic *was* back, and it was warning him.

"Must you go now?" Magnus asked, something like disappointment in his voice.

That stopped Agrippa, but their stern face betrayed nothing as they nodded. "The birds are a sign. Part of a threat detection spell placed on my partition of the Collectio's archives."

Calix took a moment to put that together. "It's the security alarm on the Collectio," he said, stunned.

"Correct, Calix." Agrippa motioned to the glass over their heads. "It means someone has entered the Collectio without my permission, but also that they absconded with something."

"A rather bold thing to do," Magnus said, "considering who guards it."

"An *impossible* thing to do," Agrippa corrected. "At least, impossible for any mortal with any version of human magic."

Calix hated that he understood the moment Agrippa's words left them. "But not for a Dreamwalker who has been traveling the *demimonde*."

Those galaxy eyes on the exiled Guardian blinked. "Exactly so."

Calix felt lost. In the span of a few hours, his entire world was on the brink of incredible, terrifying change. Lawton was leaving with Agrippa, and Agrippa had a break-in and theft to investigate. Magnus was returning to the Collectio to assist in the investigation. Aubrey was taking a leave of absence from his work. And Ethaniel was trying to locate his uncle, who seemed to have disappeared into the city with no trace. In the heat of everything, Calix had also lost track of Richard, who had vanished from Rosehill.

Missing people. Mysterious missing item or items from the Collectio. Pain and heartbreak and renewal all wrapped around each other.

Calix did not know what to do with himself. There was at least one very hard conversation to be had, goodbyes to be said, and a new relationship trying to blossom in the face of odds that should have broken them apart.

Convergence was gone, either lost to the gray mists of the *demimonde* or picked up by some creature or being that lived there. Isme was untraceable, at least for now. And Vincent, battered and bruised, his ego mortally wounded, would wind up in Agrippa's care.

So, what was left? And after everything that had happened, who was he now?

"It's as though I can feel those gears in your mind turning," Ethaniel said in his ear. Calix was watching Lawton sort through boxes of clothes, in anticipation of needing to take at least a few things with him to Agrippa's portal home.

Down deep, where soul and body met, Calix felt something *crack*. The world he knew wasn't the same anymore. He was adrift in a sea of confusion and conflagration. But here was this man, a kind, somewhat stubborn, patterner with a great deal of magic and the biggest heart. And he was asking after Calix's wellbeing.

Calix didn't know what to say. He simply turned into Ethaniel's welcoming embrace and kissed him, sweet and soft and over far too quickly. "I want to go home, back to the city," he said quietly. "But I have something to deal with right now."

Ethaniel nodded. "Agrippa has offered to take us back when we're ready. My shop and apartment are yours, dove. Or we can go to your apartment. Or a hotel. Whatever you want."

Calix wanted to *weep*. He wanted to cry out all the exhaustion and stress and heartbreak, until the pillows couldn't take another drop. He wanted to sleep for a week.

He wanted someone to hold him.

Hands slid down his arms and now Aubrey was behind him, nestling Calix between his and Ethaniel's bodies and it felt right. He would have stayed here forever, if possible.

"I heard what Ethaniel said," Aubrey whispered in his ear. "Take your time. Let us know when you're ready."

They slowly let him go, but not before Calix kissed Aubrey as well. The little smile Aubrey gave him warmed Calix in places he hadn't realized were cold.

He could do this.

"Lawton," Calix said as Lawton stood and brushed off his trousers.

Lawton's face bore no expression, but there was a darkness in his friend's eyes that made Calix worry. But he couldn't be that for Lawton any longer; not the sounding board or the one to pull him off the ledge of another hare-brained idea. Not the one to hold him close and tell him everything would be all right.

Because everything was different now.

Lawton didn't say anything. Instead, he closed the distance between them and embraced Calix as though it was the last time they'd ever see each other. Calix could only return the hug and try to keep his tears to himself.

"It won't be forever," Lawton said, lips pressed to Calix's temple. "I have penance to do, and I want to do it. I want to come back to you a better man. Someone worthy of your good heart and kind spirit."

That did it. Lawton's words broke the fragile dam Calix had constructed, and his tears quickly soaked the shoulder of Lawton's shirt. Lawton wasn't immune; Calix could feel the warm, wet drops on his neck.

When they separated, Lawton kept his arms around Calix's neck. His face was splotchy-red, but there was a clarity in his expression. Calix saw hope there, too. "Are you going to talk to her?" Lawton asked.

Calix nodded. "Agrippa will let me in to see her when I'm ready."

"Good. That's good."

The silence between them was a half-constructed bridge. Time and peace of mind might make it whole. Calix could only hope. "I love you, Lawton. My oldest friend," he managed to say. "My first lover. The one who taught me so much."

Lawton chuckled at that. "You mean, taught you many, many bad habits."

"And many good ones, too." Gently, Calix pressed his lips to Lawton's cheek. "Please stay safe."

Lawton's hands, warm and soft against Calix's jaw, were a grounding thing against how fleeting his thoughts felt. "I will. I swear. And I love you, too."

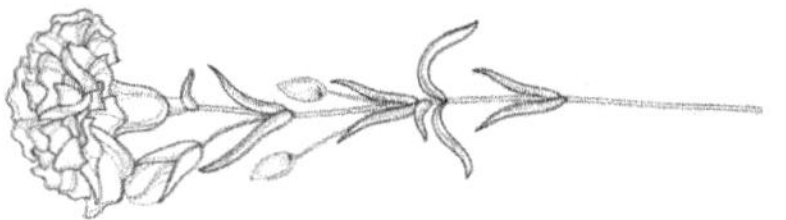

Agrippa came to Calix a bit later, via a portal that snapped open in the bedroom he was busy cleaning up. Calix bit back on the instinct to jump out of his skin, but he doubted Agrippa would have noticed or cared, one way or the other. They seemed to operate, at least partially, on a different plane than humans.

Agrippa gestured to the slowly churning silver portal. "I can give you only a small amount of time with her. Despite the fracturing of her soul, your mother is quite strong."

Calix heard what they did not say: *I fear she may try something if you spend too long in her company*. And he had to agree; if not for his own safety, but for his sanity. Seeing her one more time and getting to close the door on a relationship that had never been merely between parent and child was what he needed. For once, Calix didn't give a damn about what her needs might be.

"I'm ready," he said, and then stepped into the portal.

There was no upending of reality this time. No strange, jittering waves in his sight or nausea-inducing lack of gravity. It was no worse than stepping from one room to another in the estate.

As soon as his vision cleared, Calix saw her. A wispy, ghostly form in a high-necked dress, her hair piled on top of her head, hands laced together in front of her. It looked as though she had been waiting for him.

Calix could only stare. Seeing his mother once more felt like a slap in the face, and also the closure he needed.

"You came," she said, her voice unnaturally high and atonal. "That being said you would."

"I don't back away from my promises," Calix replied swiftly. Anger was already flaring up in him at her simple greeting... but it wasn't so simple, was it? He heard an implication in her voice, as if she doubted he would stick to his words.

What right or reason did she have for that?

None. None at all.

So, he kept his distance. This was a piece of his mother; a hollow-eyed, barely corporeal remnant of a woman who had loved fiercely and had made many mistakes. She'd grabbed power for herself, and in a desperate attempt to help Calix, had overreached. She'd trusted the wrong people. Dallied with magic she didn't understand. Tried over and over again to save herself from a terrible fate and tried to keep Calix from meeting the same one.

He could hate her. He should.

All he wanted was to forgive her. And standing before her now, he realized it was within his right, and his power, to do so. He didn't need to wait for her permission to be kind to himself.

Calix stepped forward and took her hands. They were cold in his, but solid, and he held them tightly as he said, "I forgive you."

Her entire form shuddered in his grasp, and Lily let out what sounded like a half-choked sob. "I can't believe you would forgive me, after all I've done."

Some part of Calix gnashed his teeth at the thought. That he shouldn't cave so easily, that he should interrogate her for every unanswered question or wonder from the time he'd been aware enough to know something wasn't quite right. He *deserved* answers. But what he wanted, more than anything, was finality. To shut the door on this whole dreadful affair and greet the next day with optimism and opportunity, graced by the luck and joy of new love.

Because he did love them both. For different reasons and for some of the same. But Ethaniel and Aubrey were a part of his life now, and he wanted to move forward without the regret of glancing back.

"Forgiving you is the grace I deserve, and the grace you deserve, too," he whispered as she sobbed into his shoulder. "I don't know what will happen after this, but I cannot move forward with my life if I stay mired in ugly thoughts. I have to make peace with all of it."

Calix pulled back so he could see his mother's face. She looked so thin, so fragile, and as much as it hurt to see her like that, he was not at fault for her condition. Or her demise. "I understand," Lily whispered back. "And I'm so glad I was able to see you one more time. To see the man you've become, and to see the ones you've met who love you as much – or maybe more – than I do." She cradled his face in her hands and Calix wondered what she saw when she looked at him that way.

But one thing stuck in the back of his mind. "Is there anything, anything at all, I should know? Anything you didn't tell me that might keep me and Aubrey and Ethaniel safe?"

Lily stared at him for a long moment. "Uriel is incredibly powerful," she whispered. "They were meant to be a tool, a way for me to seek information and magic from the *demimonde*. To keep you safe, yes, but to also keep myself from falling into the fate that meets so many Oracles. I discovered much too late that Uriel had plans even beyond what I could imagine. They want into our world, Calix. But the reason why they want that is beyond me. I had guesses: to take our magic, to conquer us, to break the barrier between realms. What you should understand is that they *know* who you are, and that is my fault. And because they know you, you will always be a target."

"I am not going back to the *demimonde*," Calix said. "None of us will."

Lily shook her head, her expression creasing with sadness. "Not willingly, you won't. But Uriel is a creature driven by purpose, and I don't know that you will be safe so long as they exist, in any realm."

Calix leaned in and kissed her forehead. "It's a risk I'm willing to take, if it means living my life the way I wish."

"My dear boy. Calix." Her voice drifted now, as if caught on an invisible wind, and Calix looked down. Her form, already pale white, was slowly evaporating. "You always meant the world to me. And I loved you before I even met you, darling child."

Calix watched her figure waver, and for the first time since his mother had passed, he was able to step back and watch. Eyes and heart open despite the pain of letting her go.

"Goodbye, Mother," he whispered to the last time he'd ever see her face.

They left Rosehill behind after sending a letter to Calix's attorney, letting him know that the estate, grounds, and all property were to be sold. Calix didn't tell Ethaniel or Aubrey what he would be doing with the money, but he already knew. He knew before he'd ever put pen to paper for that letter. And before Magnus had used Agrippa's portal to return to his home, Calix had told him to expect communications in the near future.

"I'll let you keep your secret, for now," Magnus said with a smile. He was back to his pristine self, and there was a light in his eyes that only ever appeared when Agrippa was nearby.

"Good, because I'm not going to tell you now," Calix teased. They embraced, and once Magnus said his goodbyes to the others, they were alone. Alone in the place that had inscribed itself into Calix's memory, into his very life and soul, and the place that deserved its own send off.

Calix met Aubrey and Ethaniel at the front door, their bags packed and ready to be whisked away by Agrippa, who was grousing under their breath about being a delivery system. Calix hid his smile at their grouchiness and turned toward his lovers.

"It's a pity you couldn't see this place without all the drama and darkness," Calix said as the two other men crowded close. "It was a lovely place to grow up."

"So you're selling it? Truly?" Ethaniel asked as he ran his hand over the fine woodwork around the front door. "I'm sure someone will want it."

"Maybe don't disclose what's happened here over the last days," Aubrey said as he straightened his coat.

"Definitely not," Calix replied. "Besides, Rosehill deserves a proper sale and a new owner. Leaving out what's happened isn't against the rules, but even if it was, she should have better. There should be a family here, with children that can run outside and try to climb up on the roof to see the stars." Calix glanced up at the ceiling, to the panes of glass that had been cleaned off with a bit of carefully applied magic from Aubrey. "She deserves to see love again." Calix turned to them, pulled both men close, and kissed their cheeks. "And I deserve it, too."

Aubrey grinned at him, his pale green eyes alight with mirth and admiration. "You have it. I won't speak for Ethaniel, of course." When Ethaniel elbowed him in the ribs, Aubrey only chuckled. "I am besotted with you both. And I think we fit together rather nicely."

"Rather nicely, he says," Ethaniel teased. "As if he doesn't already know." Ethaniel ran his fingers down Calix's cheek, bringing with his touch a warmth that rivaled nothing else Calix had ever felt. "I adore you both. Admire you both. And I love you both, in every way I could and every way I will show you."

Calix folded himself into their embrace, his body and mind, heart and soul, alive once more and looking forward to a future that was just the three of them.

Acknowledgements

To Željka Dobras for the incredible work she has done for the covers and additional artwork for this trilogy. Her brilliance cannot be overstated.

To my friends who read this book early and kept me going, all my love.

And to those who stayed for the whole thing, those who wanted to read it before I ever put a chapter heading in my formatting software, and to those who pick these up long after publication. *Thank you*, sincerely.

ALSO BY HALLI STARLING

Wilderwood

Twelfth Moon

Ask Me For Fire

A Brighter, Darker Art

When He Beckons

The Way We Wind

Always There For You

Pose for Me

Venor

(The Werewolf Novels, Book 1)

Coup de Coeur

(Oracle, Tailor, Curator trilogy, Book 1)

Demimonde

(Oracle, Tailor, Curator trilogy, Book 2)

About the Author

Halli Starling is a queer librarian fascinated by the occult and strange history. She lives in Michigan with her spouse, feline supervisors, and is always surrounded by books. When not writing, she co-hosts The Human Exception podcast, plays D&D, and dives into secondhand bookstores. She is a video game fan, preferring RPGs and strategy games, particularly the old school Bioware games like Dragon Age and Mass Effect.

Halli spent over a decade working reference desks in public libraries, then switched to working in another part of the book world while still supporting libraries and the freedom to read. She started writing her debut book, WILDERWOOD, during the pandemic, after spending years trying to find the right story to tell. While she writes books across genres, Halli always puts characters first.

For updates on future publications and more, follow Halli on Instagram @hallistarling.

Website: hallistarlingbooks.com